BEWITCHED

No, wait, I didn't mean. . . . The self-serving lie caught in her throat. If she had not meant this to happen, she'd hoped it would. If this was frightening, it was in the way that roller coasters and water slides were frightening—for the sheer delirious, jubilant intensity of the plunge into unknown excitement.

"You know what—I mean who—I am," Diana said in a trembling voice. Witch and woman and traveler out of time.

"But I and thou are apart from this," he said softly.

He lowered his face to hers and she opened her mouth to him at once; desire that had become a physical presence made her nip at him, seeking to hold him to her with her mouth alone. She heard the rasp of a faint moan caught deep in his throat and the sound of it sent joy blazing through her body. The fierceness of her desire to give him pleasure was a part of her need to have him, to envelop him and possess him utterly.

Wiccan belief held that every lovers' meeting was a microcosmic reenactment of the Great Marriage—that celestial embrace of heaven and earth, male and female, the paired opposites that were the cornerstone of all Creation—but Diana had never quite understood why until this moment.

She pulled at his shirt, tugging and tugging until finally it came free of his waistband. When he felt it slip over his shoulders he pulled away from her. "Wouldst see me?" he asked. "In the light of day?"

Diana realized that he was giving her one last chance to refuse him. But it was already far too late for that. Daylight . . . moonlight . . . candlelight—if she could not have him it would be a sorrow as great as death.

"Yes," she said. "Yes."

DANGEROUS GAMES   (0-7860-0270-0, $4.99)
by Amanda Scott

When Nicholas Barrington, eldest son of the Earl of Ul-
combe, first met Melissa Seacort, the desperation he
sensed beneath her well-bred beauty haunted him. He
didn't realize how desperate Melissa really was . . . until
he found her again at a Newmarket gambling club—being auctioned off by her father to the highest bidder. So,
Nick bought himself a wife. With a villain hot on their
heels, and a fortune and their lives at stake, they would
gamble everything on the most dangerous game of all:
love.

A TOUCH OF PARADISE   (0-7860-0271-9, $4.99)
by Alexa Smart

As a confidence man and scam runner in 1880s America,
Malcolm Northrup has amassed a fortune. Now, posing
as the eminent Sir John Abbot—scholar, and possible
discoverer of the lost continent of Atlantis—he's taking
his act on the road with a lecture tour, seeking funds for
a scientific experiment he has no intention of making.
But scholar Halia Davenport is determined to accompany
Malcolm on his "expedition" . . . even if she must kidnap
him!

*Available wherever paperbacks are sold, or order direct from the
Publisher. Send cover price plus 50¢ per copy for mailing and
handling to Kensington Publishing Corp., Consumer Orders,
or call (toll free) 888-345-BOOK, to place your order using
Mastercard or Visa. Residents of New York and Tennessee
must include sales tax. DO NOT SEND CASH.*

MET BY MOONLIGHT

Rosemary Edghill

Pinnacle Books
Kensington Publishing Corp.

http://www.pinnaclebooks.com

PINNACLE BOOKS are published by

Kensington Publishing Corp.
850 Third Avenue
New York, NY 10022

Pinnacle and the P logo Reg. U.S. Pat. & TM Off.

First Printing: February, 1998
10 9 8 7 6 5 4 3 2 1

Printed in the United States of America

Chapter 1

Salem, Massachusetts, October 31, 199-

It was going to be a dark and stormy night—and that, Diana Crossways thought, was the ultimate cliché. Tonight was October 31st—All Hallows' Eve ... Halloween—when even the least romantic soul thrilled to the presence of the Unseen. Diana gave the black volume of storm clouds visible through the bookstore windows a dubious glance. This year even Dame Nature was dressing the part; it was only three o'clock and the sky was already dark. Diana just hoped the rain would hold off for another few hours.

"Bye, Diana." Molly Murray, Diana's clerk, was small and dark, her looks the exact opposite of Diana's blonde cover-girl legginess. At the moment Molly's expression was that of someone who was certain she'd forgotten something vitally important.

"Later," Diana said, her mind still on the storm and its possibility for ruining the evening.

"Will I see you at coven tonight?" Molly asked, lingering in the doorway to the shop.

What an odd question.

"When did I ever miss a Grand Sabbat?" Diana answered

lightly, smiling to cover her sudden unease. She'd sponsored Molly into the Craft; Wicca was a religion dedicated to the positive aspects of Nature, and Diana's coven concerned itself with works of healing and empowerment for those who came to them, but the coven meeting tonight would be only for celebration. She and Molly had spent most of the afternoon going over plans for the party that would follow tonight's celebration of *Samhain*—the Wiccan Feast of the Dead—which both women would attend. There was no reason for Molly to ask Diana a question like that.

Molly still hesitated, staring at Diana with worried violet eyes. "Are you sure?" she asked.

"Of course I'm sure," Diana said. *No I'm not.* "Molly, are you getting one of your headaches?" she added suspiciously.

Amelia Murray—Molly to her friends—suffered from shattering headaches, but tied to the headaches was the unnerving gift of clairvoyance. If this were one of those occasions . . .

"No. Of course not," Molly said quickly. "It's the storm. See you."

"If I don't show up, start without me," Diana joked. Molly flashed her a fleeting smile and scurried out. The bell on the door jingled as it shut behind her.

Diana stared around the empty bookstore, her unease stronger than ever. "Forget this," she said to the deserted room, coming to a sudden decision. "I'm closing early."

Diana strode to the front of the store and pulled down the heavy green shades, blotting out both the view of the storm and the silhouetted witch-on-broomstick painted on the glass.

Witch Hunt (open ten to six Wednesday through Sunday) was a bookstore that stocked the latest books on Wicca and Neo-Paganism, but what gave the store its name—and paid most of the bills—was the fact that it specialized in booksearching and restoring rare and out-of-print occult books.

Its owner, Diana Crossways, was twenty-eight years old, tall, blonde, and blue-eyed; the perfect all-American girl. She'd been a Witch for nearly ten years now, having been introduced to the worship of the Goddess while she'd still been in college.

Diana had graduated from Price Challoner's book design course at the Boston College of Arts and Crafts and worked for two years in the Harvard University Rare Book Collection. She could have gone on the bibliographic fast track and buried herself in some museum's documents collection at a nice salary; but having thought the matter over very carefully, Diana had opted out of the corporate arts rat race and into *Witch Hunt*. The friends who thought she was wasting her time had dropped away, and Diana was mostly satisfied with her life as it was. The faint sense of something yet to do nagged at her occasionally, but she trusted in the Goddess to send the answer to that in Her own good time.

Diana frowned, trying to shake the feeling of unease that Molly's casual question had given her. It didn't seem to be a premonition. She'd never considered herself particularly psychic. In Diana's experience, psychic gifts had to be paid for somehow—if not by a disability like Molly's, then in some more subtle way—and Diana was just as glad not to have that extra burden. And besides, she believed that the magic made in a Wiccan circle carried with it a burden similar to that of Molly's gift: with all power came responsibility.

Diana shot the three locks on the front door and put the "Closed for the Holiday" sign in the window. Just as she did, the first thunder rumbled, and Diana sighed. No hope of beating the storm now, even if she left the store immediately. Diana walked back through the store toward her workroom, pausing to straighten a few books and switch off the hot water under the tea urn. She could empty it in the morning; right now she'd tidy up, she'd get her things, she'd get out of here, and she'd shake this sudden case of the creeps.

Diana felt better as soon as she reached her crowded workroom. Books in every possible stage of repair were stacked on every available flat surface, and the room smelled of linen and glue and disinfectants. Quickly Diana tidied away her various projects, cleared her worktable, and switched on the answering machine. As she worked, the first gust of rain spattered against the window, followed immediately by another. A second rumble

of thunder came hard on the heels of the first, followed by a
nearly subliminal snake-tongue of lightning.

The light subsided. The noise did not. After a moment Diana
recognized it as the sound of someone hammering at her front
door.

"All right, all right: *'I come, Graymalkin,'*" she muttered.
Elizabethan drama was Diana's secret vice.

She opened the door to the sight of a young man in soggy
motorcycle leathers holding a large rain-spotted package and
a clipboard. Diana knew the sight of a book at thirty paces;
she snatched the package out of the startled messenger's hands
even before she ushered him in. Quickly she tore open the
brown paper and pulled out a large bundle—tightly wrapped,
thank the Goddess, in sheets of waterproof plastic. She set it
down carefully on the counter beside the cash register.

"Diana Crossways?" He had a foghorn transatlantic accent:
working-class Brit or a terrible cold. "Sign here."

She glanced up. Gold-spangled hazel eyes stared into hers
as fixedly as if their owner thought she was going to run off
with his package. For a long moment Diana stared at him,
mesmerized by the certainty that she knew him, or *would* know
him. . . .

Then the moment shattered like the raindrops on the paving.
She sighed the form on the clipboard. Her signature blurred
into illegibility along with everything else on the dampened
sheet. What *was* this, anyway? A book she'd ordered? An
unnanounced repair job?

"Thanks." The messenger tipped two fingers to his cap,
confirming Diana in her guess of English origins, and stepped
outside again. The next thunderclap was prolonged by the sound
of the motorcycle engine as the messenger raced away. Fresh
rain hit *Witch Hunt*'s wooden front like a shower of pebbles.

This is no night to be out on a bike, Diana thought. *I hope
it doesn't go over on him.* She locked the door of her shop
again and picked up her prize. She could feel the outlines of
a book even through the layers of wrapping that cocooned it.

Diana went back to her workroom, this time stopping to

turn out the lights in the front of the store to forestall further messengers. She set the package on her worktable and began unwrapping it. The rich bitter smell of ancient bookbinding wafted up as she laid back the last protective layer ... the sweet autumn scent of rotting vellum. The leather was glazed and cracked with age, and tiny chips of its surface flaked away like paint from a long-neglected wall.

She held her breath as she cautiously opened the book itself. The first page was filled with ancient handwriting, its precise spidery loops of once-black ink faded brown by the passage of uncountable decades. She hadn't ordered this. She couldn't *afford* this; a handwritten book this old would cost hundreds—thousands—of dollars. Someone must have sent it for repair.

Diana closed the book and looked carefully through the wrappings, but there was no enclosed letter or return address. At least she had her copy of the delivery receipt; she'd call the courier service first thing in the morning and find out what maniac had handed a book that must be at least three hundred years old to a motorcycle messenger to deliver in the middle of a rainstorm.

As if her thoughts had roused it, the storm grew wilder, the rain coming in gusts that mimicked the rhythm of ocean surf. Suddenly the room flared with impossible brightness. Diana clutched the book to her in a useless automatic gesture of protection as the sound followed the lightning almost instantly—a roar louder than any thunder had a right to be, a disorienting wave of sheer noise loud enough to make the windows rattle in an eerie soprano counterpoint.

And all the lights went out.

Still cradling the book against her chest, Diana groped through a fog of purple and green floating afterimages for the dangling chain of the overhead light. As if it had only been waiting for the lights to go out, the storm struck now in earnest. Finally, the chain wrapped around her searching fingers and she yanked it. Several times. Nothing happened.

Circuit breaker? Fuse? Is the power out all over? The windows were sheeted with rain. They rattled with the impact of the wind and leaking water all along their old wooden frames. The lightning flashed constantly, the flashes coming so close together that they seemed unrelated to the thunder that pounded like war drums. The rational part of her mind assured her that the blackout was a temporary nuisance and nothing more; but if Diana had not had the book to clutch, her hands would have been shaking uncontrollably. Deafened and terrified, Diana was jarred from her numbness by a blast of cold, wet air.

The front door—it's open!

She ran from the workroom with the book in her arms, thinking as much of escape as of denying entrance to the storm. As she reached the doorway, the lightning struck again, coruscating with a sizzling, air-tearing sound, and Diana, blinded, passed through.

As soon as her feet skidded on wet grass, she stopped, her mind desperately offering any explanation other than the truth. The grass was blown in by the storm. The storm had stopped. The outside door was open; the lightning had dazzled her so that she couldn't see. . . .

"Cover her face; mine eyes dazzle; she died young." The quote came automatically to her rebellious mind; soothing syrup for the soul.

"She died young."

Was she dead? Diana stared around herself with the stunned reasonableness of shock. She was a Witch and accepted magic as a part of her daily life, but *this* . . .

The storm was gone. Come to that, the *store* was gone and the city street and the city itself. *"The cloud-capp'd towers . . . the great globe itself . . ."* Oh, GODDESS . . .

Diana stood in the middle of an open field. It was night. Faint luminous scraps of cloud drifted by overhead and a full moon edged, cold and white, toward midheaven.

No.

Diana turned around quickly, as if the workroom should still be behind her. It wasn't. There was no building of any kind behind her—only more field, faintly hillocky and unkempt, leading off into vague tree shapes at its edge. Diana turned back. There was another patch of woods ahead, a tangle of darker shadow punctuated by the faint upright grayness of trees.

No.

She was breathing hard and fast, gasping in sheer outrage at the impossibility of this, the book still clutched tightly to her chest. But the ground was real under her feet, muddy and faintly moist; the night air was real, chill but curiously soft, filled with thick, green summer smells that had no place in Diana's October. She could hear the whisper of wind through leaves, smell distant wood-smoke.

Where was she?

When was she?

Diana took a cautious step, as if to move would shatter this new reality. To her faint surprise, her body obeyed her and the world stayed as it was. She struggled to control her breathing and make sense of things. She didn't see anyone else panicking, did she?

She didn't see anyone else, *period.* Common sense and instinct clashed and quarreled, riding the tidal wave of fear whose undertow threatened to drown her. Instinct told Diana that her best hope of safety lay in this direction; common sense swore that these woods were dark and dangerous. But the terrible thought that she might be utterly alone—that there might *be* no one else anywhere—was what drove Diana forward into the darkness.

The undergrowth between the trees was springy and treacherous; the black slacks and orange blouse that had seemed so appealingly seasonal in the bookstore left her shivering and unprotected here. She could feel every stone and twig through the soles of her thin leather shoes, and the flats offered no protection against the sucking damp of the forest floor. Diana shivered and hugged the book against her breasts as if it could warm her. Even such slow headway as she managed to make was exhausting.

After what seemed like a small eternity, Diana leaned against an ancient tree in a tiny clearing and wiped icy sweat from her forehead with the tail of her ruined silk shirt. She realized now that what she probably should have done in the first place was simply to find a place to sit down and wait for dawn. Surely the sun would rise *sometime,* and in the daylight she would see that this was all just some sort of mistake. . . .

Diana's mouth twisted in a grin on the edge of tears. *Just some sort of mistake. What sort of mistake—Stephen King's?*

Her eyes had adjusted now to the forest gloom; what had been pitch-dark before now seemed merely dim. Even so, she had been staring at the man standing motionlessly beside her for several seconds before she actually saw him.

His image coalesced like an optical illusion, as if he'd only just appeared. His face was a pale oval, as exquisitely beautiful as that of a fallen angel; and though she could not see the color of his eyes, Diana could see the dark feathering of the lashes that fringed them. She saw those eyes flicker as they focused on her suddenly, and the stress of his regard was like a physical touch. His eyes locked with hers, gazing down into her as if all her soul lay behind her eyes.

Diana's heart hammered. There was a misty green radiance gathered in the depths of his eyes, golden green as Midsummer morn, that seemed to radiate a warmth, drawing her in and comforting her. She had never been studied with such intentness, as if she were the most important thing in this dark, silent man's world. Diana stared at him as if he were her reflection in a mirror, fascinated, willing him to reveal more about himself. For this enchanted moment she forgot that she didn't know where she was and how she had gotten here: discovering who this man was and what he wanted with her was suddenly more vital than anything Diana had ever done before.

"Who are you?" Diana whispered, her voice shaking.

Why didn't he say something? How had he gotten this close to her without her knowing it? Who was he? *Who?* What was he doing in the forest at night? Everything else was abruptly insignificant; all the terror, all the dislocation of time and space, had occurred solely so that they two could meet. In this brief fantastic instant Diana realized that the wholeness the Goddess promised Her children was possible, if only she could master the tantalizing riddle of this man.

"Please . . ."

His face was inches away from her own, his warm breath a soft night breeze against her face. She sensed but could not see the mass of black-clothed body, as close to hers as if they were fellow travelers on a rush-hour train. He would only have to move his hand a few inches to touch her. In her imagination the caress had already taken place, and she could feel the heat of his knowing hands burning through the torn silk of her blouse. His breath smelled of flowers; to kiss that mouth would be to kiss ripe apricots drowned in honey by the sun.

Diana's lips parted in sympathy to her dream. There was a sudden white blur at the corner of her vision. Her head jerked toward it, and her lips touched his outstretched hand.

Hot and chill . . . soft and rough . . . SWEET . . .

The shock of the sensation made her clutch at his hand; but instead of flinging it away from her, all Diana was able to do was cling to his hand as if it were a lifeline and she were drowning. His skin was sun hot under her fingers, supple and hard with muscle, and his fingers reflexively tightened over hers.

"Righ-malkin," the stranger whispered, his voice soft and yearning.

Now fear and longing filled Diana equally; she stared at him, spellbound in the truest sense of the word. Unable to move, holding his hand.

Then, suddenly, he cried out and jerked his hand away.

Diana saw the white flash of teeth as his lips drew back, and suddenly the greenwood light was gone from his eyes and all that was left was embers—black embers and the eyes of an angel in hell, his teeth bared in the silent howl of a forest wolf at bay.

"I will *not*—" he cried, his voice slurred by passionate denial; Diana could only guess at its source.

He flung up his hand to ward himself from her, and sharp electrical pain flared through Diana's body—ice to drive out fire. He gestured again, and a phosphorescent afterimage of the sign seemed to hang in the air between them, burning as frigidly as the sudden fear that sluiced through her veins. She saw him smile then, but there was no happiness in it, only strangeness.

And rage.

GO! LEAVE THIS PLACE! RUN! his voice shouted in her mind. With a cry, Diana flung herself away from him.

Pure terror flushed all fatigue from her muscles and sent her fleeing blindly through the wood. She lost both shoes almost immediately and never considered stopping. Unseen branches tore at her face and clothes, tangling in her hair and ripping at her skin, but it was more important to run than to protect herself. She careened off trees, scrambled over fallen logs, slid and clawed and barely stayed on her feet while the commandment seared like acid into her brain: *RUN*.

At last, exhausted muscles betrayed her. A fallen tree blocked her path. She jumped and failed to clear it; rough bark scored the skin from her instep and she twisted, scrabbling for a balance she couldn't retain. She fell, and the book—the precious book—slid out of her grasp, sledding across the short-cropped grass of the clearing. Diana uttered a despairing wail.

The drumming stopped.

Diana raised her head and stared around her, only belatedly understanding the information her mind had registered while she ran: the light from bonfires and lanterns; the sound of the drums, now silent; the people gathered there.

Rough hands grabbed her and lifted her to her feet. Diana struggled feebly, but her blood pounded in her ears and the world wavered as if it were under water.

"Peace, Jankin, is she not one of ours?" The voice held the same swallowed inflections that the young bike messenger's had: English. Diana looked down and saw the silver pentacle she always wore—the five-pointed-star-in-circle that marked her as a Witch—lying against the speaker's leathery hand.

"She do be wearing the goosefoot cross. Who else would

dare these woods at night bearing such a sigil?'' The hand released her pendant, and it fell back against Diana's skin.

"Oh, you're Witches!" gasped Diana, giddy with relief. "Thank the Goddess!" Another wave of relief-fueled dizziness swamped her senses, and she slid gracefully to the grass as her handlers released her. After a moment she was able to raise her head and look around.

She wished she hadn't.

The clearing was about the size of her living room back in Salem. It was lit by fire and candles. Most of the people gathered in these midnight woods were women, dressed almost identically in long dull-colored gowns with full skirts and long sleeves. Close-fitting linen caps concealed their hair, and over the caps one or two of the women wore high-crowned flat-topped hats that made Diana think of Pilgrims and Thanksgiving. Two of the men wore thigh-length tan smocks and leather breeches that came to just below the knee. Their feet were bare. Diana looked around instinctively for her chance-met companion of the woods, but he was not there. She could not tell if the sharp pang that struck through her was relief or loss.

And against her will, Diana could see that the trees that the dancers had filled with lanterns were in full summer leaf—thick and green and impossible to find anywhere in the autumn she'd just stepped out of.

"Please . . . who are you?" Diana whispered.

"Thou hast named us, Mistress," said a deep voice.

The man who spoke wore black square-toed shoes with silver buckles and white silk stockings that disappeared into silver-buttoned knee breeches of soft dark cloth. His long matching full-skirted coat had wide white cuffs, and a narrow sword was belted at his waist. In his hand he carried a tall carved wooden staff, and his face was covered by an elaborate mask of carved and painted wood. Horns—the antlers of the Forest Lord—branched out from a hide-covered helmet. The deerskin cascaded down his back like a medieval coif. The mask's eyes were round holes, and through them Diana could see the eyes of the man beneath. The carved face stretched longer than a human face; the chin of the mask, with its grimacing mouth, brushed the wearer's chest below the wings of the starched white linen collar that covered his shoulders and chest.

For one mad hopeful moment Diana was certain she had stumbled across a coven of historians who had decided to take up Wicca. She'd read about costumes like the one this man was wearing; two centuries ago it would have marked him as the High Priest of the coven, only they hadn't used to call them that. . . .

"Magister, it do be the Book!"

"Hey! Give me—" Diana started to scramble to her feet at the sight of the book in the hands of strangers, but a wave of weakness forced her back to her knees. "—that back," she finished faintly.

But the Magister already had it, flipping through it as carelessly as if it weren't a priceless antique.

"It is the book that we did set into the Summoner's hands, he that was slain at Landsdown in the King's service four years gone," he said. His voice was deep, made hollow and echoing by the mask but with the same swallowed vowels as the other speakers.

"And how came you to this grammarie, child?" asked the woman who had first spoken to her.

"A messenger—" Diana said, and stopped. A murmur ran through the party, and all at once a tension Diana had not realized was there vanished. The woman smiled.

"Then be welcome here," she said. "Will dance with us, Maiden?"

The Maiden was one of the officers of the medieval coven, Diana remembered, along with the Summoner and the Magister. She opened her mouth to reply, to protest, to demand some reasonable explanation, but the woman seemed to take this for assent.

"No, wait—" Diana said, but the Magister pounded his staff on the ground and the rhythm of the wooden drums began again. Strong arms pulled her into the dance, spun her and caught her, robbing her of speech.

After a few moments she stopped fighting and let the dancers do what they would. Her heartbeat was the beat of the drums, and her mind drifted far above her battered, exhausted body. She didn't want to ask questions. She didn't want answers. She was safe now, and now was all that mattered. Diana threw herself into the dance that spun and whirled about the fire, until all that was left was the memory of the burning black eyes of a fallen angel met in a midnight wood; and at last that memory rose up and enfolded her like a lover, bringing the oblivion she so desperately craved.

He was damned.

The man stood in the forest, trembling as with fever. The power that was the remains of his disavowed heritage had protected him from her, but he was weak, tainted. The Master had sent him here to find the Malignants, knowing he would not fail because the dark cancer in his soul called out to the corruption of the despoilers and led him to wallow in their evil. His own successes showed him again and again that all his strength was lies, that the Princess of this World had set their mark upon him, making him forever unclean. Only the Master could save him, only the Master could protect him. Only the Master could cut away the taint in his soul until what remained was pure and lightborne.

His breath came in great wracking sobs now as he felt the darkness coiling around him, sliding like silk and night over his skin as it claimed every inch of him for its own and took his body for its plaything. . . .

As the Master had taken everything from him.

No.

As he would take the woman.

No!

But it was true. Memories that he did not want ripped at his mind—of all that had been taken from him, along with his name, his *true* name—

NO!

—taken from him . . . taken from him . . . Once he had been powerless to resist them, but now the power beckoned, calling to him, if he would only seize it. . . .

He felt sanity begin to slide away, like the deck of a storm-tossed ship from beneath her master's feet, leaving him at the mercy of—

Of the woman.

He clutched at the memory of her as if she were his salvation instead of the enchanting gateway to a private hell. The nightwings receded as he thought of her: soft flaxen hair that glowed like the sun, eyes the vaulting azure of the summer skies, and her hot silken skin as soft and yielding as the breast of the swan.

His body spasmed with the whipsaw of hot desire transmuted into pain. As hard as he fought against it, the vision printed itself on his inner sight. . . .

He felt the hot satin of her skin slide over his as she struggled against him, laughing. He growled, deep in his throat, and pushed her down to the soft green moss of the forest floor. He knelt between her thighs and gazed down at her, feeling the pressing clutch of her muscles as she urged him down and in to her. And now he laughed and put a hand upon her breast, feeling the melting softness of her skin beneath his touch, seeing the shadow of his fingers against her whiteness. He followed the path of his hands with his open mouth and breathed in the scent of her that was hot flowers and wildness. . . .

The tree trunk against his back was suddenly shockingly rough; all his senses shocked to hypersensitivity by the vision of her, his *righ-malkin.*

His.

He would have journeyed long to find her, stolen her away from clan and kin and claimed her past all denial, courted her and tamed her and made her his own. He—

He whimpered deep in his throat, a desperate animal hungering. His hands shook with the intensity of his need to hold her, *now,* to pull her against him and lose himself in her body, to see her eyes go wide and soft with pleasure and feel her soft begging cries against the skin of his throat.

"No—"

He clutched his hands into fists and gasped against the savage need for her while his traitor mind insisted that kissing her would be like kissing flowers, soft and white and cool, *cool* against his fevered flesh.

But she was not his. She could not be his—and it was a measure of his damnation that he should want her. The hot-blooded madness receded, leaving him trembling and aching in its aftermath. She was a witch. All who walked these midnight woods were Malignants, servants of the Evil One who worked for England's doom. She was a witch.

And he still wanted her.

The man in black drew a long shuddering breath and compromised with his ghosts once more. He thought of the sunlight woman's youth and strength and beauty, the hope of joy he had seen in her eyes. He wanted her, all of her, heart and hope and strength and passion, even knowing what she was.

But she did not know what *he* was. And if he cherished her at all, he must pray that he never saw her again.

For her sake.

The dark man pushed himself away from the sheltering tree. For a moment his shoulders sagged, as if with the intolerable weight of an enormous burden, then he forced them straight.

He was what he was. What Man had made him.

God help them both.

Chapter 2

The New Forest, England, June 23, 1647

She stood in the forest clearing where she had seen him last, but he wasn't there. The moon rode full and high; her body tingled in its light as if it knew what she did not.

Then suddenly she saw his eyes flare in the darkness before her like captured moons and she was in his arms. There were lips upon her breasts, silken hair that slid over her skin in a teasing caress; she reached for his shoulders to pull him up to her kiss and his body slid through her fingers like moonspun silk and starshadow and he was cold; it was cold, cold black water closing over her. . . .

Diana woke up.

Her body yearned after the dream. She was still cold—that much of the dream had not faded—and as she rolled over, the cold air hit the previously protected parts of her anatomy and shocked her the rest of the way awake.

Diana stared around the clearing with sinking despair. This wasn't her cozy attic bedroom in Salem, Massachusetts. She was still here. *Here* was still here.

She sat up and realized that sometime between yesterday evening and now her silk shirt had lost most of its buttons. She wrapped it closed as well as she could and looked around. It was barely light; the foxy false glow of early dawn was only enough to show that the clearing where the dancers had whirled the night before stood deserted and empty.

Almost.

"So thou'rt awake."

Diana recognized the voice as the woman who'd done most of the speaking the night before.

"Where is the man in the mask?" *And the man in the wood? Where am I, come to that?*

"The Forest Lord is gone back to the forest, and best we be to our houses before good Christian folk are afoot."

"I'm from Salem!" Diana blurted out desperately.

"And I from the town hither and best be on my way. Merry met and merry parting, good mistress." The woman turned away.

"No, wait!" Diana cried. "I don't know where to go. . . . I don't know where I am. I was in my shop and the messenger came with the book and there was a storm so I ran out. I didn't mean to come here . . . and there was the man in the woods and I want to go home!" Diana finished in a rush.

The woman stared at her, weighing Diana's words more carefully than she had.

"I'm not from here," Diana whispered again. "I don't belong here."

"My grandam did say that those that come out of the Hollow Hills don't find it so easy to get back in," the woman said at last. "Art banished from Erlhame then, girl?"

"I don't know," Diana said miserably. She didn't even know where Erlhame was.

The woman sighed. "Then best thou stop with me until thy own come for thee, for thou did do a great deed for our Covenant in bringing back our grammarie." She held out her hand.

Diana took the outstretched hand and got stiffly to her feet, wincing at the pain from aching muscles and battered feet. She looked down. Blood from thorn-scratches had mingled with mud and sap to coat her injured feet in a sticky glaze. There was a spectacular blue bruise across one instep that hurt her just to look at it. The effect was rather colorful, really. And it hurt.

Diana looked up again to find the woman regarding her clothes with disapproval, as though seeing them for the first time. ''Thou'rt best rid of those seely clothes, if thou'd go about the town unremarked.''

Diana had no idea what ''seely'' clothes were, and the woman's accent gave her the treacherously unreal sensation that she was an extra in a Monty Python skit. But at some time in the night just past, Diana had abandoned the hope of this being some dream, some hoax, some spasm of her imagination.

''I don't have anything else,'' she admitted miserably.

The woman sighed, as if she'd only expected as much.

''Then bide here until I come and bring thee suitable dress. I shall say thou'rt my niece. How did they call thee in the Hill?''

''My name is Diana. Diana Crossways. What's yours?'' Diana asked.

''They call me Mistress Fortune that do speak of me, and my parents did see fit to name me Abigail when they stood before the town priest. As for thee, 'Diana' is too unchancy a name for these times. I shall call thee 'Anne' for my sister's child who died, though thou might find it best to take a new name that those who name themselves 'Pure' will approve of.''

''Like what?'' As Mistress Fortune had just renamed her, Diana hardly saw the point of changing her name yet again.

''Oh, they do call their children by all manner of unchristian newfangledness, as 'Praise God' or 'Helpmeet' or 'Preserved.' It might do thee good to have a name that no one could find fault with. I shall think on it.''

The names Mistress Fortune had told her woke dim frightful memories in the back of Diana's mind. ''What is—'' she began and could not force the words past the dry horror in her throat. *What YEAR is it?* Automatically she clutched at the silver pentacle around her neck for comfort.

''And bury that deep, Mistress Anne, for it is plainly out of

Erlhame, and to wear the goosefoot cross where townsfolk can see it is to wear the halter.''

"What?'' Diana asked blankly. She simply didn't understand.

Mistress Fortune stared at her in exasperation. "Do they know thee for elfborn and witch, Mistress, they'll hang thee for the sin of witchcraft.''

This can't be happening, Diana thought in horror. "What year—what year is this?'' she managed to croak. But Mistress Fortune had already tired of her questions and walked away.

Abigail Fortune did not return until the sun was high overhead; and before then, thirst had driven Diana to find a nearby stream. It was barely a trickle, and muddy besides, but Diana didn't care. She drank until she could hold no more, then slid her feet into the delicious coolness. She'd rather die of weird diseases than hang.

And it seemed they hanged Witches here.

Diana knew a little Wiccan history. In England there had been laws against witchcraft as late as 1953; and from 1200 to 1700, nine million European women had been executed for witchcraft in every way men's inventive courts could devise. In England and Salem they had hanged them.

For the sin of witchcraft.

"Thou shalt not suffer a witch to live,'' said King James's Bible.

"No,'' Diana said pleadingly to the bright summer forest. She had always believed that everything operated by some natural understandable law—even magic. How could she explain what had happened to her last night? Even if it were possible that she'd been struck by lightning and carried with the book in her arms back to whatever century it belonged in . . .

Stubbornly, Diana refused to believe it. There must be some other explanation. Some *reasonable* explanation.

"The time is out of joint; O cursed spite, that ever I was born to set it right."

"Mistress Anne!"

Diana scurried out of the brush and back into the clearing. Abigail Fortune regarded her dubiously when she appeared, as if she had only just now realized what a problem Diana represented. Seeing her rescuer in full daylight for the first time, Diana could understand her feelings.

Diana saw a woman some years older and several inches shorter than herself, wearing a dress of close-woven brown wool that was cinched in at the waist with a wide leather belt. The dress's sleeves were long, but the smock beneath showed at wrist and throat. She wore a wide straw hat, and beneath it there was a caul-cap of creamy homespun snugged tight around Mistress Fortune's head and tied with neat strings beneath her chin. On her feet she wore wooden clogs, and she carried a staff in one hand and a basket slung over her other arm.

And what must Mistress Fortune see? A woman freakishly tall, wearing the remains of a blouse of no natural color, cut, or fabric—and slacks. Not to mention the goosefoot cross. No wonder she looked worried. Diana smiled crookedly.

Mistress Fortune smiled in return, revealing strong, even teeth.

"Ah, I did think thee gone to the Hills again, Mistress."

The Hollow Hills. Elfland. Or Erlhame, if you preferred.

"I'm not an elf," Diana said wearily.

"Ho, and thee with the mark of the Shining Ones set fair on thy brow and eye? With hair so bright and lashes yet so dark? Give over Mistress, that cock won't fight, though I did not think to see thy kind in man's world again. Now come and garb thee in earthling clothes."

I owe it all to Maybelline, Diana thought. *The mascara guaranteed to survive fire, flood, and time travel without smudging or flaking.*

Mistress Fortune spilled the contents of her basket on the ground. A gray bundle, a white bundle, and a second pair of clogs. Clothes. Native dress. Diana wiggled her aching feet in the grass.

"And we will bury thy seely garb deep, and there will be nothing to mark thee out," Mistress Fortune continued in satisfied tones. She took a small wooden trowel from her basket, knelt, and began to dig in the cold ashes of the fire.

Diana walked over to the bundles on the grass and selected one at random. She shook it out. A dress. And a smock, an apron, another pile of cloth, something else whose purpose she could not guess at, and a cap like Mistress Fortune's. Each piece was beautifully finished, all the tiny stitches set by hand, and the cloth had the faint creamy unevenness of hand-loomed homespun.

As Diana stared at the fabric in her hands, Mistress Fortune came and shook her. "This is no time to be dawdling, Mistress. Cover thyself like a decent Christian and I will lesson thee to be my goodniece Anne."

"But I'm not a—" Diana began, and gave up. The tattered buttonless shirt slid off her shoulders, and in the sunlight the silver pentacle hanging on its chain between her breasts flashed and shimmered.

"Never say that," Mistress Fortune whispered hoarsely, glancing around her as if someone might hear. "As thou do love thy skin whole, Mistress, curb thy prating elfish tongue."

Diana stopped in the middle of removing her shirt. There was no mistaking the grim terrified urgency in Mistress Fortune's voice.

"I'll remember," Diana said, throat dry. She snatched the smock from the pile and pulled it over her head. It fell to the ground in a billowy tent, and Diana began removing her clothes beneath it.

Mistress Fortune pounced on each article of clothing as Diana discarded it: shirt, slacks, underwear. Diana pulled off her wristwatch and carefully removed the tiny gold crescent moons she wore in her ears before finally—reluctantly—unclasping the chain that held her pentacle around her neck.

Mistress Fortune took the pentacle and gazed at it reverently.

"Do not fear to lose this, Mistress; we but keep it safe for thee. And should thou wish, I'll stand thy sib and prick thee into our company at the next Covenanting."

Diana stared at her, knowing that she should say something, even if only to mention that she didn't understand a word Mistress Fortune was saying, but she was too bewildered by shock and exhaustion to respond. Mistress Fortune grimaced at her confusion and hauled up her mass of skirt and petticoat. She pointed at a mark beside her knee, her sunburnt earth-stained hands dark against skin never exposed to the sun.

Diana saw a faint blue smudge and, leaning closer, made out the blurred tattoo of a five-pointed star.

"Sealed to the Covenant with the goosefoot cross," Mistress Fortune said proudly, dropping her skirts. Something stirred in the back of Diana's mind, a flicker of bright fear gleaming through the fog of shock.

"What year is this?" she forced herself to ask once again. This time she was determined to get an answer.

Mistress Fortune regarded her balefully. " 'Tis four years gone that we did send the book to Landsdown, and not five months past did the King come into the Great Nose's tender keeping, he that was plain Noll Crummel ere he stooped to treason."

Noll Crummel. Some quirk of Diana's mind allowed her to unriddle the name given in Mistress Fortune's old-fashioned dialect. Noll Crummel. Oliver Cromwell, ruler of England's Commonwealth government, who'd lived three centuries before Diana had even been born.

Mistress Fortune plucked the watch and earrings from Diana's hand and dropped them into the hole along with the pentacle and the scraps of Diana's clothes, then set the turves back into place and began to walk back and forth over them, pressing them into place. Diana picked up the dress and began to pull it over the smock.

Cromwell.

She was in the *past.*

"Nay, child, stay! Anyone would think thee a babe unweaned, for all thou can dress thyself." Grumbling amiably, Mistress Fortune helped Diana into the bewildering array of garments, lacing Diana fiercely into a canvas stay that flattened her bosom and pinched her hips before tying several petticoats and a cylindrical pillow around Diana's waist. Only then did Mistress Fortune drop the gray dress over Diana's head, smoothing down the narrow fitted front absently as if Diana were a dressmaker's dummy.

"There," she said in satisfaction.

Diana looked down at the sweep of gray cloth, pushed out from her hips by the layered petticoats to fall in wide folds about her legs. She had an apron tied about her waist; the dress was obviously one of Mistress Fortune's; instead of hanging to Diana's ankles as the other woman's dress did, it came to midcalf.

"Happen we will let that down betimes," Mistress Fortune muttered, staring at Diana's ankles. The small cap that she handed Diana to wear on her head made Diana feel like one of the Pilgrim Mothers in the Thanksgiving play. The only thing missing from the costume was the starched linen collar and cuffs.

She wondered if the Pilgrims had left for America yet.

"Nay, not that way, child! Thou would leave thy hair a snare to catch angels in," Mistress Fortune scolded next. Diana knelt so that her mentor could unlace the cap and tuck every scrap of Diana's shoulder-length blonde hair safely out of sight before tying the cap firmly beneath her chin again.

The last item of Diana's new wardrobe was a pair of clogs like Mistress Fortune's. She slid her feet into them and stood gingerly, but the thick sheepskin lining made them bearable on her bruised feet, if still not something she'd pick to go jogging in.

"Well, come if thou'rt coming, Mistress Anne," Abigail Fortune said briskly.

* * *

Diana clumped along behind her hostess—whom she must now learn to think of as her aunt, for both their sakes—as Mistress Fortune rattled on about her sister Mary, her sister's goodman John, their large and hopeful family, the summer fever in London-town that was probably not Plague come again, praise God, the fact that suppliers for the army never paid but left worthless chits that would not buy so much as one copper coin's-worth, the wet spring and last fall's spoiled harvest, and other things.

Diana listened with only half an ear. The sun was high and the air was warm, with a salt tang that made Diana think she must be near the ocean. The track along which the two women walked was barely a foot wide, the trampled white clay dissolving to tough wiry grass at the edges. And everything was in bloom; Diana filled her lungs with sweetness. She did not recognize any of the places she'd been the night before, and that night seemed now as if it had been a thousand years ago.

"Yon's Talitho, Mistress Anne."

The road ahead sloped sharply down the hill; and the sea, penned by headlands on either side, stretched its shining path ahead of her. Automatically Diana looked around for a road, a town. When she finally saw what Mistress Fortune was pointing at, the sight was a wrenching shock.

The town of Talitho was a community of about two dozen buildings grouped at the edge of the ocean. From this distance, the white-washed, thatch-roofed buildings all seemed the size of dolls' houses; Diana could see only a handful that looked as if they had a second floor. There were one or two fishing boats pulled up on the shore and a short stub of dock reaching out into the water. There was nothing else in sight.

"As fine a town as you will see anywhere in England," Mistress Fortune said proudly.

Diana began, hopelessly, to cry.

She was trapped in the past.

* * *

In an unbelieving despair too deep for pain, Diana allowed herself to be led down the hill. She was lucky, she realized much later, that Abigail Fortune considered her a half-mad changeling out of the Hollow Hills. It was the only thing that could have either excused or explained her behavior.

Mistress Fortune did not go through the town, but around it, and at last brought Diana beyond the town to one of the cottages that seemed to have been dropped on the rolling coastland like a giant child's blocks, facing here and there without rhyme or reason. The cottage to which Mistress Fortune led her was tiny but whitewashed, with a green-painted door and a large garden behind a white-painted fence.

Mistress Fortune flipped up the small iron hook—there didn't seem to be a lock—and the door swung inward.

"Enter and be welcome, Child of Air," she said.

The ground floor of the cottage was one room and dark, despite the brightness of the afternoon. As her eyes adjusted, Diana saw that the cottage had a wide-planked wood floor and a huge stone fireplace at one end flanked by long high-backed wooden benches. She took a few steps inward, and Mistress Fortune bustled past her to open the door leading through to the garden.

At the opposite end of the room, beneath the windows, were an enormous spinning wheel and a complicated, boxy thing that looked like a piano turned inside-out but was probably actually a standing loom. A table, two chairs, some stools, and an immense oak hutch completed the furnishing. Diana sat down at the table. Along the back wall, a narrow ladder led through a hole in the ceiling to . . . something.

Welcome to the English Civil War. I suppose a civil war is better than a rude one, but I'd rather not have any war at all, if it's all the same to You, Bright Lady. . . . Diana thought lightheadedly.

"Drink this," Mistress Fortune said, setting a quart-sized pewter tankard down on the table in front of her. Diana curled her hands around it. It was warm, and the liquid inside was the exact golden color of Häagen-Dazs Honey Vanilla ice cream.

"What is it?" Diana asked suspiciously.

"Only a posset," Mistress Fortune said soothingly, "and nothing to harm thee. Now drink, and then to bed."

Diana drank, suddenly remembering that since last night she'd missed dinner, breakfast, lunch, and a number of between-meal snacks. The drink tasted of honey and brandy and cream, laced with an unfamiliar herbal bitterness. She drained the tankard quickly and set it back on the table.

"And now to bed," Mistress Fortune said firmly, "for tomorrow is the Lord's Sabbath and we must be to church."

Diana tottered to her feet. Her head seemed to be full of feathers, and her feet were leading a willful life of their own. "That's ridiculous," she pronounced. "I don't *do* Sundays."

Mistress Fortune simply ignored this, taking Diana by the elbow and leading her toward the ladder that led to the second floor.

The bedchamber was built up under the eves, and the ceiling slanted sharply down to the windows that looked out over the sea. The center of the chamber held a four-poster piled high with blankets. Diana wandered toward the window, which looked out over the sea and garden. The ocean seemed to be bouncing up and down far more than the calm day could account for and Diana's head felt unbearably heavy.

I'm spifflicated, she realized belatedly. *Potted. Drunk. What was IN that thing, anyway?* Much more brandy than any time-traveler should drink on an empty stomach, that was for sure. She wavered back into the center of the room and sat down on the bed. She didn't notice that Mistress Fortune had left until she came back, a jug and basin in her hands and a towel over one arm.

"Now wash thy feet and I shall unlace thee, and call upon sleep to heal thy disordered wits."

" '*Sleep that knits up the ravel'd sleave of care,*' " Diana muttered. " '*When in disgrace with fortune and men's eyes/I all alone beweep my outcast state—*' " A sob of pure self-pity choked her.

"But thou'rt not outcast, Mistress Anne—not while the Covenant claims thee," Mistress Fortune said gently. She eased the clogs off Diana's cut and swollen feet, poured water into the bowl, and began to bathe the broken flesh. Diana plucked at her cap-strings and finally got them untied. She pulled the cap off and shook her hair out, then sat numbly, letting Mistress Fortune have her way.

Chapter 3

The Thorn Inn, Manningtree, Essex, June 28, 1647

There were three men and a woman in the chamber. It was the parlor above the taproom—snug and secure with its separate exit, a place where information could be taken and informers come and go in perfect secrecy. There was a table and a desk such as any lawyer might envy and a glass-fronted case of books in German and French. Toward the middle of the room, with the windows behind for light, there was a dais, and on it a broad and comfortable leather chair.

The woman sat on a bench against the wall, and beside her stood a man with a full jack of ale in his hand. They both watched the second man, the one who sat in the kingly chair of state and gazed down on the last of them, who knelt, head bowed, before the chair. He had been kneeling that way for the past seven hours, as the others came and went and took their ease.

"Tell me again," the seated man said. His voice was light and fond, a voice for the giving and taking of secrets.

The kneeling man stared up at him. His eyes were wild. He wore only shirt and breeches, and his long black hair fell down his back in a tangled silken skein. Across the back of his shirt were thin rusty lines, ruler straight, where fresh whip-scars had opened and bled. Now, as the others watched, he struggled with the effort of speech.

It did not surprise them. They knew what he was and that human speech did not come easily to his kind.

None of them suspected he was lying to them.

"I did see angels going to and fro above the earth. . . . I am on my Master's business, walking to and fro in the world, seeking whom I may devour, and he took me up into a high place, and—"

"He's raving, Matthew. You'll get nothing out of him but deviltry," the standing man said in bored tones. "You must force the Devil out; I've told you that long and long."

"And by saving one petty soul imperil all?" The seated man toyed with the pair of white leather gauntlets he held and shook his head in mock dismay. "What of the great work, Johnnie? What of the soul of all England? Now. Tell me what you saw," he said, returning his attention to the man who knelt before him.

"I saw. . . . I saw—" The kneeling man choked upon the effort to speak—or not to speak. "I did see the angels going to and fro above the earth—" The words were cut off by the wet sound of leather against flesh. Matthew sat back and dropped the gauntlets into his lap. The kneeling man hung his head.

"Goodwife, the bottle."

The woman leaped up and seized the flat brown bottle from the table. With the ease of long practice she caught the kneeling man by his hair and jerked his head up, thrusting one knee against his back to hold him still. She forced the bottle into his mouth, pouring raw spirit down his throat while he coughed and choked and swallowed. He did not resist. At a sign from Matthew, she jerked the bottle away and let him go. He crouched on hands and knees, still coughing, his long hair a dark curtain about his face.

The foul taste of the liquor burned his mouth and throat, but he welcomed the promise it held of escape. He had kept from speaking as long as he could, and when he did speak, had kept the *righ-malkin* out of his tale of the Malignants in Talitho. But it had taken all of his strength to keep from following Matthew's honey-voice into his labyrinth of half-truths and confessing everything Matthew wanted to hear.

True or not.

Matthew's empire was built upon lies, but sometimes truth was needed—sand to the mortar in the architecture of fear. And then Matthew would send him, hellhound, creature of the midnight woodland, to penetrate the night's deepest secrets and bring back the strands of names, numbers, meeting places that Matthew used to weave his poisonous webs.

The light hurt the kneeling man's eyes, driving glassy splinters of pain into his aching brain. That which he was and that which he should have been warred for mastery within him, and to give that banished Other Self dominance now would doom him surely. He must hide it from Matthew's gaze, as he had hidden the *righ-malkin*.

He felt a chill hand upon his cheek as Matthew raised his head to look into his eyes. Matthew saw every rebellion, every departure from the path of righteousness. Matthew had made him what he was. Surely Matthew would see the rebellion in his heart and destroy him.

"You went into the wood on Midsummer," Matthew coaxed, "to discover the Malignants who trouble the good people of England."

But Matthew did not see, and the rebellious angel in the kneeling man's breast spread its starry wings.

"I went into the wood," he agreed. The gin burned in him, slurring his words, but that did not matter. Like the ancient warrior of his people who rode to battle with the Lady's image painted on his shield, he would keep the image of his *righ-malkin* before him. She would protect him while he guarded her.

And with her help, he would be free of Man's tyranny.

"And you saw them," Hopkins prompted.

"I saw men gathered in the wood. I saw the Devil in the

likeness of a stag.'' The words came easier now, carried on the crest of oblivion. The light behind Matthew's head was splintering into aureoles, spinning circles filled with angels, and the kneeling man felt the dark undertow of oblivion pulling him, at last, out of the world in which he had never belonged.

''I saw them all.''

And he had seen her there, but he would never tell that, never. As he slipped into the darkness he seemed to feel, once more, the imprint of her lips upon his hand.

Matthew Hopkins gazed down at the form of the dark-haired man lying insensible upon the floor and absently wiped the hand he had used to touch him upon the fabric of his fine broadcloth breeches. It had been more difficult than usual to get the information from his hellhound—almost as if the creature were resisting him. Matthew shook his head sorrowfully. How sad it would be if this most valuable of his secret agents were nearing the end of his usefulness. Something would surely have to be done.

But not now. Now he and his representatives must determine how best to spend the information they had gotten so that they could be summoned to do the Lord's work in Talitho.

Chapter 4

Talitho, Hampshire,
July 21, 1647

One day melted into the next for Diana as the full moon waned and then waxed again. Long periods of dull peace were interspersed with stretches of jarring strangeness. She woke each dawn in the bed she shared with Mistress Fortune— the only bed in the house—and after a while Diana stopped expecting to see her own familiar bedroom when she opened her eyes. Her own time and place began to seem almost mythical, something so strange and unlikely that it wasn't even worth talking about. America wouldn't even exist as a sovereign nation for another one hundred and twenty-nine years.

Shock as much as prudence led Diana to immerse herself in her assumed identity until at times she forgot that Diana Crossways of Salem, Massachusetts, had ever existed. There was only Mistress Anne Mallow of London, niece to Goodwife Fortune. If Diana let herself think about anything else, she felt she would surely go mad.

But despite her determination not to think and not to remember what had gone before, she found herself pinning her hopes for returning to her own time on the approaching Sabbat—or, as Mistress Fortune referred to it in her infrequent comments, the "regular night." Surely when the moon was full once more and the coven had gathered, Diana would be able to go home to her own century. After all, what she'd apparently been sent to do—to return the book to the coven—was done, wasn't it? Surely now, the power that had sent her here would return her to her proper place.

But if she went home—*when* she went home—any chance of seeing the stranger again would be gone forever.

That was the only thing that dampened her anticipation of returning to her own time, for try as she might, Diana could not banish the memory of the man she had met in the forest on the night of her arrival here. When she closed her eyes, she could still see his face, his dark eyes burning into hers, his lips half-parted as if he were about to disclose some urgent message. At night as she lay in the feather bed beneath the eaves, she imagined the imprint of his body on her own. She felt his breath, warm and scented, against the nape of her neck when she stood alone in twilight rooms.

But for all Diana's asking, Mistress Fortune did not know him, and Mistress Fortune knew everyone in Talitho and most of the people in the neighboring villages of Christchurch and Milford-on-Sea.

"Be done with asking, Mistress Anne!" Abigail Fortune had said at last, wearied by Diana's repeated questions. "Many's the unhouseled spirit roaming the wood of a night. Be thankful only that he did thee no ill!"

But Diana was not done with asking. The man she'd seen was no spirit. He was real. He'd come to one midnight meeting in the woods. Surely he would come to another. She did not let herself think that she had found him only to lose him.

Because she meant to find him, no matter what.

"Aunt Abby, what shall I do today?" Diana gnawed industriously at a piece of manchet-bread, then, giving up, dunked it in her wooden mug of goat's milk to soften it. It was barely two hours past dawn, and this morning already she had milked

Mistress Fortune's two goats—a newly-acquired skill—and gathered up the eggs the chickens had seen fit to leave scattered here and there. Life in Talitho was one long round of chores, but they were all so unfamiliar to Diana that she enjoyed them. Just as long as they were a holiday vacation, and not for the rest of her life.

Diana was about to repeat her question when the door of the cottage was thrust open and a boy Diana had seen on her visits to the town burst in. He was barefoot, wearing the knee-length pants and baggy smock that were the almost universal male costume here, and the paleness of his face made his freckles stand out like mud spatters.

"The Lambs, Mistress Fortune! The Lambs are coming to Talitho! Squire Adcock at the manor asked for them—and Dr. Grimsby, who's staying with parson. They've paid them twenty silver pounds to come!"

Twenty pounds? Diana thought in shock. Twenty pounds was more money than most of the villagers would see in a lifetime; the seventeenth century equivalent of a rock star's ransom.

"When?" Mistress Fortune's voice was a harsh crow-caw.

"Tomorrow . . . soon." He plainly did not know, jittering up and down with the need to spread the news.

"Go." Mistress Fortune flipped her apron at him and he vanished from the doorway, running on his way to the next cottage.

She turned back to Diana, and suddenly Mistress Abigail's face was that of an old woman. "The Lambs," she said. "The Lambs are coming here."

"What Lambs?" Diana asked, bewildered. "Aunt Abby, tell me."

"The Three Unspotted Lambs of the Lord," Mistress Fortune said bitterly. "They that never do leave until they have borne false witness against some hapless victim, as they did in Cambridgeshire not three months gone. Did I dare without the Magister's leave, I should lay such a knotting upon Old Adcock and Grimsby—that righteous man of God—as would tie up their bowels until Christ should come again!''

Though Diana tried, she could not get Mistress Fortune to tell her anything more. Either Mistress Fortune was afraid even to talk about it—and in Diana's experience, Mistress Fortune feared very little—or she felt that she had explained the matter perfectly clearly and Diana was just being difficult.

"But I don't understand! You know I don't!" Diana protested.

"The blackberries are ripe for plucking, did thou but know how to recognize them," Mistress Fortune said meaningfully, jerking her head toward the door.

Diana sighed, recognizing defeat as well as a reminder of her other shortcomings. Anytime she was tempted to believe she belonged here, the list of skills she lacked would change her mind. She could not sew or spin or weave; her attempt at making butter had been a particularly spectacular failure; and though Diana knew a good deal about the properties of herbs, she had no idea what most of them looked like in their natural state.

"Okay," Diana sighed, "I'll go and get the bucket." *And maybe when I get back, you'll be willing to tell me what it is about lambs—with or without spots—that has everybody so upset.*

The rope-handled leather bucket was three-quarters full of ripe, half-crushed blackberries—and so was Diana—when she finally stopped to rest. Her berrying expedition had carried her several miles up the coast from Mistress Fortune's cottage, and she might as well have been on the moon for all the sign of civilization she could see. No airplanes overhead, no superhighway just beyond the trees, not even an abandoned beer can. The only sound that reached her ears was a drowsy humming composed in equal parts of bees, surf, and the sound of the wind through the trees.

Diana walked away from the berry patch and sat down next to a rock, leaning back against it and digging her bare toes into the soft sandy dirt. Most of the inhabitants of Talitho saved their shoes for Sundays or rough weather, and Diana had not found it hard to follow the local custom.

It's so pretty here. No drugs, no crime, no pollution. No traffic problems, no terrorists. These people don't know how lucky they are. Diana ran a scratched and berry-stained hand through her sun-warmed hair. The irritating caul-cap that Mistress Fortune made her wear was stuffed safely into her apron, to be extracted at need.

On the other hand, there's no penicillin, no chocolate—and no books.

In fact, the only book Diana had seen since her arrival in Talitho was the church Bible, and she hadn't been allowed to touch it. When she'd asked Mistress Fortune about books, she'd been firmly told not to bother her head with such things.

" 'Books in the running brooks, Sermons in stones, and good in everything,' " Diana quoted to herself wryly, staring sleepily off into space. " 'Sweet are the uses of adversity.' "

Her eyes closed, and her hand slipped from the rim of the berrying-bucket to her lap. Diana was asleep.

She stood in the forest clearing where she had seen him last, but he wasn't there. Moonlight spilled like silver cream from the dark pitcher of midheaven and she wove the beams into a gown, argent, soft, and fine. Her hair was the golden corona of the sleeping sun.

The leafsong stilled and he was there, standing among the trees. He wore a jeweled collar about his throat and his black hair swept over his shoulders like a curve of raven's wing. On his head was the horned crown of the Forest Lord, each branching tine gleaming gold. He smiled, and she saw the feral flash of his curved teeth.

"Well met by moonlight, proud Titania," he said. His voice was soft and low, binding her will in velvet shackles. Her pulse fluttered in her throat; fear and anticipation.

"You come at an inconvenient hour, Lord Oberon."

"And yet I do find that you await me." His smile widened and he took a step forward.

"Stay back!" she cried, but it was a protest only meant to incite and they both knew it. He laughed and lunged for her. She turned and ran, fleet as a white deer—but not as swift as he.

She saw his eyes flare in the darkness and then she was in his arms, crushed against the silken velvet of him as his hot expert hands opened her gown to the night.

The earth beneath her was living and yielding, and she could feel its heartbeat and his and her own. There were lips upon her breasts, silken hair that slid over her skin in a teasing caress. Her body ached with the urgent need to enfold him, to bring him safely home. She needed his weight upon her, his body hot and desperate inside her. She needed him.

She reached for his shoulders to pull him up to her kiss. His body slid through her fingers like smoke and sorrow and he was cold. It was cold, cold black water closing over her. . . .

Diana jerked awake with a gasp. Something had wakened her, but what? She shook her head, trying to clear the last of the dream from her mind. It was then that she heard the hoofbeats on the sea road and suddenly remembered Mistress Fortune's visitor of the morning. Strangers were a rarity in Talitho, but hadn't the butcher's boy said that someone was coming to town?

She ran to the edge of the cliff to look and saw four riders on the road below. They would pass directly beneath her vantage point in only a few moments.

The leader rode a gray horse. His cloak was edged in silver buttons and faced in white satin. She thought he must be a nobleman, for by now she knew that it was unlikely for anything other than inheritance to make one so young so rich. Behind him, on what Diana thought of as two horse-colored horses, rode a man and a woman.

The woman rode astride, and even at this distance Diana could see fine point-lace edging the revealed petticoats. Beneath cap and sheltering hat, the woman's face was coarse and boiled looking; and as she turned in the saddle to cry out to her companion, Diana could see the gaps of missing teeth.

"Ea, John, how long must we ride?"

The man addressed was large, his garb a shade less fine than the leader's. He had thick sausage fingers, his hands folded calmly one over the other as if he were in a pew in church.

"We ride on the Lord's business, Mary, and such work shall last until the Day of Judgment."

Moron, Diana thought. At least these weren't the Unspotted Lambs Abigail Fortune was worrying about; there were four of them, not three.

And the fourth rider she knew. She saw him every time she closed her eyes.

His horse was tied by a leading rein to the one called John's saddle. The animal lugged along behind, neck outstretched. The man on its back did not seem to notice.

He was garbed all in dark-colored cloth unrelieved by silver button or buckle and wore a broad-brimmed hat just as the others did. He rode with his head down, as if he did not care where he went, and all she could see of him at first was the shine of the sun on his long black hair. It spilled freely over his shoulders, where other men would have tied such long hair back; and in the hot light beating down, it shone with the iridescent glory of the raven's wing.

Then he looked up.

Diana jerked as if she had been jolted by electricity. It was *him*—the man from the forest—and at last she knew what color his eyes were: black amber, with only the faintest hope of gold to relieve the ravening darkness.

The world spun like a diving falcon and suddenly Diana was not on the cliff—she was looking *up* at the cliff, at a barefoot woman whose unbound hair was a golden flag in the sun and whose soft red mouth bore berry stains like the imprint of wanton kisses.

She was looking at *herself.*

The shock of recognition broke the connection, and Diana was in her own body again, looking down on the man who had haunted her every moment since she had come here. Now, at last, he was within her reach.

She was filled with unreasonable joy: He had come back for her; she would see him again; and this time, she'd find out his name. . . .

She raised her hand—to hail him, to call out, she was hardly sure—but when she moved, he turned his head sharply away from her and stared fixedly out to sea. Shutting her out.

Slowly Diana lowered her hand and walked back to the berry bucket. The hoofbeats faded as the riders passed around a curve in the road; and suddenly, unreasonably, standing alone in the bright summer sunshine, Diana was terribly afraid.

Even walking briskly, it took her the better part of two hours to retrace her steps to Mistress Fortune's cottage. When she arrived, Diana was surprised to see that her usually solitary mentor had company. The three women sat together at the table; Diana recognized both of Aunt Abby's guests from her reluctant, compulsory church attendance: Lettice Forster and Jemima Skelton. Lettice was the town midwife; Jemima was married to the miller who lived in the direction of Christchurch. The mill was several miles away; Mistress Skelton must have come by horseback to be here so late in the day.

"Hi—um, good afternoon," Diana said, dropping an awkward curtsy. It was only then that she realized she hadn't put her cap back on and scrabbled in her apron to retrieve it.

"Back so soon?" Mistress Fortune regarded her balefully. Diana set her bucket inside the door, wishing it were fuller.

"I saw some riders heading for the village—three men and a woman," Diana said, awkwardly trying to tie the cap back onto her head.

"The Lambs," Goodwife Forster said.

"God keep them," Mistress Skelton added quickly.

"And hurried to ask what business they had with you?" Mistress Fortune said to Diana tartly. Diana set her jaw and remained silent. Abigail Fortune had done too much for her for Diana to return rudeness for rudeness now, when the older woman was so obviously upset.

"Well, thou can go see to it in the town; there's a bottle of cider I'll be wanting from the Moon and Lantern, an' thou feels able to fetch it," Mistress Fortune said.

It was only then that Diana remembered that the Talitho coven met tonight. She stared at Mistress Fortune; mouth half open in surprise.

"Go!" Abigail Fortune said.

Since she'd gotten here, Dr. Grimsby's depressing—and gradually lengthening—Puritan sermons had become longer and grimmer with each succeeding Sunday. These days the parish of Talitho could expect to spend from morning till night on its knees searching out its imagined sins—and anything you looked for long enough you were sure to find, whether it had been there in the beginning or not. Not counting the mandatory Sunday pilgrimages to Talitho's despoiled church, Diana had been to the village less than half-a-dozen times since she had found herself marooned here.

In a way, she was happier to stay away; she could tell herself that such a cottage as Mistress Fortune's might have survived into Diana's own time relatively unchanged, but each sight of Talitho was a crushing reminder that she was a stranger in a strange land.

In future centuries, no doubt Talitho would develop urban sprawl: paved streets lined with shops—milliner, tobacconist, bookstore, grocer, sweet shop—apartment and office buildings, and in its suburbs, neat streets lined with cottages, each with its flower-bordered square of lawn. But the Talitho Diana walked through now seemed oddly unfinished: the public-house and the church looked much as they would in the future, but there was a wide green apron of open yard around the tavern and a stable behind and the church was a good distance beyond the town with nothing but grass around it. It was set on a low swell of ground, its graveyard spread around it like a widow's skirts.

What would someday be the village's fashionable High Street was scarcely a city block long, crammed with narrow timber-and-plaster buildings: butcher, baker, candle-maker; the trades that every village needed, no matter how small. But doctor, lawyer, and the closest thing to a grocery store that existed here were ten miles away in the town of Christchurch. There was a market day there every two weeks, a hiring fair in the spring and a harvest fair in the fall, and a court which met once each quarter to try the offenses of the previous three months. The cloth for the dress Diana was wearing—as well as the linen for her cap and smock—had been bought at Christchurch Fair, along with needles and pins, sugar and spices, and all the expensive luxuries that were common stock in any drugstore of the twentieth century.

There was no bookstore in Christchurch. The printing press itself was less than two centuries old, and a rich man's cherished library might consist of less than twenty volumes. What literacy there was in places like Talitho was confined to primitive pamphlets and printed broad-sheets—as if the entire stock of human information had been reduced to one issue of *TV Guide*.

Stop thinking about that, Diana told herself crossly. The summer heat beat down on her primly covered head, making the layers of clothing she wore damply uncomfortable. It wasn't as if there were *no* books—in fact, if she had ten times Squire Alcock's fortune and could get to London, she could buy the plays of Shakespeare and Marlowe and rare Ben Jonson, peruse the philosophy of Francis Bacon and the poetry of Edmund Spenser. This was an age rich in literacy and learning, so the history books agreed.

If you were in London. In London, and rich. Here in Talitho the black beast of medieval superstition still prowled, seeking what it might devour. . . .

Will it even be safe to go into the woods tonight? Diana wondered as the path went from beaten earth to cobblestones beneath her bare feet. The coven met in the woods a few miles outside of town—how could it be safe for them to gather with the danger Mistress Fortune feared holding court in Talitho itself, at a time when all the village would be tuned to noticing the slightest strangeness?

Still brooding, Diana arrived at her destination and went inside. The inn was unusually crowded for late afternoon; in a world where artificial light was expensive and rare, the villagers labored by the light of sun and daylight hours were precious.

Diana tried not to inhale too deeply. The inn's common room was hazy with the smoke from clay pipes—King James I had already said that smoking was hazardous to your health, but it would be three centuries before anyone took him seriously.

You could have anything you wanted to drink at the Moon and Lantern so long as it was beer or cider; there were three enormous barrels—hogsheads—laid along the back wall, each bunged with a carved wooden tap. The trestle table before it was the precursor of a later century's bar. Hesitantly, Diana approached the innkeeper.

"Mistress Fortune's girl." The tapster turned toward her, wiping reddened hands on a clean white apron. "Hast come to see the sport? Master Matthew Hopkins of Manningtree in Essex is with the squire now. We'll have the Devil out of Hampshire just as we did the King."

Laughter from the men around the bar greeted the witticism; and despite her avowals of bravery and detachment, Diana flinched from the coarse merriment. The name the innkeeper spoke woke faint uneasy memories in Diana, and instinct told her that the group of idle men were perilously close to being a mob.

And mobs weren't noted for being reasonable.

"Has the Devil been here, then?" Diana asked coolly, though her heart hammered in fear. She searched her memory for the man's name and found it. "I'm sure you'd know if anyone would, John Landlord."

There was an angry rumble from the men in the inn's public room, and Diana saw John Landlord's face grow dark with anger—and fear.

"I'm no Malignant," he growled swiftly. "And you'd best stop your mouth, Mistress Anne, lest the Devil fly in it."

"I've come for a jug of hard cider," Diana said, keeping her voice even with an effort. "May I have it?"

There was the rumble of talk from the far end of the room; an observation made at her expense, followed by laughter. Deliberately Diana did not react, holding John Landlord's eye and staring him down. At last he looked away, shouting for the serving boy and bending to swing up the trap door that led to the cellar. The boy dashed in from the kitchen, red-faced and grubby, and soon the stoneware jug of cider was sitting on the bar.

"Thank you," Diana said levelly.

John Landlord glared. "Best mend thy London ways, Mistress, or you'll get no husband here."

Diana nearly snatched the jug off the bar, and staggered at its solid heaviness. "Thank you so much for sharing that with me; I really appreciate your input," she said with poisonous sweetness. Before the tapster could get the last word, Diana swung her burden up onto her hip and swept out of the inn.

The Devil and Matthew Hopkins. Diana hurried back toward Mistress Fortune's cottage, her mind a whirl of disbelief and dread as she remembered where she'd heard the name before. He was one of the most notorious criminals in Wiccan history—hundreds of innocent harmless people had died during the English Civil War because of Hopkins's self-serving crusade. He'd made thousands of dollars—pounds sterling—out of fraudulent manufactured accusations of witchcraft.

Witchcraft.

You might just as well say AIDS, considering the unreasoning terror the word provoked. Filled with fear, the citizens of

Talitho would soon begin to accuse one another, delivering their neighbors to the knife, the whip, and the rack.

The shadows stretched. Without her banished wristwatch, Diana wasn't quite sure of the time: four o'clock, or maybe five. In a few hours it would be dark. She was passing the last of the houses along the high street when a hand seized her and yanked her backward into an alleyway.

Diana opened her mouth to scream; a hand covered it. She struggled silently in the narrow darkness between two shops, her bare feet skidding on the sloping stones that paved the surface beneath them. The alley was little more than a gutter separating the buildings on either side of it. Though she'd dropped the stone jug of cider, the alleyway was so narrow that it was still wedged between her thrashing body and the wall, pushing her harder against her attacker's body.

Sheer terror and lack of air made her dizzy; it took her several moments to realize that her assailant was only holding her and had made no attempt to hurt her or tear her clothes. She stopped fighting, and the grip upon her mouth loosened enough for her to draw as deep a breath as her tight canvas stays would permit. The stoneware jug slid down her body and clunked to the alley floor. Cautiously she pulled away and turned to face her attacker.

The upper stories of the buildings formed a roof over the passageway; the only light came from the street beyond. But she recognized him, even without knowing his name.

A faint scent of salt and sun clung to his clothing; he wore neither collar nor cuffs, and the neckband of his shirt was open, exposing the pale skin of his throat. His long dark hair was pulled severely away from his face and his eyes were nothing but shadows in the gloom, but Diana sensed he gazed on her with feral intensity.

The narrowness of the passage pressed their bodies gently against each other. Even through the damp layers of linen smock and petticoats and dress she wore, Diana could feel the summery heat of his body, its outline as sharp and plain to her senses as if neither of them wore anything at all. A prickle of sweat broke out along her hairline; she tried to back away, and the wall behind her plastered the soggy stays against her moist back. Its clammy coolness sent a calming chill through her.

"Can I . . . can I help you?" she asked ridiculously. She felt faintly unsteady—not afraid, but as if she were on the verge of a surrender so powerful that to yield to it would change her completely. She opened her mouth, gasping for breath against the canvas corset that suddenly chafed her. What did he want? He'd been in the woods that night.

Had he come to take her home? Was that why he was here? Still he said nothing.

"Talk to me," Diana whispered.

She raised one hand to push him away, moving as slowly as if she were under water. The sweat-soaked linen of her petticoats clung to her thighs when she moved, and all she could do was sway against him in the cramped space, imprinting his body with her own.

She did not really want to move. She did not want to escape. He had obsessed her from the first moment she had seen him, and now he was close enough to touch. He'd given her permission to touch him by his actions; he had sought her out deliberately. . . .

She pressed herself against him harder and he did not move; she felt the cloth of his shirt slip against his sweat-slick skin, and in the darkness she heard the sudden stifled intake of his breath. Sweat ran down her forehead and beaded ticklingly on her upper lip. She could almost feel his mouth covering hers and leaned forward, willing him to kiss her.

This is stupid! Diana's mind yelped, jerking her back from the offered intimacy. She flinched and banged her head on the alley wall. "Who the hell are you?" she snarled, frightened more of herself than him.

"I would thou did not dance." His voice was soft and hoarse, as if it were a thing rarely used. She could feel his breath against her face, hotter than the summer night that surrounded them.

"Dance?" Diana recoiled in shock; whatever she'd expected from him, it was not this. "What do you care if I dance or not? Who are you?"

"Good Christian folk lie abed and do not dance; dancing is lewdness and heathenish."

The bizarre senselessness of his calm pronouncements finally broke through to her, and Diana felt as if she'd been punched in the stomach. She stood pressed against him in a space no wider than a phone booth; his heart beat against her own, and she felt each irrational word he spoke vibrate through his chest as he spoke it. Now that she'd found him again, how could he talk like this?

"I would thou did not dance." She ought to have been afraid, but somehow she did not feel as if she'd been accosted by a stranger; the illogical conviction remained that this was her own, her true love, and she wanted to anoint the salty flesh of his throat with kisses. . . .

But they were strangers, and she couldn't.

"You were in the woods the night I came. You spoke to me then," Diana tried to remind him. But had he? She could not remember those events clearly now; all that remained was the touch of his hand, the sound of his voice urging her to run.

Her left hand was still trapped against his chest. Diana raised her other hand, but could bring it no higher than his hip. She rested it there and felt the trembling that passed through his body as a gust of wind through a forest. The impulse to rub her body against him like a cat beneath a stroking hand was nearly irresistible.

"Did you bring me here?" she asked. "Was it you? Who are you?"

"I—" He tried to jerk away from her, but the unforgiving walls of the alley pressed their bodies teasingly against each other. "I am a black crucible of corruption; the Malignants have laid their spider's kiss upon my soul; they have ransomed my salvation from the angels and I am their hound to hunt the night. And I would thou did not dance.''

''*Damn* you,'' Diana breathed. An anger and sorrow barely distinguishable from fear made her savage. Only now, when the meeting she'd dreamed about had finally come to pass so disappointingly, did she realize how much her imagination had invested in it. She'd thought of him as an angel who could take her home, had supplied her dark woods-lord with every desirable quality. In her heart, he'd become the perfect stranger she'd always longed to meet, to touch, to kiss. . . .

And now she found out he was crazy.

''Leave me alone!'' Diana began to struggle against him in earnest, trying to claw past him to reach the street beyond. If she screamed, someone would surely hear her.

Then, suddenly, she was free. She scrambled from the alley's mouth into the open air. Her hair tumbled brightly about her face; her cap had come off in the struggle. With shaking hands she smoothed her hair back from her face, ready to scream, to run, to fight if he followed her out of the alley.

But he didn't. She took a few steps into the street so that she could see squarely into the alley's mouth. The late sun slanted across it. She could see the jug of cider resting against the wall.

There was no one there.

Diana expelled a long shaky breath. The alley ran straight until it backed upon another house. There was nowhere he could have gone.

Could she have imagined it? Diana hugged herself tightly, trying to slow the hammering of her racing heart. The fear that this whole experience was just some sort of madwoman's dream was never far from the surface of her consciousness—but no. She could still taste his scent on the air. It had been real. *He* had been real.

Tears of frustration and disappointment prickled behind Diana's eyes. No. He wasn't real. The man in her fantasies and the man she had met had nothing at all to do with one another. Fighting back her tears, she stepped into the alley to retrieve the jug of cider.

Chapter 5

Talitho, Hampshire, July 21, 1647

She was here.

The hunter lay upon the worn slates of the rooftop, stretched full length upon them to keep from falling. He had the power to dazzle men's minds to pass among them unseen, to make them dream the dreams he chose, but he had not needed to exercise those black gifts. The rough brick of the wall at the alley's end had been easy enough to climb, and the hunter did not go about openly among Man if he had a choice, just as he did not call upon the powers of Hell. Stretching his body, he slithered another handspan forward along the angle of the roof. In another few inches he would be able to see the street.

The stored summer heat radiated into his body just as the wind from the ocean cooled him; he lay suspended between hot and cold, a part of neither. At last he gained the edge of the roof and gazed down upon his *righ-malkin*.

She was still there. Her hair was an unchaste golden tumble about her shoulders, and he had felt the heat of her living flesh as she had writhed in his arms; his body still ached for her in proof of her sinful power; darkness calling to darkness. His fingers tightened around the fragile linen square of her cap, and he ground his body against the unrelenting stone in awkward frustration, held as irrevocably prisoner by the mere chance to look at her as if he were bound in nets made of her hair.

Thus were the angels trapped by the wiles of the wanton daughters of Men; thus was sinful Man caught in the Malignants' toils.

And she was of their number.

He pressed his body harder against the slate roof, this time to shut out the pain that thought brought him. His body tensed. His hands closed into fists, but nothing could blot out the knowledge: she was corrupt beyond the things of this world. She was his special prey.

Mistress Anne Mallow, they had named her in the village, but it was a lie. She was his lady of the hidden sun; she had danced in the wood beneath the full moon and had opened herself to the night. He brought the scrap of linen to his nostrils and inhaled the scent of her hair.

She was. . . . She was. . . .

Why did she stand so still in the street below? Why did she not run? Tonight the moon was full once more. The Malignants' covenant would meet and dance; and he had told her not to go, had warned her not to dance, not to flaunt her white body to the insistent power of the drums, not to allow their pagan heartbeat to caress her flesh and rouse the hot blood beneath the silken skin.

But she had not listened. She would go tonight, to dance before the fallen altars of the body—and he would follow and mark all who joined her there and bear his witness to his Master so that the outer evil that mirrored the corruption in his own soul could be destroyed.

And she would be taken. Perhaps not this night, but surely the next time they met. Taken. Stripped, beaten, forced to confess and bear witness to her evil . . .

The hunter thought of John Sterne's hard hands upon her glorious golden body and shuddered. He had seen the lies Sterne had wrung from living flesh with needles and hot irons. Sterne could make a stone cry out and fill the air with lies.

He would not let that happen.

His own rebellion was as stark as a dagger in the heart, as unyielding as the bright deadly blade of cold iron his kind feared most. Though she was his master's lawful prey—as others were not—she was truly guilty, he would save her.

If he could.

If Matthew did not read his hunter's heart and find her there.

He saw her turn and step back into the alley. He saw the sun-kissed bronze of her bare feet, dusky with earth, and the paler golden flash of her ankles as her skirts swung up. She came back out of the alley with the stone jug she had carried upon her hip.

She looked up toward the roof, and he saw the long angle of her tawny throat gleaming with sweat. A lock of her hair lay across the skin like a necklace, darkened to the deep gold of autumn leaves by the dew of her skin. She brushed it away and shrugged.

He imagined he could see her flesh move independently of the covering garments; imagined the caress of linen over the curves of her sweat-dewed body, the clasp and flex of her limbs, the perfume of her silken hollows, like the scent of sea and storm. He watched as she walked up the road in the long summer twilight; and as her gray dress blurred into the pale sand of the cliff road, he began to work himself slowly backward along the roof. Soon it would be night, and the moon would rise.

And he would hunt.

It was twilight by the time Diana returned to the cottage, and Mistress Fortune was not there. She set the heavy jug of cider down with a sigh of relief—she wished these people would invent the backpack—and looked around the room.

Tomorrow she would look back on this as if it had been a dream, Diana told herself hopefully. She tried to summon up the memory of her sunny apartment, the Salem bookshop, but the memories would not come. Instead, the sights and smells

of the cottage around her presented themselves with sudden
vividness.

The loom in the corner had been strung a few days after she
had come and now held a half-finished piece of cloth. The
spinning wheel opposite it stood with a half-full spindle of fine
white thread upon it—Mistress Fortune's work, as all Diana's
attempts to spin an even thread so far had been worthless—
and a puff of carded flax lay on the bench beside it.

A cauldron of soup simmered over the fire, heating the
already close air, and the room was heavy with the smell of
recent baking. Diana sniffed appreciatively and then followed
her nose to a covered basket set by the back door. She lifted
the bright kerchief that covered it and looked inside.

Most of the inhabitants of Talitho bought their bread from
the baker, whose closed brick ovens ensured a superior product,
but these cakes could not be bought there. Diana stared down
at the basket full of hand-sized cakes. The recipe was in her
own Book of Shadows, handed down through the centuries—
honey, wine, salt, meal—and just as Diana would three centuries from now, Mistress Fortune marked each cake she made
with a five-pointed star.

No matter what happened here in the Burning Times, Diana
knew that the Craft had survived to her own time, slowly changing as it was handed down through the centuries until it took
on the form she knew. But knowing that didn't make her any
more content here.

I want to go home, Diana thought with a sudden burst of
homesickness. Home, away from this—away from *him.* She
sat down at the table and put her head on her arms. Why
couldn't she have kept her illusions? Why couldn't he have
stayed a pleasant dream instead of a disappointing truth? When
she'd seen him again, she'd been able to believe, even if only
for just one shining moment, that her dark woods-lord, her
demon lover, was *real.* . . .

"Ah, Mistress Anne, I did not look to see thee before nightfall," Abigail Fortune said, coming in from the garden. She

brushed her work-coarsened hands on her apron. "Did'st go about the town so uncovered?"

Slowly Diana raised her hand to her head. Her cap had come off in the scuffle in the alley, and she'd been so upset she'd managed to forget that the first thing she should have done coming in was go and get a fresh one from the clothespress. Everyone in Talitho had seen her walk back here without it, too.

She shrugged helplessly.

"Ah well, that's gossip for another morning," Mistress Fortune decided. "Did get what I did send thee for?"

"The hard cider," Diana said, indicating the jug. The disturbance at the inn returned to her in a rush. "They're talking about . . ." She faltered, surprised at how hard it was to go on. "About having Matthew Hopkins drive the Devil out of Talitho," she said helplessly.

Mistress Fortune snorted derisively. "Out through the door and in through the window," she said, "until the Lambs have had their fill. But there is nowt we may do to stay the Lord of this World. Tell me instead, Mistress, would be pricked into our covenant this night?"

Pricked into the covenant. Diana stared at her mentor in confusion until the memory of the faded blue star Mistress Fortune had showed her on their first meeting came back to her. Pricked into the covenant. Initiated into the coven.

"But I already am. . . ." Diana faltered.

"Under hill among the firstborn of the Hidden Queen," Mistress Fortune supplied for her. "Wilt go back there this night, then?"

Under hill . . . Diana remembered that Mistress Fortune believed she was one of the Fair Folk, the elves that the country-folk still believed in though their city brethren had discarded such outworn knowledge, and she wanted to know if Diana was going home again, now that the moon was full.

A wave of homesickness that seemed more like terror shook Diana. She *would* go back. She *had* to! She couldn't stay here, in this crazy world where they hanged Witches and witch-hunters rode through the countryside like travelling gunslingers. She didn't belong here. This wasn't any of her business.

"I don't know," Diana said raggedly.

Mistress Fortune sighed. "It is not ours to will, but theirs . . . but I would thy seely brethren came for thee soon, Mistress. But now eat thy soup and then rest awhile. We do not stir from here until the moon shall show us our way."

Mistress Fortune ladled soup from the kettle into a pewter bowl and set it on the table beside a wide-bowled carved horn spoon. Diana accepted the soup reluctantly and dipped her spoon into the bowl. Mistress Fortune turned to the sideboard to cut slices from a loaf of bread and pour Diana a cup of goat's milk.

"Are you sure it's safe?" Diana asked, when they were nearly finished eating. "To go out tonight?"

Mistress Fortune set down her own spoon and looked at Diana as if she'd gone mad.

"I mean, with Hopkins in the village. I mean, if they're just looking for an excuse . . ." Diana's voice trailed off.

"But 'tis never safe, child," Mistress Fortune said quietly. "Each time we go forth by night, there is that risk of discovery; we can but trust in our Queen to protect us from the Lord of this World."

Their Queen: the Hidden Queen, the Goddess of the Wicca. Diana couldn't even begin to speculate who the Lord of this World was, though the phrase sounded familiar somehow. She looked into Mistress Fortune's stern shining gaze and felt vaguely ashamed. In her own time, to be Wiccan only meant risking a little ridicule. For *her* beliefs, Mistress Fortune faced death every day of her life.

"And now that thou has supped, thou must rest, for there will be much gaiety at the regular tonight."

A 'regular' was what Mistress Fortune called the coven meeting; for all her questions, Diana had not been able to find out a regular *what*. Diana had never felt less like gaiety in her

life; but if she stayed downstairs, she knew she would only
end up telling Mistress Fortune about the man who'd dragged
her into the alleyway, how she suspected him of being in league
with the bloody-handed Matthew Hopkins, who was going to
drive the Devil out of Talitho. And that, she knew, would gain
her nothing but a fierce scolding.

Diana set her bowl in the bucket full of water to await later
washing and trudged up the ladder to where the solid four-
poster lay beneath the open window. After giving her dirty feet
a cursory scrub in the basin on the washstand, Diana undressed
to her smock, relishing the play of the cool air over her damp
skin.

For a moment she stood before the open window, staring
out at the mirror-bright sea in rebellious confusion, then she
flung herself down on the bed and tried not to think. Finally,
unwillingly, she slept.

*She was in a vast lightless cavern; a world where there was
neither sun nor moon, where a river made of all the blood shed
on Earth produced a roaring like the ocean wave. With the
irrational conviction found in dreams, Diana knew that HE
was here somewhere and that she had to rescue him before it
was too late.*

*The stone beneath her feet was slick and cold as glass; and
as she ran, the walls of the cavern narrowed until she fled down
a corridor lined with all the instruments of the Inquisition—
the rack, the boot, knives and needles and thumbscrews, all
illuminated by the sulphurous blue-burning torches that lined
the walls.*

*"Where are you?" Diana cried out helplessly. She had to
find him, help him, free him. . . .*

*She forced herself to stop, to search among the grisly relicts
of that ghastly exhibition, searching for him. . . .*

*The human monsters who had built these things had a sense
of humor. Why else would they so lavishly decorate these objects
designed to crush and maim? Here was a Spanish Boot; it*

would pulp and splinter the bones of the leg and foot, yet some malefic artisan had ornamented its surface with gold and embellished its heel with a spur. The standing rack's pulleys were sculpted with gargoyle faces, and the impassive surface of the Iron Maiden was adorned with a serene woman's face, her downcast eyes and madonna smile presiding over the horrors within. Fearfully, reluctantly, Diana approached its cabinet and reached for one of the handles crafted in the likeness of folded hands that were set upon its front.

The doors fell open without her touch, and she saw the man within. Crouching, naked, he snarled at her as his body began to flow, to change, to sprout fangs and talons and long gray fur. . . .

Diana sat up with a jerk, her heart hammering with the panic of her dream, and stared wildly around at the too-familiar room. The chest and clothespress were barely visible in the blue of the early summer night. She shook her head, pushing back her sweat-tousled hair from her forehead.

What had she dreamed? Something about a chamber of horrors, a wolf . . . something like a Marquis de Sade retelling of Little Red Riding Hood. But the wolf had been the dark man—she didn't even know his name—or he had been the wolf; and despite the threat, the fear, she still had the nagging dream-intuition that *he* had been the one in danger, not she.

Diana swung her legs over the edge of the bed and stood, reaching for her clothes. She had been here so long that the clothes no longer seemed strange; she pulled the sleeveless stay around her ribs and tightened its front-lacing with a single expert pull. *Not too tight,* she cautioned herself. She'd be dancing tonight.

The thought of dancing brought back her humiliating conversation that afternoon with a vivid immediacy. His talk of dancing would make sense if he had spied on the coven at its last meeting. If he had . . .

But he couldn't have, Diana realized with a pang of relief.

If he knew anything of the Talitho coven, surely he would have reported it weeks ago. She'd seen him in the forest, true; and while she didn't know how far she'd run after she'd seen him in the woods, he obviously hadn't followed her. All his talk about dancing was just Puritan party line.

He doesn't know anything. Diana felt herself relax. She reached for her petticoats and bumroll and tied on, first the sausage-shaped pad stuffed with horsehair, then the layers of cream-colored petticoats—one, two, three—stitched to a wide linen band.

She groped about for the hated linen caul-cap before remembering once again that she'd lost it in town. She was sure Mistress Fortune had another, but she wasn't going to bother with it tonight. To be caught in the woods at all tonight would be disaster. She couldn't be twice as dead for not following the dress code.

"Cover thy seely head until we're away," was Mistress Fortune's only comment when she saw Diana's freshly brushed and uncovered hair. Despite the summer heat, she handed Diana a large square shawl dyed a dusky gray green with lime-slaked woad. Grimacing, Diana wrapped it around her head under Mistress Fortune's demanding gaze, pulling it well forward. Mistress Fortune did the same with her own brown-and-red shawl and picked up the basket of cakes and a covered lantern to guide her way. Diana tucked the cider jug under her arm, and the two women slipped out the door, heading across the downs to where the forest met the fields.

Diana had no idea of what time it was—full dark and with the moon that would be overhead at midnight just rising, a fat golden pearl over the church spire to the east. It had been weeks since she'd been up this late, a seeming lifetime, and the roads and meadows that looked familiar by day took on a whole new appearance here at night. Without Mistress Fortune to lead her, Diana would not have been able to find the coven's dancing ground again at all.

It took longer to reach there than Diana remembered—perhaps Mistress Fortune was taking the long way around or perhaps her own memory was at fault. When they finally reached the clearing, some others had already arrived—men and women in the plain simple clothes of farmers and laborers, come to keep faith as their mothers and fathers had before them, back to the dawn of time.

In her own coven Diana would have known just what to do, but here everything was strange. There was no altar, no candles, no High Priestess with her silver crown—only a bonfire already burning merrily, providing as much light as the scattered lanterns did, the country people in their everyday clothes and two leather-wrapped bundles at the edge of the circle. All the trappings of High Magic that Wicca had picked up between this time and Diana's were stripped away, leaving behind only simple fealty to the Great Goddess and her Horned Lord.

"What am I supposed to do?" Diana whispered to Mistress Fortune as they went to place their offerings of food with what others had brought. Suppressed excitement made her hands shake; was it possible that she could just walk out of the woods and be back in her own place? Home as simply as that?

"Dost worship the Queen in the hills no longer, then?" Mistress Fortune said at last. "When it was we who had it from thee, Her first children?"

Diana remembered that Mistress Fortune still believed that Diana came from the Hollow Hills—a member of the Court of Elphame.

"We ... do it differently there," Diana compromised, remembering with a sharp pang of longing her own coven. They met at whoever's house had the largest living room; with their incense and Lady-statues, they'd probably be taken for Catholics here, not witches!

"Take no fear," Mistress Fortune told her, "we owe the *seely* kind a great debt—for all that they have sent us thee," she added with harsh fondness.

Diana had puzzled for a long time over that word "seely." For a while she'd thought it was merely Mistress Fortune's way of calling her a silly girl, but finally she'd ferreted out the truth. *Celidhe . . .* blessed. Folk tradition held that the Fair Folk had once been angels; they had fallen from Heaven with Lucifer but had not been wicked enough for Hell, and so they remained on Earth, neither good enough or bad enough to leave it again. *Non angles sed angelii.*

It seemed a very few minutes until the clearing was full. There were a dozen people, only a few of them wearing the leather or wooden masks in the shape of animal faces. This time, unlike the last, Diana recognized many of the unmasked faces. Some of their identities surprised her; some did not.

At a signal unknown to Diana, the whole congregation stilled, turning northward and watching with hushed expectation. Two of the coven pulled the leather covers from the shrouded objects, revealing drums. Squatting behind them, they began to play softly, an echoing rhythm as deliberate as a heartbeat.

A figure appeared through the trees. Diana gasped. For one stark transported moment she was convinced it was her dark man; but this angel's beauty was from a more voluptuous Renaissance, his dark eyes and dark curls merely the legacy of some Spanish grandfather shipwrecked on these shores in the time of the Armada. Unlike the others, he was no one Diana could remember having seen in the village. He was dressed in the height of fashion, and his silk stockings were held up by the silver-belled red garters that proclaimed him one of the coven's officers—the Summoner, the one that the trial records usually called the Man in Black.

He was followed by the Magister, in carved antlered mask, who carried his tall staff and wore a sword belted at his side. His face was covered, but this time Diana wasn't night-dazzled and disoriented. She knew him.

Blessed Lady . . . that's Reverend Conyngham! No wonder the local coven had felt itself safe for so long, if Edmund Conyngham, the parish's own priest, was its leader. But if he was, indeed, so sympathetic to the Old Ways, how had Matthew Hopkins ever gained his invitation here?

It must have been Grimsby. Simon Grimsby of the endless

sermons, the more-Puritan-than-thou visitor whom Conyngham had hosted so reluctantly. Grimsby's unquestionable orthodoxy had protected the little hamlet from the doctrinaire inquisitions so common to these troubled times. *Until now. And I bet Grimsby's got Squire Alcock wound round his little finger. Nothing like a good witch trial to pump up revenue.* But tragic as it was, after tonight none of this would matter to her, Diana reminded herself. She'd be gone.

Pastor Conyngham—only here she must think of him as 'Magister,' Diana corrected herself—stepped forward to the urgent patter of the drums. In the bright light of the fire and the lanterns, the carving of the mask of the Forest Lord seemed to take on a sort of harsh oracular beauty, as if something more than human invested it. The assembled worshippers bowed. The Horned Lord of the Forest had come to his flock. Diana curtsied awkwardly, still watching him.

"As the sun rises in the east to open and govern the day, so do I open and govern this meeting which sets the Craft to work and gives it its proper instruction."

"So mote it be," chorused the villagers.

The Magister unbuckled his sword belt and held out the belt and the sheathed blade it bore to the Summoner. "Receive the implement of your office," he told the younger man, "to keep and discharge your duty."

The Summoner bowed low, taking the sword and disappearing into the trees.

"Is there any communication to be made?" the Magister asked.

A woman several years younger than Diana stepped out of the circle and came to his side. She wore a plain boxy gown of unbleached linen; it made her look like an angel in a Christmas play. On her head was a wreath of wildflowers. With a deep curtsy, she took the forked staff from the Horned Lord's hand and stood beside him.

"That the Hidden Children have kept to the Covenant from regular to regular and have set the Craft to work."

"And otherwise?" he asked again.

This time it was one of the congregation who answered him. Each time someone finished speaking, the Magister asked again to be told of the fruition of some spell worked at the previous covenmeet, of some small intercession, or to answer what seemed like ritual questions about the blooming of the flowers or the ripening of the grain. Beneath the murmur of question and response, the drums beat, quiet and regular as a ticking clock; and despite her best intentions, Diana's attention wandered as she waited—for what, she wasn't quite sure.

The clearing was lit by the lanterns the coveners had brought, illuminating the pale trunks of the trees and the tall summer grass. Beyond the rim of the firelight she could glimpse fugitive movement, and once, low down, the shine of some night-roaming predator's eyes. Did her road home lie somewhere out there, beyond the light?

A change in the Magister's voice claimed her attention.

"As the sun in the south is the beauty and glory of the day, I call the Craft from labor to refreshment to labor again, that they may have pleasure and profit thereby."

"There is one in darkness who seeks light, who comes free born and duly qualified, seeking us out with no thought of gain," the Maiden beside him said.

"Children of the Hidden Queen, is it your wish that she stand forward?" the Magister asked.

There was a low rumble of assent, and a girl stepped into the center of the clearing. She was barely out of childhood, daughter of a local farmer, looking small and determined in dove gray homespun and the nearly universal cap. She strode boldly up to the Magister and pulled her skirts up above her knee.

"I be Sarah; Mam Forster is my dame and gossip," she said, her soft voice clear and steady.

"I take away the name of the Lord of this World; among us, you will be *Id'ho,* the Yew."

"Mark me. . . . I shan't squeak," Sarah/*Id'ho* said, taking a deep breath.

"I receive you then upon the point of a sharp instrument," the Magister said.

The operation that followed took only a few minutes and produced a mark similar to the one Mistress Fortune had showed Diana. As the coven watched, a patch of the girl's skin was covered with a woad paste and the outline of a goosefoot cross pricked into her skin with a sharp skewer.

Id'ho dropped her skirts and kissed the Magister upon the mask's grimacing mouth. Lettice Forster came forward and stood beside her daughter with pride as the Magister took out the great book and wrote both *Id'ho's* names in it and *Id'ho* made her shaky mark in witness. There was a brief exchange too low for Diana to hear, then the Magister closed the book again and set it aside.

He closed his hand about the stave that the Maiden held and thumped it sharply upon the ground. The congregation turned toward him expectantly.

"Is there any further communication to be made?" he asked.

There was a stirring among the people, but nobody spoke. After a moment, the masked man went on.

"A great trouble has come among us," he said. "As ye well know, we are harried like hares in the fields by this Witchfinder-General who comes to take us up like a heron feeding among frogs. Be brave, keep faith. If you are taken, tell nothing or, if you cannot keep silent, tell any but the truth. Help will come. It is a dark time, but never doubt that you are the Stepchildren of the Moon, beloved of the Harvest, and if you die, it is only to come again to live among those who love you."

"So mote it be!" the worshippers replied.

"Then dance for the Lord and Lady!" the Magister cried, and the complex double-valued rhythms of the drums surged up.

Though everything about the evening's ritual was strange to Diana, it was obviously quite familiar to the witches of Talitho. The people on either side of Diana took her by the hands, and round and round they went in the spinning twisting dance that, Diana remembered, would someday become the waltz.

When the moon was visible directly overhead at midnight, everyone was glad to rest, to sit in threes and fours upon their grassy dancing floor and share the bread and cakes, mutton and hard cider, they had brought. The mildly alcoholic cider went directly to Diana's head; she sat on the grass and regarded the people around her giddily.

When the drumming resumed, a fiddler joined the music. Though many got up to dance—this time in couples—Diana saw others slip away in twos and threes to the edge of the firelight. She looked away from the fire, out toward the darkness, as if she'd been called.

Someone was waiting for her. Someone out there, somewhere . . . someone, some*thing* unlike anything that had ever happened to her before.

The sound of the drums was quickly muffled as she passed through the trees. The illusion of light persisted longer; it was only when she stumbled that Diana realized she was walking through the dark.

No. Not the dark. High above, the lady Moon glowed against midheaven, turning the sky about her the color of midnight velvet and picking out in sharp relief the trees and the fields beyond. Only the ground underfoot was dark; everything else was drenched in the illusory brightness of moonlight. Diana's skin glowed with it as though she were veiled in blue silk.

In the Tarot, the Moon is the mistress of illusion, Diana reminded herself. The drumming of the coven behind her was no longer any louder than the beat of her own heart. Everything around her looked familiar with the eerie, sharp-cut insistence of dreams.

It was near this place that she'd first set foot in Talitho. She looked down at her grubby, callused, bare feet, then up at the moon. If she could set foot in that same place again while the moon rode high, could she go home? Back to her own life, her normal, quiet life, and away from all this confusion and harm?

Diana's heart raced with anticipation and a painful hope. Once she was past that stand of trees on her right, she'd be there. Beyond them was the open field; when she'd come, she'd run through it just to the edge of the trees.

The edge of the wood. It was where she'd come from.

But as she approached the spot, her steps slowed; she hesitated.

She wasn't sure. That was what it all came down to. Until a month ago, her life had been composed of the same orderly certainties as anyone else's. Then, in a flash of lightning and a roll of thunder, it had been turned unthinkably upside down, and standing here in the midnight wood, Diana realized that she was afraid, paralyzed with fear, some careless reckless courageous part of her cut away by a knife so sharp she hadn't even felt the wound.

Until now.

That was when she saw him.

This time it was from a distance. He stood in the grove of trees that was the last obstacle between her and the fields. The moonlight made his uncovered face and hands glow with the same blue fire as her own skin.

She forgot the hot humiliating disappointment of their last meeting. It had not been real—only this was real. Once again he was the lord of the midnight woods, mantled in secrets, and she ached for ... something ... that only he could give her.

He wore a loose open shirt, not white—some dark indistinguishable shade—without the covering coat that most men wore. The shirt's soft fabric molded to the line of his chest, and it was open at the throat, exposing a white line of moonkissed skin that made Diana vividly aware of what the thin shirt covered. He stood as if he had been waiting for her, and for a moment she expected to see the tines of the Horn Crown upon his brow.

"What do you want?" Diana asked, and found her voice was trembling.

Had he come to take her home? He did not belong here, either. It was so plain, that she wondered why she hadn't realized it earlier. His long lean body did not seem to be cast from the same mold as those of the townsfolk. His face, his

bearing, all marked him as completely a stranger in this time
and place, as exotic as she was.

He did not move. She took a few steps forward until she
could see him clearly. His face was serious and unsmiling; he
watched her as closely as if he had been sent to judge her.

"What do you want?" she repeated. Hope made her voice
ragged.

"Good Christian women are abed," he said. His voice was
low, and hoarse as if from disuse. "Not flaunting their white
bosoms to the moon."

The sudden shock of disappointment nearly made her weep.
No, not a stranger here—just like all the rest. He was not her
rescuer. Not her ally. He was just one more trap laid out in her
path.

"I could say the same thing about good Christian men,"
Diana responded sarcastically. "What are you doing here?
Come to dance with the devil in the pale moonlight?"

Sudden fear made her muscles tense. If he was not her
rescuer, why was he here? If he *did* really belong to this time,
what was he doing out here in the woods at night? She dared
not look back, but surely the fire of the covenmeet was visible
behind her. He only had to see the coven to know what it
was—and then denounce it to Matthew Hopkins.

She had to keep him away from the coven.

Distract him, Diana told herself. She'd taken another step
toward him as she spoke, and so she saw him recoil as her
words reached him. And it came to her in that moment that
she'd said the worst thing she possibly could if she wanted to
keep the witches of Talitho safe. She'd mentioned the Devil.
He'd take her mocking words for the literal truth.

He turned and fled.

Past the stand of trees, through the hedgerow, out into the
wide sheep meadow. Though she could think of no way to
undo the damage she had done with her thoughtlessness, Diana
ran after him.

Out in the open, the moonlight gave everything a false clarity,
illuminating his swiftly retreating figure. Diana ran faster. A

month ago she would not have been able to manage it, but a month ago she had been living in a world where human muscle-power had been replaced by the power of the machine.

She had just reached him, was reaching out her hand to grab his shirt, when he caught his foot upon a tuft of grass and fell. Diana fell with him, too close behind to do anything else, and her falling body slammed against his with bruising cruelty.

She lay atop him in the meadow, gasping for air, feeling the thunder of his panicked heartbeat slam through both their bodies. At last she gained enough oxygen to roll off him, but he did not move. *Oh, Blessed Lady, I've killed him*, Diana thought mistakenly.

He lay where he fell, only his strangled breathing giving any indication that he was still alive. Staggering to her knees, she rolled him over onto his back. His body was a slack limp weight in her hands, and so she thought he must be unconscious; but when she had rocked him onto his back she saw that he was watching her, his dark eyes wary. The fixed intensity of his gaze made her think of some trapped wild thing—a wolf or a lynx, most dangerous when cornered.

What could she do to repair the damage she'd done? What should she say? What *could* she say to keep him from making his disastrous accusation of witchcraft? In the town, he'd babbled about angels and the forces of darkness; could she possibly *scare* him into silence?

"Hello?" Diana said tentatively.

Still he didn't move. How badly had she hurt him when she'd fallen on him? Her own ribs ached with the fall, and she'd been on top. Cautiously she took his hand in both of her own. The fingers were icy, even in the warm summer night, but they curled slowly over hers; she could feel the strength in them, even though they trembled as if he were in the grip of a high fever.

"I didn't mean to hurt you," she said.

The moonlight slid over the arch of his chest as it rose and fell. He was breathing fast, almost panting, though by now Diana's breathing had slowed and his should have as well. The night air was summer-warm and soft; moonlight glinted on the sweat that beaded his upper lip, and Diana could feel the tingle of imaginary salt on her own tongue.

Still he said nothing.

"Look," Diana said, more frightened with each passing moment as he continued to say nothing. "What were you doing out here? I'm sorry if I startled you. I was just out for a walk." The babbled lies sounded flat and unconvincing. No one from here would believe them. If her hands had been free, she would have wrung them.

"I . . . I . . ."

His jaws worked as he swallowed; she could see the muscles tense beneath the skin. His fingers tightened over hers.

"I—"

She felt him gag on the words, heard the desperate rasp of breath in his throat as he struggled to breathe past them. *"Righmalkin . . . mor righ ban sidhé . . ."*

The words were in a language she didn't know, their tone passionate and despairing. His breath caught on a sob. He clutched at her hands with both of his, as if he were a drowning man. "Go," he whispered. "Go. Do not dance."

In that moment, surrounded by darkness and his soft whisper, everything changed. He wasn't crazy. There was something terribly wrong here, something she did not understand, but he wasn't crazy. For a moment she forgot everything—the moon, her topsy-turvy world, the coven—and accepted the truth her heart already knew: That from the first moment she'd seen him, he'd become the most important thing in her life . . . simply, irrevocably, as quiet and inevitable as the change of seasons, and as impossible to stop.

"Oh, blessed Bright Lady, who *are* you?" Diana moaned. She held his hands tightly between both of her own and thought only that she wanted to understand, to *help.* "If you know . . . if you know, then *why? . . .*" she faltered.

All that answered her was a wordless groan and the thrashing of his head from side to side as he struggled for speech.

"Hush," Diana said meaninglessly. "It doesn't matter."

She tried to unwind his fingers from hers, but he clasped her hands tighter. After another small eternity of grim struggle, he found his voice once more.

"Righ-malkin," he repeated, as if the word should have meaning for her.

"I don't understand," Diana said helplessly. "I don't know who you are."

Though he still clutched at her hand, he turned his head away as if what she'd said had hurt him badly—as if her denial were only pretence, as if she'd rejected someone who depended on her out of nothing more than casual cruelty.

She tried to make herself believe that he'd mistaken her for someone else, but it didn't seem ... probable, somehow. Yet how could he possibly know *her?*

"I'm sorry," Diana said. She managed to work one of her hands free of his clutching grasp and laid her palm against his cheek, cradling his head and trying to turn his face back toward her. Touching him made her want to smooth back his hair, to kiss him, to feel his body on her own, *in* her own. . . .

She felt a breathless spreading warmth, the sudden longing to lie down beside him in the summer grass and take her pleasure with him as simply, sweetly, and uncomplicatedly as the beasts of the fields—the fox and the vixen, the hart and the hind. . . .

With a deep breath, she wrenched herself back to the moment. To reality.

"I don't know you. My name is Diana Crossways. I'm from Salem, Massachusetts. I don't think I'm who you think I am," she said.

He closed his eyes. His lashes skimmed her palm in a butterfly's caress, making it suddenly hard to breathe. "Blessed art thou," he said.

It was close enough to the greeting the Wiccans used among themselves to make Diana wonder now if she'd been wrong to worry at all, if he were somehow connected with the coven. But that couldn't be—could it?—when she'd seen him riding into town with the witch-hunters. Every time she was certain she'd figured him out—Puritan bigot, alien lunatic, figment of her imagination—he turned into someone else ... but if he had only just arrived today, how could she have seen him here in the woods on the night she'd come here?

Nothing about him made any sense. And if she sat here looking at him for one more moment, she'd do something that would tangle things even further.

"Can you get up?" Diana asked. "Are you—are you hurt?" She rocked back on her heels and rose, pulling him with her. He came to his feet easily and stood looking down at her, his long hair blowing across his face. Her fingers tingled with the need to fill her hands with it, to ...

"What am I going to do with you?" Diana muttered, trying not to think of what she *wanted* to do. They were just standing here holding hands like two children in a schoolyard. If he touched her in earnest, she thought she'd melt.

But he didn't. She drew another deep breath, trying to think clearly.

She didn't dare take him back to the coven—not without knowing more about him. She couldn't just walk off and leave him here; he might follow her back to them. And she couldn't stand here forever. It was already past midnight; soon the moon would set and it would be too dark to find her way.

"Goodbye," she said hopefully. He let her pull her fingers free, but made no other move.

And if she left him here alone, where was he likely to go but right back toward the coven?

She couldn't risk it. She wasn't sure whether he was friend or foe, and the stakes were too high to take a chance. *You don't want to risk it,* her thoughts answered.

"Come on," Diana said on a sigh. She took his hand again and began to walk back toward the village.

It was an odd and companionable thing to be walking along the familiar goat-track leading into Talitho with this tall, lithe companion silent beside her. She could pretend there was nothing strange about the situation—or him.

But there was everything strange about him. She knew by now what belonged in this place and time and what didn't. She knew that she didn't belong here—and neither did he.

But if not here, where? She'd thought at first that he might be a fellow time-traveller, but he hadn't seemed to recognize "Salem" or "Massachusetts," and she'd been afraid to say anything more explicit or ask him any more direct questions. When she thought too much about him, the uncomfortable burden of desire threatened to make her do something that would make him run away again—or laugh at her. Diana clenched her hands into fists. An emotion composed of equal parts of frustration and wild excitement filled her and made her tremble—and kept her from doing anything at all.

The small bulk of Mistress Fortune's cottage loomed up ahead, its whitewashed lathe-and-plaster walls gleaming eerily blue in the moonlight. The faint ruddy light of the banked hearth-coals shone through the small-paned windows. Diana took the door off the latch and opened it, pulling him inside with her.

After the freedom of the open air, the air inside the cottage was warm and close. Diana released his hand and went to take a paper spill from a bundle on the mantle. She coaxed it alight at the hearth, then lit the two beeswax candles in their heavy pewter chamber-sticks. Their gilded glow made Mistress Fortune's snug cottage nearly as bright as the midsummer moonlight outside.

Now that she'd brought him inside with her, Diana wondered if that had been such a bright idea; after all, she wouldn't have brought a total stranger picked up off the street into her apartment at home. She pressed her hand to her forehead, closing her eyes tightly. *"Neither fish nor flesh nor good red herring,"* her mind quoted whimsically. She'd abandoned the survival mechanisms of twentieth century America without picking up the ones of seventeenth century England, and she was going to get herself killed. She felt a passionate tension draw her body tight, demanding expression even in anger.

"Well," Diana said with sudden acid brightness, "can I get you a cup of coffee? A Coke?" The quick fury comforted her, eliminating fear and the need to judge.

Her companion stared at her with bright, watchful eyes, saying nothing.

"Well, let me see. I know you speak English. What's your name? What do you want? Were you looking for me?" The unexpected uprush of hope that came with the last question daunted her.

"Upright." When he spoke at last, it was another surprise; Diana jumped. "Upright-Before-The-Lord. He has named me."

"Oh, they do call their children by all manner of unchristian newfangledness, as 'Praise God' or 'Helpmeet' or 'Preserved'. . . ." Mistress Fortune's words on that first morning echoed in Diana's mind. Upright-Before-The-Lord. Her midnight woods-lord was a Puritan witch-hunter.

"I am—They say I am . . ." His voice faltered.

"Are *what?*" Diana snapped, frustrated more with herself than with him.

"I am damned," he said harshly. "For the shadow is on me and my soul dwells in the foulness of the Malignants. And thou art no good Christian soul, but a temptress from the Pit itself," Upright continued desperately, "luxurious, and—and—"

"Carnal," Diana supplied helpfully. She smiled. She couldn't help it. This was so ridiculous; they were like two children in the school play, parroting lines neither of them believed in or quite understood.

Upright took a step toward her. "Carnal," he agreed seriously, becoming calmer. "Woman is a beast unperfect, wanton and lascivious, given to the passions of the flesh and . . . carnal indulgences." He shrugged, palms out, a half-smile upon his grave, composed features. It was a gesture that she had not seen anyone else make here; it said that this was how things were, there was no point in getting upset about something so patently impossible to change. . . .

Something caught in Diana's chest, in her throat; a painless tearing, filling her with a sense of pressure and light, of sudden irresistible craving, a need that would no longer be ignored. She'd never before in all her life realized that a person could ache simply from the lack of a particular other person to hold close, had never realized that love was the unreasonable hunger that could be satisfied in any place so long as one person— one specific, unique person—was there.

"Well," she said in a voice gone suddenly hoarse, "isn't that just peachy for the indulgences?"

She'd meant it to come out bold and mocking, a ringing defense against her uneasiness and tension. But there seemed to be no air in her lungs; all she was conscious of was the steady regard of his black amber eyes, resting upon her face like a caress, the close heat of the room, and the beat of the dancing drums that still swirled through her blood.

He took another step toward her and now he was close enough that the electricity of his body made her skin prickle, close enough for her to smell his sea salt and wildflower scent, to see the candlelight ebb and flow over the breathing skin of his neck and throat like liquid sunsets.

His hands came up from his sides and settled about her hips, folding the fabric of her dress in against her skin as gently as if she were made of spun sugar. Her entire body throbbed at his touch; she felt a melting tickling heat that made her press her thighs together hard, denying it. He spread his fingers wide against her back, and that tiny motion made her breasts ache, fired her skin with maddening sensitivity until she could only think of being touched by him . . . as if his body had been made for her, and hers for him.

She reached up; her fingers skimmed the side of his neck and she felt him shudder like a man under the lash. Then her fingers found the silky tangle of hair at the nape of his neck and clutched it to draw his face down to hers. The touch of his breath on her face made her lips open in thirsty yearning. She suckled at the sensitive flesh between her lips.

This was ridiculous—madness. *Stupid . . . stupid . . . stupid . . . oh, Diana, DON'T. . . .* a despairing inner voice wailed.

The first shock of contact sent a pang of wanton heat through her body that stole the air from her lungs. Her mouth glided over his, savoring the warm, clean wetness. His hands slid down over her back, pulling her slowly, inexorably against him, locking their bodies together as their mouths were bound. She pressed against him, wanting to be naked for him, wanting him to touch her in that intimate place where her need for him was a ticklish, melting, quivering torment. Her body ached, needy for the gentle violence he could bestow upon it, and Diana pressed herself against him, needing, seeking, craving the release that he could give her.

She felt his tongue graze the soft surface of her inner mouth, feeding upon her as if he were discovering her taste, her breath, her soul. She could feel his teeth within the matrix of their kiss, turning her from seducer to seduced before she realized it, her mind caught and held in the web of the moment by her body's overmastering demand. She felt him draw up the hem of her skirt so that his bare hands could print themselves upon her naked flesh. She moaned helplessly, needing him, dropping her hands from his neck to his hips to urge him against her.

And he shoved her away.

"What? . . ." Diana asked groggily, reaching for him again.

Upright-Before-The-Lord jerked back as though her body were made of red-hot metal. Staring at him in shock and dawning anger, Diana could see the moment when his face changed, his expression shifting to one of near panic, as though he discovered himself having stepped into quicksand, sinking fatally and inexorably beyond human help.

"And I did stretch out my hand and loose the third seal, and below me all flesh became dust, at one with the corruption of the earth." His voice rose in a frantic robotic cadence that cloaked real emotions in meaningless gabble. He took one step back, then another.

The chill that cut sharply through her wiped away the cobwebs of her sensual haze as if it had never existed. Diana could see his chest rise and fall with the violence of his breathing, and despite the heat of the little room, gooseflesh rose on her neck and arms. Had she actually been on the verge of offering herself to this madman?

"Stop it," Diana said desperately. Despite the relative isolation of the cottage, someone was sure to hear and come to investigate, and how could Diana explain to anyone what he was doing here?

Upright took another step back and was at the door. He reached behind himself, clawing it open. The wash of moonlight backlit him, making him into a darker shadow cut from the fabric of the night.

"And where were you in that hour, daughters of Jerusalem? You opened your bodies to corruption and rutted in the earth. And the clay that shaped you—"

"Shut up!" Diana said again. "Stop it! Upright—"

"The fire will come," Upright said in a low voice, "and who in that day will be safe?" He turned and ran.

Diana heard the pounding of his retreating footsteps. She took a step toward the open door before a shaky feeling of faintness and nausea made her clutch at the back of one of the narrow settles flanking the fireplace. She groped around to the seat, moving slowly, and lowered herself shakily to the bench before the fire. She didn't even quite know what had just happened, yet it made her heart ache unbearably.

It was nothing. It was nothing to do with her. She didn't care who he was, or what he thought. By sunrise she'd be gone from here, plucked back to her own time with the moon's setting.

And so she told herself while she washed and undressed and drank the cup of wine that replaced the meal she would have shared with the coven. And then, because it seemed so reasonable to do so, she went up the ladder to her solitary bed and did her best to shut out the world that had just hurt her so badly.

Chapter 6
Talitho, Hampshire,
July 22, 1647

The morning sunlight woke her. Diana stared sleepily around the familiar bedchamber—the timbered, slanting roof, the tiny leaded-glass window open to the sea—thinking that there was surely something she was forgetting. Automatically she washed in the basin, tied on her petticoats and padding, and flung her dress over her head. Thinking to please her benefactress, she rummaged in the clothespress for a clean cap and brushed her hair up snugly out of the way before tying the cap's starched immaculate linen over her head.

She went barefoot down the steps, ticking off the list of morning chores in her head. Milking. Egg-gathering. Feed the chickens and the goat, then perhaps there would be time to make yesterday's berries into a pie or conserve. . . .

She was halfway down when she saw that the cottage door was open. Mistress Fortune entered, a basket over her arm and her shawl pulled well up to protect her from the early morning chill, only now returning from the coven's meeting. She looked up. Her eyes met Diana's.

I'm still here. The ridiculous, obvious, delayed realization slid through Diana's consciousness like ice water through her veins, something that had not even occurred to her until this moment because it was too big, too awful to safely think about.

She was still here. Still marooned in the third-world country of the past. And now, with no assurance that she was ever going home.

Ever.

It was a toss-up, Diana reflected with grim humor, as to which of the two of them was more appalled by this turn of events—Diana or the woman who sheltered her. Diana had sleepwalked through her familiar tasks, infuriating Mistress Fortune to the point where that good lady told Diana sharply to take herself off and not return until she had her seely wits about her.

Now Diana stood upon the back step and looked out over the ocean. Here a month and she hadn't hit the beach yet. She squared her shoulders and strode off to find the path that led down to the sea.

Though the fields surrounding the village were given over to rye—where they did not pasture sheep—Talitho depended also on a small fishing fleet. Even in this turbulently Protestant England, Fridays were still fish days, and a welcome relief to palates grown tired of mutton prepared in every possible variation. Spying the boathouse in the distance, Diana walked toward it.

It was a bright summer day. A few low clouds described the horizon, but overhead the sky was a clear unlikely blue. Diana tried to fill her mind with its beauty, to take pleasure in the simple animal sensations of the smooth sea pebbles beneath her feet and the hot sun above, the clean glassy green of the small waves that purled in to the shore, lifting the stones to clink softly against each other.

She'd been subconsciously counting upon this being a brief vacation, Diana realized ruefully, treating Talitho and its peculiar ways as some sort of quaint anthropological field trip, its local problems as ones that did not touch her. But now she realized that they did, whether she wanted them to or not. She no longer had the illusion of choice.

From here she could see the ocean stretched out before her like cut velvet; Diana wasn't quite sure what part of England she was in, but whatever land lay beyond the water—France or Ireland or even America—it was too far away to see.

Just as her own time was too far away to see.

Diana stared into the sky, feeling the weight of all that future that had once been only pages in a history book press down on her, as if she sat like some amphibian at the bottom of a well filled with time, gazing up at the freedom she would never reach.

Tears prickled behind her eyes. Diana turned away from the ocean and strode quickly up the beach.

The boathouse was farther away than she'd thought, past the village and nearly to the church. The boathouse door stood open and the tall wooden racks for the drying of nets were empty. Only one hull remained on the shore, its battered and unseaworthy condition ample explanation for why it had been left behind. When she reached the boat, she took the opportunity it provided to sit upon its sun-warmed surface and rest for a moment, tucking her skirts up between her thighs and dabbling her feet in the water.

It was there that Upright-Before-The-Lord found her.

Diana started as his shadow fell over her, bringing a chill that had nothing to do with the sun. She stared up into his face, blinking owlishly.

His face was a perfect carving in an ivory that had never been kissed by the sun. He regarded her gravely, his dusky hair hanging down over his shoulder like hot black glass, a few fugitive strands lifted by the sea breeze.

"Go away," Diana said sullenly.

Upright hesitated. "Concerning dancing—" he began.

"What *is* it with you?" Diana cried. "Do I look like Ginger Rogers? Go bother somebody else!"

"The burden was laid on the servant in the bones of the world to serve until the bones have worn away, and the world with it," Upright said calmly.

Tears sprang to Diana's eyes and she angrily blinked them away, telling herself it was the sun-dazzle. She was only deluding herself if she thought she could talk to him at all. Every time she tried, he started spouting nonsense.

"Does it matter to you what you do?" Diana asked wearily. "Oh, never mind. How can it? From one point of view, it's all already happened. Years and years ago, set as the stars in their courses."

"That the stars instruct thee is witchcraft," Upright-Before-The-Lord said sharply, "and though they dance, their dance is not for thee."

His hands clenched and unclenched. Diana could see the tension in every line of him, in the way the strong muscles of his neck were hard and tense beneath his skin, in the hard line of his mouth. Something had upset him just now—what? Her talking about stars?

No. He kept talking about dancing. Every time she met him, every time he sought her out, he mentioned that. "What do you care if I dance or not?" Diana asked boldly. She stood up and he backed away, stepping into the water.

"Good Christian folk lie abed and do not dance; dancing is lewdness and heathenish," Upright said flatly.

"I danced in the morning when the world was begun. I danced in the moon and the stars and the sun. Dance, then, wherever you may be; for I am the Lord of the Dance said He. . . ." The words of a lovely Shaker hymn not yet written skirled through Diana's mind. However much the Puritans might shun the dance, the prohibition was not universal.

"Are you so good a Christian that you can give lessons? I don't *think* so," Diana said mockingly. The taunt's effect exceeded her wildest expectations. Upright took another step backward, his boot making a dull plunking sound as it sank into the water.

"I—" he said. His eyes were wild, and sweat sparked on his skin like a sudden wash of starlight. "I am damned," he gasped out, almost stammering.

He turned to run, wading clumsily out of the water. He moved like an unstrung puppet, with all his leopard grace reduced to jerky, fitful motions, as if the very existence of his body was a sudden terror to him.

"That's right! Run away! *Coward!*" Diana shrieked after him in abrupt fury. And when he had vanished from sight, she sank to her knees and laid her face against the warm weathered wood of the boat and sobbed as if her heart were breaking.

The sun had slid to the west, leaving behind it the long summer twilight. With the sun's departure, the constant wind off the sea had turned cold, and Diana finally roused from a timeless contemplation of her misery to find she was hungry and shivering with cold.

But worse awaited her at the cottage.

"Art returned?" Mistress Fortune asked sharply. "The grace of the Lord of this World upon thee—and thy seely heart shall be well-lessoned in the ways of God-fearing men this night."

"What?" Diana stood in the doorway, dazed with a long day of sun.

"The Unspotted Lambs of the Lord, whose coming thou didst well mark, have business with all the town and they will instruct us in it, as thou shall shortly find. Squire Adcock has bidden all Talitho to a meeting this night, that Master Hopkins can acquaint us all with the hazard that hides among us like a wolf in the fold."

With an angry grunt, the older woman set bread and cheese upon the table and glared at Diana, fists on hips. "Master Hopkins," Diana echoed dully. Matthew Hopkins of . . . of . . .

Concrete details danced tantalizingly out of reach of her jack-daw memory. Witch-hunter. Mass murderer. And not safely tucked away in a history book, but here, *now,* and real.

Under Mistress Fortune's baleful gaze, Diana sat down at the table and picked up her cup. She took a sip and choked in surprise when she found that it was not the mildly alcoholic cider that she expected, but strong and highly spiced wine.

"Happen thou will need it to strengthen thee," Mistress Fortune said. Her face had settled into harsh lines of anger at an unseen foe. "Sup you, and we will go."

The village church had been Catholic once, and under the New Learning of a previous reign it had not been much changed; but with the coming of the Puritans, its significant symbols and welcoming Pagan heritage had been stripped from it so aggressively that what remained resembled a bomb site.

The walls had been crudely chipped smooth and white-washed; the niches for the saints were plastered over; the carved wooden altar and the high narrow windows of colored glass had been smashed and removed, just as they had been in churches all over England. Now there was a plain table at the front of the church beneath an unadorned wooden cross and a pulpit with the town Bible chained to it with a brass chain. Aside from the manor house and possibly the mill, the church was the largest structure in all of Talitho. Makeshift window coverings of oiled parchment gave the stark white hall a grim sallow illumination by day. Tonight it was packed, jammed near to bursting with every member of the scattered parish. The great iron wheels studded with candles—the chamber's only light—were lit and hoisted high overhead; the walls had become one long, claustro-phobic blur, with no escape anywhere.

She and Mistress Fortune had come in just a few minutes ago, circling the church, as was their usual habit, to come in by the north door up near the front of the church. Though Diana had read about this ancient Wiccan custom in the trial records of the Burning Times, she'd never in her life thought that someday she would be following it herself.

Diana fidgeted, watching the empty pulpit. For them to use the north door was an obvious symbol of Mistress Fortune's apostasy—too obvious to be safe in such a dangerous time—but as a result, the two of them were sitting near the front of the church now, in a cluster of Mistress Fortune's friends and fellow coven-members. Diana shifted in her seat again and Mistress Fortune pinched her.

"Bide thy ways!" the older woman hissed from the corner of her mouth.

Diana sighed and looked toward the blind parchment-covered windows, wishing she could see out. But even clear glass was expensive, so replacements for the smashed windows of Popish colored glass would not come soon.

There were a couple of hours of summer twilight remaining; Diana guessed it was somewhere around seven o'clock. Since the most reliable clock in Talitho was a sundial, she'd slowly gotten over the need to always know exactly what time it was. *Whatever time it is, it's always later than you think,* she told herself cynically. But she was three hundred years early for all of *her* appointments. . . .

The murmur of the townsfolk stilled as the north door opened once more and four men entered.

Dr. Grimsby she recognized at once; Pastor Conyngham's ecclesiastical guest preached sermons that were full of hellfire and sin to the point that Diana wondered if he'd read the New Testament at all. She recognized Squire Adcock from churchly Sundays as well, dressed in austerely elaborate finery that made him perspire damply in the July heat. Here in church he, of course, wore no sword, but the satin and lace and silver buttons of his costume and the bright cock-feathers trimming the felt hat he held awkwardly before him proclaimed his lofty rank as clearly as a billboard.

Pastor Conyngham stood behind the two men, sober in the stark vestments of the Puritan Church and looking as if he wished he were anywhere else. Seeing him in this setting, it was hard for Diana to connect him with the masked Forest Lord who had led the dancing of the Talitho coven only the night before. He stared out at his congregation, both Wiccan and Puritan, without a trace of irony on his face.

But it was the fourth man who instantly drew all of Diana's attention. He was not Upright-Before-The-Lord, but there was a haunting familiarity about him, as if he were someone she knew.

He was dressed in stark black and white—and true black, Diana had found since her arrival, was an even more expensive hue to wear than scarlet or saffron or royal purple. He wore no sword nor any lace edging to his brilliant linen collar, but the back-turned edgings of his cloak were faced with white satin and the white doeskin gauntlets he carried looked expensive even from where Diana was sitting. He ascended to the pulpit as if he belonged there and gazed silently out at the assembled parishioners with a pale basilisk gaze.

"Some good many of you know whereof it is that I am here," he said. "I am Matthew Hopkins, by act of Parliament the Witchfinder-General of all England and by my act and writ I am come among you to punish the doings of the Malignants that suck the blood of honest Englishmen." Witchfinder-General—not a military rank, Diana knew, more of a description. Witch-finder in general. General-purpose witch-finder.

And it's all lies. You haven't got any permission from Parliament or anyone else to do what you do. I know it.

Diana hoped she didn't look as frightened as she suddenly felt. Seeing Hopkins in the flesh was like seeing a nightmare come to life: more than three hundred women had been arrested as a consequence of only one of Hopkins's witch-hunts, and over a third of them had died in prison before ever being tried. In all the annals of the Wicca, Hopkins's was the blackest name. The one thing all the historians she'd read had agreed on was that the *soi-dissant* Witchfinder-General's crusade had been motivated by little more than greed; he'd made sixty thousand pounds from the slaughter of the helpless—an inconceivable amount when translated into 1990 dollars. He didn't

even have the authority from Parliament which he claimed—
it was just another lie.

An excited murmur welled up from the crowd, washing over
the last few words of that lying mellow voice. Diana shot a
glance toward Reverend Conyngham and the others. Grimsby
and the Squire looked positively triumphant, but Reverend Conyngham's face was carefully neutral. Diana prayed to her Lady
Moon, mistress of illusion, that her own face showed nothing
of her thoughts.

Hopkins waited until the mutter of the crowd had died down
before he resumed speaking.

"But be easy in your hearts, good people, for I do not ask
you to sit in judgment upon your neighbors. Christ has laid
this task solely upon me, for as it is truly written, 'He that
justifieth the wicked, and he that condemneth the good, even
they both are an abomination to the Lord.' Therefore, let my
experience guide you in your accusations."

Even the Devil can quote Scripture! Diana thought scorn-
fully, trying to slow her wildly beating heart. She glanced at
Squire Alcock and the Reverend Doctor Grimsby again. It
wasn't hard to guess who was responsible for Hopkins's presence—and what could Reverend Conyngham have done to stop
them? In this age, refusing to believe in witches could be as
dangerous as being one. Hopkins made his accusations based
not on truth, but on a canny knowledge of what his hearers
would believe. He'd neither known nor cared whether his victims truly were Witches so long as he was paid. And he'd been
paid twenty silver pounds to come here and find the witches
in Talitho.

Hopkins was still speaking.

"But tomorrow, when I begin my inquiries, there may be
those among you who say, 'Who is this man that he should
have ways to ferret out the evil in a Malignant's heart? Who
is he that the Devil's own book should fall into his hands to point
the way to those partisans of the *summa daemonologiae?*'"

*That's a damned good question; pity nobody's going to ask
it.* Diana couldn't believe that no one saw through him, that

no one was going to leap up and denounce Hopkins and his Joe McCarthy tactics. Why couldn't this nightmare stop before it went any further?

"And I say to those doubters this: That God in His holy righteousness has sent me gifts," Hopkins's mellow practiced voice continued. "Such hounds as course the Devil's own—" He gestured, and two men entered through the north door.

"Here is John Sterne, a mighty man of God—" Sterne towered over Hopkins by a good head. He had broad florid features, small suspicious eyes, and a nose reddened by drink or acne. But it was to the man whom Sterne shepherded before him that Diana's eyes were drawn.

"—who brings before you Upright-Before-The-Lord Makepeace, a young divine brushed by angel's wings so that his eyes are turned always to the glory of the life beyond— and to the evil in this world."

It was Upright-Before-The-Lord. Diana's midnight woods-lord was one of Hopkins's hellhounds. How could she feel what she did for him if this was what he was?

She could barely restrain herself from running up to the altar and shaking him until he told her it was a lie, a mistake—that he didn't belong to them; he belonged to her. A feral possessive fury unrelated to her danger shook Diana. *He's mine. He's mine, in the Goddess's name, and YOU CAN'T HAVE HIM....*

A crushing anger shook her, making it hard to breathe. In another moment's time she'd be on her feet, and she dared not call attention to herself that way. Grimly, Diana forced herself to study him closely, really seeing him for the first time.

Upright-Before-The-Lord was dressed as a gentleman— which meant in a less-expensive version of the clothes Hopkins and Squire Alcock wore. Next to Hopkins's raven's-wing garb, Upright's coat and breeches looked faded and muted, the blacks rusty and gray. It made him seem less substantial, as if he were one of the masonic carvings that had once adorned these walls,

come back to survey the destruction of his home. He stood
with eyes downcast, his whole posture ill-at-ease.

Look at me, Diana pleaded silently. And as if she had spoken,
Upright-Before-The-Lord, Hopkins's hound, raised his head
and looked into her eyes.

Once again Diana felt that eerie sense of discontinuity. The
chapel flickered around her, and she felt him as close to her
as if he whispered in her ear.

*Darkness . . . open fields . . . the moon and the hellhounds
following, following, following . . . escape; you must
ESCAPE. . . .*

The coolness of the night wind was on the nape of her neck,
and the small hairs on her skin rose to meet it. For an instant
the walls around her dissolved and she stood alone in the forest,
open to the night, with the Wild Hunt gathering around her to
hunt, to harry, and to *take. . . .*

With a gasp, Diana jerked free.

Mistress Fortune kicked her sharply in the ankle with a
hard leather shoe and Diana flinched. Upright-Before-The-Lord
shifted nervously where he stood, staring away from her. A
faint blush of color stained his pale cheeks.

"He speaks only in the tongue of angels and in that good
Scripture which is a lessoning to us all—but his eyes are as
keen as angels'," Sterne rumbled meaningfully in his slow
country accent.

"Aye." Hopkins could not long relinquish being the center
of attention. "Keen to see down into that charred and blackened
pit where the blasted souls of those who have covenanted with
the great Enemy dwell."

Diana shifted position again and was rewarded with a fero-
cious pinch from Mistress Fortune, her hand concealed by
Diana's skirt. Diana sucked in her breath and held very still.
What Mistress Fortune had told her was true—any wriggling
about in her seat while Hopkins spoke might well be taken as
the prickings of a guilty conscience, and she was in enough
trouble already. For the first time it occurred to Diana that she
herself might fall prey to Hopkins's accusations. She sat and

stared forward unflinchingly until her eyes teared with the exercise.

Finally, after a pious homily by Reverend Grimsby that would have set the Archangel Gabriel's teeth on edge, the congregation rose to go. Despite the lateness of the hour, there was still a thin line of light upon the horizon as the people of Talitho shuffled out of the church. The tide was out, and the salt smell was strong in the wind that blew landward across the flats.

Diana looked around but didn't see Hopkins and the other men of rank among the inhabitants of Talitho spilling from the church. Mistress Fortune stood off to one side, talking in low tones to Lettice Forster and her daughter Sarah, but the congregation did not break up into little knots and stop to talk to one another as they did on Sundays. Hopkins's words were already starting to sow fear and distrust among them.

First, the suspicion. Then would come the accusations, the torture, the hangings.

And no one would be safe.

"Did you see how he looked at the woman in the church tonight?" John Sterne asked.

The Moon and Lantern was Talitho's only inn, there at all by virtue of the presence of a harbor that could accommodate deep-water craft as well as fishing vessels. There was a common room, private parlor, and kitchen below and six bedchambers above, two of which were reserved to the use of the landlord and his family. Hopkins and his advisors occupied the other four, John Sterne and Mary Phillips each alone and Hopkins keeping Upright in his own bedchamber. The fourth room was for private meetings, and Hopkins had also reserved the parlor below to his exclusive use.

"I saw the woman, Johnnie—golden hair and roving eye and a body that would tempt the Angel Gabriel himself to sin."

Outside the parlor's small glass windows the short summer night had fallen at last, and the uneven panes reflected the candles burning on the table as a shower of fragmented sparks.

"It is not like him, Matthew. The witch is in it," Sterne persisted.

His companion laughed, as merrily as if they were not here upon the Lord's most holy business. "The witch, indeed; she will make a pretty witch—and we must pray that the wanton and all her handsome kindred are delivered into our hands." Hopkins sat back comfortably in his chair and drew upon a pipe of tobacco.

"It is not our hand that will slay them, but the righteous hand of God," Sterne objected, as he always did. "Yet I do fear that Upright's will is no longer to that work—for has he not gone to roam the downs without thy command, bent upon what harlotry I know not?"

"It is true that he has been less dependable of late," Hopkins said, considering the matter thoughtfully. "I am very much afraid that Upright seems to be losing his battle with the great Adversary. Who knows but that in Talitho he will fall to the Malignants entirely and become, in death, a great warning and reproach to others?"

It was hours later, and still Diana had not slept.

The doors and windows of Mistress Fortune's cottage were all open in acknowledgement of the summer heat, but even the Atlantic breeze and the soft sound of the waves could not lull Diana's aching head. She felt as though something that could have been wonderful was over before it had begun; the Burning Times had come to Talitho, and Upright-Before-The-Lord Makepeace wasn't just crazy. . . .

He was a mass murderer.

With a sigh, Diana finally gave up on sleep for tonight. She slipped out of bed and groped her way over to the ladder that led down from the loft. With the ease of long practice she let herself down the rungs until she stood on the cool packed earth floor of the cottage's only room.

Even in summer the fire burned. There was nothing else to cook over, after all. Diana swung the hook that held the half-full kettle in over the fire. While she waited for the water to heat, she took down one of the bunches of dried herbs hanging on the wall and began to shred leaves into a clay cup. A little mint tea never hurt anyone.

I want to go home.

The homesickness that she'd managed to hold at bay for the last several weeks returned full-force. Suddenly Diana missed everything familiar with a longing that was nearly pain.

It wasn't because of Hopkins. The thought of him and his self-serving crusade was scary enough, but it was a cause for fear, not melancholy. No, the thing that filled her with such a sense of loss was Upright-Before-The-Lord.

She'd kissed him, wanted him, dreamed about him. She'd made up a beautiful fancy about him, thought he was that magical and special creature that she'd been hunting all her life—and even now, when she knew beyond doubt that the reason he seemed out of place here was because he was mad, that his ravings were the meaningless babble of insanity, she'd managed to delude herself that there was some untouched part of him that she could still reach. But what she knew now about him now placed him beyond redemption. The hands that had caressed her had tortured and killed women for being accused of witchcraft; the lips Diana had kissed had spoken the lies that had doomed them. He was nothing that could have anything to do with her—ever. Just another bigoted, intolerant, half-mad witch-hunter, she told herself angrily. The man she'd imagined was light years from the man she'd met—like meeting a rock star, only far worse.

The kettle boiled. Moving carefully because it was heavy, Diana took it from the hob and poured water painstakingly into her cup. She hung the kettle back on its hook and swung it away from the fire, then picked up the cup.

Her eyes closed as she inhaled the minty steam, and he

appeared again before her mind's eye. Not as he was, she told herself firmly, but as she wished he were—standing tall and proud and noble before the fire like some ancient warrior, his dark eyes arrogantly commanding her. A faint smile curved his lips as he watched her, and Diana could feel the thrill of his fingertips on her skin as he undid the ribbons of her smock and let it fall to the floor. Her skin tightened in response to its exposure, anticipating the piercing sweetness of his lips and tongue. He opened his mouth; Diana could see the white wolf-gleam of his teeth.

"Righ-malkin—"

Diana's eyes flew open; jarred from her waking dream, her hand flew to her throat as if her nightgown's ribbons really had been untied, and the unthinking gesture slopped hot tea across her thighs. She swore, a hissing sound under her breath.

Someone had called her.

It hadn't been a real sound. She tried to tell herself that she'd imagined it, knowing that she hadn't. The voiceless summons was insistent, bringing her to her feet in search of the source. *Hopkins?* But no; midnight Gestapo raids weren't his style; Matthew Hopkins pretended that everything he did was legal and liked to do his work in broad daylight.

Diana felt herself drawn toward the garden. Setting down her half-empty cup, she crossed on silent bare feet to the door that led out into the garden.

In this time and place a garden wasn't an ornamental luxury; it was where Mistress Fortune grew the herbs and vegetables that fed her through the year and went to make the cordials and tonics she sold at Christchurch Market. Neglect of the garden now would mean privation in the coming winter.

Diana stood upon the doorstep and looked out. It was midnight and the moon was a cold bright coin in midheaven, distant and serene. Beyond the edge of the garden, fenced to keep the goat and chickens out, the tough sea grass grew down to the edge of the cliff. Below the cliff was Talitho's rocky beach and the sea road that connected the village with the neighboring towns.

There was someone on the edge of the cliff. Standing—no, *crouching*—a barely visible silhouette at the cliff's edge.

That sight shocked Diana out of the last of her self-protective sensual daze. There was something so deliberate about that half-concealed watching that she felt its motive could only be sinister; yet despite her professed certainty of malice, Diana did nothing, only stared in the direction of the crouching figure, willing it to move. Somehow she was not surprised when she saw that it was Upright-Before-The-Lord.

He'd freed himself from the confining formal clothes he'd worn at the church and wore a smock and breeches like any village farmer. He came toward her, holding something in his hand. Reflexively, Diana glanced toward it and stared at it for several seconds before she identified it as a pair of hares. Two months ago she would have been revolted; now she simply wondered how he'd caught them. He hadn't been in Talitho long enough to set snares; had he stumbled on someone else's by accident and looted them?

"Witchcraft is high treason against God's Majesty, and so they are to be put to the torture and made to confess; and he who is found guilty, let him suffer all the other tortures prescribed by law in order that he may be punished in proportion to his offenses," Upright said harshly. "Therefore, let the woman take heed, and be comforted."

Infallibly, he made her angry the moment he opened his mouth, as if he were playing cruel tricks on her, pretending to be what he was not. Inwardly, she frowned, inspecting her own emotions. Who did she think he ought to be, if not who he was?

"And a good evening to you, too, Upright-Before-The-Lord," Diana said tartly. "Poaching?"

He seemed to notice the hares in his hand for the first time. "That thou would eat from my hand," he said, holding them out.

"No," Diana said, taking a step backward toward the safety of the doorway. She wasn't sure what he meant. It sounded personal, though, and degrading—and she was damned if she was taking presents from a man who murdered Witches.

Upright continued to hold out the rabbits for a moment longer, as if it took him that long to understand that she wouldn't take them. Then he lowered them to his side and dropped them in the dust.

"Thou knowest me for what I am, then," he said in a low voice.

Yeah, sure, right, whatever, Diana thought spitefully. "Just tell me what you want," she said aloud. A scrap of rhyme flitted through her head, written of a queen yet to be born. *". . . or if that effort be too great, then go away at any rate."*

He spread his empty hands before him, staring down at his spread fingers as if he'd never seen them before. The loose sleeves of his shirt fell back from his wrists, baring his forearms. The tendons stood out in his wrists and on the backs of his hands. Then he raised his head, meeting her gaze, and held his hand out to her, miserably.

"Go away," he said.

The words were an eerie echo of her thought. Diana felt an impact at her back and realized she'd backed up until she bumped into the doorframe of the cottage.

"Go away?" she echoed blankly. *Go WHERE?* The small towns of England were networks of kinship she couldn't penetrate except with help; London or the great cities of Europe would be entirely beyond her ability to deal with. She had no money, no skills, no way to survive on her own. Where could she go, even if she wanted to risk leaving Talitho?

"I must work the works of him that sent me while it is day." His voice was soft and hoarse, fatally reasonable. At the church, they'd called Upright-Before-The-Lord, the Witchfinder's hound. Shouldn't he be hunting?

Was he out hunting?

Diana felt a thrill of absolute fear. "What do you—"

"But the night cometh, when no man can work; yet for a little while is the light with you. Walk while ye have the light, lest darkness come upon you. . . ."

"What are you *talking* about?" Diana demanded, frustrated and frightened. "Upright, um, Before-The-Lord? What do you *want?*"

"Silver and gold have I none," Upright said. Though the words were plainly mad, the tone was serious and sane. "I have been about my Father's business, walking up and down in the world. . . ."

Diana could not escape the sense that despite all that Hopkins had said of him, Upright-Before-The-Lord was not her enemy. He seemed to honestly be trying to tell her something—but what? She knew that rationally she ought to have been afraid, but somehow she did not feel as if she'd been accosted by a stranger; this was her own, her true love, and she wanted to feel his bare body beneath her hands, wanted him to kiss her and tell her this was all a mad game. . . .

"Please!" Diana begged. "Please, tell me who you are, what you want. Hopkins is—" The awful reality of what she was about to say made the words dry up in her throat. *Matthew Hopkins is going to kill us all. Help me. Help us!*

"I must work the works of him that sent me while it is day," Upright repeated.

What had Hopkins said? That Upright Makepeace spoke only the words of Scripture? But she'd heard him saying other things; at least, she thought she had. The first night he'd come here, he'd told her to run; and in the church, he'd spoken to her.

Hadn't he?

"And where were you in that hour, daughters of Jerusalem?" Upright continued, rambling from text to text as if to outrun some interior monologue. "You opened your bodies to corruption and rutted in the earth. And the clay that shaped you—"

Before she could censor herself, Diana stepped forward and picked up the dead hares from the ground. "Cut to the chase," she snapped. "Just what do you want, other than to be the Puritan version of Meals on Wheels?"

The hares were a slack cool weight in her hands. "Never

mind. I don't want them anyway. Here.'' She held them out
to him, taking another step forward.

Upright cowered away as if she had offered to strike him.

''The true faith teaches us that certain angels fell from heaven
and are now devils. By her pact with the devil, she is changed
in body forever. By their very nature, witches can do many
wonderful things which we cannot do—''

Diana could see his chest rise and fall with the violence of
his breathing, and though the night was warm, hackles rose at
the back of her neck at the sheer terror in his voice. It ought
to have frightened her, repelled her, but it didn't. The more he
tried to drive her away, the more she came to realize how much
he had been hurt. A fierce need to protect him made her reach
for him. She would protect him—but from what? What was
there for *him* to be afraid of? No one should have to stand in
the dark and be so afraid. . . .

''No. No. No.'' Her words were only meaningless syllables
as she put her arms around him—her love, her child. ''Hush,
hush, hush,'' she soothed, pulling him tighter against her body.
He seemed to surrender all at once, sinking to his knees and
pulling her down with him. Kneeling in the sandy soil of Mistress Fortune's garden, Diana held Upright's body against her
chest and rocked him as gently as if he were a child, feeling
the uncontrolled galloping of his heart. As she held him, the
shuddering that racked his body slowly passed to stillness.

The chance just to hold him soothed her as well. She pressed
her cheek against the top of his head, feeling the soft warm
sleekness of his hair. She didn't understand anymore. If he
wasn't Hopkins's hound, who was he? Was he in danger?
Matthew Hopkins had careened unchecked through the south
of England. . . .

For how long? Diana frowned, distracted for a moment from
the warm clinging weight of the man in her arms. She tried to
remember what she'd read. Hopkins's career would have ended
sometime, even if only with his death—but when?

''Hello?'' she said to the man in her arms. For one giddy
moment she wanted to ask him the date of Hopkins's death,

but then the harsh reality snapped into focus around her once more. This wasn't a footnote in a textbook. This was her reality. And the end of Matthew Hopkins's reign of terror was in her future now, not her past.

He stirred, but not as if he wanted to move, and sudden animal consciousness of her position rushed over Diana like a wave of raw sensation. Her skin tingled, a seduction at once so pleasurable and so fraught with danger that she hung suspended between the two extremes, unable to act. She'd never thought of herself as a reckless woman. Danger held no allure for her. She'd never understood the temptation of the dark and dangerous bad boy; if something was dangerous, you didn't do it. You didn't *want* to. And if some*one* was dangerous . . .

"I think you'd better go," Diana said weakly, and didn't move. They were as secluded as possible here in the midnight darkness. Her hands tingled with the thought of how easy it would be to push his unresisting body backward in the sandy loam, to unsheathe him and mount him as easily as she could straddle a chair, to impale herself on his sleek hardness and ride him with panting sweaty violence to her freedom.

The hot longing the image kindled made her breath come in short ragged gulps. Her cheeks were flushed, and she was glad he couldn't see it. No man in her life before had ever struck her with this thunderbolt of sexual obsession. If he moved to take her now, she would not even hesitate.

No. That is not who I am.

"Wake up. C'mon. Let's go," she said faintly, hoping he would not sense the shameful completeness of her surrender.

"Aye." His voice was muffled. When he spoke, she could feel the warm puff of his breath across her skin. "I would thou wouldst go, but thou will not," he said heavily.

"I can't," Diana said. "There's nowhere to go."

Slowly he pulled away from her. Diana knelt, watching him, willing herself not to cry out, to cling to him or beg. These feelings were out of a book, not from her life, and she didn't like them. She didn't even like him, she told herself again and again, as though the sentence were a charm against the raw physical sorcery of his body.

He rocked back on his heels and stood, retreating from her with the silent grace of a stalking panther.

"If thou do not run, thou wilt surely die," he said softly.

And then he was gone. Diana blinked at the darkness, unable to believe it. She was left staring at the explicit record of his bare feet in the soft earth. He'd just vanished.

"The fire will come, and who in that day will be safe?" His voice came to her faintly, borne on the night wind.

It was a long time before she could bring herself to move, to gather up the hares and go back into the cottage.

Chapter 7
Talitho, Hampshire,
July 23, 1647

Who will be safe? It was a question Diana asked herself many times the following day as, groggy with missed sleep, she went on the errand Mistress Fortune had given her.

It would take her most of the day to make the journey on foot, and she suspected that was the reason she'd been sent on it. At least it minimized Diana's chances of running into Upright-Before-The-Lord again.

The weather was hot, the sky lightly dotted with small clouds, as if to emphasize its blueness. Mistress Fortune had spoken of the village's hope of six more weeks of such days to let them get the harvest under cover without spoilage. Last year had been wet, she said, the harvest poor.

As she walked, Diana worried at the soft flesh of her underlip, brooding. The moon had waxed, the coven had met, and she was still here. What if she were trapped here forever? With Hopkins loose in Talitho, forever might not be very long at all.

Cudgelling her brain as she walked, Diana thought about Matthew Hopkins. He was the architect of one of the darkest chapters of Wiccan history, so she knew a good deal about his career—the spies he'd paid for, the false claims, the false

accusations, the notorious sadism of his assistant, John Sterne
. . . the fine details of dates and places were missing, but she
knew enough—all but the most important thing.

*When does he die? HOW does he die? You used to know,
Diana. . . . Think!* And if she did remember, could she change
the future that was her past?

Did she dare?

Diana stopped, pressing her palms to her throbbing temples.
She touched the linen cap that seemed to be the badge of her
shipwreck on this lost island of the past and groaned. It wasn't
fair; it wasn't right. Her own time had its ups and downs, but
she was *used* to it. Throwing her into the 1640s, where she
knew just enough to know she was in trouble and not enough
to protect herself, wasn't fair.

Diana glared rebelliously at the deserted summer landscape.
It wasn't fair. It *wasn't*. She wanted Hershey bars, Coca-Cola,
and MTV. She wanted to go *home*.

And what about Upright-Before-The-Lord?

He's nothing to do with me, Diana told herself, and knew
that she lied. But no matter what she felt for him, she didn't
know what he was. She didn't even know what side he was
on, not really. After another moment she heaved a deep sigh
and continued on her way.

Miller Skelton and his wife Jemima worked the mill that
ground rye, millet, spelt, and the occasional measure of wheat
for the inhabitants of the surrounding countryside. The mill
stood in a rolling sheep-scattered meadow where shadows from
the small puffs of cloud overhead chased across the ground
and a light breeze caused the grass to ripple like a cat's fur.

Mistress Fortune had sent Diana to buy flour; the silver
pennies she had sent her with jingled faintly in Diana's apron
pocket as Diana stared at the mill.

She had only been here once before—making the five-mile
round-trip by cart—but on that occasion, the mill had been a
place of meeting and bustle, reminding Diana of a backwoods

country store of her own time. Now the place was deserted, and Diana saw that the door was not closed against the breezes that might blow the ground flour about, but hanging open.

When she saw that, her first impulse was to turn and run—but what would she tell Mistress Fortune if she did? Jemima Skelton was her friend, a member of the Talitho coven. Mistress Fortune would want Diana to see if anything needed to be done. Reluctantly, apprehensively, Diana headed down the path to the millhouse.

"Mistress Skelton? Master Skelton? Hello? Is anyone here?"

Diana stepped inside. Walking into the mill was like walking into a giant timepiece: a tall central spindle that was surrounded with carved wooden gears and lead down to two enormous millstones that—when the mill was running—rotated in opposite directions to grind grain poured into the sluice from the catwalk above. A beam struck out from the grindstone at right angles. That was where the mule was yoked when the mill was working, but right now not even the mule was there.

"Hello?" Diana said again. The smooth plank floors of the mill were soft underfoot, cushioned with chaff and the tailings of spilled flour. Barefoot, Diana padded across it, leaving faint footprints behind her. For one brief anachronistic moment she wished she could have phoned ahead; obviously both the miller and his wife had gone off on some errand.

Both? Together? Diana shook her head. It didn't seem reasonable somehow.

"Come to gloat, have 'ee?" came a harsh male voice from behind her.

Diana let out a startled yip and spun around. The speaker was a man she didn't know—but whoever he was, he wasn't Miller Skelton.

"Gloat? I didn't know anyone was here. Mistress Fortune sent me for flour," Diana said, holding out the two silver pennies on her palm as proof.

"Well, thou'd best be having it, then. There'll be little enough business with Caleb and his goodwife haled into town."

The speaker was a heavyset man with a young-old face and a body shaped by a lifetime of grinding manual labor. He bore a faint family resemblance to the miller, in the way that most of the people in this inbred, isolated corner of Hampshire did.

"Haled—hauled—called into town?" Diana stammered, translating the seventeenth-century dialect to twentieth-century English with difficulty. "Why? Who are you?"

"And who'm but Caleb's own born brother Hiram? Take thy meal, Mistress Anne from London-town." Hiram Skelton stepped heavily across the threshing floor to a lidded barrel and, pushing the cover off, scooped meal into a burlap sack without measuring it.

That profligate gesture, as much as anything, convinced Diana that things were bad, indeed.

"Was it Hopkins?" she asked through a throat gone suddenly dry. "Did someone—"

Hiram turned on her, his face flushed. "That the harvest's bad and the rye spoiled needs no witch in it—aye, nor King nor Cromwell either. All the parish knew—and there was no one to blame. . . ."

"Spoiled?" Diana asked, baffled.

Hiram reached into the barrel next to the one he'd scooped the flour from and drew out a handful. He rubbed the kernels between his fingers and then showed Diana his hand. The palm was covered with black smudges, like fine soot.

"Damp-rot, Mistress, and no good harvest even before it. But if we was to plow it under, what would there be to eat, with the Army to feed?" Taking up a large needle already threaded with a length of twine, he began sewing the top of the sack shut, talking as he did.

"And so this one or that comes forth to say that Caleb's Jem was about the fields by night, and what should fall out but that she needs go to Talitho to answer it? . . ."

"And is bound over to be examined," a new voice said. Caleb Skelton pushed open the door and stumped in, harsh marks of anger and weariness lining his face. " 'Tis Matthew Hopkins himself who will try the truth or falsehood of the charge laid and my Jem to bide at Parson's until she is found innocent, by the grace of God.''

But none of Hopkins's victims ever was found innocent, Diana realized with a chill of horror. By community standards, the miller was a wealthy man. If Jemima confessed to witchcraft, it was beyond belief that she wouldn't implicate her husband—and a condemned Witch's property was divided between her accuser and the town. The mill—Caleb's property—would be Hopkins's prize.

"But surely no one can believe it?" Diana burst out.

Both men turned to stare at her.

"Dost deny that the Wicked One works upon the Earth?" Hiram asked heavily.

Diana froze. The question was a loaded one, and she didn't know if Hiram—or even Caleb—was a member of the coven. In these times, to deny the existence of Satan was to deny the existence of God as well, and if anyone denounced her for it, Diana would be easy prey for Hopkins's Inquisition.

"I won't deny that there is evil in the world," Diana said slowly. Hiram Skelton thrust the sack of meal at her. Numbly, Diana walked forward and took it.

"Then keep thee close, Mistress, lest thee fall into his nets," he said. "Come, Caleb, strong ale to tide thee." Putting an arm around his brother's shoulder, Hiram led his brother away from Diana into the back room of the mill.

It was a relief to get back out into the sunlight. Enmeshed in the chill horror of the mill, Diana had nearly lost faith in the daylight's existence.

Taken for examination! Was Jemima Skelton the first of Hopkins's victims or were there others already that Diana had not heard of? *"You cannot be a Witch alone,"* so the persecutors of the Old Religion had always said, and—in a pattern followed by later, more secular witch-hunts—each victim a witch-hunt took was forced to give up the names of others. Few had the stamina to refuse long under the torture or the strength to object to the names their tormentors put into their mouths.

How long until Mistress Skelton named the other members of the coven—Pastor Conyngham, Lettice and Sarah Forster, and all the rest?

Named *her*.

Suddenly her fear was a selfish, real, and personal thing. Mistress Skelton would break under torture and name Diana along with the rest of the coven. She could die here, die for greed-fuelled superstition, die before she'd ever been born.

The sun seemed to darken as a wave of sudden, irresistible panic washed over her. Diana stopped on the path, gasping for breath, pressing her hand to her side and fighting the stiff canvas stays for every breath of air.

Slowly the spasm of terror passed. The power that had brought her here had not done it only that she should die, Diana told herself. She took a deep breath and fretfully smoothed back the hair concealed beneath her linen caul-cap, forcing herself to be calm. There was nothing she could do. As she'd told Upright last night, she had nowhere to run.

Diana managed to get lost along the way and take the wrong path, arriving to the west of her destination. To cut back east and strike the sea road, she had to pass by the Rectory.

The Rectory was a substantial building; perhaps, Talitho had been a richer parish once. Like the church itself, it was a harsh angular building built of the local stone. What was quarry now had been sea bottom once; the ivory whorls of fossil shells embedded in the stone stood out brightly against its soft, pocked surface. Diana looked toward the windows, seeing only the uneven surface of the thick rolled-glass panes. Was Jemima Skelton in there? What were they doing to her?

And who was going to be next? Diana hefted the sack in her arms and hurried homeward.

Chapter 8

Talitho, Hampshire, July 23, 1647

Upright-Before-The-Lord Makepeace stared out the window of the Rectory in the direction of the retreating figure. Though she wore the tight linen cap of godly womenfolk, one coin-bright lock of hair had escaped to brush against her cheek and his imagination painted the rest. He had *seen* the rest, seen her flaunting her unbound body in the moonlight, torturing him with promises of a sweet agony too exquisite to bear. . . .

"What are *you* gawking at, mooncalf?" John Sterne growled. As he spoke, Sterne mopped his neck with a sodden kerchief and looked about the room for beer.

Upright turned away from the window, keeping his face smooth. The horror of his soul was for none but Matthew to see; Matthew, whose bright fire was a sword to cut away the rot that ate at him, confining the use of his powers to the small enchantments that could be turned to Godly use and not allowing the great magics that would open the gates of Hell itself.

Sterne's gentlemanly coat and hat were discarded in the heat of his work; he stood in trousers and a sweat-stained linen smock with rolled sleeves, looking like any country butcher.

They had been waking the Skelton witch all night; it was thirsty work, even with as much help from the town as Matthew could command, and it might be as many as three days before the Malignant opened her soul to Matthew's cleansing fire.

"Well?" Sterne snarled.

Upright hurried to the sideboard where a pail of beer sat beside half-a-dozen country loaves and a joint of mutton. He hurried to fill a gleaming pewter tankard with beer and bring it to Sterne. Sterne drank it off quickly and thrust out the mug for a refill, and Upright moved quickly to get it. The part of him that leapt to serve was his brute nature only, isolated from the clever torment of his thoughts. His disorientation and despair were familiar things to him now, nearly comforting. He was two men . . . three; his name was Legion, for he was many. . . .

The sunlight gleaming on the pewter dishes splintered into hosts of angels, and for a moment something *alien* moved beneath the surface of Upright's mind, rendering his entire existence a masquerade in a foreign language. To live indoors and wear these thick constricting coverings over every inch of skin—had he ever been free, a creature of fog and mist and storm? . . .

"Well, Johnnie, what news?" Matthew's voice shattered the moment of grotesque certainty, leaving only the pain behind. Working through haloes of angel wings, Upright refilled the tankard and brought it humbly to Sterne once more.

"The Malignant resists our good council yet," Sterne said with slow deliberation. "Mary has sought the marks upon her—"

"And found?" Matthew said eagerly.

"No mark, yet a burn she says she got of cooking fat may conceal such; it is a known Malignant trick. She has made no confession, nor could Mary find any marks upon her such as the Evil One loves to brand his servants with. She claims to have no imp or familiar spirit—"

"Then she will not sleep until she claims otherwise. I say the woman is the pawn of Hell, for have we not been told that one here thought she saw Goodwife Skelton in the fields by night—and giving short weight beside,'' Matthew said merrily. All at once his mood darkened. ''But I must have names! You! You have seen the Devil covenant here with his familiars. Did you see Mistress Skelton among them?''

''I saw. . . .'' Upright began. The woman crowned with the sun filled his mind; the feel of her body beneath his palms blotted out all other images until he wished he could turn his skin to run wolflike through the fields and howl to the mocking moon. He had seen her with them, dancing, her face flushed and her hair tumbled as if she were caught in the act of love. He stopped, gagging on the words.

He must help Matthew root out the malignancy that cankered the rose-heart of England. Only in searching out their evil could he find his own salvation. He was damned . . . *damned*. . . . But the Lady of the Sun had not looked upon him as if she saw his evil. She had looked at him and seen . . .

The pressure grew behind his eyes until he had to speak.

''Dark,'' Upright croaked. ''Darkness erupted from out the bowels of the Earth and mine eyes were blinded, covered as with a shroud.'' He trembled as he felt Matthew's eyes on him, but he had told this lie once before and Matthew had believed it. From that small victory he wove another now. ''Mine eyes were blinded.''

''Then open them now,'' Matthew snapped. ''Go and listen in the town. Tell me who the villagers speak of as lucky or unlucky. It may be days before that silly gossip opens her heart to Goodman Sterne and discovers her error, and I mean to have cause for celebration long before that time.''

It was a little over two miles from the churchyard to Mistress Fortune's cottage. Diana had already walked several miles today and her muscles ached. But her mind ached worse, spinning around with its unanswerable questions like a gerbil in a cage.

Mistress Skelton was taken, and that endangered all of the

Talitho coven. Hopkins knew nothing for certain yet— how could he?—but Diana wondered urgently whose testimony had placed Mistress Skelton in the rye fields by night.

Spies. Hopkins used paid informants to gather material for his accusations. She wished she'd paid more attention to her history lessons when it hadn't mattered. But she did know that Hopkins used spies—and Upright-Before-The-Lord Make-peace, Hopkins's hound, had been outside Mistress Fortune's cottage early this morning.

He'd told Diana to run away and save herself. He must have already *known* about Mistress Skelton's arrest. Diana felt her head begin to swim with the seductive treachery of shock and sat down quickly on the warm pebbles of the beach, bending forward to place her head on her knees. *What did he know and when did he know it? Ah, there's the question. . . .*

Did he love her? Did he lust after her? Could she trust him at all? He'd told her to run away, but that might just be another trick. She couldn't trust anyone. She wasn't sure any more *what* she knew. But she did know that Hopkins's Devil was a fraud, a sham, a tissue of lies that Hopkins wove for his own enrichment—as was the Inquisitor's writ he supposedly held from Parliament. *Someone should do something. There must be some way to expose him!*

I should do something. The sudden realization made Diana sit up straight, her giddiness forgotten. She knew that somehow, some*when*, Matthew Hopkins had been brought low, his bloody career ended. Why not here and now? Perhaps *that* was what she had really been brought here for: to bring Hopkins down.

And not to meet Upright-Before-The-Lord at all.

Perhaps that's the reason I was sent, Diana mused thought-fully. The thought was obscurely comforting; she could safely ignore her own obsession with the dark man, secure in the knowledge that he had nothing to do with her, after all. She could ignore him.

But what could she do to change something that had already happened long before she was born? *Only it didn't happen a long time ago. It's happening NOW. And the first thing I can do is tell what I know.* Diana got to her feet, brushing sand and tiny pebbles from her skirts. She'd better get moving. She still had a long walk before she reached the cottage.

And on her way she could decide how best to enlist Mistress Fortune in her plan to expose the "Witchfinder-General of all England" for what he truly was.

She heard the steady sawing drone of the spinning wheel even before she reached the cottage. Mistress Fortune was spinning. Diana slowed, hefting the sack of meal higher in her arms. She dreaded the thought of going inside and telling her mentor that Goodwife Skelton was in Matthew Hopkins's hands, but there was no help for it. Diana squared her shoulders and walked into the cottage.

"I'm back," Diana said. She found the flour barrel and opened it, yanking the sack open with a jerk and pouring the meal into the barrel.

"Ah, Mistress Anne. I did not look to see thee before nightfall," Abigail Fortune said. She rocked back and forth as she worked the foot pedals of the spinning wheel. There was a fluff of carded flax in her hand, a mechanically even thread coiling on the spindle.

Was it Diana's imagination or did she stress the syllables of Diana's assumed name? Diana glanced over her shoulder to see if anyone were watching, but could see no one. She turned back. The older woman's head was bent to the task, her head turned away from Diana. "Did get what I did send thee for?"

"I went to the mill," Diana said, the fear and anger welling up afresh. "They've arrested Mrs.—Mistress Skelton. For witchcraft."

"Aye, that tale has gone around the town. She did overlook the rye," Mistress Fortune said placidly. Diana stared at her in shock. Overlook. What Mistress Fortune meant was that Jemima Skelton had *cursed* the rye.

"Or so they say." Mistress Fortune made a face, as if the words tasted bitter. "But arrested? Nay, Master Hopkins only

examines her for her soul's health and maun bind her over to
the Assize if he finds cause.'' The steady drone of the spinning
wheel did not falter.

"Examining?" Diana said. Whatever reaction she had
expected from the older woman, it was not this.

"Aye. They do here no more than what they have done
elsewhere: Wake the witch or, failing that, tie her so she may
not find ease and see what imps come to her call.''

Diana sat down quickly, fighting a wave of nausea. Hopkins's
methods were the same tortures the Nazis had used: Take a
person, keep them moving, awake, unable to sleep; and when
the hours stretched into days without sleep, eventually the agony
of sleeplessness would make its victim confess anything, admit
to any crime, no matter how fanciful.

"They're torturing her," Diana said helplessly.

"And there's nowt that thou or I can do to save her without
bringing doom upon ourselves," Mistress Fortune said with
harsh pity. She brought the wheel to a halt and stood up, shaking
her skirts out. "I have it in mind to make a cased pie for Pastor
Conyngham's supper and bring it to him. Thou mayest roll out
the dough.'' Mistress Fortune crossed the room to the cupboard
and began removing bowls and measures to place them on the
table.

"But—" Diana began.

Mistress Fortune ignored her.

"You can't just—"

"With coney and bacon and onion for relish, 'twill be just
such a savory dish as a man might like, and done to a better
turn than his own cook might, with such evil doings beneath
his roof.''

Moving about her kitchen, Abigail Fortune collected eggs
gathered fresh from the chickens that morning, goat's milk
from a cheesecloth-covered jug, butter from the larder. The
hares that Upright had brought to Diana the night before hung
already in the chimney, skinned and cleaned and ready to be
made into a pie.

With quick deftness Mistress Fortune measured ingredients

into the large mixing bowl and then handed the bowl and a wooden spoon to Diana.

"There. 'Twill be hard for thee to spoil that."

Reluctantly, Diana began the long process of mixing the dough. "Look," she said when it was clear that Mistress Fortune considered the subject of Jemima Skelton closed. "If Hopkins isn't stopped, he's going to rip through here tossing accusations around—and some are going to stick—and then just ride off scot-free. We can't let him do that."

Abigail Fortune expelled her breath with an angry puff. "He is a godly man, a man of the Lord of this world, an' should we work against him in public, all are endangered, not merely some. 'Tis the Art that must survive, not us," Mistress Fortune said.

It was a measure of her distress, Diana knew, that made her mentor speak so plainly. Before she'd been one week in Talitho, Diana had learned that there was no surer way to cast Mistress Fortune into a towering rage than to say anything at all about the Wicca or rituals performed in the forest by night. But if Mistress Fortune was upset, then so was Diana.

"So, you're going to just walk up to the noose and stick your head in it because you think he's sincere?" she asked exasperatedly. "That's just stupid. Matthew Hopkins isn't any more pious than your chickens, and he sure as hell doesn't have Parliament's approval to go around doing this! He's just another con man. He's after the money, and he doesn't care what lies he tells to get it!"

Mistress Fortune studied her sharply. "Is this what thy kind says of him under Hill?" she asked.

"It's the truth," Diana repeated stubbornly, willing to use Mistress Fortune's belief in her otherworldly lineage if it would get her what she wanted now. "He's a self-serving fraud. And everyone's going to know it . . . someday," she finished lamely.

"Ah." Mistress Fortune seemed to come to a decision. "We do not work against the Lord of this world, Christ's twin who fell from Heaven for the sin of pride, for he is powerful and his servants are many. But if the witch-finder is not his creature, then it may be that we can work against him and I shall tell our Master so.''

''When?'' Diana said eagerly.

''Why, when next I see him, child. But mind thy blending. Thou dost leave flour lumps in thy dough.''

It was several hours work to make the pie and its filling of rabbit, bacon, onion, and turnip, but at last it was ready. Mistress Fortune packed it carefully into a woven basket, adding one of her precious bottles of brandy. Last of all, she ascended the stairs as Diana watched curiously and a few moments later came down carrying a tiny bottle.

It was glass and no longer than the palm of Diana's hand, corked and stoppered with wax. The light of a candle gleaming behind it showed that the liquid it contained was a bright, startling green.

''A cordial,'' Mistress Fortune said curtly when she noticed Diana staring. She did not add it to the basket, but tucked it into her apron instead.

''Get some soup for thy supper, and mind you not bolt the door against my return,'' Mistress Fortune said.

It was only then that it occurred to Diana that her mentor meant to go off on this errand alone.

''I want to go with you,'' she said quickly.

It wasn't completely true. Diana had walked a long way that day and she was tired, but the thought of being here alone if Upright-Before-The-Lord chose to come back was enough to make her want to be anywhere else.

It was not that she was afraid of him. It was that she was afraid of what she might do if she saw him again.

'' 'Tis a long walk,'' Mistress Fortune said. Diana shrugged.

''Well, come then, if thou art of such a mind. But none of thy cat-squalling or seely tricks. And thou mought carry the basket.''

* * *

Mistress Fortune's good tin lantern gave a surprising amount of light though the two women wouldn't really need its help until the return journey. Diana was a little surprised that they took the longer road that led down by the water, but Diana supposed that Mistress Fortune simply didn't want to pass by the inn. God knew *she* didn't, with Hopkins and his crew staying there.

The thought brought her mind inevitably around to Upright again. No matter how she tried, Diana couldn't make everything settle down into proper shades of black and white. He was one of the enemy. He spied on all of them in the woods by night. Then why did she feel as if he were her only ally?

Because you're a jerk, Diana, she told herself, trudging along in Mistress Fortune's wake. The basket was heavy and her muscles ached from all her healthy outdoor exercise. And once they gotten there and delivered the pie, there'd still be the long walk back.

When Mistress Fortune made a wide circle around the Rectory in order to come to it by the less-watched back door, Diana began to realize that their errand was a secret one, though for her very life she could not imagine what could be so secret about delivering a bunny potpie to the Parson.

Mistress Fortune knocked at the door, and they were admitted by a kitchenmaid who looked scared out of her wits. "Is thy master at home?" Mistress Fortune asked curtly.

The kitchen girl bobbed a nervous curtsey. "Doctor Grimsby from London-town speaks a special lesson for our deliverance in the chapel; but Dickon and Hob that's own brother to Jenny—they two are a-waking of the witch while Master Hopkins has his supper, and Pastor Conyngham prays over them that they be not taken."

The kitchen of the rectory was much grander than the one

in Mistress Fortune's tiny cottage, with a flagstone floor, two hearths, and an oven. The hooks on the wall held enough oil lamps to make the room quite bright by local standards. There was a railing running along the lime-washed wall with shining pewter platters and cups upon it, a long wooden table running the length of the room, and shelves and niches and cupboards all around the room holding all the ingredients of a well-appointed larder. Suddenly, it all looked unbelievably primitive to Diana.

"Does it not worry thee to abide beneath the same roof as the witch?" Mistress Fortune asked the servant girl with great solicitude. "Who knows what she might do to thee whilst thou sleep? And her imps likewise, if she cannot herself command them."

Diana, staring at Mistress Fortune in stunned surprise, barely saw how the girl's complexion faded to a pasty white.

"Well," Mistress Fortune said, still in that false kindly way, "happen the Malignant will not suck forth all thy blood, or ride thee as her horse to some Devil's Sabbath, at least while Master Hopkins bides beneath this roof."

The maid gulped and bobbed up and down again. Mistress Fortune, seeming to see nothing of this, set her basket on the table and began emptying it.

"I—I—It is past time I'm gone home to my mother, and give you good evening, Mistress."

The terrified serving girl scampered for the door and out into the night. Mistress Fortune calmly walked across the kitchen and bolted it.

"It wasn't very nice of you to scare her that way," Diana said reproachfully.

"I?" Mistress Fortune said innocently. "I merely said what all say. And now, since that witless girl has gone, I must go myself to tell our good pastor what I have brought." She walked away, leaving the basket on the table beside the rabbit pie and the bottle of brandy. Unwilling to be left alone anywhere in the house, Diana followed Mistress Fortune.

The door from the kitchen led into the dining room, which had an enormous carved sideboard and enough real glass windows shrouded behind its velvet curtains to make Diana blink. Though she'd left the basket of food in the kitchen, Mistress Fortune had retained the lantern, and by its light she guided them through the dining room and into the room beyond.

Although she supposed that the Rectory wasn't particularly grand by local standards, Diana could not help but be impressed. In her own time, original art, handwrought sterling silver bowls, and handmade furniture were marks of great luxury. Here, *everything* was handmade.

"He hath an unchancy dearth of servants," Mistress Fortune grumbled—odd in one who had done her best to frighten off the only servant Diana had seen, "but he was ever a marvelous frugal man."

The next room was a small parlor. In it, the candles had been lit, burning away brightly with no one to care, and—even more sumptuous to Diana's eyes—a rug lay upon the floor and tapestries hung over the polished oaken panelling. The trees that had given up their lives to these walls had been old when William the Conqueror had sailed from France; in building the houses and the fleets of England, King Henry the Eighth had deforested England to such an extent that the woodwork of a house like this could never be replicated at any price by future generations.

They thought there would always be enough, Diana realized with a small shock of recognition, *just as we do.*

Mistress Fortune stopped in the middle of the room, scowling around herself fiercely. Coming to a decision, she thrust the lantern at Diana.

"Now, bide thee here—and touch nowt!"

Diana nodded and Mistress Fortune strode off to tell Pastor Conyngham about his pie. Diana looked around, mindful of her promise, and decided that there wouldn't be anything wrong with doing her touch-nothing waiting if she sat down to do it. She crept into the corner and the comfort of a chair turned with its back to the room. She heard a creaking from the floor above, and her skin crawled in horrified sympathy. Try as she might, Diana could not keep her imagination away from what was happening to Jemima Skelton at this very moment only a few rooms away.

It wouldn't be so very bad yet, Diana thought cravenly. Mistress Skelton had been arrested only today—yesterday evening at the earliest. If they were doing nothing but keeping her awake, it wouldn't be so bad yet, would it? Diana felt tears come to her eyes and bit her lip to keep from making a sound. She'd always thought that when she saw something like this happening, she'd leap in and *stop* it. But now it was happening right in front of her and all she did was wring her hands and whine that somebody should *do* something.

She heard the men's voices only an instant before they entered the room, and all she could do was lift her feet quickly up onto the chair-seat and hope they wouldn't see her.

"—want our dinner, too," the first voice said.

"I confess I thought it would be better sport. All the sow does is weep and pray. Why should she not summon her imps?" the second speaker said.

"She be too canny for that, but she fails hourly. And tomorrow Goodman Sterne will have her naked and prick her before the town—"

The voices stopped as they passed through the doorway and out of hearing, and Diana uncoiled with a strangled sob of relief. That must have been Dickon and Hob, Hopkins's assistant torturers. From what they were saying, Pastor Conyngham must have sent them down to the kitchen to eat—leaving Mistress Fortune and the Pastor alone with Jemima Skelton.

Everything that had puzzled Diana about this became clear— why Mistress Fortune should suddenly decide to cook dinner for the Parson and walk two miles to bring it, the surreptitious nature of their visit, why Mistress Fortune had taken such care to drive off what must be the only other servant in the house. It was so that she and Edmund Conyngham could be alone with Hopkins's victim.

They must be going to rescue her, Diana thought in sudden hope. Rescue Mistress Skelton, take her out of here, *hide* her somewhere until this madness was over. . . .

Diana's reverie was interrupted by the sound of footsteps upon the stair. She sprang to her feet, remembering only at the last minute to grab the lantern and take it with her as she walked out into the hall. Mistress Fortune was descending the great staircase alone, one hand clenched in her apron pocket.

"Come, we'll begone," she said, seeing Diana.

Diana stared at her, confused. "Where's Mistress Skelton?" she asked.

"Where should the witch be?" Mistress Fortune barked, "but hearing right humbly her lessoning in the Lord of this world's grace. And thou, witless seely child, must come away."

Mistress Fortune took the lantern from Diana's hands and swiveled the tin shutters until the lantern was hoodwinked. Then she walked away, still holding the dark lantern, to the front door. It was unbarred even at this hour, with so many of the house's inhabitants absent, and she tugged it open easily.

Diana followed her. With the louts occupying the kitchen, they had to go out by the front way, but the quenching of the lantern's light was proof that Mistress Fortune didn't want them seen. They'd be known to have come—secrets were impossible to keep in a village the size of Talitho—but the rabbit pie provided a cover story for the visit, even if it was a flimsy one.

Diana breathed a sigh of relief when they reached the sea strand and Mistress Fortune uncovered the lantern again.

"And now home in good hour," the older woman said, "that we may rise up and be about our ways in the morn."

She reached into the folds of her apron and threw something out to sea; Diana saw the brief sparkle of moonlight on the small glass flask before it vanished beneath the waves.

The sun was noon high when Diana awoke. It blazed whitely in through the open window, chiding her with remembrance of tasks undone. Why hadn't Mistress Fortune awakened her? Was something wrong? She'd meant to raise the question of what had been decided during Mistress Fortune's conversation with Pastor Conyngham the night before, but the pace Mistress

Fortune had set coming home was too fast for idle conversation and once they'd reached the cottage Mistress Fortune was in no mood to talk, merely all-but-forcing a posset down Diana and putting her inexorably to bed.

Without stopping to dress, Diana gathered her nightgown tightly around her and descended the ladder to the kitchen below.

"—aye, died as they waked her, and never uttered a word," the stranger who leaned in the cottage's door said. He held a mug in his hand—common hospitality to any caller—and chattered on amiably to Mistress Fortune.

From some impulsive reflex, Diana coiled herself into a small ball at the top of the stairs, crouching down to peer at the visitor.

He was too well dressed to be one of Mistress Fortune's friends. The sun gilded his black curls and brought out the brightest possible colors from his neat plain dress. He was dressed in sober green except for the May Day brightness of the red-ribbon garters showing at the tops of his stockings. He held one hand awkwardly behind him, out of Diana's sight.

She'd seen him at the coven, Diana realized, though the garters this time were plain, without silver bells.

"—but I take *his* word and have far to travel to do it, so I will bid thee and thine good day, Mistress Fortune." He handed back the tankard and stepped back onto the path, turning away and swinging himself up into the saddle of the horse he led. He chirruped to the beast and as it began to move away he began to whistle. Diana heard the fluid, birdlike notes overlaying the horse's hoofbeats for a few moments before both sounds faded away into the distance.

"*. . . died as they waked her . . .*"

With an awful premonition of what the words must mean, Diana scrambled to her feet and shinnied down the rest of the ladder.

"Who was that?" Her voice came out harsh and confrontational, not at all the way to gain the cooperation of the mercurial Mistress Fortune. "I mean, why did you let me sleep so late?"

But Mistress Fortune didn't seem to notice. She turned blindly away from the dooryard, the tankard in her hand, and sat down upon the bench.

"Jem Skelton is dead," Abigail Fortune said in a bare, ragged voice.

As if it were suddenly before her now, Diana recalled the green gleam of the flask of cordial—how Mistress Fortune had not trusted it to the basket meant for the village lads, how she had thrown the flask empty into the sea on their way back.

As if the flask had contained something so deadly it could not be reused.

"You *poisoned* her," Diana said in incredulous shock. "You *killed her!* But she was your *friend!* She was—"

"And could I have given her better gift than this?" the old voice asked wearily. "They would have made her speak. She had time to lay hot iron on her mark and take it away, but she could not stop her tongue."

"Couldn't you have taken her away? You and Pastor Conyngham were the only ones in the house!" Diana cried.

"Take her to thy Hill, perhaps?" Mistress Fortune's voice was hard. "Thou did not offer that, and there is no place of Man's device that would succor her. Could she seek Sanctuary in the church who stood accused of witchcraft? She had no kin to go to away from here, nor could she come back to us so long as that charge stood. And thou knows full well she could not be found innocent."

"So you just—" Diana couldn't find the words to speak of it. She felt shock and anger, fear because anyone in Talitho could be next—and guilt that she did not have the refuge to offer that Mistress Fortune assumed she had. Diana waved her hands in helpless agitation.

"You superstitious *idiot!*" she finally sputtered. "I told you Hopkins was a *fake*, a *fraud*. He has no legal authority; he doesn't know anything. Half of England already knows he's a charlatan and the rest is going to figure it out soon, and you just—''

Diana felt nauseated with the violence of her feelings, as if she were going to cry or scream or go mad all at once. She'd been so sure last night that they were on a mission of mercy, that Mistress Skelton was to be rescued. . . .

"Why?" Diana demanded plaintively, gulping back tears.

"And could I leave my good-sister bereft, and her husband and children and those she might tell of? They would have names of her by eke or ill, did she live to tell them." Mistress Fortune bowed her head, and Diana saw the tears that etched the lined old face in silvery seams. Her own tears spilled over; Diana crossed the room and knelt to put her arms around the older woman, knowing at last that there were no more words to say.

A few moments later Mistress Fortune pushed her away and scrubbed at her face with the hem of her apron.

"But come! We must turn our hands to housework and our minds to pleasanter matters or our neighbors will come and ask what reason we have to be mourning the death of a Malignant."

"Okay," Diana said. "You're right."

Diana sat back on her heels, wondering how she could ever have thought this place safe and peaceful. Her anger with Mistress Fortune was gone, but the grief and uneasiness of Jemima Skelton's death remained. And now they had to dissemble for their lives, just as if this were Nazi Germany, lest one of their neighbors decided that two women living alone had something to hide and denounced them to Hopkins.

"Break thy fast then, Mistress Anne, and remember that tomorrow is the Christian Sabbath and we must to church to pray for the souls of all those stricken by witchcraft."

Diana stood up and went to the pot beside the fire to dish herself up some cereal. *Pease porridge hot, pease porridge cold, pease porridge in the pot and where are Kellogg, Nabisco, and Post when I need them?* her mind rhymed idly. She took her pewter bowl to the corner and sat down on the settle, picking at the warm porridge with her fingers. Mistress Fortune handed her a horn spoon.

Diana took it. *The spoon's all right, but there's lead in the pewter,* her mind protested, *and in the crystal as well. They don't know to pasteurize the milk, and there's no way to refrigerate the eggs. Salmonella, botulism, trichinosis, TB, something wrong with the rye ... the real miracle is that anybody here lives long enough to be hanged.* With the realization that she might never leave this time, all the things she'd forced herself to ignore suddenly demanded her attention. This wasn't a theme-park attraction. Life in mid-seventeenth century was a short, hard thing, usually cut short by violence or disease. Even for the rich, the conditions of existence were brutal by twentieth century standards.

"I'm not hungry," Diana muttered.

"Eat!" Mistress Fortune snapped. Diana jumped, startled, and stared at her.

"Would thou accuse as well as being accused? Take care, Mistress Anne, that thou do not waste away, nor change color, nor fall down in fainting fits. For by such cause and no more are people hanged for witches. Eat."

Numbly, Diana began to stuff herself with porridge, gulping it past the burning lump in her throat though she choked and gagged on each mouthful.

"You were to watch her!"

The blow, though anticipated, was delivered with enough force to knock Upright-Before-The-Lord from his feet and send him sprawling to the floor. He crouched in the corner and stared up at his master.

Matthew Hopkins was filled with a cold fury that clamored for outlet. He could not even exercise it upon his prisoners, for he had been less than a week in Talitho and had not yet made the rich harvest of victims that experience had taught him to expect. And the one subject that he'd had under examination

had died in the arms of the country louts who were supposed
to be keeping her awake!

Dickon and Hob had sworn they had not left Mistress Skelton's side for even so much as an instant. After much pressing
they had admitted they had left her to eat, but still only for a
moment and the Reverend Conyngham had been with her. More
tellingly, Hopkins had looked in on her himself when he'd
returned from his dinner and could swear that it was God's
own truth that the Skelton bitch had been alive *then.*

"How dare you fail me?" Hopkins raised his hand to strike
again.

Upright stared at him, his expression curiously remote. His
passivity inflamed Hopkins, who stooped over him, taking
Upright's jacket in his hands and shaking him so that the supine
man's head struck the wall in an arrhythmic thudding.

But it would not do to kill his hellhound—not here and
not now, at least. He straightened and stepped away to the
sideboard—Pastor Conyngham's sideboard, a rich living this,
with everything of the best. Hopkins wondered if it were possible that Conyngham himself was tainted with witchcraft and
heresy. Simon Grimsby would support him in finding it to be
so; it was Grimsby who had talked the Squire into sending to
Manningtree for his services and Grimsby who would inherit
the living here if it suddenly fell empty.

His hellhound, in the odd puppet way of their kind, was
striving to answer his question even now. It was an odd literal-
mindedness that those folk had which could be trapped with
words as stoutly as good Christian men could be with iron bars.

"How dare you fail me?" Hopkins repeated to drive the
question home.

"The night—" Was the creature trying to speak to him of
what had happened here last night? Hopkins already knew the
names of everyone who had passed in and out: the witless
kitchenmaid, a village girl, had fled swearing the house was
populated with imps of Satan and the only visitor had been a
woman of the village bringing Conyngham his dinner—a

woman against whom he had not yet been able to obtain any accusations.

"The night cometh, when no man may work," Upright gasped. "I must work the works of him that sent me while it is day, but the night cometh—"

More of his elfish prattle! Hopkins aimed a booted kick at Upright's ribs and grunted in satisfaction when he felt it connect. He'd left the hellhound there on guard, watching through a spy-hole that led into the chamber where Skelton was being waked. And Upright had told him nothing!

He drew back his foot to kick again and withheld himself. Hopkins was by nature an ascetic; his vices were wealth and power, not fleshly indulgences. He would abstain from this small pleasure now, in the hope of greater pleasures to come.

He wondered, for example, how that blonde wench that Upright had gazed on in the church would look, well-stripped and singing out to the strokes of the lash. He turned away from the contorted figure curled on the floor and left the room.

Upright-Before-The-Lord coiled away from the kick, welcoming the pain, welcoming the shame, knowing they were not enough to allow him to properly do penance; he must have more. He heard the slamming of the door and knew himself alone, trapped within doors until it should be Matthew's pleasure to release him. It was only a small punishment—the room was large enough to cause him little discomfort; it was not like the times Matthew had shut him into a coffin-box as punishment for his transgressions.

Such times lay ahead, for Matthew worked to purify Upright's Godly part and Upright knew that if such a part had ever existed it was gone now past all retrieval. He had lost himself—lost the voice in his thoughts that said "I," that named itself Upright-Before-The-Lord and feared for its soul. That voice was gone, and try as he might, he could not summon it back. In its place stood one who was lord of illusion and trickery, who could call the storm and turn men and women to horses for his riding and wolves for his hunts. One who could claim powers that Upright was terrified at the thought of using.

But even that one was not free. He was tormented by the vision of a woman with hair like sunlight and a body sweeter than honeycomb, and his mind was filled with disordered visions—of the time before Hopkins, before his imprisonment in the Other Place, of a time when shining beings with the faces of angels had loved him, had called him their child.

Child of Hell!

He got to his knees, then to his feet. It was hard to think at all when the words went slipping away . . . unfair, when he'd had English words enough beaten into him.

"—speak a good Christian tongue, ye damned Erse cata-mite—" A snatch of an old hated voice. A child's terrified cries. Scraps of memory from a time even before he had been imprisoned in the Other Place, memories of salt ocean and a rocking journey in a small boat.

His head began to hurt. There was a part of him that took a certain smug satisfaction in the pain, satisfaction in the known and familiar. His head had always begun to hurt when he tried to think, when he tried to piece together the jumbled scraps of memory into a whole cloth that he could rely upon. Perhaps, if he tried to make the pain *increase,* if he welcomed God's just and heavy hand upon his sins? . . .

In order, then, from now to the earliest memory he had. Now was sweetest; it held the touches and caresses of his sun-hot woman. *Righ-malkin,* jewelled queen; her skin that tasted of silk and flowers, salt and musk, all heat and delight. Perhaps she had taken the hares he had left for her so that he could claim to have fed her. He must feed her. It was the Law: No man could take a wife he could not feed. His father had told him that. . . .

His thoughts were spiralling off into dreams and wishes now, the sick chill breaking over him in waves. Pain lanced through him like beating lightning; cold and hot warring over the battle-field of his body. Upright forced his mind away from the present,

from his pain and from his imprisonment here and even from
the memory of his *righ-malkin* into the past.

*"And I think that Upright-Before-The-Lord is a good godly
name for such as thee, and we will add Makepeace to commemo-
rate the owner of this excellent hospital."*

Matthew's voice, giving him his name, giving him the safe
"I"-voice in his mind whose orders he must follow without
rebellion, taking him away from the Other Place where he had
spent so long. Memories of the Other Place were easily got
but strangely fluid. Each day might be any other day, in cold
and pain and beatings and hunger, sleeping in wet and soiled
straw as the seasons wheeled swiftly like the stars through their
heavens, alert for the occasional foolish and overconfident rat
. . . shackled so he could not run.

But the questions that circled about those memories like the
souls of the hungry dead frightened him too much to linger
there. Who was he? Who were his kin? Where had he come
from and where was his place?

Who was he? *Who?*

Memory was a chain, each memory a link between two
others, like a bridge between its past and its future. He took
another step along the bridge to his past; now the pain was a
hammering spike in his brain, blinding him to the point he
could neither see nor speak. He who had seen Malignants run
through with red-hot needles, their bones crushed in vises,
could not imagine their pain to be any greater, for God in His
holy mercy allowed them to faint of the flesh's torments and
he had no respite, none.

A jarring impact shook his body; blind and nearly insensible,
he knew from this that he had fallen and began to crawl along
the floor, his cheek to the smooth-sanded planks. If he could
reach a wall, he could reach a window; if he could reach the
windowsill, he could stand again.

But who was he?

Memories writhed against his skin, unpeeling beneath his

thoughts as if they were the layers of an onion, memories moving backward through time. Matthew, who had taken him from the Other Place. Matthew, who had given him his identity and name. Before that, a time of living as wild as a fox in its earth, in naked terror of any human contact. Before that, his escape from the man who had caged him; before that, a long time that held only disjointed images of pain and his own screams, of demands that he speak an incomprehensible language, that he abide by alien ways. Here was where memory always faltered.

But there was one last memory, earlier than capture, escape, recapture, imprisonment, and enslavement. One memory—or dream or myth—that made all the agony it took to retrieve it worthwhile.

The Place, the Place against which the Other Place was measured.

The pain was a distant thing now, and the coldness subsumed in a sinking, tearing weakness that came over his limbs, a sensation that he welcomed as the forerunner to unconsciousness, uncaring of how horrible the waking would be. And as the void filled him with the emissions of demons, the last jewel-bright vision came clear.

It was the morning of the world, and he stood on the mountain's crest to welcome the day. The slopes of the surrounding hills fell so steeply that it would be easy to think the valley they guarded was not there at all. Some ancient settling of the earth had left this perfect cup-shaped indentation, and generations of busy hands had worked to dig into the body of the hills, bringing wood and stone from miles away to shore up the tunnels, hollowing man-made caverns, smoothing natural caves, until the very hills were hollow. On a misty May morning the clouds walked the hills; the valleys were filled with silver air and the mountaintops crowned with sparkling mist.

It was home, home, *home*. He had lost it once, and if he could only hold it in his mind, find it again, he would go home. . . .

Home.

* * *

Mistress Fortune had put Diana to work weeding and tending the garden, an act of charitable faith on her part as Diana had shown no previous facility for telling weeds from what was actually supposed to grow there. With the industriousness of one who wished to blot out thought, Diana knelt and grubbed in the dirt, cautiously murdering anything that looked as if it did not belong. The sun beat down on her back, and the wind off the ocean was a constant cool stream.

Three hundred and fifty years would not change this. If she'd had a garden at home, Diana would have been down on her knees in the dirt in just this way, gently spreading the green plants that thrust up out of the pale sandy earth and searching among their roots for upstarts and outlaws. She'd done the vegetables earlier, now she was tending to the herbs.

Mint she recognized, and fennel, by its licorice scent; but was that flourishing thing parsley, or something worse?

"Fillet of a fenny snake" . . . *Billy Shakespeare, a man for all seasons; quotes for every occasion* . . . *"Eye of newt and toe of frog, wool of bat, and tongue of dog, Adder's fork and blindworm's sting, lizard's leg and howlet's wing. . . ."* *Molly told me these were all old-time herb names.*

Which of these herbs had gone into the cordial Mistress Skelton had drunk?

The sudden thought killed all the pleasure she'd been able to find in the day and her handiwork. Diana sat back on her heels and wiped at her brimming eyes with grimy wrists. Jemima Skelton was dead. Jem Skelton, the miller's wife, whom Diana had seen at the mill, in church, in Mistress Fortune's kitchen, at the coven's meeting—a living, breathing woman and not a nightly news statistic.

But Goodwife Skelton was only the first of many who would become statistics here. There might even have been other arrests today. If she could bear to go into the village and listen to the gossip, Diana could know for certain.

Hopkins had to be stopped. Though she knew that the coven

would not act without the Magister's permission, Mistress Fortune'd had the chance to speak to him last night. Diana hung her head in shame for being so pragmatic as to think about practical details in this time of grief. But maybe he'd given the necessary permission for the coven to act.

"Did you talk to him?" Diana asked. The inside of the kitchen was too dark for her eyes to adjust to its dimness quickly; she'd listened outside the door before she spoke to be sure Mistress Fortune was alone. *How swiftly the habits of the persecuted come to us,* she thought bleakly.

"To Pastor Conyngham? About Hopkins?" Diana persisted.

Mistress Fortune seemed to ignore the questions, seated at the great spinning wheel, her feet tirelessly working the pedals, spinning industriously until Diana despaired of an answer. *Straw into gold, lies into truth, hate into love, and old age to youth . . .* But fairy tales couldn't save them now.

"Aye," the older woman said at last. "I did speak with him on thy lessoning as to the Godly man being the poppet of the Lord of this World."

"And?" Diana prompted when it seemed no more would be forthcoming.

Mistress Fortune considered for a moment, her lips pursed as though what she was about to say was entirely obvious to anyone. "Wherefore it has been said that we may summon a Grand Coven together upon this Lammas Night, there to raise havoc against this false ungodly witch-finder, which all may take for the judgment of the Lord of this World upon him."

It took Diana several minutes to digest and untangle this, and when she thought she had it figured out, she felt a sinking sense of despair. Lammas was the Wiccan festival that fell on August first, less than a week from now, and a Grand Coven was a meeting of all the covens within a certain area, but . . .

"Raise . . . havoc?" she asked, hoping Mistress Fortune didn't mean what Diana thought she did.

"In the Hill did thee never work to call down favor to

thyself and confusion to thy enemies?'' Mistress Fortune asked curiously.

"Yes . . . I mean, no. But you don't need any magic spells. I mean, if you just come out and tell everyone he's a fraud . . . You just have to stand up to him, refuse to cooperate. Everyone doesn't believe in witches. . . .''

Diana's voice trailed off. Mistress Fortune snorted derisively.

"There's belief enough in Talitho to see half the town tried at the quarter-session, and what good does it do them to gain release in September, an' they come to find their neighbors' minds poisoned against them? No, it is better that the Lambs go at once.''

Diana fought off the childish impulse to stamp her foot and howl with frustration. Whether or not she believed in her heart that Wiccan magic would have any effect upon Hopkins, Lammas was a week away, and much of the damage he could do would already be done by then.

"He's a fraud,'' Diana pleaded miserably. "He has no authority. You don't need magic to prove that!''

"We do only what we did in my grandam's time to keep the Spanish from these coasts by raising a great havoc upon them so that they could not sail,'' Mistress Fortune said soothingly. "Thou need not fear that our hand in it will be exposed to the sight of the common folk.''

The drone of the spinning wheel did not falter. Mistress Fortune seemed to be able to feed in strands of flax and steady the emerging thread no matter what else she was doing. How many years had she been doing it? Diana wondered suddenly.

How many years more would she live to do it if Hopkins were let to have things his own way?

"That wasn't what I meant,'' Diana said. "I'm sure it would work just fine,'' she added feebly. From Abigail Fortune's point of view, casting a magical spell on Matthew Hopkins was the logical thing to do. *She thinks I'm the one who's crazy,* Diana realized in despair. "But you need to do something more, all of you. If you'd just gather the villagers together and—''

"I have said it was decided,'' Mistress Fortune said in a

tone that plainly signalled an end to all discussion. "If thou would exert thyself upon a matter, then study how thou would return under Hill or say when thy own will come for thee."

Diana closed her eyes. "I wish I knew."

Chapter 9

Talitho, Hampshire,
August 1, 1647

It was late afternoon on a cool misty day a week later. The summer days had taken on a sort of edge, a bitter undertone as though Nature Herself were commenting on events in Talitho. Even the bright days lately seemed less bright, and today the fog seemed to magnify the sound of the surf until it seemed to thunder and rage just outside the door of the cottage itself. The fine weather the farmers had prayed for had not materialized; the rain fell and the rye rotted in the fields, and no one was sure how much of the crop could be saved.

Diana lingered in the doorway of the cottage, savoring the contrast between the wild day outside and the warm tidy orderliness of Mistress Fortune's kitchen. Tonight was the Grand Coven. And whatever the covenors planned it wouldn't work, it *couldn't,* and the horror would just go on and on.

Hopkins's nets had spread across the parish. Five woman had been taken, though none as prominent or as wealthy as Jemima Skelton. One had even turned herself in, claiming she was much tormented by devils and wished to be free. Goody Mather had confessed to being the bride of the Devil, to blighting the crops, and even to the murder of a number of village children who were still very much alive. She had owned to the possession of a dozen familiars whom she sent forth to do her bidding. But she had not named any of the other villagers as her accomplices.

Today Diana was alone in the cottage. Mistress Fortune was off on a round of visits—to the families of the accused, to the accused themselves if she could manage it. Diana didn't know if anyone who'd been taken was Wiccan. She didn't want to know. She didn't want to know who might have died suddenly, inexplicably, in custody after a visit from Mistress Fortune.

She didn't want to know anything. She'd tried to get Mistress Fortune to denounce Matthew Hopkins, but she hadn't succeeded. As Mistress Anne Mallow of London, she was not enough of a leader in the social life of the village to put her own opinions forward if her *soi-disant* aunt would not. She dared not even go directly to Reverend Conyngham to plead her case. As the coven's Magister, he risked the most of all, and she would not do anything that might implicate him.

Face it, Diana Crossways, when it comes right down to it, you're a coward.

It was a bitter truth to unearth about one's self, but she supposed it was better to know it now while there was still something she could do to correct it. She surveyed her preparations, laid out here on the kitchen table.

A shawl, Mistress Fortune's scarlet wool riding-hood that she could bundle up to sleep in at need, her fleece-lined wooden clogs. She should have done this weeks ago; but at first Diana had waited for the turning of the moon to whisk her out of here, and after that, she'd been too scared to leave.

Diana took down a woven willow basket from its hook on the wall, lined it with a cloth, and filled it with bread and cheese, apples, boiled eggs, and a small stoneware bottle of hard cider. She wished there were some way to pay her mentor back for the food and clothing she was taking away; all Diana had done since she'd come here was take, and the only thing she had to give was her absence. If she left, she wouldn't be here to draw attention to Mistress Fortune by her strangeness. It was the only gift she had to give.

Diana had thought long and hard about where she could go and decided on London. She'd been wrong to think she couldn't survive on her own there. She *did* have skills this era could use. She could bind books, restore books. The craft of hand-bookbinding that she had so patiently learned had changed hardly at all in three centuries. With only a little luck, her skill would keep her. She could walk there—people did—and she wouldn't seem so out of place in the greatest city of the age, where everyone was an immigrant.

And someday the war and Cromwell's Commonwealth both would end and Charles II would ascend the throne; that much she *knew*. The madness would end, and she could come back here. . . .

Go before she comes back. Diana didn't dare leave a note explaining where she was going. She didn't even know if Mistress Fortune could read, and what if someone else got to it first? Better just to go. She'd go by way of the village so that someone would be sure to see her leaving and the word would get back to Mistress Fortune. Maybe she'd even think Diana had gone back into the Hollow Hills.

I wish.

Diana tucked the cloak down over the food in the basket and closed the cottage door behind her. Humming softly to herself—the tune of an early hit single by the Liverpool trouba-dours whose first hit lay three hundred and sixteen years in the future—Diana walked down the road that passed through the village.

Neighbors—in their gardens, at their looms, at their spinning wheels or churns—looked up as she passed, but greeted her in guarded tones. To hail a neighbor today might be to have greeted a Malignant tomorrow.

Since Hopkins had come, Talitho's life had pulled inward despite the fact that by August the ripening fields needed every man to watch over them and the time of the biggest fishing catches was now. Most of the villagers found some reason to head into the center of town at least once each day—for news or perhaps only to assure themselves that the spreading web of slander had not yet touched them and theirs. Diana was sorry for that, but she knew that once the ''Witchfinder-General'' had gone, the village folk would be able to settle back into their accustomed patterns once more.

Those who were left.

Diana's clogs clattered over the cobbles as she hurried through the village itself, past the shops, past the inn, and on up the gentle rise that led to the church. She passed the parsonage, where Dr. Grimsby served as jailer of the accused, with Reverend Conyngham's unwilling help.

Mistress Jemima Skelton had been buried—with Pastor Conyngham's intervention—in the churchyard. There had been talk against it, or so Diana had heard. Many felt a witch should not be buried in consecrated ground, no matter that Mistress Skelton had not been convicted of that so-called crime. But Pastor Conyngham had prevailed, and so the service for the dead was properly held, though many had stayed away.

The path climbed more steeply once she passed the parsonage, the brown sandy earth giving way to white clay and chalk, the ungiving marl of the Downs. Ahead, the gray stone church raised itself from the land like a shout and the path branched: the broad way to the East Door, the narrow way to the North Door, the twisting way that cut through the burying yard. In the corner of the churchyard, far from any other graves, Diana could see the fresh-turned earth of Jemima Skelton's burial place.

On impulse she turned into the graveyard to pay her last respects to a woman who had been, at the very least, her sister in the Art. She stepped over the low stone wall that marked the sacred ground from the unhallowed and found the path.

The better gravestones were slate and marble; slowly dissolving tablets of soft chalk marked the graves of the poorest. The fresher graves were mounded with green grass growing thickly over them. The older ones were nearly anonymous, faint depressions in the earth, if that. Diana walked past them all to the grave so fresh that grass did not yet grow on it, the one without a stone.

Goodbye, sister, Diana said to the soft earth. *Come again in springtime, born again to the Goddess.*

She stood at the edge of the turned and mounded earth, looking down at it. She was as numb as if she stood in the still eye of the hurricane, her emotions raging around her but just out of reach. Distantly, as though it were someone else's problem, she realized this crazy plan of hers would fail. She'd never reach London alive or be able to survive there alone.

But she had to try. She didn't even have the luxury of staying in Talitho to denounce Hopkins; if she did stay and spoke out against him, it would only bring the awful weight of suspicion down on Mistress Fortune.

But there was one other person she could tell. One person she could trust because he already knew so much she could not possibly incriminate herself further. And besides, she needed to say goodbye.

Diana looked around as if she expected to see him standing right behind her and shrugged when she realized he was not. *Just like a man,* she thought, taking a deep, rallying breath. *Never around when you need him.*

And she *did* need him. But where was Upright-Before-The-Lord Makepeace?

Beyond the churchyard, the land rose to a headland undercut on the seaside and crowned with a stand of hardy pines. The coarse unbarbered sea grass swept up the hill, becoming underbrush and new growth forest as it retreated from the headland. Diana began to climb.

She'd never come so far in this direction before. Here the land made a sheer drop off to the sea below, the wind that swept from sea to land was a constant push at her back, and all trace of civilization vanished like a blown-out candle. Diana stopped near the crest of the hill and looked back. The church dominated the view. Beyond it, Talitho lay, its houses scattered along the land above the beach like a handful of thrown stones.

From where she stood, she could see everyone in the village below.

A scrap of a poem yet to be written passed through her mind: *All I could see from where I stood/ Was three long mountains and a wood.* But Edna St. Vincent Millay'd had an American vista of the first decade of the twentieth century in mind, not this ancient, half-familiar world.

Conflicting impulses warred in her. She could always cache her supplies here and go back to find and talk to him, she told herself. Or she could leave now, before her meddling made the situation any worse than it was already.

She spread her skirts and sat cross-legged in the grass, pulling the shawl around her for warmth against the constant sea wind and easing her feet out of the uncomfortable clogs. She'd sit here awhile, Diana thought, and watch the village and see if she spotted Upright skulking about. After a few moments, she hauled at the strings that tied her cap in place and pulled it off, shaking her hair free with a sigh of contentment. She tucked the cap into the withy basket—she might need it later, but she didn't have to conform to anybody's antique standard of propriety right now. Once it was safely packed away, Diana leaned forward, stretching out the muscles in her back and combing her fingers luxuriously through her hair.

That was when she saw him.

He might have been a shadow, except that the sunless day cast none. He was lying in the tall grass only a few yards down the slope, as motionless as a leopard in deep cover. It was only slowly that the eye discovered him at all, even though he was dressed, as usual, in rusty, gray-faded black.

The breeches-cuffs that had once been meant to button at the knee over silk stockings were open. He wore no shoes or stockings or coat; other than the breeches, his only garment was a plain shirt, such as any man from clerk to king might wear beneath his elaborately stitched and cuffed and buttoned coat.

Though he must know she was here, Upright-Before-The-Lord had not acknowledged her presence by so much as an eyelash's flicker, and Diana had nearly stepped on him coming up the hill. It was as if he felt that if he pretended not to see her, Diana would go away.

For a moment she was content merely to watch him, puzzling out the reason for his presence. She had not seen him since that night in the garden when he'd brought her the brace of hares, and had been almost glad of it since the raging storm of emotions he raised with his mere presence gave her no pleasure. But now, in this suspended moment when either of them could choose to turn away, she could gaze at him to her heart's content; see the pale shine of skin on his bare legs, the swell of calf and curve of ankle, the dusty arch of callused sole as he lay full length on the ground, facing down the hill.

Hopkins's hound, on Hopkins's business.

But no.

Diana considered the matter with fine twentieth-century suspicion. Too many things just didn't add up—his behavior in the garden, his insistence that she leave Talitho. Twice now, she'd seen him near where the coven met, but if Hopkins had possessed any real information on the witches of Talitho, he would have acted at once. And so far, no one that Diana knew to be a member of the coven had been arrested except Jemima Skelton, and *she'd* been accused by a jealous customer. Could Upright know about the coven and yet not have told Hopkins what he'd seen?

But why wouldn't he? He worked for Hopkins. Hopkins had said so, had showed him off to the entire congregation when they'd arrived—him and John Sterne and Mary Phillips, his whole cast of young upwardly mobile persecutors.

Hopkins and Sterne and Phillips and Upright-Before-The-Lord Makepeace. John Sterne was someone Diana thought she understood—a religious fanatic and a sadist. Hopkins's female assistant, Mary Phillips, was the sort who'd enjoy hurting others as long as she didn't have to take responsibility for it. Hopkins was a psychopath, plain and simple.

But Upright-Before-The-Lord? . . .

Through village gossip, Diana knew that both Sterne and

Hopkins held court in the Moon and Lantern each night, dining lavishly at the town's expense, and Mary Phillips had attracted the sort of hangers-on that a woman like that always did, but no one at all had reported seeing Upright after his first show-appearance.

Show-appearance: show-trial. The association formed a teasing significance in Diana's mind. Show-trials, legacy of the Cold War. When did you have a show-trial? When it didn't matter if the defendant was guilty or innocent, but only that he be *seen* to be guilty or innocent. . . .

But the significance of the thought slithered away even as she gained that much from it. Diana shook her head in frustration. She knew that Upright-Before-The-Lord roved at night, and she'd bet she could sit here until Doomsday and he wouldn't look at her.

There was nothing for it. Diana gathered her skirts together and stood up.

" *'Ill met by moonlight, proud Titania,'* " Diana quoted, sitting down beside him. The sex and the sentiment were wrong, but she thought she deserved points for coming up with even a vaguely appropriate Shakespeare quote.

He twitched when she spoke, just like a cat who realizes it can ignore someone no longer.

"It is day," he said after a pause, still not looking at her.

"So it is," said Diana with feigned cheer. "A beautiful, bright, sunshiny day."

Upright raised himself from his prone position and rested his weight upon his forearms to look both left and right in eloquent silence at the heavy, gray, misty afternoon.

"No," he said after some consideration and lay down again, still not meeting her gaze. "Thou'rt mad."

Diana repressed a small blurt of startled laughter at the joke he might not even have known he'd made.

"What are you looking at?" she asked. She leaned closer and found she had to resist the temptation to put her hand on the hollow of his back where the thin fabric of the shirt molded the outline of taut ready muscles. Sitting beside him, out of the wind in the small hollow, she could feel the heat that radiated from his body warming her where her body brushed against him.

The very normalcy of this meeting made her feel paradoxically surreal. In the brief time she'd known him, Diana had been dragged into alleyways by him, encountered him when half-asleep, chased him through the woods at night, and collided with him when she'd just fallen through a time warp. She'd never had the chance just to sit quietly beside him in broad daylight, making awkward conversation by fits and starts.

He ducked his head shyly.

"Hello?" Diana said hopefully. "Come on, can't we have a civilized conversation like normal people?"

He looked at her then, and Diana almost wished he hadn't. The intensity of his gaze was a direct challenge, demanding that she meet it with an intensity of her own.

"I and thou—" His voice was soft, slurry with some sort of mysterious accent around the edges. "—we are not people."

Diana was willing to let the conversation get as bizarre as he liked; his voice was the harsh soft velvet of a panther's coat and made her imagine that same velvet upon her bare and willing skin—and at least it was a *conversation,* not hysterical weeping or religious rantings.

"All right," she said reasonably, taking a deep calming breath against the traitorous flutter of yearning in the pit of her stomach. "We're not people. Then what are we?" And could she manage to work the conversation around to Matthew Hopkins, charlatan, while they were at it?

"I—" Upright seemed to be having trouble with the question. He sat up, abandoning his scrutiny of the town in order to study her more easily. His hair was a true blue-black; Diana was close enough to see the fine furrow drawn between his raven brows by his solemn frown before he relaxed, seeming to come to a conclusion.

"I am damned," he said with what sounded to Diana like a faint note of relieved satisfaction in his voice. "And thou—"

Before Diana realized what he was doing, he had reached out to touch her face, his fingers skimming gently along the line of her jaw beneath the tumble of blonde hair unconfined by a tight linen cap.

"Thou art beautiful."

"I—well—um—" Flustered by the touch and the directness, Diana pulled away, putting her hand up to touch the place that still tingled with his phantom caress. Served her right, she supposed, for taking off her cap. Loose hair seemed to be the local equivalent of naughty Victorian underwear. "But that isn't really what I wanted to talk to you about," she said clumsily.

Upright Makepeace regarded her steadily. It was—Diana realized in a rush of discovery—one of the sources of his strangeness. When Upright looked at her, he was concentrating on her with every iota of his attention, as if she were the only thing in the world.

All Diana's life, all her formidable social skills had been spent learning how to get people's attention or how to escape it. But with Upright, there was no way to avoid his attention and no need to compete for it. He was not thinking of what came next, of how to seduce her or how to leave. He was simply and demandingly *here,* and they could go on to what came next.

Only she wasn't sure she knew what came next or if she really wanted to go there.

"Well," she said awkwardly. An errant gust of sea air blew a strand of hair across her face, and with the same silent concentration Upright brushed it away. And suddenly Diana knew what was going to happen, knew it with the same certainty she knew the moon was going to rise tonight.

The knowledge brought a tingling rush of awareness to every portion of her body, as if she were suddenly more present in the world. She felt the yielding unevenness of the grassy slope beneath her, the shifting heaviness of her skirts and petticoats against her thighs. In her mind, halfway between fantasy and imagination, was Upright-Before-The-Lord—the weight and feel of him, the pressure of his muscles sliding over her own; the soft invasion and the clasp of oiled bodies gliding on an upwelling spiral of delicious tension, of tastes and kisses. . . .

If she got up now and ran away, she could delay it, postpone what was about to occur for only as long as she could run and twist and dodge and hide from him and from herself. But it would find her in the end. *He* would find her.

No! Diana told herself sternly. These were ridiculous things to be thinking—unseemly, undignified, unsafe. And she didn't have *time.* She had to deliver her warning about Matthew Hopkins and leave.

"Well," Diana said again. Upright merely gazed at her. *As if,* Diana thought rebelliously, *he's sure of just what's going to happen and all he has to do is wait for it. Well, wait forever, buster.*

"You must be hungry," she said with bright politeness. She bit her lips together, denying the possibility of a kiss. "Would you like some lunch?"

Without waiting for an answer, she tucked her skirts up and scrambled up the slope to get her basket. But even that didn't work out precisely as she expected it to.

"Thou feed'st me?" Upright said as she pulled back the cloth to expose the bread and cheese and dried apples and boiled eggs she'd brought with her. *"I have fed thee,"* his ghostly satisfied voice murmured in her memory. *Great. Stuck in the seventeenth century with the Galloping Gourmet.*

But even flippancy could not defuse the tension Diana felt growing between the two of them. It was as irresistible as gravity, and she had no idea of what to do about it.

"Yes, yes, yes. Have something to eat," Diana said hastily, "and then tell me what you know about Matthew Hopkins."

Upright paused with a piece of dried apple halfway to his mouth, his lips already parted to receive it. Diana, watching him, felt the angry clutch of a hunger in her chest that had nothing to do with food. She wanted to own him. She wanted to belong to him.

She wished he were dead.

"He is a learned physician to the soul of all England," Upright said at last, and sank his teeth into the fruit.

Diana regarded him uncertainly. Had he meant to be funny? Was this a joke or deadly serious? And what could she say that he would understand as she meant him to?

"He's a witch-hunter."

"The Witchfinder-General of all England," Upright corrected her. "Appointed to this office by the Parliament, so he hath said often."

"But he wasn't appointed by Parliament," Diana said. "That's a lie. He just appointed himself."

"I would not dispute him," Upright said in neutral tones. He reached for one of the eggs and began to peel it, his fingers white against the brown shell of the egg.

"He's a fake!" Diana burst out passionately. "All his legitimacy, his so-called appointment, is just made up. He doesn't care whether there are witches or not. All Hopkins wants to do is *persecute* people."

"And be paid."

The quiet of the words undercut her own passionate fury whipped up out of fear, a passion that was meant to protect her from the slower and more irresistible passion. Diana stared at Upright, goggling with the surprise of it. He had taken away every single one of her arguments with that single phrase.

"So, you know," Diana said stupidly. Upright shrugged, flinging the shell of the egg away in one long unbroken scale-skin. He bit into the egg, his teeth shearing irresistibly through the glistening white meat.

"Eat," he said.

He knew Hopkins was a fraud. He'd known all along—and he'd said nothing.

"Why don't you care? Why don't you do something about it? Why don't you stop him?" *I hate you, I hate you, I hate you,* Diana chanted to herself, as if it were some holy litany that would protect her.

"Are there no witches?" Upright asked cryptically. "Do

their doctrines not work wickedness in the world to rival that of the Pope himself, who is the father of lies?''

He held out the other half of the egg toward her, offering it. Diana could see the exposed yolk, bitten cleanly in half, its center a dusty goldenrod yellow edged in dark olive green. She grabbed the egg out of his hand and threw it down the hill with all of her strength.

Diana's eyes filled with tears of anger as she watched the small white speck sail out over the grass and fall, slowly, slowly, to bounce and roll nearly all the way to Mistress Skelton's fresh-turned grave. *There are no witches,* she longed to say. *There's no one slinking around in the dark casting evil spells on people.*

But there were, and there was. No matter how benign, how innocent, there were witches in Talitho who were going to bespell Matthew Hopkins tonight if they could—wickedness by the world's standard, even if it was only self-defense. Diana closed her eyes and swallowed miserably.

As she sat there, eyes closed, gathering her strength to go, she felt his touch, as light as an autumn leaf. She shivered as his fingers skimmed over her hair, down her back, hesitating at the edge of the canvas stays and then sliding lower, the contact fainter through the insulating layers but no less piercing. It slid through canvas and linen and skin and flesh to touch her heart and goad it to a quicker rhythm.

''But I and thou are apart from this,'' Upright said softly. His hand rested on the horsehair-stuffed bumroll at her waist; the caress burned as though it were against living flesh.

I should go. It's afternoon. I've got a long way to go. It's going to be dark in a few hours. I should get away from here. I need to find the main road. . . .

''You know what—I mean, who—I am,'' Diana said in a trembling voice. Witch and woman and traveller out of time; she had to know that he *knew.*

''Thou hast come to me; I have fed thee and I do take thee and I will keep thee,'' Upright-Before-The-Lord answered with quiet certainty.

He was seated beside her, his thigh pressed against her own

and his arm across her back. Her hands and face were cool with the sea mist of this summer's day; where their bodies touched she was warm.

Beneath her clothes, she burned. Longing and shy and humiliated by the force of her own desire, Diana discovered that she was the prey of a force as inexorable as physical pain, a force that demanded relief with the urgency of physical starvation. His hand made its slow progress up her back again, questing, learning.

Diana bent forward in submission, savoring the pull and weight of her head, grown suddenly heavy, against the muscles of her neck. But she was used to the dresses of her own time that were made to be fastened and unloosed from the back. Her dress, the imprisoning stays, both closed in front.

She was safe.

His hand upon her back reached higher, brushed the heavy weight of tumbled hair away from the nape of her neck. She felt the cool of the sea air upon the bared skin, and then she felt his mouth there.

He tasted rather than kissed; she felt the gentle stroke of his tongue over the bone, the gentle pressure of teeth. As if he would caress every inch of her this way, learning her flesh in sightless seeking. Diana shuddered, feeling the map of her nerve endings suddenly printed brightly upon her skin, a vulnerability that made her tremble. She closed her eyes, locked within her body in a prison of demanding appetites, of flesh that pleaded for touch.

His fingers slid away from her hair, slid beneath the neckband of her dress and followed it around the curve of her throat. The gesture pulled him toward her until his chest brushed gently against her back and his free hand slid up her arm, over the fabric of her dress, to trace her neckline from the other side until his fingers brushed against each other beneath her chin and she was clasped in the circle of his arms.

The neck of her dress was tied close with a ribbon tab. Below it were ten buttons from the neck of the gown to the waist, ten small carved bone buttons that fitted through loops to close the front of her dress snugly over the betraying flesh.

It was not a Sunday; Diana did not wear the stiff formidable collar that armored her bosom in an unyielding shield of starched linen. There was nothing beneath Upright's hands but the soft fabric of the gown itself.

In silence he drew open the string that held her neckline closed. Diana gasped for breath as the tie came undone.

The air spilled over the sweat-moist skin at the hollow of her throat. His fingers slid through the opening he had made and touched her skin, sliding over the dampness as he traced the shape of her flesh.

She raised her hands from her lap—her hands only; her wrists and arms seemed borne down by some secret weight too heavy to shift. As if that tiny motion had possessed the force of a shouted command, his fingers slid out from beneath the cloth to work at the first of the ten small buttons, worrying it free of its closure with maddening patience.

His breath tickled the dampness at the back of her neck where his mouth had been; his breath stirred the fine tendrils at her hairline until they danced over her skin with a feathery caress at each expelled breath.

The neck of her dress slid open farther with the first button's release. His hands moved lower, finding each button in turn and drawing his body forward until his cheek rested against the back of her neck.

Paralyzed by the force of the craving that demanded all her attention, Diana watched his hands as they moved over the buttons—the flex and clench of the tendons and muscles, the movement of his fingers strong and sure as they slid over the small round buttons and teased them gently free. Her cheeks were flushed and each breath was an effort to drag useless air into burning lungs.

She was afraid. She didn't want him to be this real, to have the power to draw such response from her body. But he wasn't locked up safely between the pages of a history book. He was here, and so was she, and nothing in all her life had been as real as the touch of his hands on her body.

Upright nuzzled at her throat; and when he turned his head, the tail of his bound hair slid forward, over his shoulder and hers, striking her breast with a soft whiplash. Diana wanted to reach up, to touch its ebony softness, but she was shaking so hard she didn't dare move. Her breath was a rasping sound now, louder, with a catch at the top of each inhalation as she struggled to fill her lungs fuller than they would hold.

He reached the last of the buttons and worried it free in that insanely methodical fashion. And then he put his hands on the shoulders of her gown and slid it open, slid it down, trapping her arms at her sides.

The stay came high beneath the arms to flatten the bosom. Above it, Diana was covered only by the single layer of her smock. He tightened his arms around her, running his palms down the smooth front of the stay as if testing its resilience.

At the sight of the touch she could not feel, the sound of his hands rubbing over the stiff canvas, Diana pushed herself backward, pressing against him. Her own movement pulled loose the lace-strings that tangled between his fingers; the knot came free and the stay opened enough to slide against the smock beneath.

He moved then, rising to his knees behind her. His hands on her shoulders pulled her backward to lie in the warm nest their bodies had made. For a moment he knelt beside her, silhouetted against the misty silver of the sky, and then lay down next to her, his arm across her body.

This has gone too far. A tardy note of warning sounded in Diana's mind. She struggled to sit up or at least free her arms from the dress, but Upright-Before-The-Lord had no interest in allowing her to do either. When she began to struggle, he rolled on top of her, ignoring her breathless squeaks of reproach.

His arms were on either side of her, pushing her arms tight against her ribs and thrusting her breasts at him, making the stays gape still further as the lace ran free. The horsehair pad in the small of her back thrust her pelvis against him; as she struggled to free her arms, his leg slid between hers, spreading her legs—imprisoning her and opening her and making a hard pressure between her thighs where she most needed to be touched.

Diana held herself motionless, fighting the need to rub her body against Upright's like a cat in heat. Her leg was clasped between his thighs. She could feel the muscles flex as he shifted position, feel the hard solidity of his readiness pressed between them.

No, wait, I didn't mean ... The irresponsible, self-serving lie caught in her throat. If she had not meant this to happen, she'd hoped it would; if she had not hoped, she would have left the moment she saw how he looked at her. If this was frightening, it was in the way that roller coasters and water slides were frightening—for the sheer delirious jubilant intensity of the plunge into unknown excitement.

Diana struggled again, this time to reach up and *feel* him through all the suffocating weight of fabric that lay between them. As she did, Upright tore at the lacing of her stays, arching his body over hers and pulling until the lace ran free, yanking the whole string loose with a faint pop and flinging it aside. The long trapezoid of stitched canvas fell open, sliding away to curl in the folds of Diana's open bodice; and when Upright saw the plain white fabric of her smock, he let out a long shuddering sigh and bowed his head.

His hair had come loose of its ribbon sometime in her struggles and fallen around Diana's face like a silken curtain, straight and soft and clean. The paleness of his face glowed against its darkness, and Diana's whole world had narrowed to the elemental longing for him to kiss her.

Upright lowered his face to hers as if he feared to bruise her. She opened her mouth to him at once; frustration and recklessness and a desire that had become a physical presence bordering on pain made her nip at him, seeking to hold him to her with her mouth alone.

She heard the rasp of a faint moan caught deep in his throat, and the sound of it sent joy blazing through her body. The fierceness of her desire to give him pleasure was a part of her need to have him, to envelop him and possess him utterly. His body rocked against her and Diana arched her back, taking more of his weight, pressing him harder against her. She could feel him trembling with need as his tongue touched hers, sending a bolt of pure liquid desire along her nerves.

Finally she freed one arm from its imprisoning sleeve and at last she could touch him. She dug her nails into his shoulder, holding him and pulling him down to her, not caring how she hurt him because she could not imagine how she could survive if he stopped what he was doing.

But Upright was stronger than she was; he was able to push himself up off her, arching his back even though she clawed at him. Diana moaned a wordless protest, and he took her lower lip gently between his teeth and worried at it, tormenting her with flickering caresses of his tongue. Whimpering deep in her throat, Diana reached higher and twined her fingers in his hair, pulling and twisting and attempting to force his mouth back to hers.

He let her push him against her, but he released her mouth, bending his head lower. She writhed, freeing her other arm and clutching at his shoulders with both hands, but his mouth upon her took her by surprise, closing moistly over her breast, where the taut nipple showed darkly through the thin fabric. His touch seemed to dissolve the fabric like morning mist; it was as if she were naked.

The bliss of what he was doing made her arch her back and force her body against his; the flickering heat of his tongue, the spreading heat in her loins merged into one sweet, demanding ache. She yipped and jerked as if she'd been bitten instead of merely tongued. All the reasons why she must not do this were gone, made insignificant by the need to have him, to melt and dissolve and blaze in his grasp until the two of them merged into one creature, one life.

She was drowning; she was dying, licked and suckled insistently as if she were sugar, as if he could draw nourishment from her flesh. In this sweet, airless languor that meant that she had forgotten even to breathe, the things he was doing to her, the things that he was were an insistent demand that she could bear to delay only because the outcome was so inescapable.

He nuzzled at first one breast, then the other as she squirmed and gasped and writhed beneath him, forgetting shame, forgetting pride, forgetting restraint, already on the edge of the dissolution that would complete her.

Unable to undress herself, Diana pulled at his shirt, tugging and tugging until it came free of his waistband and slid up his back. When he felt it slip up over his shoulders, he pulled away from her. She stared up at him, her hands still full of the rough homespun of his shirt.

"Wouldst see me?" he asked. "In the light of day?"

Diana nodded, her mouth dry. Upright pulled away, bunching the shirt in front of him to pull it off; and suddenly, through the breathless weight of her arousal, Diana realized what they were about to do—and where.

"No!" She caught at his wrist. "No. We can't. Not here. They'll see. Isn't there somewhere we can go?"

He stopped what he was doing but did not move, gazing at her with a new light in his eyes, as though the sleeping angel she had always known was there had finally wakened.

"No," he said. There was amusement in his voice. "They will not look. It is Man's way not to look, not to see. The grass hides us."

Amusement—and scorn.

"Wouldst see me in the light of day?" he asked again, and Diana realized that he was giving her one last chance to refuse him. But it was already far too late for that. Daylight . . . moonlight . . . candlelight . . . if she could not have him, it would be a sorrow as great as death.

"Yes," she said. "Yes, I want to see you."

He pulled the shirt off over his head and paused, holding it in front of himself. His body was pale, the muscles hard and seasoned; but his skin carried no hint of bronzing from the sun.

Diana sat up to shove the stays out of her way, feeling shy

and wanton, both at once. He was right; no one would see them unless they came as far as the churchyard, and not even then if they didn't look.

Upright dropped his shirt in a careless ball and began to work at the fastening of his breeches, and Diana found she was gazing at him in expectant rapture, as though he were the Forest Lord himself come to life before her.

Wiccan belief held that every lovers' meeting was a microcosmic reenactment of the Great Marriage—that celestial embrace of heaven and earth, male and female, the paired opposites that were the cornerstone of all Creation—but Diana had never quite understood why until this moment. But the divine fire burned in him, and Diana felt as if she were seeing something she was not meant to, as if the gods had shed their masks to appear here naked to her mortal eyes.

He'd sat down, pulling his breeches and smallclothes off together. He made no move to cover himself, as innocently aroused as a wolf in the wild.

The tenderness that melted her was more intimidating than passion; she wanted to love him and bind him to her and keep him—and feed him, oh, Blessed Lady, yes, if that was what would make him happy. She loved him. Even if it was against all reason, even if it was wrong.

Even if it was the stupidest thing she'd ever done in her entire life.

"Come here," Diana said, in a small, wavery voice, holding out her hand to him as she sat on the hillside.

His naked body was all ivory-and-pale-blush velvet. He took the hand that she held out to him. His skin was pale against her sun-browned flesh, his grip strong and sure, and suddenly she didn't know what came next.

He did not hesitate, tugging her toward him, onto her knees, kissing her mouth over their clasped hands. He pulled at her skirts, pushing them up around her waist, and then his hands were on her hips, urging her to move forward, to straddle him where he knelt.

Flesh on flesh, with her skirts bunched between their bodies and his silken male heat pressed hard against the soft swelling curve of her belly, he rocked back, taking all her weight, pulling her even farther forward, and suddenly Diana was sitting on his lap. Her heels skimmed the grass of the slope, and the coiled muscles of his thighs were a hard presence beneath her own. It was not a position that gave her any leverage; he'd trapped her neatly, and all she could do was cling to him as he began to rock against her.

The touch of his body pressing against her where she was open and vulnerable made her body burn. His movements made his hardness slide against her soft, yielding essence over and over, the silken movements oiled by sweat and by desire.

If he did not take her soon, she would not be able to stand it. She tried to raise herself enough to bring him inside her, but she could not get her feet under her with the position he'd put her in and her squirming attempts only increased her helpless desire.

He would not let her hurry or rule him. His movements against her body became slower and deeper; now each motion rubbed the whole length of him against her portal until her blood beat there in time to her heart. With merciless restraint, he resisted all her attempts to escape, to urge him on, to end this slow exquisite torment until she trembled on the brink of shattering and she had yielded to him utterly. At last Diana could only cling to him and tremble, her struggles forgotten.

Then he slid his hands beneath her, raising her until she was nearly standing and then slowly lowering her. When their bodies touched, he groaned with the effort it took to hold himself back. His arms trembled as her body slowly sank onto him, filling her as she sobbed wordlessly in frustration.

The sensation of being opened and filled, of his prolonged irresistible conquest, built suddenly, stunningly; Diana cried out as the fire suddenly blazed up, breaking her with soft quick hammer blows that seemed to stretch to eternity. Her surrender was more a surprise to her than it was to him; she heard him laugh, a small growling wolf-chuckle in his throat, as she clung to him, dazed with the swiftness and force of it, her face pressed against his neck.

And then, before she'd had time to recover, the hill was solid against her back and he was a durable weight and a delicious pressure on top of and inside her, moving in her, not yet so caught up in his pleasure that he could not watch her. His gaze was fixed on her as if he were trying to draw her down into a world of his own creation.

She lifted her hips to meet his thrusts—pressure and heat and salt and desire, a sweet building ache that forced words from her throat in time to the rhythm their bodies made.

"Don't leave me. . . . Don't leave me. . . . Don't leave me. . . ."

She kept her gaze fixed on his face as all his senses were enchanted away at last by the irresistible heat of their private dance, as his eyes closed and his body tensed and spasmed against hers, and then Diana, too, was whirled away again, taking him, all of him, into sweet oblivion.

He'd slept only a short while, but it was enough to change the light and for his *righ-malkin* to turn a little away from him in sleep. Di-Ana, she had named herself on Full Moon Night; *di'anu*, the woman. His woman. He lay content, watching the sky darken, listening to her breathing, and considering what they would do next.

She was his now, beyond argument. She had given herself to him; there might even be a child of their making growing already in her womb. A child who would be free.

Free.

He knew enough now to make it so. He knew the language of Man—their clothes and their food and how to pass among them. He would not be taken and chained again. He would take her north of here, and west, away from cities. Somewhere in the world were the mountains and green valleys of his painful tangled dreams.

He had heard it said that there were mountains in the West.

He would call the mist and the rain to cover their tracks, and he would take her in search of them. They would live free. And Matthew would not follow them. Not after tonight.

He looked toward his *righ-malkin*. He had heard them talking about her, Matthew and John, of what a pretty witch she'd be to prick with their needles, to strip and flog naked through the town in proof of God's power in this world. It would have been easy enough to find accusers for her, to put words in the mouth of the tormented Malignants Matthew already had beneath his hand.

But now that would not happen. She'd come to him, knowing somehow that tonight was the night he meant to come for her and take her away—tonight, the occasion of Matthew's greatest triumph. He had been willing to use any means to make her come away with him, but there had been no need. She had come to him freely.

And now they would both be free. He turned and coiled against her, holding her body against the body of the earth, and dozed again, waiting for true night.

Her movement woke him. She was on her knees, blindly seeking her discarded shawl to cover herself against the evening chill. Without thought he rose behind her, pushing her skirts up over her back until he had exposed her. Her scent and his, mingled, came off her skin, hot and strong where it had been trapped by the layers of fabric; and he felt himself filling and tightening for her, an engorged and naked hunger that called to its sheath.

Without any of Men's words he took her, curling his fingers around the bone of her hip and pulling her back against him, filling her with one easy movement, placing his other hand against her belly so she could not pull away. He slid his fingers down, finding the cluster of curls at the root of her belly, dampness and softness and woman's secret. She knew him and did not struggle as he pressed into her, his chest resting against her back, holding her between his body and his hands.

With careful fingers he traced over the folds of flesh still slick with his seed, feeling the pressure of his body carried through her flesh. His fingers roved on her until he could touch the entrance to her womb, touch himself sheathed within her, feel how her delicate flesh was pulled with each small movement he made.

He traced his fingers carefully along the folds of her body—the inner and the outer, the delicate mysteries of her fashioning—seeking. He knew when he found what he sought by the way her body stiffened, the way his fingers grazed a proud hardness amid the sleek engulfing flesh. He probed gently and found his reward in her ragged moan, a shudder that startled her body out of his rhythm.

He pushed himself against her, hands and body together, until no matter how she moved she thrust herself against him. Small movements, small, slower and slower until he stopped. He was not sure he could bear it, waiting with the hot tightness of her flesh burning all around as her body nursed at his with rhythmic demanding pressure, drawing his very spirit out of him with his essence.

He forced himself to remain motionless, holding all of him still except the fingers that moved between her thighs, circling and pressing and teasing at her ready, helpless flesh until at last she could not move at all, could only arch her body back against his in unbearable tension.

Her breathless whimpering was the anguished sound of a creature in need as he drew her tighter, *tighter. . . .*

She gave a choked cry and worked herself upon him, but he would not let her have her deliverance yet. With both hands he clamped her hips against his thighs, taking the rhythm from her and forcing it faster, riding her mercilessly to climax as she gasped and cried and he died in the incandescent hammer blows of bliss.

When he came back to himself she had collapsed and he lay on top of her. He moved only enough to drag the shawl over both of them and slept, suddenly and absolutely, curled protectively around her with one hand shielding the entrance to her womb.

Chapter 10

Talitho, Hampshire, August 1, 1647

It was full dark now and the wind had changed. Diana moved, disoriented and groggy, dazed and sated with the aftermath of physical pleasure. Upright-Before-The-Lord lay against her back; gingerly she pulled herself out from beneath him and got to her knees.

Her dress was twisted around her hips and her smock was stuck to her thighs with his spilled seed. When she moved she could feel the bruised sensitivity that came from violent loveplay. She winced, pulling her clothes into some semblance of order and wishing for the convenience of a twentieth-century bathroom. She thought of going down to the sea to wash, but she didn't dare move very far; in the dark with no lantern she could see almost nothing. The village, too, was nearly dark; the brightest light she could see was the torches burning outside the inn.

What had happened here, what it meant, was still too new to think about. Diana concentrated on the present moment, putting her arms through the sleeves of her dress and pulling it around her, wondering where her stays and bumroll had gotten to. She'd never been corseted very tightly, so the bodice buttoned up easily enough, though she almost missed the support the stays had given. She ran her hands through her hair, straightening its tangles, and then began to grope carefully around the darkened hillside for her shawl.

A hand over hers stopped her. Upright. Without a word he handed her the shawl, then moved away to retrieve his own clothes. Diana sat on the hill, pulling the shawl around her, feeling the awkward ache of strained muscles, and watched the movement of the faint, pale shape in the darkness as Upright found his clothes and dressed. As he covered himself he seemed to vanish, a mistwraith in the wind.

What had she done? She didn't know what she felt. She didn't know what she should do. She wasn't even sure this was love; her emotions were too keyed up to settle and give her any clue. She could put her hand against the place in her chest where the feeling burned, hot and strident, and try to press away the ache, but it wouldn't go away.

She stared at the man she had given herself to, thinking that only now did that oft-used cliché seem to have any meaning. "Given herself" . . . That was what she'd done. Given herself to Upright-Before-The-Lord, seventeenth century—what? She didn't know that either. They were from two different worlds— another cliché that was literal truth.

She felt as if she'd died and been reborn, and her confused feeling for Upright-Before-The-Lord were a hot miserable joy in her heart. What did *he* think of what they'd done here this afternoon? What did he mean to do now? Surely he didn't mean to just go away and leave her here?

"Upright?" Diana whispered, a note of panic in her voice.

He appeared again, coming close enough for her to see him, both hands full of the heavy scarlet wool of the riding-hood he'd retrieved from her wicker basket. He knelt as gracefully as a courtier and offered it to her.

"Hail, thou that art highly favored, the Lord is with thee: blessed art thou among women."

A pang of sudden unease shot through her at words that even Diana knew.

"No," she said.

She was still more worried than afraid, but certainly she was disturbed. He'd seemed to come back to her and himself here this afternoon, but a small traitorous voice of caution counselled that it could be an accident, an illusion, temporary. And he could be the gentlest creature under heaven; but if he were not capable of being responsible for his actions, he might do anything.

"They are the words that Man has given me, but it does not matter," Upright said, setting the cloak at her feet. "I will not use them. Eat, and then we will go."

He'd brought the basket, too, and his own offering: a leather flask, such as the shepherds carried, filled with strong red wine. He broke off pieces of the bread and cheese and fed her. Diana discovered she was hungry, ravenously so, for what seemed the first time in days.

"Go where?" Diana said after her first hunger had been satisfied.

"To the mountains. You will come away with me and all will be well, for us and for the child to come. Matthew will not follow when he has the others."

It took her a moment, distracted by his easy certainty that she was pregnant, to focus on the rest of what he was saying.

"What others, Upright? Those poor women he's arrested?"

"The covenant," he said, cutting through the suggestion that was, even as she said it, only a faint hope against the reality she suspected and dreaded. "The regular of Malignants which meets this Lammas Night."

He knew. Oh, blessed Bright Lady, he *knew.*

"He's going to arrest them?" Fear made her voice harsh. Fear wiped away every other emotion as if it had never been.

"Do they not meet in a Grand Covenment this night to work against him who calls himself my master and those who are still his servants? They plotted it before my very ear, while I lay concealed, and so I did carry this intelligence to Matthew, telling him wherein he might discover them, that we might go free."

He must have been at the parsonage the night Mistress Fortune gave the cordial to Jemima Skelton. Diana covered her mouth with her hand in horror. He'd betrayed them all. How could she have trusted him? *How?*

"They're my friends," she said in a muffled voice. Every coven within fifty miles was out there in the woods tonight—because of her. She'd told them it was safe to meet. She'd done nothing to stop them. It was her fault.

"They are Malignants, and will hang for it," he answered. "But we—"

"No!" Diana cried in swift, instinctive revulsion. She scrambled away from him. He'd betrayed the coven to Hopkins. He'd betrayed *her.*

She had to warn them.

Without conscious thought, she was on her feet, half-running, half-falling down the hill. Miraculously, she reached the bottom without injury. Without the padding and the stays, her skirts hung trippingly long; as soon as she reached level ground, Diana scooped up her skirts, orienting herself upon the white shine of the gravestones. The overcast of the day had broken into scudding clouds; behind her the moon was rising, sovereign gold as it left the horizon. It was a waning moon, but in an hour it would cast enough light to see by.

She didn't have an hour. She had to find the coven *now.*

Where were they? Would they meet at their usual dancing ground? That was where Matthew Hopkins would go. Where he'd been *told* to go, by the man she'd spent half the afternoon rutting with.

Tears prickled behind her eyes, and a passionate knot of emotions rose up in her throat, gagging her with their fierce intensity. She couldn't see. Betrayed . . . betrayer . . . guilty . . . bereaved. The needle of her emotions gyrated wildly about the compass-rose of possibilities. She struck out blindly in the dark, a hurried walk that would become a run once she reached clear ground.

Upright-Before-The-Lord appeared out of the darkness, grabbing her arm with as much certainty as if he could see her plainly. A scream strangled in her throat as he dragged her to a stop, choked to silence by fury and grim determination not to let him see her afraid.

"You cannot save them."

His face was close enough to kiss, the words spoken with the slow weight of utter conviction.

"Let me go!" Diana tried to pry his hand off her arm; if he would not let her go, what could she do? Scream?

"He will have them, I tell you. *Di'anu,* do I not know his ways? Once he has come to a place, there must be blood . . . victims and coin . . . and survivors to name him great. He has spies who come to him in his places; I know not how many, but do you not think he could find us again if he hungered to? Only give him this great triumph and he will let us go. *Righmalkin,* if you go to them, you will only die with them."

"I have to!" Diana shrieked, striking out at him, taking refuge in any emotion that would seal away the ache of utter betrayal in her heart. "I'm one of them! Let me go, damn you. Let me warn them. There's still time—"

Without another word, Upright released her and stepped back. The wolf-light shine in his eyes was a trick of the light, vanishing when he glanced away. And because she wanted so much to stay, to be *safe,* she gathered up her skirts and ran, ran as though all the devils in hell were pursuing her.

Ran away from him.

He—he did not have a name to think of himself by other than the one Matthew had given him, and he would not use it—crouched down in the shadow of a gravestone and rested his cheek upon the cool marble. He would not weep. His kind had no tears, so Man's tales of them ran; and if he could be true to his kindred in nothing else, he would be true in this.

There had been one moment when he might have seized and dazzled her, carried her away helpless, but he had been unable to seize it. The years had made him too much a part of Man's world, and there had been no one to teach him what he truly was. The chains Matthew had placed about his spirit had held, and he had failed her.

Anger made a cold stone of his heart, but he could not hate her. Her quest was hopeless. It was already too late to save the coven. Matthew had meant him to guide his agents to their meeting place, but Matthew did not need him for that. Any villager knew where the forest's edge was; and once Matthew and his eager helpers reached it, the Malignants were lost. Three dozen people, or nearly, could not hide or flee in such cover as was available there. Matthew's hunters would capture as many of the Malignants as they could hold.

And Matthew would take his *righ-malkin*, too.

Better he had never seen her. Better that Upright-Before-The-Lord had not seen her and wakened his nameless self from his spirit's sleep. The poor creature who lived in the name Upright was broken to its bondage, but the sight alone of her had been enough to waken *him*—he who was *not* Upright-Before-The-Lord—to wake him and make him who had no name yearn for freedom.

If he failed to gain his freedom here tonight, he knew now that he did not have the strength to fight the Upright-self for the chance to make another attempt. He would die to himself, and his body and that which lived in the name Upright would live a brief while longer as Matthew's cringing servant.

Freedom had nearly been within his hand, and then *di'anu* had escaped his will and fled from him. There was nothing he could do to save her. To follow her was a futile errand; she would run into the trap herself trying to win freedom for Matthew's victims. And only if he were very lucky could he save himself—by running now, as far and as fast as he could, and pretending that the moon had never risen upon the day that he'd seen his *di'anu*.

He rubbed his cheek against the harsh surface of the gravestone, then rose to his feet, testing the wind. The silvering moon rose higher, into a cloud-choked sky, and the sea mist

4 BESTSELLING HISTORICAL ROMANCES BY YOUR FAVORITE AUTHORS CAN BE YOURS, FREE!

Kensington Choice brings you historical romances by your favorite bestselling authors including Janelle Taylor, Shannon Drake, Rosanne Bittner, Jo Beverley, and Georgina Gentry, just to name a few! Each book is filled with passion, adventure and the excitement of bygone times!

To introduce you to this great club which is part of Zebra Home Subscription Service, we'd like to send you your first 4 bestselling historical romances, absolutely free! And once you get these 4 free books to savor at home, we'll rush you the next 4 brand-new books at the lowest prices available, as soon as they are published.

The way the club works is that after your initial FREE shipment, you will get our 4 newest bestselling historical romances delivered to your  doorstep each month at the preferred subscriber's rate of only $4.20 per book, a savings of up to $8.16 per month (since these titles sell in bookstores for $4.99-$6.99)! All books are sent on a 10-day free examination basis and there is no minimum number of books to buy. (And no charge for shipping.) Plus as a regular subscriber, you'll receive our FREE monthly newsletter, *Zebra/Pinnacle Romance News*, which features author profiles, subscriber benefits, book previews and more!

So start today by returning the FREE BOOK CERTIFICATE provided. We'll send you 4 FREE BOOKS with no further obligation: A FREE gift offering you hours of reading pleasure with no obligation...how can you lose?

*We have 4 FREE BOOKS for you
as your introduction to
KENSINGTON CHOICE!
To get your FREE BOOKS, worth
up to $24.96, mail the card below.*

FREE BOOK CERTIFICATE

Yes! Please send me 4 Kensington Choice (the best of Zebra and Pinnacle Books) Historical Romances without cost or obligation (worth up to $24.96). As a Kensington Choice subscriber, I will then receive 4 brand-new romances to preview each month for 10 days FREE. I can return any books I decide not to keep and owe nothing. The publisher's prices for Kensington Choice romances range from $4.99-$6.99, but as a preferred subscriber I will get these books for only $4.20 per book or $16.80 for all four titles. There is no minimum number of books to buy and I may cancel my subscription at any time, plus there is no additional charge for postage and handling. No matter what I decide to do, my first 4 books are mine to keep, absolutely FREE!

KF0298

Name _____

Address _____ Apt. _____

City _____ State _____ Zip _____

Telephone ( ) _____

Signature _____

(If under 18, parent or guardian must sign)

Subscription subject to acceptance. Terms and prices subject to change.

already walked the streets of the village, creeping up over the land. He took one step, then two, in the direction *di'anu* had gone. Three steps. His fate was upon the face of the bright Lady of the Night, and he began to run in the direction his *righ-malkin* had gone, loping low and fast along the ground, like a hunting wolf.

If she kept the moon at her back, she was sure she must be going in the right direction, toward the forest and the Witches meeting there. Mist hung in the air, reflecting the moonlight and making everything strange. In her wake, the fog from the sea rolled over the land, offering concealment . . . and refuge? Please let it shield them. She'd never make it. She couldn't run far enough, fast enough.

She had to.

There were moments when Diana was sure this was a horrible hallucination, a dream before waking. *"How many miles to Babylon? Threescore miles and ten."* Scraps of poetry flitted like fireflies through her exhausted mind. *"She was a child and I was a child, In this kingdom by the sea."*

Diana ran, across the sheep meadow and past the animals clustered for sleep in a wooly grayish pack, over the stile that kept them out of the ripening grain. When she paused to gasp for breath, the sudden rush of weakness she felt was a new bright layer to Diana's gnawing fear. She couldn't faint. She had only herself to count on. If she failed herself, she failed everyone. She stood very still and gasped for air, forcing her will upon her body. After a moment, the world steadied.

With quivering hands Diana ripped at the bodice of her dress, tearing it open. Buttons went flying as she dragged at the cloth, pulling and yanking until she could step free. She'd be less encumbered without it. Her petticoats and smock came only to the bottom of her calves; they wouldn't get in her way as the yards of heavy fabric in the dress would. And she couldn't afford to fall.

Diana kicked the dress away from her, biting her lips shut

to stifle the sound of her own breathing so she could listen for drums, scanning the field with desperate eyes to find any trace of passage through it. Then, like a white owl hunting through the night, she ran again, driving herself past exhaustion, past the hollow fire in her throat and the pain that felt like iron bands around her chest, past the trembling weakness in her muscles and the sick pain in her heart.

She could hear voices, and the power they raised was a tingling wash over her skin, like the energy that precedes a storm. Even from this distance, Diana could hear the strike of the drums, see the flicker of movement as dancing bodies passed before the fire; and the energy they raised was almost tangible, a golden fog of heat and passion that she could wind through her fingers like silk and lace.

She'd found them.

Diana was stopped before she reached them. She saw the bright flash of a blade in the darkness and realized it could all end here, on the Summoner's steel. When she stopped moving forward she seemed to lose all strength, swaying unsteadily on her feet and fighting for each inadequate breath. Finally she surrendered, gasping for air as she sank to her knees in a welter of ripped and grimy petticoats.

"Merry meet." His words were cautious, but he'd recognized her. "Mistress Anne?" he asked, putting up his sword and staring at her curiously.

"Run," Diana croaked. "They're here." She raised her hand weakly, as if to ward him off. Her voice was an inaudible whisper.

He could not even have heard her, but the Summoner did not hesitate.

"Run!" he bellowed in a voice like a sudden shout of stormwind. "We are discovered. Save yourselves!"

The gathering power vanished, disappearing as the witches did in a flurry like partridges exploding from cover. Diana heard the babble of their voices and, over them, a rising chorus of shouts and the high keen shrill of a signal whistle.

She was too late. Hopkins was already here.

The Summoner would have stayed for her, but she waved him away, shaking her head. After an instant he ran, a pretty boy in lace and velvet, the Magister's rapier naked in his hand. Behind him, the grass of the now-deserted dancing ground was trampled to its edges, littered with hats and caps and even an expensive embroidered glove.

Diana had thought she was utterly spent, but the sound of the trap closing gave her new strength—the cold, chill strength of stark terror. She leapt to her feet as though jerked by invisible strings.

Don't let them catch me; oh, don't let them catch me.

She ran with the flagging strength of utter terror through the edge of the wood, shock and exhaustion and disorientation all conspiring to make her reckless of the thorns that gouged their bloody track across her flesh. When she gained open ground at last, she saw the wind-whipped flicker of the torches carried in the hands of the hunters and shied wildly away, running in any direction that promised darkness and safety.

She seemed to be fragmented into a multitude: The one who ran; the one who wept and begged, half-mad with fear; the cold part beyond terror that showed Diana, in pictures of ripped flesh and splintered bone, what Hopkins's people would do when they caught her. They would torture her to death for witchcraft, and there was nothing she could do to stop them.

Behind her, Diana heard a cry go up and knew it was for her. She wished with frantic despair for the powers legend ascribed to her kind. Oh, for a horse of air, a broomstick, an eggshell boat to whisk her far away from here!

A flung stone struck her between the shoulderblades and she staggered, unable to keep her balance. Another hit her and she fell, struggling to rise even as the heavy booted feet ran over the meadow toward her, as the hard hands yanked her to her feet and her captor cried his victory for anyone to hear.

* * *

He was as fast as she, had paced her like the shadow of a wolf as she raced her miles across the fields. He could have leapt from cover and seized her at any moment—and knew if he did that her shrieks would rack the night, alerting hunter and hunted both.

In the end, it was that final hesitation that cost him everything—he let her reach the Malignants, and then they were scattering like frightened birds and he heard the whistles and shouts of their pursuers. The trap was sprung. It was too late.

He ran recklessly among the hunters then, trying to find where she had run, knowing that neither of them could escape but wanting to be the one who captured her so there would be at least that much of a chance for her.

But even that was to be denied him. By the time he found her, she was struggling in another man's arms; and before he could reach her, she lay bleeding upon the ground, sprawled insensible at the blow from a meaty fist.

It was nearly dawn in the tiny coastal village of Talitho, but none of its inhabitants had slept. Torches burned up and down the fog-shrouded High Street, and The Moon and Lantern was brilliant with candles, every window shining golden light out into the night.

It was difficult to know what to do. The countryside had been torn by civil war for more than half a decade; the delicate web of sheriffs and magistrates, justices and courts, had been torn into tatters by bloody revolution so that few could say who truly held either the High Justice or the Low in any place in England. Once Simon Grimsby had returned to the town with his tale of a great army of Malignants subdued in the fields, the commander of the local garrison had been called. Captain Shackleton was a good Puritan and no freethinker; he was terrified at the first mention of witchcraft and turned to Matthew Hopkins for advice and support. At Hopkins's command, Shackleton sent a rider to the Warden of Christchurch Gaol so that the Malignants could be properly imprisoned and questioned and bound over for trial. He ought to have sent to the Sheriff of Hampshire and notified the local justice of the peace; but in these unsettled days, neither post held the consequence it had when the King had reigned and might both lie vacant.

Within the village itself, people gathered in the streets, daring the cloak of ocean mist in their disquiet, dumbstruck at the enormity of the disaster that had befallen them. The Devil was among them. They demanded that their neighbors' houses be opened to them so that they could see who had fallen prey to the darkness gathered around them and who still walked in the light of God's Grace. The local thugs who had been Hopkins's army fondled their slings and cudgels as they drank at Talitho's expense in the taproom and on the street and regaled villagers and each other with tales of their great valor.

And in the Moon and Lantern, Matthew Hopkins, Witchfinder-General of all England, held court.

The low ceiling of the private parlor captured the coils of smoke from tobacco and candles and made it a thick pearly blanket just beneath the age-blackened timbers of the ceiling. The room imprisoned sound as well as smoke, the sound of many men laughing and talking loudly together to cover their fear.

He could smell it on them, their fear. It burned his nose with its harsh piss-vinegar rankness, even over the smells of gin and beer and burning leaf. The Devil rode out in Talitho, and the sons of Man were afraid.

And he, who knew that the only Devil was here in this room, was also afraid.

He had seen *di'anu* fall and had done the only thing left for him to do. He had gone and found Matthew, who was standing at his ease while John Sterne and the others did his work for him. He had come up to his master like a whipped and penitent cur, hoping that mere presence would be enough to provide him his readmittance into this charmed circle of Hell.

And Matthew had smiled in that easy knowing way of his and touched the head of his hound, but had said neither yes or no, nothing that could be used to judge his mood. And so his creature could do nothing save follow, hovering at the edges of those that mobbed the man they saw as their salvation as Matthew took command. Matthew, who had fought the Devil and stolen his Black Book; Matthew, whom the Evil One could not kill; Matthew, who knew every secret in the traitorous hearts of the damned; Matthew, who reigned over them all, giving his orders with the practiced assumption of privilege.

The endless night had dragged on toward morning, and he had not dared leave Matthew's side, afraid to speak in case the words he had left to him were not the right ones. News came in scraps, swirled around the room like the sea mist that lay heavy on the land. the Malignants were taken, shackled, laid in the cellars of the Rectory to await transportation to the Christchurch jails.

He dared not go there and try to carry her off, not now when men with horses and sabers stood ready to ride the two of them down at Matthew's sole word.

With the coming day the candles became pale ghosts of their nighttime selves, the haloes of light around them shrinking until their flames were only brilliant sparks lost against the greater fire of the sun. The last tankard was drained, the last pipe smoked, and Matthew's fulsome delight in his victory seemed to come at last within bounds and give pride of place to the demands of the mortal flesh.

At last Matthew stood, his fine satin cape still set about his shoulders, and spoke to the few townsfolk who still attended him, saying he would go up to bed.

It came then, the gesture *he* had been waiting for: the careless flick of the hand summoning him in. To be within walls was bad enough while all his body cried for freedom; to go to one of the tiny rooms upstairs would be worse. But he welcomed even this suffering, knowing it brought him closer to a way to free his *righ-malkin.*

Gratefully he rose from where he had been crouching by the wall and followed his master up to bed.

"Where were you tonight, my faithful servant?"

The directness of the question was startling, disorienting him even while he was still trying to deal with the dread that entering the small, low-ceilinged room gave him. He had thought to lie down in his place but stopped, head hanging, confused at what was suddenly required of him.

"Surely you can answer. The Devil's power is broken in Talitho, the whole network of Malignants brought out into the light for the greater glory of the Lord. And where were you?"

He could not answer. He dared not. He hung his head and kept his eyes downcast, hiding his true self from the master's eyes.

"Johnnie." Matthew raised his voice only a little, but the door opened again and John Sterne stepped through. In his hand Sterne held the short truncheon of leather-wrapped shot that could shatter a kneecap or break all the fine bones of the hand with one weighted blow. Within his skin, the creature named Upright-Before-The-Lord gibbered in fear when he saw it, another thing to fight against here in what felt so much like a trap.

"Our young friend harbors a rebellious spirit within his heart," Matthew said. His rich voice was filled with nothing but kindly concern, but its victim knew that tone—and dreaded it.

"We must aid him to cast it out."

Sterne advanced on him, the truncheon in one hand and, in the other, a braided leather loop such as was used to leash hunting dogs and drag them away from the downed quarry.

He backed away from that loop, eyes wild, searching for the right words. *"Thou hast made me a table in the presence of my enemies; I will fear no evil. . . ."* some frightened part of his mind gibbered, but the words lied. He did fear. He feared Matthew.

"Come, boy." Sterne's voice was neither cruel nor kind. "Come and submit to Master Hopkins like a good Christian. We'll beat the Devil out of you yet."

At those words he relaxed slightly, trying to watch Sterne and Matthew both at once. If it were only a beating that was the price of Matthew's final forgiveness, that would not be so bad. He had been beaten many times before. The pain always passed, and Matthew took care not to hurt him too badly.

So he stood without moving and let Sterne take him, reaching the noose toward his neck.

"Humility, pup," Sterne said, slapping him lightly upon the cheek to make him bend down for the leash.

The wild fury that rose up in him at the harmless blow was nearly his undoing. It was agony to lower his head in meekness, and feel the cold slickness of the leather circle his neck. The killing fury that filled his throat made his words appropriately strangled and disjointed.

"Submit," he gasped, though he nearly choked on it. "Meekness—"

Then Sterne jerked the loop tight, cutting off further speech.

He forced himself to follow docilely as Sterne led him to the empty bedchamber that Matthew had reserved for private interviews. The hearth was cold, the shutters closed, and only one meager stub of lighted candle gave any illumination to the room. Head down, intent on playing out his role, at first he did not see what else the room contained.

A box.

A narrow wooden box.

Small, suffocatingly small, set on two trestles as it had been brought from the sawyer's, so narrow that a man inside would press against the wood on every side, so narrow that the lid would crush him into place, sealing him away from all light, all air. . . .

He flung himself backward, away from Sterne and the box. He collided with Matthew, knocking the other man off balance.

Then Matthew shoved him forward and Sterne dragged at the leash with all his enormous strength, pulling it tight about his throat.

They were going to put him into the box.

Fear wiped away the disputing voices in his head, blotting out the distinction he made between himself and Upright-Before-The-Lord. He thrashed in pure animal terror, but he'd let them put a leash about his throat and now Sterne used it. Sterne dragged him to his knees, choking him ruthlessly as he struggled for air; and the light from the small stub of candle darkened to blindness and numbness and the roaring of the sea rose in his ears.

Dimly, he was aware when the choke loosened. He tried to move, but his body was a distant thing and would not obey him. Sterne lifted him as if he had no more weight than a babe and bore him up—over—down—

His back hit the raw wood bottom of the narrow box and he lunged upward, feeling the box rock unsteadily on the saw-horses. Breath whistled in his bruised throat, and each moment he was stronger.

In another instant he would have been free, but Sterne laid a light stroke of the truncheon along his head and the world exploded in sickness and stars. It took him away for only a few seconds, but that was long enough for him to come back to rough wood upon his palms as the lid of the coffin was pressed down over him, sealing him away from even the candle's faint light.

In the last extreme of desperation he fought it, his furious terrified howls ringing from the walls with the sounds of a trapped animal, but all of Sterne's weight lay upon that unyielding piece of wood, crushing him in as Matthew's clever fingers tightened the screws to seal the box around him.

He could not move. *He could not move.* His arms were crushed against his sides, his hands forced against the lid above him. There was no part of him that was not pressed by the box; his chest was forced against his forearms with each breath he took. He was stifling. . . . There was no air.

He heard a voice.

"Little changeling."

Matthew's voice, coaxing and fond. He forced himself to hold silent, to listen and hear. This was only another punishment, he told himself desperately—worse, horribly worse than a beating, but they must let him out in the end. Surely they must let him out.

"Little changeling," Matthew said again, "did you think you could dispute with me?"

Inside the box, he shook his head wildly, the only movement left to him. *No, no, no.* He did not wish to argue with Matthew; he'd only wanted to run away. If he could tell him that, would Matthew let him out?

He tried to form words, to *tell* him, but all he could do was moan, a terrified high-pitched keening like a wounded animal. His breath rebounded against his face; if he lifted his head only a little, he touched the wood above him.

"You set your will against mine," Matthew said sadly, "though you knew your nature was tainted, that your only hope of salvation lay in submission to my will."

The casket creaked as the man inside shoved against it, but the cover did not shift above his hands. He was helpless, immobilized, clinging to rationality by only the frailest of threads.

"But you have rebelled." Matthew's rich voice reached him only faintly; he whimpered at the soft drumbeat that meant Matthew had laid his hand on the box's outer surface. Only an inch of wood separated their hands. It might have been a thousand leagues.

"And in rebelling, Upright-Before-The-Lord, you have died to Grace, and so suffer the fate of all dead men.

"You shall be buried alive."

Then there was only silence and the dark for some uncounted eternity before his prison was lifted and carried away.

* * *

Sunk into a fitful sleep on the cold cellar floor, Diana dreamed that she was buried alive, dying strangled and suffocated in the cold eternal dark. . . .

With a gasp she woke herself. For a moment she did not know where she was, then she tried to move her arms and remembered. And the reality was so much worse than the phantasms of sleep that for a moment she wished she were back in her dream of the coffin sealed beneath the earth.

She was wedged between two other bodies. She did not know whether they were men or women, alive or dead. She did not know how many shared this room with her; she hadn't dared to raise her head to look because she knew they were watched.

The floor was cold, the stone rough and gritty with the sand and dirt tracked across it by the tread of many booted feet. She lay face down on a floor of fitted slates. Her wrists and ankles were lashed together with the same thin, strong twine that was used to weave the fishermen's nets, and her hands and feet had long since gone numb. There was a scrape on her face from where she'd been thrown down, and a bruise upon her jaw. Her head hurt, and her back, too, where the thrown stones had struck her . . . how long ago?

In the pool of yellow light cast by the thick wax candle burning in a wall sconce, Mary Phillips sat in a chair near the door. There were a handbell and a gin bottle on the floor beside her. When Mary rang the bell, it summoned men with clubs who lashed out until they dispelled all resistance.

The men had come once, a few hours before, when Diana was first conscious; and some of the prisoners had still tried to fight back, even if only with words. Now the only sound was that of fitful breathing, and the moans and whimpers of those who were more badly hurt than Diana was.

Carefully, she tried to shift position to ease her cramped frame, fearful of drawing attention to herself. Fear sharpened her senses to painful acuteness, made her mouth dry and metallic, caused her heart to race until it was an active pain in her chest. Why hadn't she realized how badly things would end when she'd run off to warn the coven? She wanted to think she'd have run to warn them anyway, and in her shame she had to admit she wasn't sure she would have, if she'd known. She was a coward. She'd always been a coward, the worst kind of coward—one who thought herself brave, supposing her courage would never be put to the test.

She'd known—intellectually she'd known. She'd read the accounts of the Burning Times in books, had read the eyewitness accounts of her own century's Holocaust. But she hadn't known just how frightening and uncomfortable it was to lie on a floor somewhere, waiting to be tortured to death. Now it was all real, and immediate, and happening to *her*. It wasn't a book or a movie or a tale told by a survivor. She did not know how this story would end.

They didn't get us all, Diana told herself, desperate to find some consolation. It was true. There hadn't been enough of Hopkins's thugs to take the entire covenmeet. She didn't think they'd gotten more than ten or perhaps twenty people out of maybe three times that number. Her warning had been that much help.

She vowed that when Hopkins demanded she name names she wouldn't give any, and wondered bleakly how long she could really hold out.

They were going to kill her. *They were going to kill her. . . .*

Think of something else, she told herself. Something nice. Something good.

Her mind lifted and wheeled like an owl upon the night wind, seeking comfort for her. She thought of Upright-Before-The-Lord, his strong knowing hands and his strong body whose touch was pleasure. He'd wanted to save her from this. She ought to hate him for betraying the coven's meeting to Hopkins, but she didn't have the energy. What else could she have expected from him?

Think of Upright, but not of that. Think of the sunlight on his hair, of the pale silk of his skin. Think of his kisses, the warmth of his body, think of wind and sunlight, a picnic on a grassy hill, of *freedom*. . . . She visualized it with a longing that carried the passion of a prayer. *Gone. Free.* Whatever happened to her, Upright was safe. He'd known the danger better than she had; surely he wouldn't have followed her into it.

Free . . . She allowed her mind to spin out the details of her hope. He had to be miles away by now—gone, safe, somewhere that the horror to come would not touch him. He'd made his escape from Hopkins under cover of the arrests, just as he'd planned.

And because he was free, a part of Diana was free as well. She could think of him and know that there was something still beyond Hopkins's reach. She held to that thought, clinging to it in spite of herself, because here in this place she needed to believe in something to protect her from the dark.

Sir Wilmot Jekyll, the warden of Christchurch Gaol, had sent an open cart to convey the Malignants from Talitho to Christchurch, where they could confess and repent before sentencing. Though there would be a trial as well, it was already certain beyond dispute that the accused were all Malignants and heretical imps of Satan, caught in the very act of their unholy worship and blasphemy.

It was well known that by the sinful pact with the devil the witch's God-given body was replaced by one of the Devil's, so that the sin of the body required the repentance of the body, just as sins of the mind required the repentance of the mind. And once body and mind had both done sufficient penance, each Malignant would die and the power of the evil they had done in the world would end with their deaths.

The sun had burnt off the morning mist by the time the prisoners had been hooded and loaded into the cart and the rest of the little convoy had been assembled. It was decided that the prisoners must be hooded for their transportation to the prison lest they should use the opportunity of their journey to work *maleficium* upon everything that met their gaze.

There was an escort of soldiers from the garrison to convey both the prison cart and to provide an honor guard for the Three

Unspotted Lambs of the Lord, who would be called upon to finish their work in the district by the examination of the Malignants—and by obtaining their full and complete confessions, of course, by any means necessary.

Matthew Hopkins drummed the tail end of the rein against his thigh as he rode, thinking of that day, not long in the future, when he would be able to examine the comely blonde girl that Upright had looked upon with such favor.

Hopkins did not think of Upright himself at all.

Diana did not know how many hours she had stood hooded and blind in a jolting disorientation that she'd finally identified as a horse-drawn cart. She'd been jammed in with an unknown number of weeping, praying prisoners who cried out their own names and those of their families, as if who they had been had the power to save them now. When the cart had finally stopped, Diana had been jerked from it still hooded and half-dragged, half-carried over rough cobbles and down stairs. The fitful daylight that had filtered through the coarse weave of the sack had vanished; in the darkness, the flames of torches were erratic dazzles of light. Then she and her captor had stopped; she'd heard a jingling of keys and the creaking of hinges and had a moment to collect herself before she'd been flung, sprawling, to a floor covered with damp straw.

Now it was entirely dark. Diana lay on her side and listened to the door close and lock, to the soft scrape of retreating footsteps. When it was quiet again, she got to her knees.

Her feet had been freed for the ride in the cart, and the binding on her hands had been loosening all day. She groped her way to a wall, where half an hour of patient rubbing against the cold, rough stones made the hastily tied knot come free so she could turn her attention to the blinding, choking hood.

When she finally got the hood off, her eyes were already well adjusted to the dark. Enough illumination came in through the door that she could see her surroundings fairly clearly—a small windowless chamber about six-feet square, with lime-washed walls and a straw-covered floor. The straw that covered the floor was damp and smelled foul, but there was a wooden stool in the corner. She could sit on that and did, holding her petticoats out from her legs in what even Diana recognized as a doomed and pathetic effort to dry them.

She rubbed at her wrists where a deep, red welt still showed where the cord had cut, blessing the miracle that had left her sensation in her hands. She rubbed at her eyes, grateful to be able to do so. Such small things had become luxuries in the course of a day.

She continued her inventory of the cell. There was an empty pot with an obvious purpose shoved in the corner—and, half buried in the straw nearer the door, a clay jug and a tin plate with a slab of bread on it.

Diana pounced on the jug and almost wept to find it full. She'd never been this thirsty in her entire life. Bread and water, and stale at that, but Diana fell on them greedily. She ate and drank, finishing every drop and crumb, having already learned the first lesson of the victim: Save nothing for later, because at any moment it might be taken away.

When she'd finished, she continued her explorations, using anything she could to occupy her mind and to keep herself from thinking about the future. The wooden door had a small observation grate in it. She looked out into the hall and saw doors much like her own stretching off in both directions, a low beamed ceiling and a slate floor, and the iron baskets of burning cressets that provided her the illumination to see all these improving sights. She watched at the door for a while and then went back into the dim recesses of her cell and sat on her stool.

She had never been so lonely in her life.

As far back as she could remember, Diana had prized self-sufficiency. She'd never wanted to depend on other people to meet her emotional needs because, in some place deep inside of her, she'd always suspected that people would somehow fail her when her need was greatest. Of course she'd had friends, and one or two of them had become casual lovers, but she'd liked them—she hadn't needed them. The many carefree contacts of her daily life, the Salem coven, Molly, her circle of friends had made up in number what they'd lacked in intensity, and she'd been content.

When she'd come to Talitho, Mistress Fortune had taken Diana in, her hospitality so complete and so all-encompassing that Diana had felt instantly befriended. The Talitho coven had made a family circle of a sort. She did not know them well, but she knew that she could call upon them at need. And there had been Upright-Before-The-Lord in all his maddening contradiction, a riddle and a game and a challenge all mixed in together.

Now all of them were gone. The coven, gone. Upright, gone. The coveners were dead, or scattered. Diana had kept herself from thinking about Abigail Fortune in an act of will, but surely the older woman had been at the meeting and now was dead or damned by Diana's own guilt. Even her hope of Upright's freedom did not comfort her; she would never see him again, and knowing that was almost a greater pain than anything else that had happened.

Gone, all of them. Gone and cold and dead.

I'm sorry. It's all my fault and I'm sorry. . . . The tears she could not weep for herself gathered in Diana's eyes as she stared unseeing at the hard, unyielding prison walls.

Some time later—her mind insisted, on no evidence, upon naming it morning—Diana was awakened by the clatter of keys and the sound of voices in the corridor outside.

Rather than sleep on the wet, rotting straw—and unable to sleep perched on the stool, no matter how much she wanted to—Diana had swept the straw into the corner and lain down on the bare floor in the shreds of her petticoat and smock. It had been cold, but she'd been too tired to care.

For a long moment now, Diana lay dazed, not quite certain of who she was, or where. Then reality resumed and she sat up, wincing at the pain in her cold, stiff muscles. It seemed as if her entire body had become one solid, aching bruise. Her eyes were hot and swollen with a night's weeping, but her hands were so dirty by now that she dared not rub them.

The sounds were stopping outside her door. Diana flinched back, clawing her way to her feet with painful slowness. She wanted to be brave in the face of what came next, but she was possessed of too vivid an imagination.

The door swung inward. There was a man with keys, and another man with a broad-brimmed hat. The turnkey stepped in to her cell, holding up a lantern.

"Is this 'un?" he said.

The second man took a quick look. "Aye," he said briefly. "Come out of there, lass. It'll do thee no good to cower from John Sterne."

Chapter 11

Christchurch Gaol, August 1647

Helplessly, Diana walked down the corridor between the two men. Walking hurt her bruised and battered feet, but she didn't hang back. She was afraid to. With the turnkey in the lead and Sterne prowling along menacingly behind her like a great bear, Diana ascended the stairs at the end of the corridor and found herself in an open courtyard.

The bright summer sunlight dazzled her eyes; involuntarily, she slowed, unable to see, and was rewarded with a shove between the shoulder blades that struck her in the same spot the thrown stone had. The casual cruelty did what nothing else in the last two days had been able to do to her.

It made her angry.

Diana stopped dead, digging her heels into the cobbles and turning around.

"Don't you *touch* me," Diana told her tormentor. Her low voice throbbed with fury.

Sterne's placid expression faded as Diana glared at him. He frowned, his face darkening with anger, and raised his hand to strike her in earnest. She did not flinch, and it was Sterne who looked away. A surprised laugh escaped from Diana, a flagrant crow of triumph.

He would have hit her then, but Diana skipped out of reach, running after the retreating turnkey and away from Sterne. By the time she caught up to the turnkey, her quick spurt of anger and triumph had faded. She'd bought herself nothing but trouble, and made a deadly enemy of Sterne by making him look a fool; but even so, Diana found it hard to regret her actions. Sterne was already her enemy. He and Hopkins were going to kill her. Why should she make it easy and comfortable for them?

With Sterne's harsh-breathing bulk at her back, Diana hurried up the stairs at the far side of the courtyard and along a gently curving corridor with smooth, plastered walls. On her left hand, tall narrow window slits filled with a patchwork of tiny panes of leaded glass showed the green-gold of the summer countryside. Ahead was a door, its wooden surface elaborately carved and oiled, surmounted by a coat of arms worked in plaster. The turnkey strode up to it and threw open the door without knocking.

Diana balked. She didn't know what was in the room beyond the door, and she didn't want to, either. As she hesitated, Sterne seized her by the scruff of the neck, his brutal fingers twisting in her hair and nearly dragging her off her feet as he shoved her through the opening.

The room was airy and spacious, larger than Mistress Fortune's entire cottage. The left-hand wall followed the curve of the outside corridor and had tall windows that let in the sunlight. The other walls were panelled in a coffered golden oak, and the most enormous Persian rug Diana had ever seen covered most of the floor. Beneath the windows was a Jacobean sideboard set with tall silver candlesticks and a massive bowl filled with fruit. There was a desk standing before a locked bookcase filled with books. On that same wall were two more doors as elaborate as the one she'd entered through. It was somebody's office, someone rich and powerful. Offices didn't change that much, even in three centuries, and an office of Diana's own time might very well have looked much like this if it had belonged to a rich man with a taste for antiques.

Sterne pulled her to a stop and yanked her even higher so that Diana was forced up onto her toes, her chin pushed down into her chest. She fought to raise her head, battling a wave of nauseated fear.

"Here's the vixen, Matthew."

Matthew Hopkins sat behind the desk, toying with a pair of white kidskin gauntlets. He looked up as she entered.

She tried to hold on to her anger and use it to shield herself. His pale eyes made her think, unpleasantly, of snakes; and as he continued to stare at her, Diana became uneasily aware that she was nearly naked. Her smock and petticoat—all she was wearing—were torn in a dozen places.

"Well," Hopkins said. "Here's a pretty child. What is your name, little mistress?"

I'm not your little mistress or anyone else's! Diana bit back the first flip retort that came to her mind. Hopkins was her enemy—a hypocrite, but by all the reports that history had left behind, a dangerously clever man. She didn't want to make him angry without a good reason. She'd already made that mistake once.

"I don't see," Diana said after a moment, "why I should tell you."

And Hopkins laughed, which frightened her more than anything had yet. She hadn't needed to worry about making him angry. He wasn't afraid of her as Sterne was. But then, John Sterne believed in witches. The punishing grip he maintained on her hair was proof of that. Sterne *believed.*

And Matthew Hopkins did not.

Still laughing, Hopkins dropped the gloves atop a pile of vellum sheets inscribed in a beautiful, even secretary hand and walked around the desk to stand before her. Diana, who restored antique manuscripts of all sorts, knew what she was looking at. A bill of indictment against the witches of Talitho.

"Be bloody, bold, and resolute" Diana quoted desperately

to herself. *"laugh to scorn/ The power of man, for none of woman born/ Shall harm Macbeth. . . ."*

Matthew Hopkins was barely taller than she was, especially with Sterne dragging at her hair until she stood on tiptoe. Before she was quite certain how to react, Hopkins took her chin in his hand, his thumb pressed against the bruised softness of her lower lip.

"So, little hellcat," he crooned, pulling her face toward him. "You'd show some spirit, eh?"

A bubble of insane laughter rose in her chest. She knew that if she once gave in to it she'd never be able to stop; but if Hopkins kept on acting like the villain in a Grade B horror film, she didn't know if she'd be able to help herself. Diana shoved at his chest with all her strength, shaking her head free of his grip on her chin at the price of a burning wrench to her scalp.

For one moment a cold glare of surprise and fury transformed his face into something truly frightening, but then Hopkins smiled again . . . as if he were so far removed from her that nothing she could do would touch him.

Hopkins leaned back against the edge of his desk and waved Sterne away with a languid hand. "Oh, Johnnie, let her go. Anyone would think you were hanging a Christmas goose."

The punishing grip on her hair was abruptly released. Diana staggered and lost her balance. She found herself on her hands and knees, regarding the plush surface of the carpet from very short range. Dust motes twinkled in the sunlight. *Be still,* she told herself. *Just be still.* The words of Julian of Norwich skirled through her mind. *"And all shall be well, and all shall be well, and all manner of thing shall be well . . ."*

"I require from you a confession of witchcraft and the names of those others in your village who have likewise fallen prey to this most monstrous error," came the voice from above her head . . . trained, confident, arrogant. Diana found herself hating him in a new and different way from any she ever had before.

"Forget it, buster," Diana said briefly. She wanted to smash that sanguine smirk, silence that gloating voice.

There was a pause while Hopkins puzzled out the unfamiliar idiom, and then the hateful, unruffled voice began again, as if Matthew Hopkins had all the time in the world.

"You will sign this document; you will make a public confession of your sins, and you will name your accomplices."

Cautiously Diana got to her feet, trying to watch both men at once. Her scalp burned where her hair had been pulled. She raised her hand carefully and touched it; there was soreness but no blood. Sterne was behind her, and she was afraid he was going to hit her, but he did nothing.

"And what's supposed to be in it for me?" Diana asked.

She'd meant to sound like a heroine, but the words came out in a timid squeak. She felt dizzy and light headed once she'd stood, but she was determined to face down Hopkins with dignity for as long as she could.

"*Whore!*" Sterne snarled, reaching for her. "Do as thy master lessons thee!"

Diana ducked away from Sterne, backing away from both men and praying she could keep her feet. She barely glanced at the door through which she'd entered. She didn't have a hope of reaching it; and even if she got out of *here,* there was no way for her to escape the prison.

And nowhere to go if she did.

"Why?" Diana shouted back, finding her voice. "Why should I? Give me just one good reason!"

"Why, to improve your soul through humble obedience to the will of the Lord," Hopkins said lightly. "To repent you of your sins and be returned to a state of abiding grace in the bosom of the Lord."

Diana stared at him, wavering where she stood when every blind instinct urged her to run as far and as fast as she could . . . as Upright-Before-The-Lord had urged her. Run before it was too late.

"But I can see you are possessed of a stubborn heart," Hopkins continued playfully. "Still, perhaps there is someone here who can compel you to change your mind."

Hopkins tugged at the embroidered bellpull; and after a

moment, one of the doors behind the desk opened and a third man stepped into the room. He regarded Diana with chill, accusing eyes.

He was tall and dark, dressed in sober Puritan dress from his silver shoe-buckles to the hank of black ribbon that pulled his black hair sleek and taut against his skull. He gazed at her with utter contempt. His face was set in the harsh lines of a warrior-saint's, and there was not the faintest gleam of recognition in his black amber eyes.

"Harlot," Upright Makepeace said.

Diana stared at him, knowing that she had gone white with shock, knowing that Hopkins had noted her reaction and set it down to use as a weapon against her.

"Master Upright has some experience with recalcitrance," Hopkins said suavely.

"I have been a great sinner," Upright said. "I am not worthy of the grace I have been shown." There was no trace of the low huskiness or hesitation she remembered in his voice. It was strained and harsh, filled with pain. He stood with his head bowed.

Diana tried not to cry. She'd thought he was miles away, and safe. She had never thought she would see him again—nor see him here, stark and plain in white silk and black velvet, the stiff linen wings of his starched collar lying over his breast like armor, gazing at her as if she were his sworn enemy, as if their tryst on the hillside had existed only in her imagination.

Everything about him was changed.

"What have they done to you?" Diana whispered. She took a step toward him, unable to believe in the evidence of her eyes. He didn't even look the same. Harsher. Less human. But still so important to her that the moment he'd entered the room he became the center of her universe. The most important thing in it. Her heart, her hope . . .

She reached out her hand to touch him.

"Bitch." His hand came from nowhere to knock her sprawling. "Do not seek to ensnare me with thy practiced tricks. Let the woman conduct herself with all humility, so saith the Lord, that she may gain salvation thereby.''

The blow was a shock and a betrayal too deep even for pain. Diana stared up at him from the floor, feeling a new emotion well icily up from within her, freezing everything it touched. More than fear, more than anger. Grief. *Despair.*

Hopkins had killed him. Upright-Before-The-Lord stood here before her, but this wasn't the man she'd known. They'd caught him and destroyed him. Because of her. In shock, Diana raised her hands to her face and stared at them as if she expected them to be covered with murderer's blood.

''Yes,'' Hopkins said, ''I believe that Master Makepeace will provide excellent guidance to you, Mistress.''

Upright-Before-The-Lord hauled her to her feet and put heavy iron cuffs on her wrists. Then he took her from that luxurious, well-appointed room to the hideous place where Time would come to flow, to change, to slip away from her reckoning.

The room she learned to know as the Long Gallery was a hundred and twenty feet long by thirty feet wide—so clean, so quiet, so monstrous in its implications. Pulleys dangled from the bare crossbeams high above, and along the smooth, lime-washed walls there were iron rings set into the wall at various heights. The streaks of rust trailing down the white plaster surface looked terribly like fresh blood. Down the center of the room were a number of stout tables, some with straps, and chairs with high backs and legs that were bolted to the floor.

And there were other things, things that Diana refused to allow herself to see.

Even through her terror, she knew that she should have been grateful. There was no rack, no Iron Maiden, no Spanish Boot. The pulleys at the center of the room were unlikely to be used for the *strappado* or the *penne forte et dure*. The gothic excesses of the European Inquisition were far from the scope of this simple room. Torture was quite forbidden in England—but the things that the law of this so-called civilized time and place did not yet consider torture were bad enough.

"Please, tell me," Diana began once they'd stopped, but the words dried in her throat. Tell her what they wanted? She already knew.

Please, tell me how they caught you. Tell me what they did to you. Tell me how to help you, Upright, PLEASE. . . .

"Confess." He would not look at her. "Name your fellow witches."

Diana raised her hands. The chain clinked; the stirrup-shapes of the shackles on her wrists were a bulky iron weight.

"I can't," she whispered.

"You will admit your guilt; you will name your confederates, and you will do penance." He faced her again, but his eyes were still focused past her, beyond her, fixed on some vista she could not share.

His remoteness was frightening. It was as if he refused to be here with her. Only now, seeing him this way, did Diana realize how intensely his every action before had been bent on communication—of some message beyond appetite or danger that she'd never understood, had not even known to heed until now, when that constant urgent communication was withdrawn.

Please . . . you have to talk to me. Please, Upright-Before-The-Lord, please . . .

"What happened to you? Why are you here? You should have—" Unexpected tears filled her throat, making her next words blurry. "You should have run away. You told me you were going to run away. You *told* me!"

He did not respond to her words at all. It was as if they had been spoken in a language he no longer knew. After a brief hesitation, he spoke.

"The woman is a beast imperfect, of a creation below men and the angels. Therefore, she will bend her neck in all humility. Confess. Confess. *Confess.*"

"I'm sorry!" Diana shrieked, drowning out the sound of his voice because she could not bear to listen any longer. "I'm sorry, I'm sorry, *I'm sorry!* Is that what you want?"

"Confess," Upright said woodenly.

"Damn it, answer me!" She raised her hands, and the weight of the iron at her wrists pulled her off balance, sending her staggering into him.

He caught her. Skin to skin, the palms of his hands were warm and rough on her bare arms, and for a moment he looked *at* her, not through her. And in that brief instant Diana knew that the trap that was laid was a trap for both of them.

If he won her confession, she died. If he failed, they both died. But the stakes were even higher than that: If he won, she did not die alone. Admit to being a Witch and she damned everyone who'd ever spoken to her. *"You cannot be a Witch alone"* was the first tenet of the inquisitor's craft. Everyone she knew would be accused by the fact of her guilt.

"Please," she whispered. "Don't ask me to—"

"Only by confession can you be saved. Only through purification can you escape the jaws of Hell," his voice responded mechanically.

Upright pushed her inexorably away. Diana would have tried again, but the sound of a door opening stopped her. She glanced toward it.

The newcomers were a man and a woman. The woman regarded Diana with nervous hatred; the man looked toward Upright with an unreadable expression. For a moment Diana had thought they were some of Hopkins's other prisoners, but now it was clear what they were.

"Do we walk 'er, Maister?" the man asked.

"Yes." Upright stepped back. Hours later, when the first couple was replaced by another, Diana realized they did not mean to stop.

Ever.

They meant to break her by not letting her sleep—a torture that was not quick, but sure. Upright had not even asked her again for her confession. It was as if he had not wanted her to cooperate.

Diana dreamed of burial as she walked, of being trapped beneath the earth and screaming for release. Every time she tried to stop walking, her jailers hurried her on, pinching her to keep her awake. She did not know how long it was before she began to babble helplessly, as though speech could replace the sleep her body longed for; and when she did, she cloaked her pain in borrowed words: Marlowe, Jonson, Beaumont & Fletcher, all the Shakespeare she could remember, run together in a slurred and meaningless stream of sound.

"Give sorrow words; the grief that does not speak/ Whispers the o'er-fraught heart and bids it break. . . ."

The world shrank to the space before her feet, the sound of her own voice, and Upright's infrequent questions. How long had she been a witch? How many had she killed with her sorcery? What were the names of her demon lovers?

Sometimes he left her to lie where she fainted; sometimes she even slept for a few precious minutes, only to dream of burial, and after a while, the pauses between interrogations became longer and longer, as if it were Upright's endurance that was failing, not Diana's.

And slowly, as the days and then the weeks ran together, Diana came to realize that though she was neither particularly strong nor very brave, Upright-Before-The-Lord would not get the confession he sought, even if he killed her with waking.

"And be these juggling fiends no more believ'd,/ That palter with us in a double sense;/ That keep the word of promise to our ear/ And break it to our hope. . . ."

Because Diana Crossways didn't believe in witches either.

Not in the way these people of the seventeenth century did. When she was out of her mind with exhaustion, driven beyond her endurance and willing to tell him anything if he would let her sleep, she quoted poetry and sang the theme songs of every TV program she'd ever watched, told him about UFO's and fudging on her income tax, her childhood failures and humiliations. . . .

But no matter how long he harried her with the list of Inquisitor's questions, Diana could not summon up that whole tangled nightmare of demonic congress, black sabbats, and evil spirits who flew through the air. The information Upright insisted on was so alien that his demands just swept past her exhausted mind and left her in a howling stillness, able to say nothing.

"Wilt thou confess thyself?"

With some difficulty Diana focused on him as he stood in front of her, immaculate and judgmental. He gazed into her eyes—no, not into them, *past* them, at that thing he saw that was beyond her comprehension.

The minders holding back her arms seemed almost not to exist, to vanish as if her arms held themselves at that painful angle of their own accord. Even though Upright-Before-The-Lord was the enemy, she felt an obscure comfort in his presence, as if he guarded and defended her even here.

"Confess!" Upright hissed.

"You first," Diana whispered hoarsely.

He'd flinched as if she'd spit at him and raised his hand—but not to strike her.

Chapter 12

Christchurch Gaol, September 1647

Diana lay coiled in a ball of aching misery in the corner of her cell trying to remember that she was lucky to be here and no longer in the Long Gallery. She did not know how many days—weeks—she'd been imprisoned, and just now she did not care. She was here; she could lie; she could sleep. She didn't know why, but she knew that tomorrow the inquisition would begin again. Tomorrow and tomorrow and tomorrow.

She'd pulled the single ragged blanket she'd been given around herself and was already halfway to that vague tranced sleep that was her only rest now when she heard the jingle of keys in the hall outside.

In an instant she was bolt upright, clutching the blanket around her, pushing dread and imagination out of her mind and waiting, waiting, *waiting*. . . .

The door of the cell opened, and Upright stepped through the doorway.

Diana stared up at him, expecting to be afraid, but she wasn't. It had become a habit to think of herself as afraid, but the fear had been worn away, leaving only exhaustion.

Upright took a step toward her and stopped. Even in the

darkness she could see the expression of disgust on his face as he looked around the cell, his recoil as if he'd just stepped on something unpleasant. Then he turned away again and left.

In her weariness Diana had fallen asleep again by the time he returned, this time so deeply that he had her on her feet and moving before she was quite awake. They turned left out her door instead of right—away from the Long Gallery. The turn-key followed after; she could hear the jingling of his keys.

"Upright?" Diana asked groggily.

"The woman is formed of the man and must comport herself in obedience to him." The haughty composure that he'd worn like a cloak ever since she'd seen him again seemed to have evaporated; there was a passionate rage in every note of his voice and line of his body.

They went up a flight of steps. At the top there was another corridor with another collection of doorways—another cell-block. One of the doors was already open. Upright pulled her forward and then pushed her through it ahead of him.

She was in a cell on the outer wall of the prison. Diana could tell that instantly—there was a window. High up and barred, but she could see blue sky through it and hear the harsh calling of seabirds. The room itself was more than twice the size of her previous cell, and furnished. There was a bed, a chair, a table. There was no straw on the floor, and the floor was dry and clean.

What did this mean? Diana regarded Upright warily, fully awake now. There was a plate and a pitcher on the table; she edged around to where she could reach them and still watch him.

Bread and cheese and—she sniffed at it—small beer mixed with water; her stomach rumbled. Ever-present thirst made her mouth and throat a desert in the sudden taunting presence of relief. Cautiously, Diana pressed her back against the wall and reached for the pitcher, her hand shaking. He did not take it away from her.

Distrustfully, she raised the pitcher to her lips and drank, trying to drink and watch him at the same time. The chains on her wrists clinked. Deep inside her a tiny humiliated part of herself mourned that she could have been reduced to this state of animal wariness.

Upright-Before-The-Lord stood beside the bed, watching her. His face was expressionless; there was an inhuman stillness about him that disturbed Diana to the core of her being, but she dared not watch him for too long at a time, lest she provoke him once more.

If she did not confess, she killed him. If she did confess, she killed dozens.

There was no solution.

Instead, she appraised her new situation with the suspicion of a trapped animal. There were blankets on the bed—enough to keep her warm at night—and a straw-stuffed ticking. Luxury indeed, by the standards of the time. Diana distrusted it. What could he hope to gain by this? Her gratitude?

Or was this her reward? Could she have broken and given them what they wanted to know—and not remember it?

In sudden panic Diana tried to cast her mind back over the time spent in the Long Gallery, but it was all a jumbled mass of dreams, hallucinations, and endless movement. She did not know whether she'd talked or not.

But she was measuring her captivity by the standards of the twentieth Century, not the seventeenth. Confessed witches weren't rewarded for cooperation here; they were hanged. Diana clutched that bleak comfort to herself. Whatever the reason for this sudden special treatment, it was hardly likely to have been caused by her confession.

The pitcher was empty now. Diana reached for the cheese, and froze at the sound of further noise in the corridor. As she stared at the doorway, the wedge of cheese clutched in her hand, two men came through the door carrying a large copper tub. They set it upon the floor. Neither of them looked at her.

Diana ate as they travelled back and forth to fill it with bucket after bucket of hot water. She forced herself to finish everything there, even though her shrunken stomach was almost uncomfortably distended by the bounty. Her first full meal in days brought strength and calm and a certain sense of optimism, ridiculous under the circumstances.

Made bolder by the food and drink, Diana sat down on the chair. So civilized, to sit here on this chair. As if she were a human being, entitled to the consideration human beings gave to one another. Diana felt her eyes begin to sting. In a moment she would weep from sheer weakness.

The last bucket was poured into the tub, and the men went out, carrying the empty buckets with them. This time they closed the door behind them. Diana looked from Upright to the tub, now full of steaming water.

Is this some kind of a joke? she wanted to say, but didn't quite dare. If it were some trick, some new torture, she didn't want to know.

"Wash yourself," Upright said.

She must have looked stubborn rather than confused, because he turned away to the bed without saying anything more. On the bed was a bundle she hadn't noticed before; as she watched, he unrolled it to reveal some rough ivory-colored toweling, a bundle of drab cloth, and a cake of soap, yellowish and strong smelling.

"Wash yourself," he repeated, "and dress." He picked up the cloth and threw it at her.

Diana grabbed for it and missed. The bundle dropped to the floor and the iron on her wrists threatened to overbalance her, but she managed to retrieve what he'd thrown.

Awkwardly, because her hands were chained together and the shackles were heavy, Diana shook it out—a shapeless smock, loose enough to slip over her head and so short it would probably only come to midcalf. The fabric was rough and stiff, like the Army blankets she'd used to build make-believe tents as a child.

But *clothes*, new and clean to replace her filthy rags. She resisted a sudden peculiar impulse to giggle and stood up, setting the smock aside. Lightheadedness claimed her at her first step; the room spun and reeled about her giddily. She clutched at the chair, confused by the sudden surge of warmth and unsteadiness that rioted through her veins. All the tension seemed to have drained from her muscles, leaving them difficult to command.

Come on, Diana-girl. Walk. You've been doing enough of it for the past eternity.

With enormous effort, she made it to the side of the tub and stood there, swaying slightly. The surface of the water in the copper tub shimmered, sending up veils of steam. She leaned over to test the water and only barely saved herself from a headlong plunge into the tub. Her balance had utterly deserted her. If she tried to lift her foot to step in, she'd fall.

What was wrong with her? It was almost as if she were . . .

Drunk. She was drunk. But how? All she'd had was that jack of watered beer—

And after who knew how many days of near starvation, even two pints of weak beer mixed with water worked upon her as if it had been straight Scotch. Stupid to have drunk it all.

Where was Upright? Behind her, maybe, but she couldn't look over her shoulder. And now she had to get into the tub—a neat trick when she wasn't even sure she could stand up again. But he would lose patience with her soon. She had to move.

Carefully Diana released her death-grip on the side of the tub and straightened, standing with her legs braced to keep herself from falling. She had just gotten him in her field of vision when he moved away from the wall, coming toward her.

His quickness startled her into making an unwise retreat. Her feet tangled, but before she could fall, he caught her by the chain between her wrists. Hanging from his hand, imprisoned and intoxicated, Diana stared helplessly at Upright-Before-The-Lord. His face was only inches away. She could see the grim set of his mouth, the way the pulse hammered in his throat, the faint rosy tinge of fury—perhaps—across his cheeks.

Without looking down, he grabbed the front of her smock

with his free hand and pulled. The tattered cloth split with a faint singing sound and fell into the waistband of her petticoats, and Diana was naked to the waist. She tried to pull away from him, to pull the tatters back into place again, but she might as well have been trying to pull her chains loose from the prison's wall.

He looked down as she began to struggle. Her petticoats would not give way as easily. Diana had knotted them beyond all untying on the first night she'd been in her cell to keep them securely in place, and no amount of persuasion was going to loose the knot now.

Upright didn't even try. He ignored the knots completely, moving his hands further, until the backs of his fingers were pressing against the soft shrinking skin of her belly. Diana could feel the flex of his muscles against her bare skin as his grip tightened and he pulled.

"Let go!" Diana said in a hoarse whisper. She had no way of resisting him, but the waistband of her petticoats was a two-inch-wide tape of oversewn linen and all his one-handed tug did was pull her against him.

Her knees buckled, and she fell forward with a thump, hitting his chest. She clutched at his shoulders to keep from falling at his feet, digging in her fingers and feeling human heat and warmth and the flex of his shoulder muscles as he took the waistband of her petticoats into both hands now and pulled. The linen band parted as if it were a strip of paper, and the last of Diana's tattered rags fell at her feet.

Utterly naked now, Diana still clung to him. Her unclothed state seemed oddly normal, and her rags had not provided her so much shelter that she missed their protection now. And there was no one here to see. No one but him.

The chain to her manacles stretched wide, pressing at his throat. He stepped away, but she still held her wrists out to him, petitioning.

"Take these . . . off," Diana whispered.

Was it the drink making her this bold, or the feeling she had nothing left to lose? Or the conviction, bone-deep and irrational, that he would never really hurt her? No matter what he had done to her since he'd taken her to the Long Gallery, it had been so much less than what he could have done.

He glanced toward the door—as if perhaps he were afraid that she was going to escape and overpower him if he did as she asked. Then he took another step backward, producing a key from his cuff.

The tumblers of the crude lock heeled over with a grating sound, and he pulled the browned iron open. Diana shook her wrists, and the heavy fetters dropped to the floor with a clang. She thought he might say something then, but Upright only looked silently and pointedly toward the tub.

Diana turned toward it. She wanted to feel the water cover her, to be warm, to be clean, to feel the soothing caress of the heated water on all her cuts and bruises. Absently she rubbed at her wrists, savoring their unfettered lightness. She could see red raw patches on the skin where the weight of the metal had rubbed, day after day.

The tub was a full-sized wash-copper. She'd bathed in one at Mistress Fortune's cottage, as well as using it for its original purpose on wash days. Even though it was only half the length of a twentieth-century bathtub, she'd be able to sit in it comfortably, once she got into it.

If she got into it. The giddiness came and went, the intoxication a lurking, seductive traitor in her blood. Diana bent forward and grasped the edge of the tub, uncomfortably aware of what an enticing picture she must present but powerless to do anything about it. With infinite care, she drew one knee up to her chest. . . .

Strong hands seized her from behind, sinking into the softness below her ribs as they lifted her off the floor. There was only time for one strangled yip before her feet touched the surface of the water.

It was hotter than it had seemed to her exploratory touch; her feet felt as if they were on fire and the heat of the water was almost too much to bear. It drained away the last of her strength as she sank, enfolded in the warmth; none of her joints were willing to lock and bear, and she curled forward until she was sitting bowed forward in the water, her arms clasped across her bent knees and her head pillowed upon them.

The suddenness of the change, the nested shocks of the day, were too much. Behind Diana's closed lids the room reeled drunkenly, first one way then the other, like a maddened gyroscope. She was going to faint. She was going to be sick. She was going to drown. She heard him moving around the room and could not summon up the strength of will to care.

Rustle of cloth. He was moving back toward her. Maybe he was going to drown her himself. Maybe that was what all this had been for. She could smell the strong scent of the soap. The surface of the water rippled as he dipped the soap into the tub. The small waves lapped against the islands of her knees and she opened her eyes.

He'd taken off his coat and rolled back his sleeves. His arms were bare to the elbow, the soft pale fabric of his sleeves rolled back to reveal the elegant old ivory of his skin, the blue tracery of veins, and the sparse dusting of dark hairs.

He knelt over the tub as if he were praying, the curve of his body forming a graceful arch. The shirt was open at the throat, the sleeves rolled to just below the elbows. With his empty hand he cupped water up over her shoulders and back and then, slowly, began to move the soap over her skin. His eyes were downcast, his face turned away, as if he would not permit himself to know what he was doing.

Diana curled even farther forward, and his fingers slid down her back in automatic consequence. The soap moved over her back, gliding as it lathered. With his free hand he pushed her hair forward over her shoulder.

Suddenly, defensively, she found that she could not bear her hair's unwashed state another moment. After several awkward attempts, she got her hair wet all the way through and straightened up so that she could breathe again. When she did, Upright's hands came down on her shoulders, lifting the sodden weight of hair away from her flesh and beginning to work the soap through it.

His hands moved softly through her hair, moving delicately over her injuries, his fingertips finding the knots of tension and pain and gently releasing them, and raising another kind of tension in their wake. Without hurry, he began to rinse the soap from her hair.

Diana closed her eyes, afraid he would see her watching him. She tried not to hope or to imagine the future. She would not try to find meaning or reason in any of this; she would not think of this as kindness. Better this generosity be another sort of attack, something born out of hatred. That would leave her armor intact. To believe anything else would destroy her.

The cell was utterly silent. Diana tried to hear Upright's breathing and failed because the sound of her own heartbeat was the loudest sound in her ears. It brought hot, insistent blood to her cheeks with each beat; in this place of death, she wanted life—wanted his hands on her, all over her, wanted him with an intensity that made her too weak to do anything but lie in the water and let him do what he would. She wanted *him*, and not the wooden-faced changeling they'd left in his place.

Tears mixed with the beads of sweat and the dew from the rising steam, making rivulets on her skin. She couldn't just lie here and let him wash her as if she were a doll. The chance was too valuable to waste. This was the first time they'd been alone—in the Long Gallery there were always watchers. Maybe he'd speak freely to her now.

"Upright?" Diana said. But maybe he wouldn't answer to that anymore. "Master Makepeace?"

Her only answer was a long indrawn breath, a faint groan. And suddenly the air was fraught with a new electricity, a flash of fire as the circuit of response was completed. It was a knowing that her body responded to below the threshold of language: that what she felt, he felt also. He wanted her.

His hands at her neck urged her to uncoil. She lay back, sliding down in the tub until her knees rose above the surface and the nape of her neck rested against the lip of the tub. She felt as if she were floating, all her pain soothed away.

Now she could watch him.

She wanted him. Upright-Before-The-Lord, her jailer. Her longing was humiliating in its perversity, focusing on her captor as the object of her desire. She tried to remind herself that he was the enemy; that if he'd ever been her ally, if he'd ever been as sympathetic as he'd seemed, it had been a passing thing. He'd returned to his master's camp again, dedicated to this pointless destruction of the Wicca.

Pointless, because if Matthew Hopkins and his more selfless kindred had meant to wipe out Wicca, they had not succeeded. Diana herself was the living proof of that.

Her lips curved upward in a smile. She meant to tell him as much, confront him with his failure, but then he lowered the soap beneath the water again.

Back and forth across her collarbone, and then lower, over the soft swell of her breast, touching her with the soap as perhaps he dared not touch her with his hands, pressing gently up against the curving flesh until the soap slid up over the skin in a teasing, slippery stroke.

The breath tangled in her throat. She had to stop this now, before it went any further, before she betrayed herself and her memory of him.

The soap slid down over her ribs, her stomach, up over the curve of one thigh. The faint splash as his fist broke the surface of the water sent a pang of heat-lightning to the pit of her stomach. She could feel the hardness of the slithery cake of soap, the even pressure that impelled it against her flesh; and when he stopped to rub it in small circles against her hip, the illusion of his hands in such motion elsewhere upon her caused her to whimper in faint anticipatory desire.

She could not stop him. She lacked the will to stop him. Her entire body ached for him, as if his hands were upon her everywhere that the water touched her, slipping over her defenseless flesh. When she crossed her arms over her bosom, her body was alive to her own touch and she hugged herself tightly, shuddering with feverish response.

She felt the slippery hardness of the soap travel up to her other leg and then over the upward curve of her thigh to press between them, urging her to open to him . . . to yield up all her body's responses to him.

She turned her head away. She could not bear to stop him, but she would not watch. Her legs parted slightly under his insistent pressure, enough for his hand to travel the few inches necessary for the soap to rest against her flesh, pressing against her.

When she turned her head, his other hand was only inches away. She could see the finger joints white with tension as he gripped the edge of the wash-copper, the battered redness of his knuckles, and the drastically short nails of his fingers.

All the heat of the water seemed to be concentrated at one place beneath her skin, at the place where the soap pressed, still unmoving. An instant's caress, and he would make her betray herself as she had not in all the long weeks of interrogation.

She wanted to think of something, anything else, something that would take her away from the unrelenting reality of her body.

His hand.

The tips of his fingers were silvery with strain as they dug into the wall of the copper tub. The force of his grip drove the blood from them, save where it started up in tiny beads from beneath his nails.

Bright Lady, his *fingernails*.

The small arcs of dried blood beneath the nails made a uniform pattern of dark lines against the pads of the fingertips and the bed of the nail. His nails had not been cut, they had been broken off to this brutal and uniform shortness, and his fingertips and the exposed skin abraded as if he'd been clawing at something until the skin of his fingers was worn away.

"What happened to your hands?" She hardly knew what she was saying; it was only one last defense, a fence of words to place between her and the agonizing sensitivity he was drawing from her body.

But he froze; and as if it had been her own, she felt the whipcrack of reaction jolt through him.

Hot . . . dark . . . close with pressure all around and the choking darkness lost, forever lost . . . jailed . . . TRAPPED . . .

He lifted his hand from her and stood. The soap slithered free onto her stomach and the horrible intuition of burial was cut off as if some celestial Watcher had changed the channel.

Diana splashed as she floundered upright. Her heart hammered in her chest, and darkness fluttered at the edges of her vision. She leaned forward, clutching at the soap as if it were some talisman that could save her.

"Cover yourself!"

He stood in the corner near the door, facing the wall and clutching his coat against him as if he were a violated maiden.

Something strange and horribly unexpected flowered within Diana, a savage tenderness that was half terror. All at once the rules were changed. She hated what he was doing; she was ashamed of what he was, and she loved him—*now,* not in some indefinite future when he became the man she had known in Talitho once more. It no longer matter to her whether he changed or not; pride and shame were luxuries she could no longer enjoy.

In the arrogance of her innocence she'd given Hopkins the sharpest of knives to hold to her throat. She wanted to protect Upright-Before-The-Lord with her life. It didn't even matter that he couldn't love her back.

It *hurt.*

"Upright, I—"

"Cover yourself!" he shouted at her, and it was not anger in his voice. It was terror.

Fear for him moved Diana as fear for herself could not. She scrambled out of the bath and grabbed for the smock. Only when she had pulled it over herself did she begin to feel a lessening of the horror, the crushing sensation of being trapped.

Buried alive, just as she had dreamed it, over and over.

His hands. If she'd tried to dig her way through the wall of her cell, her hands would look like that. She took a step toward him and saw him flinch, hunching his shoulders as if to ward off a blow. After that, she retreated as far as the walls of the cell would let her, dragging the chair with her and sitting down.

From where she sat she could hear him muttering to himself, his face pressed against the wall, but could not make out the words.

"Canst thou not minister to a mind diseas'd, / Pluck from the memory a rooted sorrow, / Raze out the written troubles of the brain, / And with some sweet oblivious antidote / Cleanse the stuff'd bosom of that perilous stuff / Which weighs upon the heart? . . ."

Tears gathered in Diana's eyes, and she felt a furious towering need to hurt those who had hurt him this way. What had happened to him?

"I want the book."

The private apartments of the warden of Christchurch had been taken over by Matthew Hopkins and his agents. No one had resisted this plan, least of all Sir Wilmot, who had no idea what to do about three dozen witches, though with one thing and another the number was closer to two dozen by now, and another three down with the gaol fever that in a bad season could render God's judgment on fully one-third of remanded prisoners before the Assize Court could.

Matthew Hopkins regarded his agent balefully across a table that was swathed in white linen and set with porcelain, crystal, and silver. For once the luxury that he liked to surround himself with—the visible imprimatur of power—had no ability to soothe his spirits.

Even the contemplation of his latest coup—he was already drafting the new pamphlet that would publicize his triumph over Satan in County Hampshire—had no power to delight him now. What good was a triumph if it only showed him further achievements that dangled just out of reach?

Before they'd died, some of the Malignants had talked . . . of a woman sent by the Unborn Kings of the Hollow Hills, a seely woman who'd been sent to their rescue. And of a book.

He wanted that book. At the beginning of his career, Matthew Hopkins had claimed to have wrestled with the Devil in Hopkins's own village of Manningtree and to have stolen from Lord Lucifer a book that contained the names of all the witches of England. No one had ever yet demanded he produce it, and that was just as well; there was no book, and never had been.

But now, it seemed, such a book did exist. A book containing the names of everyone in this regular of Malignants, even those not yet discovered in the confessions of the others—and if that were not enough, tying these deluded devil-worshippers into conspiracies against the godly and lawful majesty of the rightful government of England. They'd attempted to aid the now-imprisoned King Charles with witchcraft, and that was enough to make every one of his prisoners guilty of both the crimes of treason temporal and treason spiritual, and he could have them burned alive for either or both.

If he had the book.

He had no patience with the Malignant's stories of Shining Ones and Elphame—of all men, Matthew Hopkins knew to a nicety how much truth was to be found in such tales—but the girl had brought the book. She would know where the book they all spoke of was now, and maybe others like it. Such a trove would be enough to make his name beyond all hope of Gaule and the others to tarnish it, enough to give him a seat in the new government, to give him a title and a place.

And perhaps, even, to give to Matthew Hopkins the revenues and lands of those whose names might be found within the pages of the *grammarie* ... or which could be added to it at his leisure, before he produced it for all to see.

"She has not spoken of a book," came Upright-Before-The-Lord's inhumanly calm response.

Hopkins made a low sound of fury. He preferred this minion as he had been—cringing, subservient, and grateful—but Hopkins was willing to forgo small pleasures as long as the great successes could be his.

He'd wasted a month on the blonde witch, forgoing his own enjoyment and denying her to Sterne in order to break her completely but leave her whole enough to provide a good show at the trial. Only it seemed that he had sacrificed the lesser delights and would not gain the greater.

He allowed the full force of his displeasure to show plainly in his face as he stared at Upright-Before-The-Lord.

He'd known the creature was in rebellion—the meagerness of the scraps of gossip Upright had brought him in Talitho was proof of that. Upright had nearly slipped from their grasp on Lammas Eve; but against all hope he had returned, fawning on Hopkins like a dog—a dog that had been allowed one bite, and wasn't going to get another. This time, Hopkins had kept Upright sealed in that box to the edge of death.

Four days—it was the longest he'd mewed the creature up for, and every other time such imprisonment had produced an appropriate modification in Upright's behavior. Hopkins had been certain that his ministrations would turn Upright into a destroying angel who would bring his master the blonde Malignant's full confession before Upright was—sadly—felled by the witch's unregenerate power.

The plan did not seem to have worked.

"Did you *ask* her about a book?" Hopkins demanded with poisonous sweetness. "Did you stripe her pretty back with the lash or put her hand in the vise and take a nail for each impudence?"

"She will confess," Upright said. Which was nearly all he said these days, and privately, Hopkins had to admit he missed the more entertaining aspects of his hound's babble, not the least of which was the way it had frequently driven the godly John Sterne into apocalyptic frenzies.

But enough self-indulgence.

"*When?* Court convenes a week from Monday and I mean to have her confession for the velvet upon which I shall set all the rest—and daily you fail me."

"She will confess," Upright repeated harshly.

"You moved her to one of the upper cells today. You're letting her sleep. That's most unwise if you actually mean to serve me as you say you do. Or do you wish to admit your failure? Shall I give her over to Johnnie? I don't like to, you know. There isn't much left of a girl after Johnnie's brought her to salvation. But I will.''

Hopkins had thought it would be a lark, setting his creature to destroy a woman it had become besotted with, proving— were there anyone capable of sharing the joke—Hopkins's total mastery of the forces of the Unseen World.

Now he wondered if it had been a mistake.

''No.'' Upright's voice was strained, urgent. ''She will confess herself to me.''

No matter. There was still time. No woman born had ever lasted more than three days in John Sterne's hands.

''You have one more day, Master Makepeace. Then you may commend yourself and your prisoner to God.''

Chapter 13

Christchurch Gaol,
September 1647

She'd grown cold and stiff with waiting, instinct holding her silent and motionless, but he'd finally left the cell without looking at her again. Once he was gone, Diana had moved to the bed, unfolding the blankets and winding them around her. The blue sky she could see through the high, narrow window mocked her with its cheery normalcy.

She was shaking and she couldn't seem to stop; it was as if all the catalogue of horror had finally caught up to her, bypassing her mind to settle in her body and chill her so that she would never be warm again. The certainty that she was about to die had been replaced with a cornucopia of possibility; now anything might happen and she wasn't sure she could stand it. But most of all, she couldn't stand thinking about him.

Diana had never had a hostage to fortune before. But in one simple moment everything had changed.

People don't fall in love in an instant, Diana argued with herself with desperate twentieth-century common sense. Maybe what she felt for him wasn't love, she thought hopefully. Maybe she'd just gone mad from shock. Even an afternoon of love-making didn't necessarily signify love—not true love, a love that lasted, a love to die for. She wasn't even sure if "love" was the right word for this passion that made her trembling and breathless when she let herself think about Upright-Before-The-Lord, apprentice seventeenth-century witch-burner.

Maybe she *was* crazy. Didn't hostages fall in love with their captors? Stockholm Syndrome, that's what it was—and if Upright weren't her jailer, then what was he?

The argument didn't convince the part of herself that was wild with fear for *his* danger, not hers. The need to escape was an active torment now. She had to find him; she had to escape somehow and take Upright away from here before Hopkins hurt him further. He was in danger, his safety tied to her danger. . . .

I don't like this, Diana thought miserably. *I don't like HIM.* She felt as if she'd stepped off a cliff. Was this the experience people thought their lives were incomplete without?

Please, come back. Please, come back safe. I'll even make up some things to tell you. Oh, PLEASE . . .

She hated him. She hated herself.

The tub was emptied by the simple expedient of tipping it and pouring the water out. The two men who'd filled it had come and done that, then taken the tub away, sloshing over the wet floor. The water had drained away eventually, except for the few shallow puddles that still spotted the damp stone.

When it was nearly dark, a dour-faced woman had brought Diana another meal and even a candle; Diana had stared into its flame as the long summer twilight faded, willing her mind gone, aloft and away and far from here.

It was the world by moonlight as seen from the window of a 747: a pavement of pearly clouds beneath her feet, stretching off across the frosty terraces of the sky. Above, the pure air of infinite space stretched unbounded all the way to the stars; and at midheaven, the shining face of the Moon shed her silvery, brilliant light and turned everything to shades of haunting, fathomless azure.

The Bright Lady gazed down upon her, and Diana felt very small and inadequate beneath that serene and all-seeing gaze. *Why did she delay?* it seemed to ask her. *Why, when she had everything she needed to free herself and the Bright Lady's chosen one? Why did she refuse to help him?*

I'M TRYING, Diana tried to tell Her. BUT I DON'T KNOW HOW TO DO IT.

But that wasn't true, wasn't enough. There was something Diana knew, some aid she could give, there and ready to hand if only she could remember what it was.

I'M TRYING! Diana protested, knowing that she would give anything she possessed not to fail this one task. She had to find the key. . . .

IN THE HILLS, THE SILVERY MOONLIGHT WHISPER SPOKE IN HER HEART. LOOK TO THE HILLS, TO THE HOLLOW OF THE HILLS. . . .

Diana struggled awake, still sitting upright. For a moment there was the illusion of rough bark beneath her back, the sense of being surrounded by a vast cathedral wood, then her mind made the final wrenching adjustment to reality and she knew where she was.

In prison. And the scope of that calamity spread out around her in vast inhuman mathematical perfection, from her arrest to her future execution, and only one thing in all of it didn't make sense.

Upright-Before-The-Lord Makepeace.

Something there didn't fit.

Wearily Diana leaned her head back against the wall. The candle was nearly gone, the base of the candlestick filled with rivulets of creamy tallow. Through her precious window she could see a scrap of night sky and a lone star burning, far off and sapphire.

She closed her eyes. It hardly mattered if she did or not; she didn't think she was going to sleep again tonight, not with the blameworthy conviction that there was something she'd overlooked, something she could *do.*

Was Upright-Before-The-Lord the reason she'd been sent here—and not, as she'd thought, the Great Book . . . or even Matthew Hopkins? If she'd been supposed to improve Upright's life, she'd done a very poor job of it. She'd brought him nothing but pain: On the night she'd arrived, when he'd told her to run away . . . that day Hopkins had come to town, when she'd caught sight of him on the sea road and he would not look at her . . . in the town, when what had sounded then like raving nonsense seemed chillingly rational now.

Pain. Nothing but pain.

There was an answer here somewhere, if Diana could only put together all the clues. And if she couldn't, then she'd spend time with her lover in the only way she could. She forced herself to remember Upright completely: every word he'd spoken, every sight she'd had of him.

He'd warned her not to dance every time they'd met, and she'd never understood why until it was too late—but what were witches known for, here? Not for frogs or brooms or pointy hats, but for dancing with the devil in the pale moon's light. He'd known from the first just who and what she was, and tried to save her.

Angrily, Diana scrubbed the tears of weakness from her eyes, rubbing at her eyes until they ached. His fault. Her fault. It was all muddled together. There were a thousand things she should have done differently, but she couldn't think about that now. She had to think about *him.*

He'd tried to save her one last time on the night the coven was taken. He'd overheard Reverend Conyngham and Mistress Fortune plan the meeting—he'd said as much to her on the hillside—but he hadn't told Hopkins what he knew. Diana doubted Matthew Hopkins would have passed up as rich a prize as the Vicar of Talitho, no matter what the later payoff. If Upright had betrayed the coven to Hopkins, he had not betrayed it completely.

She knew that she was only trying to find excuses for what he'd done—to make his actions less horrible, to make her own disloyalty in loving him smaller. But was it possible that—if she considered events honestly—he hadn't done as much as she'd thought?

Yes. Hopkins would not be satisfied with nothing. Upright knew that. He wanted to escape Hopkins's influence and take me with him. Hopkins had studied the records of other witch-trials. He must have known there'd be a meeting on August 1. All Upright had to do was confirm Hopkins's guess.

And lead Hopkins to their meeting place—but Diana had the proof of her own eyes that Upright had not done that. He'd been with her. And though he could have told Hopkins of its location beforehand, Diana's imagination failed when she tried to visualize the spectacle of Upright—either then or now—chattily explaining to Hopkins just where the dancing ground was.

It made no sense. Diana frowned as she tried to concentrate on the events of August first. She'd left him on the hillside and gone to warn the coven. She'd run into Hopkins's trap and been brought here to Christchurch Gaol, and Hopkins had given her to Upright as a present in consideration of services rendered, so Upright must have . . .

What? Rejoined Hopkins later after leaving him in the lurch on the big night? And told him what?

That's what doesn't make sense, Diana realized with rising excitement. Upright had never held a position of authority before. When he'd been introduced at Talitho, Hopkins had passed Upright off as a half-witted curate. When she'd seen Upright riding into town, Sterne had even been leading his horse. Upright would never have joined Hopkins so wholeheart-edly. Hopkins wouldn't have let him.

With that realization, a weight she had not known was there lifted from Diana's heart. *"What have they done to you?"* she'd asked the first moment she'd seen him. He had not betrayed her. He had . . .

Been brainwashed. Upright-Before-The-Lord had been brainwashed.

And the last piece of the puzzle fell into place.

She'd seen it before: the little set speeches, the hesitations while the programming selected the closest appropriate response. . . . It had been a long time ago, in Diana's first coven, the one she'd trained in when she'd been a college student. One of the other women in the coven who was Dedicated at the same time Diana was had been named Beckie . . . a fellow student, a botany major who came from the Midwest.

Beckie and Diana had become friends, and Beckie'd mentioned once or twice, giggling with delicious alarm, what her parents would do when she came home for the summer and they found out she was Wiccan. None of them in the coven had thought anything of it, and Diana and Beckie had promised to room together in the fall. Only Beckie never came back to school, or to the coven.

Diana had only seen her once more, when she came to collect the things she'd left with Diana for the summer. Beckie had looked and sounded much the way Upright did now.

Afraid.

Because Beckie had spent her summer in the hands of one of those psychiatric quacks who preyed upon troubled parents, promising to remake their children in whatever mold they wanted. Those self-styled experts called themselves deprogrammers, but that was a lie. Beckie had been *programmed.*

Just as Upright had. And Diana could take a good guess who'd done it.

Could Diana undo what Hopkins had done? She did not have any of the advantages that Hopkins had started with when he'd turned the man she knew into this ranting puppet. She couldn't even keep Upright near her against his will.

There was only one slim hope that gave her any chance at all, and that was to believe that from somewhere within the mental cage that Hopkins had constructed, Upright would fight for his freedom just as Diana would.

Whether there was any chance for him at all—whether she threw away her last slim prospect of freedom or even survival in doing it—she had to try.

And with that resolution, some vast knot of psychic tension eased and Diana fell dreamlessly asleep.

It was rash for her to object so much to boredom when she'd found so many things that were so much worse than boredom; but when morning came and Diana was left alone and unmolested in her cell, she began to pace restlessly. Back and forth, up and down, automatically counting the paces, converting her steps to feet until she knew the exact dimensions of her prison.

Where was Upright? What was he doing? How could she reach him?

He did not come by noon. He did not come by afternoon, when Diana found that by dragging the table into the corner and balancing the chair on it she could look out the high window at the free world beyond.

The labor was a grim lesson in how diminished she'd been by her captivity: Something she could have done once in a few seconds now took minutes of exhausting labor with frequent rests to catch her breath. Lifting the chair was nearly beyond her strength, but the chance to see something beyond the walls of her cell made her persevere, and at last she achieved her goal. Diana stood upon the seat of the chair and rested her arms on the windowsill and pretended she was a dove upon the wind.

He did not come by evening, when the rattling of keys in the corridor outside alerted her in time enough to dismantle her makeshift coign of vantage and sit quietly in the corner. She'd hoped it might be Upright, but it was only another warder with a tray of bread and beer.

As the sun set and the cell filled with shadows, Diana began to fear that he was dead. She curled up on the bed and wrapped her arms around herself. It seemed so horribly possible that after his kindness—she rubbed her wrists, thinking of the moment he'd taken off her manacles—he was being punished.

Oh, Bright Lady—Diana began, and stopped as she realized that there were no promises she could make that she could believe she would be let to keep. *Oh, please, let him come back. Just let him come back.* One miracle had already invaded her life, so why not two? She had to believe that she and Upright had been brought together for some greater reason than to watch each other die.

His room was as stark as the cells of any of the condemned, lacking only a grille upon the door to be a cell in truth. Its window had been boarded over so that neither sun nor moon could enter. There was a bed, a chest, a table holding a box and a branching candlestick. The only illumination came from the hostile artificial light of candles that burned day and night, making the room into a hellish foretaste of eternity.

Upright-Before-The-Lord stood in the center of the room. His eyes were closed, his head thrown back. He clenched his hands into fists, his nails tearing the flesh. In his soul, Upright wrestled with angels.

He had touched her—the Malignant, the mare of earth—as she flaunted her nakedness, opening her thighs to him as if he were her own kind. *He had touched her.* Her skin had been soft and warm and he had felt her breath upon his flesh. . . .

He must confess the witch and gain the book, as Matthew had instructed him. When she burned in Hell he would be free. How could he doubt that she held his soul in her clutches when the mere sight of her caused a weak trembling to overtake all his limbs? It was his soul crying out to his body for reunion that made her seem to glow, even in rags, even in the filthy straw of that kennel where they'd kept her. He had done wrong to move her, but he had been terrified that she would die and take his soul with her to Hell.

The memory of the sight of her naked body, the feel of her

skin beneath his hands, hot and wet from the bath, made him groan faintly. How could he lift the witch up to the light when his body cried out to sink down into her corruption, to wallow with her in the soft darkness of iniquity?

A burning tension for which he had no name drew his body tight, and the memory of her ivory flesh burned like a candle flame behind his eyes. All his certainty had vanished the moment he set eyes on her again. Even the painful glory of his rebirth became a shabby thing when she gazed at him with pity in her eyes.

Abomination. But he burned for her in an animal-lusting for pagan fruits. He blazed with the need to go to her, to touch her, to . . .

He could not bear this. These feelings were true damnation, tempting him to the mercy that would doom him. He reached for the box, and his hands shook violently as he spilled its contents onto the table. He clutched for the object of his deliverance, but his fingers would not close and it skittered out of his reach.

He felt the darkness coiling around him, sliding like silk and night over his skin as it claimed every inch of him for its own and took his body for its plaything.

Unclean . . .

No!

He lunged for the instrument and clutched it to his naked chest. His breath came in great wracking sobs now as the hobnails on the handle bit into his palms. The long supple leather of the lashes spilled over his arm like the fall of the woman's hair.

Damned . . .

No!

He would not think of her—of her hair, soft pale silk and he'd seen it floating like a banner through the moonlight—of freedom, of escape. . . .

He brought the nine-tail cat up over his shoulder, gasping with agony and relief as the knotted cords bit into his flesh.

Her white breasts; the free air upon his skin . . .

No!

Again the lash. The body was the traitor, the enemy, and traitors must be punished. First himself—then her. He would purify her; she would gain her absolution at his hands and set him free. . . .

The rising lash sprayed a fine rain of blood upon the room's lime-washed walls as he brought it down against his back.

Again.

And again.

Diana dreamed once more of being buried alive; and when the coffin grew to become a cell, a chamber, a vast cold and echoing cave, there was still no light, no air, no warmth.

And in the darkness there were eyes, glowing green and gold with inhuman malice as the faint silver bells of Elphame rang clearly and softly. . . .

She jolted awake, still dreaming of eyes and bells. The eyes resolved into the flickers of light and shadow through the grate set into the door, and the bells into the jailer's keys.

Someone was coming.

The clutch of pure animal panic at the pit of her stomach made her gasp. Out of a restless sleep she was painfully alert, trembling with dread, her heart a panic-fuelled hammer in her chest. They were going to hurt her, she knew it; and no matter how humiliating her fear was, for that brief instant it ruled her. Diana gulped for air, deliberately taking slow, deep breaths to calm herself.

Then the cell door opened, and Upright-Before-The-Lord stood in the doorway. The light from the lantern the turnkey held made a looming shadow and cast his image over the walls like a grim promise. He gazed at Diana as if she were the last obstacle between him and entry into Paradise.

He was alive. Diana drew a shuddering breath. Relief and fear made the world seem to waver as if under water.

"Come." He gestured to her and turned away, not even waiting to see if she followed. Diana addressed another breathless, incoherent petition to the Bright Lady and scrambled after him.

The corridor seemed darker than it had before, though the same torches burned day and night in this windowless place. The turnkey fell in behind her as she hurried after Upright's retreating form, as conscientious as if this were an appointment she actually wanted to keep.

Now was the time to see if she was right, Diana told herself, but it was hard to remember the advantages her twentieth-century skills gave her when she'd been roused in the dead of night to follow Upright through the twisting corridors of this medieval dungeon.

She suspected his destination before he reached it; and despite her hopes and intentions, her steps began to slow. Without a word, Upright seized her arm and dragged her up beside him, increasing his pace until they were moving almost at a run.

The turnkey with his lantern was left far behind as Upright hustled Diana through dim passageways with the surefooted certainty of a cat. When they reached the entrance, he flung her ahead of himself into the room and yanked the door shut while she was still scrabbling for balance. The boom of its closing echoed through the long vaulting room like a thunder-clap.

The Long Gallery was empty although every torch on the walls was lit. Diana retreated until her back was against the edge of a table, wishing that a mere room did not have such malign power to frighten her.

They faced each other across the empty floor. Upright-Before-The-Lord looked like a fallen angel come to judgment and regarded her with the unflinching intensity of a hunter. She realized there was something in his hands.

She stared at what he held, as unwillingly fascinated as if it were a cobra. He slid the thongs of the lash between his fingers as if the whip were some sort of unspeakable rosary.

"Confess to me," Upright said.

Diana stared dumbly at the cat-o'-nine-tails, knowing this was the moment in which the heroine was supposed to speak up and save the day. But, surrounded by the instruments of the Long Gallery, she'd never felt less heroic in her life.

"Confess," he repeated.

"Wh—what do you want me to say?" Diana asked weakly.

She tried not to look at any of the instruments around her, lest he should take that as an invitation to use them. The tension that crackled between her and Upright now had as much to do with fear as with desire. He was different than he had been the day before. Darker, more barricaded.

Would he listen now even if she were to confess? Or did the demons that drove him only want to hurt her?

"I want the book." His hands tightened on the whip as he spoke.

"Book," Diana echoed blankly. She felt herself beginning to panic as she tried to remember if he'd ever asked about a book before. He'd spoken so little in this place, except for the recitation of endless Bible verses and the rote Inquisitor's demands that by now Diana could recite right along with him. For a moment more she was puzzled, then a pang of intuition made her draw a startled breath. The book—the coven book, the one she'd brought, the one he'd seen her with. That was what he wanted!

Where was it? If Hopkins didn't have it already, did that mean that Pastor Conyngham had also escaped the trap set for the Talitho witches? If Edmund Conyngham had escaped, there was reason to hope. But she didn't know, and she didn't dare ask.

"I don't have it," Diana said, knowing that it was the most unconvincing truth she'd ever told in her entire life.

"Thou knowest where it is," Upright said flatly. "Confess thyself a damned thing and rejoice in the mercy of the Lord."

He smacked the whip against his free hand like a truncheon. The lashes hissed and sang and coiled around his wrist and forearm. Every instinct told Diana to run; and instinct told her just as surely that if she did, she was doomed.

All that was left was attack.

"Rejoice in the mercy of Matthew Hopkins, you mean,"

Diana snapped. "And he hasn't got any—not while there's a buck to be made out of his fearmongering."

"You blaspheme!" Upright said. His hands moved restlessly over the shaft of the lash, as though he weren't quite certain what to do with it.

"Against Matthew Hopkins?" Diana asked with poisonous sweetness.

There was a frozen moment while Upright realized his mistake. Only gods could be blasphemed against, and Matthew Hopkins was not God. Upright flung the whip down onto a table and took a step toward her. Torchlight multiplied his shadow into a thousand leaping ghosts.

"Confess," he said harshly. The legal process of the witch-trials depended on confession. Without the confession, there could be no trial. If Upright could not make her confess, Hopkins could not try her.

Diana stood her ground, though her mouth was coppery with fear and her pulse hammered in her throat. It was no longer possible to hesitate, to question why saving him was so important. She had to confuse him, get him off balance, get him to *think*, or he'd follow his programmed script to their doom.

"Confess, confess . . . you keep saying that, but have you ever wondered what comes next? After I confess, what then?" Diana demanded.

"You will. . . . You are—" He shook his head, as if to drive out some unwelcome thought.

"I'll be killed," Diana said brutally, hoping it would shock him. "For dancing in the fields at night. You warned me—do you remember? You told me not to dance, but I did. I'm sorry. Are *you* sorry? *Are you?*"

A sense of menace radiated from him like a tangible corona. At any moment Upright-Before-The-Lord could explode into ruinous violence, and then there would be no turning back. The only thing that made Diana able to go on was the conviction that somewhere behind the mask of the inquisitor was the man she knew.

" 'Dance, dance, wherever you may be/ For I am the Lord of the Dance said He—' " Diana sang, her voice wavery but true. She let the music move her in the steps of the dance, knowing that would goad him like nothing else.

"Abomination." His voice was hoarse; she saw him moisten his lips with his tongue in order to speak.

"Is dancing such a sin? Then I'll confess," Diana said, taking a brave step closer to him. "I'll confess that Matthew Hopkins is a fraud; I'll confess that witches don't worship the Devil any more than Christians do; I'll confess that you tried to save my life. . . . Do you remember?"

She had to keep at him, questioning him, not letting him slip back into his rote speeches. Thinking for himself was the only thing that could save him.

"The book." Upright's voice was desperate now.

"If I give it to you they'll kill me. Do you want me dead?" Diana asked. "Answer me. Don't you remember the first time you saw me? Tell me the truth."

She reached out and took his hand, closing the gap between them. His fingers tightened over hers as his body acknowledged what his mind could not. It gave her hope.

"What did they do to you?" Diana asked softly, looking down at his raw and battered hand. "Can you tell me?"

The whip hit the floor and rolled away. Suddenly she was supporting his entire weight as his knees buckled. Her arms went around him, holding him to her, but she wasn't strong enough. It was all she could do to keep from being knocked flat as the weight of his body bore both of them to the floor.

The flagstones were hard and cold beneath her body, but she couldn't move. He was crouched almost on top of her, pinning her there as he wrestled with his demons. Her chin was pressed against the top of his head as he pushed himself against her with painful intensity. She lifted her hand to stroke his hair.

The back of his coat was damp; and her hand, when she pulled it away, was red with blood. She felt a sharp and automatic pang of dismay.

"They've *hurt* you!" Diana exclaimed.

Her only answer was an animal groan.

Hesitantly she plucked at the edge of his coat, but there was no way for her to get it off him or see what damage lay underneath. And at any moment now Upright could revert to the persona of implacable interrogator. Diana wasn't sure now if she'd ever seen his normal personality . . . except for those brief strange moments on the hillside when he'd spoken of Man as if humanity were a separate race.

"Upright, c'mon," Diana pleaded. "Upright-Before-The-Lord, I want to help you. I'm not your enemy. Talk to me." She put her hands against the front of his shoulders and pushed with all the strength she had left. Eventually he moved until she could see his face.

His eyes were glazed and unfocussed, and for one terrifying, heart-stopping moment, she thought he'd gone mad.

"*Please*," Diana whispered. "Come back to me."

When he spoke, it was in a grating monotone from which all trace of humanity had been leeched.

"Give me the book and confess to your crimes."

It was a robot's voice, a machine's. There was nothing of awareness in it.

"Upright?" Diana shook him, gently. The unfocussed gaze did not waver.

"The book. Give me the book and confess to your crimes."

She pushed herself away from him. It took all her strength to pull free, and without her support he fell to all fours.

"The book. Give me. Confess." He was on his hands and knees, head down.

Oh, Bright Lady, give me the strength to do this.

"Look at me." Diana's voice was hard, as if in that moment their roles had been reversed and she was now the inquisitor. "Tell me who you are. Tell me your name!"

"Book. Confess. All my sins." He was wavering now; she could sense it.

"Tell me your sins. Confess to me," Diana demanded. She groped to her feet. Without the table's support she would have fallen, but he wasn't looking at her.

"Look at me! Confess!" she barked at him, while she feared for his very sanity. Her heart ached with an agony of compassion. "Who do you think you are to be asking me questions? Who? *Get up off that floor and look at me, damn you!*"

He raised his head at last and looked at her at last. His long black hair had come loose from its ribbon and hung half-loose around his face. But there was awareness in his eyes, and Diana's heart leapt at the sight of it.

"I—" he began, and then stopped as if he'd forgotten the words.

"Talk to me," she demanded, pushing harder. "What did Hopkins do to you? Why did you go back to him? Talk to me. Here I am. C'mon. This is what you want, isn't it?"

He looked away from her and slowly got to his feet.

"The book," he said in a weary voice.

"No!" Diana put all her rage and frustration and fear into that shout. It rang off the walls and called back a faint flat echo from all that shadowy emptiness. "No, no, no—and you can't make me!"

It was childish, this taunting of him, safe because what he asked for she couldn't give no matter what happened. He raised his head again, watching her, and his eyes locked with hers in mute defiance.

"What's the matter?" Diana gibed. "Scared?"

She'd already taken a step toward him when he spoke. As she stared into his eyes, the mask shattered and the wolf-lord blazed out from beneath.

Chapter 14

Christchurch Gaol, September 1647

"Shall I tell thee what John Sterne will do to thee?"

His voice was as soft as the hissing of a serpent, and finally he saw her begin to be afraid.

He was rage, surrounded by fire as the salamander in its element. The magnitude of his failure mocked him as he stared at the woman who defied him now because he'd been so gentle. The fear that had caged him was gone; his fingers touched the butt of the whip and he gathered it into his hand. She would not yield to him, and Matthew's patience was gone. He had lost the woman to the hangman's noose, and himself to the dark.

"Shall I show thee?" he asked, and saw terror flicker like summer lightning across her face.

He sprang from his crouch. His shod feet slid clumsily against the floor, but he was still quick enough to reach the table before she could run. His hand and the whipstock slapped the wood on either side of her body with the finality of a blow, and he smiled murderously down at her, teeth bared.

"He will have thee naked, first."

She fought him, but he was stronger. He pulled her away

from the table and jerked the hem of her smock up over her head in one swift movement. Tell her all, frighten her with it, have her confession and her consent to the absolution he had forced his Upright-self to bring with him—an easy death, painless and quick. He flung her garment aside and heard the faint sound of it sliding across the floor.

He leaned forward, forcing her down against the table with the weight of his body until she was bent awkwardly backward, her hands pressed against his chest. She did not claw at his eyes as other women had done, but set her strength against him as if she were his equal. But to be his equal would not save her, as all his craft had not saved him.

"Godly John Sterne shall probe thy flesh with his lancet, searching out the Devil's mark. He will unjoint thy limbs and use thee as his strumpet. He will gain thy confession and then thou wilt die. *He will kill thee.*"

He bore down on her body until he heard her breath roughen and catch with pain. His back burned, but the fire in his blood was hotter; he lifted one hand from the table and set it on the sweet inward curve above her hip. The warmth of her skin burned through his palm, and he could feel the trembling tightness of her muscles. That she was helpless, that she was *here* only infuriated him. She was *his;* he had sworn to himself that he would protect her and cherish her and give her children.

And he'd failed.

"Shall I force thee, to show thee how it will be done? Wilt beg me as thou wilt beg him?" He slid his hand down further on her body, grabbed her thigh, and pulled upward with a quick jerk.

She squalled as she was flung up on the table. She writhed as she tried to gain the leverage to escape, but he pried her thighs apart and pushed his body between them until his body was pressed against the wood of the table's edge.

He could feel the trembling of her muscles as she unwillingly clasped him. When she tried to sit up, he put his hand against her torso and shoved. One hand was enough to hold her down; and though she tore at his wrist with her nails, it was all of him she could reach. With his free hand he held the whip before her face so she could see it.

"Shall I use this as he will use it, so that not even the Devil and his incubi will want what is left?"

He saw the moment when she understood what he meant and the despair of her realization that she could not stop him. Stiffly, he raised himself off her body and took a shaky step back from her, turning away to blot out the sight of her. The whip struck the floor with a hollow clatter. Suddenly he could not bear what he was doing. All his attempts to frighten her, all useless. All for nothing.

"He will *kill* thee," he repeated desperately, willing her to understand all that this meant.

One step away from her, two, and he felt the incandescent moment of clarity slipping away as the Upright-self fought to save itself, to take the body and flee. She spoke and he could not understand her words; they fell around him like leaves; his sense of self utterly deserted him. Gone, all gone, the words and the truth and the rage; he and his *righ-malkin* would die here together in this place, locked away from the wind and the stars, and there was nothing he could do to prevent it.

"Di'anu," he groaned aloud.

Diana levered herself up onto her elbows then rolled off the table, wincing at her fresh bruises. He'd moved so *fast.* . . .

She thought of what he'd said and shuddered. He'd said she was going to be given to Sterne for questioning. If not for Upright-Before-The-Lord, she would have been given to Sterne already.

She glanced toward Upright cautiously. He stood completely still, with his back to her, his entire body caught in that frozen rigidity she knew too well—as if he were made of glass and any movement would cause him to explode into a thousand pieces.

He was vulnerable now.

She couldn't afford pity. It would doom them both. They

were both victims of the same hideous circumstance that had brought them to this place and assigned them their roles. She had to attack his programming now, while he was off balance, and hit him with everything she had.

"What the *hell* did you think you were doing?" The fear in her voice came out as anger, making the question crack like a whip. Diana slid down off the table and stalked over to him, not even bothering to pick up her smock.

"Answer me!"

He stood like a statue somehow crafted of living flesh. Diana stopped in front of him, letting the maelstrom of her emotions fill her and bear her up on their crest.

"What's on the menu for today? A little rape? A little revenge? You aren't dressed for it. Take this off."

She grabbed the front of his coat and pulled. Its burst fastenings tore free and spattered like raindrops on the slate flagstones. The black fabric of the coat gaped open, exposing the rusty, tallow color of the shirt beneath. Diana yanked down on the facings in her hands, jerking the coat off his shoulders.

"And this."

She grabbed his shirt and dragged down on it. It wouldn't tear, but she saw the flicker in his eyes as they came alive again, his lips moving soundlessly as he searched for the right role to play.

She refused to permit it. She pulled again, forward and down, and he was on his knees, within reach. She knelt over him, straddling his thighs as he knelt, pinioning him to the floor with her body. He stared up at her, his face blank. A puppet without a puppeteer, emotionless.

The floor was cold beneath her knees, and Diana welcomed that because it seemed that every other part of her was numb. He'd manhandled her, abused her, hit her. She should be afraid of him; she should hate him; but whatever this all-consuming passion was, it wasn't hate. She had to make him react to her.

Diana crouched over him as he sank back on his haunches, trying to escape. She wound her hand in his hair, pulling his head back until his pale throat was stretched taut and she could see the pulse flutter beneath the skin.

And then she kissed him, as ruthlessly as if it were an assault.

She spread her free hand against his face, tugging gently at his jaw and urging him to open to her. His lips parted and she forced her tongue between them, tasting honey and wine and a faint cloying trace of something elusively sweet. The fabric of the clothes he wore was harsh against her skin as she ground her body against him, demanding some response to her merciless attack.

He made no sound, but suddenly she felt he was with her. There was a tension in his muscles that had not been there a moment before; and when she moved her hand from his face down the column of his throat, she could feel the pulse beating wildly, though his mouth was unresponsive and still beneath her own.

Gotcha! Diana exulted silently.

Without releasing his mouth, Diana moved her hand from his throat to his chest, moving her palm in questing circles until she found what she sought. She took it between thumb and finger and gently squeezed, tormenting the small bud of responsive flesh.

His back arched under the stimulation and his mouth came suddenly alive against hers, tasting and seeking. That responsive kiss kindled a subtle answering warmth she had not expected, and Diana rocked against him, her body blindly seeking a more intimate caress.

His arms were imprisoned by his tangled coat so that he could not move them; she felt his struggles as he tried to touch her, but trapped as he was, all he could do was graze the outside of her thighs with his fingertips.

Diana rocked herself against him again, this time more deliberately, and felt his whole body shudder. She pulled her mouth away from his and rubbed her cheek against his in a long, sensuous caress before turning her attention to his earlobe.

He jerked when her tongue touched it, but the grip she maintained on his hair wouldn't let him break free.

"Is this what you want?" Diana breathed, her cheek pressed to his. The contact was made slippery by the fine dew of effort on his skin. "Is this the kind of interrogation you had in mind?"

She tightened her thighs about his hips and pressed herself against him, feeling the hard proof of his arousal through the thin cloth barrier between them. His response told Diana that his body wanted what she was offering; and she wanted it, too, this sweet submission that reminded her body of other sensations than pain.

She ran her hand down over his ribs and slipped it between them. With her palm, she traced his shape through the cloth of his breeches; closed her hand over its heat and hardness and squeezed gently, rubbing and stroking him where he was most vulnerable until his breath came in rasping sobs and he bucked like a restive stallion. Her mouth was pressed against the beating pulse-point in the hollow of his throat, tasting its frantic rhythm.

She had to stop, Diana told herself. It was time to ease up on him, let him go; she'd gotten the response she wanted, now she had to use it. But she'd left her mercy too late. Melded to him as she was, she felt the transfiguration come over him like the leading edge of a storm, the crackle of ozone and electricity. She had just enough warning to pull back as the seams of his coat split with a sound like the snarl of thunder.

His hands shot forward and he seized her, pulling her against him, his hands implacable on her hips as he rocked forward on his knees and pulled her hard against him. Diana looked into his black amber eyes and saw the green wolf-light in their depths, the knowing consciousness of self in their mocking expression.

She'd prayed for him, summoned him; but now that he was here, she wondered if she might have made a worse miscalculation than she knew.

"Aye," he said in a hoarse growl. "Thou'rt mine." He arched forward, taking her mouth before she could offer it, claiming her with an absolute certainty of his right.

He held her mouth with his own as if he were drinking her soul, until he had shaped her so tightly against his body that it seemed as if she could feel his heart beating against her chest and her body hungered for a communion that almost seemed worth dying for.

"No, wait," Diana said weakly as he fastened his lips over the pulse that throbbed beneath her skin, sucking at the spot until she was dizzy with the sensation of his lips and tongue against her flesh. "I have to talk to you," she moaned as his hands slid up her back and down over the pliant curve of her buttocks, lifting and spreading, seeking access to every part of her.

"What wilt thou say?" Upright asked her, his voice barely more than a breath. "That thou dost not dance? Thou wilt dance for me."

He rose to his feet, carrying her with him in a sobering display of strength. Her feet skimmed the floor and then settled as he released her long enough to retrieve her discarded smock and spread it over the table with a flick of the wrist. He stripped the remains of his coat off and threw them down and then put his hands on her waist again.

Diana made a small sound of protest. This was not what she'd had in mind. She'd wanted to talk to him, to set him free of Hopkins's conditioning, to reason with him. . . .

"Wouldst prefer the floor?" he asked. " 'Tis colder." Without waiting for an answer, Upright lifted her and set her on the cloth-covered table. With her seated there, they were much of a height. He did not have to bend down to kiss her again.

Helplessly Diana put her arms around him, remembering only at the last moment to keep them high on his neck, away from his welted back. If she really wanted him to stop what he was doing, she supposed she could just hit him there. If she dared. She wasn't sure she did.

"Soft," he said against her neck. "Sweet." And then words in that strange other language that had the rise and fall of the sea in its short syllables.

His voice made pictures in her mind as he drew away and cupped her breasts, pressing them upward and together so that he could kiss her there, as if it were vitally important that he learn the contours of her body with his mouth alone.

"I have to—" Diana began. He covered the sensitive tip of one breast with his mouth, pushing her gently backward. The movement of his tongue sent a flash of pure liquid pleasure to the pit of her stomach and she gasped.

"I have to talk to you," Diana said breathlessly, grabbing at the edges of the table for support.

"Dance for me," he said against her flesh, and sank to his knees.

Diana's body slid forward to the edge of the table as he pulled the smock's fabric toward him. His hands parted her thighs, sliding upward along the soft inner skin, pressing them apart until she was completely open to him, until there was no chance her heels would rest against his back. Just as she realized what he meant to do, he bent forward and claimed her body with his mouth.

The bolt of pure sensation thrilled along every nerve and made her cry out. She wanted to protect herself, to pull away from this merciless delight, but she could neither close her thighs against the pressure of his hands nor retreat from the precarious position in which he'd placed her. The intimate caress of his tongue ignited her; she could not think, could not move, except to squirm helplessly as he captured her most intimate flesh in the gentle cruelty of his kiss.

She could feel the spiralling coil of tension tightening in her body as he probed her, felt the torment of arousal that clamored for release, but somehow she could not reach that moment of deliverance. He kept it just out of reach with lips and teeth and tongue, knowing just when to turn his attentions to the soft curve of her belly or the sensitive skin of her inner thigh, building the fire within her until she could not think, until she lay writhing on the table with no thought of her surroundings and the moment—and the blazing hunger were all there was.

Then he stopped.

It took a moment for that to penetrate the haze of passion

he'd woven about her senses. Diana raised her head and looked at him, her breath coming in whimpering ragged sobs.

"Are you mine? Do you belong to me?" he asked.

His fingers pressed at the delicious melting juncture of her thighs, holding back the frenzied tautness that begged for fulfillment. His spread fingers flattened on the curve over her hip, compelling her stillness. He dipped his head to touch her there once more and Diana thrashed futilely, unable to bear the agonizing sweetness of it. Her entire body ached with a pleasure at the edge of pain.

"Yes! Yes!" she gasped, as his thumb moved infinitesimally against her. "Please—oh!"

He raised his head again and stood, sliding his hand between their bodies to release himself from the confines of his breeches. Then he pushed forward and she felt him pressing against the swollen petals of her softness, sliding inward until he was just within her, until one thrust would fill her completely—and he stopped.

The focus of her universe narrowed to that molten pulsing between her thighs and the need to be filled by him. He held her against the table with both hands as she fought him with a frenzied hunger, desperate to sheathe him within her body. But he was stronger, and she could not move.

"You are mine?" he repeated. "Say it."

"I'm yours," Diana gasped. "I belong to you. You belong— oh, *please*—to me."

He made a small sound of satisfaction deep in his throat and thrust into her with a slow deliberation that made the world dissolve into a roaring heat. As if they were one flesh she could feel the aching pleasure in his loins, of ecstacy withheld almost to the point of torture, a fire that mounted until they were joined, fused together, intertwined beyond any possibility of separation.

She arched her back, finding the strength to wrap her legs around his waist to goad him into motion; but he caught her around the thighs, lifting and pushing back until her calves rested over his shoulders and she was coiled back upon herself, powerless to control the rhythm that he set.

Her thighs were pressed against his chest; his hands on her hips pulled her down to meet him. Each thrust filled her to her very core, driving into her as though in his mind there were some further barrier to breach, as though the violence that surrounded them both demanded this execution.

She could not reach him. She could not touch him. But those frustrations were swept away by the intensity of her desire. She begged him in a voice she did not recognize as her own to take her, fill her, use her in impossible ways, until at last the release she had begged for swept over her like a firestorm, annihilating her so utterly that her name, all that she was, burned away to ash.

She dreamed of a boat, of a long sea voyage that held only terror. Dimly, Diana knew that these memories were not her own. This jumble of fear and strangeness, of collars and cages and endless beatings was nothing that had ever happened to her. Through it all there was the longing for one diamond-bright image, a valley of silver and green.

Home.

She stood in the forest, but not alone. Morning mist turned all the trees to silver and crystal and the air to colorless fire. The passion of the night was over, and now she watched him as he slept, his nakedness curled in the bower she had woven for him. His muscles made a shadowed dappling against his ivory skin; she could see the long, ebony sweep of his lashes against his cheek; the soft, dreaming curve of his mouth.

UPRIGHT, she thought, but the name that echoed in her mind when she looked at him was somehow different. In a moment she would kneel down and waken him; she would feel the heat and life of him under her hands, and together they would begin the journey home.

HOME.
She reached out to him. . . .

. . . and felt only cold wood beneath her hands.

Confused, Diana opened her eyes. She was lying on her side on the table, curled with her knees drawn up against her chest. His arm was flung around her, possessive even in the dazed aftermath of love, his warm weight curled around her back; but as she came fully awake, he was already moving away.

The dream had been so real that the sight of the Long Gallery brought miserable tears to her eyes. She'd been so sure this horror was only a dream. But it wasn't.

Behind her, Upright slid off the table, a purely mundane groan of protest and stiff muscles escaping from his throat as he moved. It made him human, somehow—not a creature of fantasy, moonlight, and shadows—and that vivid awareness made Diana's cheeks burn hotly. The response he had drawn from her still pulsed faintly through her breasts and body, and she felt the spreading dampness of his seed between her thighs as she sat up and swung her legs over the edge of the table. Anachronistic thoughts of safe-sex precautions and contraception flitted through her mind, banished in the crushing weight of reality.

Upright walked into her line of vision, reaching his hand out toward her. At the sight of him, a confused clutch of emotions she wasn't ready for cascaded through her. Diana flinched away, raising her hands to shield herself.

He stopped. He was holding a pewter cup. Only that. Ashamed, she raised her eyes to his face.

No shy curate or canting witch-hunter greeted her gaze. His face was utterly still; but somehow there was a faint glint of despairing mockery in his gaze, as though he found the situation hopeless and thought that was funny. He regarded her steadily.

The desperate pain she felt when she looked at him—was that love? Knowing she would do anything to keep him safe—and knowing there was nothing she could do.

Who are you? Memories of her dream returned with jumbled urgency; Diana felt awkward, off balance, uncertain of what to do next. It made her feel shy and awkward to be sitting here naked with this stranger who was more than a lover.

He held the cup out a little farther toward her, still without speaking. Diana took it and looked down, swirling the wine around the cup and wondering where he'd gotten it. Probably the in-dungeon bar for Inquisitors.

"Drink it," Upright said.

Suddenly Diana had a flash of Mistress Fortune bringing her cordial to Jemima Skelton . . . protecting her friend in the only way left to her. Did Upright feel the same frantic desire to protect what he loved that Diana did, that Abigail Fortune had?

"Can't we escape? Can't we get out of here?" Diana asked in a small voice. She didn't want to hear the answer.

"They do not trust me."

The presence of the cup in her hands was more eloquent than any words. There was no other escape. Tears rose up in her throat. In another moment she would weep.

"I will not allow them to hurt you," Upright-Before-The-Lord said softly.

"And just how are you going to stop them?" Diana demanded in a watery voice.

Silence. She looked up into his eyes and saw the answer there.

Upright put his arms around her wordlessly. Diana set the cup aside and clung against him, trying to draw comfort from being with him; but his presence only seemed to underline how helpless she felt. In her aching heart Diana felt a last barricade against despair dissolve. She'd won—she'd gotten him back—and it didn't help.

They were both going to die.

It wasn't fair. It couldn't all have been for this. She was something more than a celestial library clerk delivering the Great Book to the Talitho Coven.

There had to be some way out.

Suddenly Diana realized she had both hands pressed hard against his back and that the fabric was damp against her skin.

"Your back!" Diana said, pulling away. Her forearms were dusky with smears of dried blood.

"It does not—" he began, but she had already pulled him around and seen.

Dark rusty stripes of blood were visible against the dun-colored linen, spread where they'd soaked into the fabric and where she'd pressed it against him. Diana tried to pull the shirt away from his skin to get a good look at the damage, but it stuck to his skin. If she forced it, she would only open the wounds again.

"They *beat* you!" Diana said, feeling sick.

"Not they. Matthew's hound, who lusts to live, even on his knees. It does not matter. When I do not bring them the Great Book, they will kill me."

It was said so matter-of-factly that for a moment she didn't realize what he'd said, then anger rushed in to fill the cold void of fear. Diana pushed Upright away from her and with a sweep of her hand sent the cup of drugged wine spinning off the table. The cup bounced across the floor, leaving splashes of sticky red in its wake.

"Did any of you people ever think there might be an alternative to noble suicide?" She heard her voice rising hysterically and didn't care. "Did it ever occur to you that since Hopkins makes up his evidence, it can't possibly stand up in court—and neither will his phony commission! Without a confession he's got nothing! *Nothing!*"

"Others have confessed," Upright said bleakly. "All named you. They say you have the Book."

"They'd have said *you* had it if they'd been asked!"

"And of all men living, Matthew should know what such confession is worth. But this time he wants to believe. He will do anything to gain such advantage. He will kill you to gain it. And I will not live without you," Upright answered.

He'd thrown away one chance of freedom to come back for her on Lammas night, and now this. She slid off the table, wincing at the cold stone beneath her feet, and grabbed her smock from the table, pulling the garment hastily over her head. The cup she'd thrown was still rolling slowly across the floor.

Upright looked at the cup, then back at her. *"Righ-malkin, there is no more."*

Suddenly the terrible absurd futility of the conversation became too much. Diana began to laugh, wracking spasms that shook her body in a mockery of mirth, a madwoman's laughter that he soothed as best he could, holding her and stroking her hair until the laughter changed to tears and all Diana could do was cling to him and weep as if he were the only safe haven in a sea of disaster. It was only when both the laughter and the tears had passed that the fear—for him, not for herself— returned, as sharp as before. It rose up in her throat and made her speak without thinking.

"We have to get out of here. We have to get the others out. They haven't done anything wrong."

She felt his withdrawal through his muscles. She must sound as if she were talking nonsense, but even though she did not know how it could be done, as much as she could not bear to remain here, neither could she stand the thought of escaping only to leave the other members of the Talitho coven to suffer the penalty of Hopkins's greed.

"There is no way." His voice was final. "Who seeks to help a Malignant can only be a tool of the Evil One."

Whether he believed it himself, it was certainly what the people of this time believed. For a moment Diana wanted nothing more than to just run away. The door of the Long Gallery was unbolted; with Upright's help, Diana told herself, there was a tiny chance that she might be able to make it out through the gates, and even Christchurch was small enough that they'd only need an hour's grace to make it to the woods. Ten miles would be an infinity; no one would know or care about Hopkins's campaign that far away. . . .

But she couldn't leave the others behind to suffer. Diana's thoughts wheeled back on themselves and then bolted off in a circle again: Escape . . . escape with him . . . free the others

. . . escape. . . . There had to be something she could do. There *had* to be!

"There's going to be a trial," Diana said slowly, feeling her way toward the inspiration of a moment before. Something about the trial and the evidence to be presented. . . . Hopkins had always screened his actions in a cloak of legality. And had vanished into history—when? How?

"In two days' time," Upright agreed. "The Malignants will confess and Matthew's power will be made manifest to all."

"Not if it's Hopkins in the dock. . . ." Diana said slowly. That was the answer. It had to be. "Denounce Hopkins as a witch and you cast doubt on all the confessions he's obtained."

She looked at Upright. His hair framed his face as he looked down at her.

"Denounce Matthew," he echoed. He moved his hands from her shoulders to her elbows, smoothing the fabric as if that motion would somehow help him to find answers. His eyes flickered, looking away as if he thought she'd suddenly run mad. But maybe it was all right to be a little mad, Diana reasoned. Maybe madness was the only possible way to be sane.

"It will work if *you* do it." Diana wasn't certain of this by any means, but she hurried on. "If *you* denounce him. Everyone else thinks you're one of Hopkins's trusted associates, even if *he* doesn't. Hopkins has enemies just waiting for him to fall."

"And he has conspired with spirits from out of the Hollow Hills," Upright said, a sudden note of hope in his tone. "But *di'anu—*"

"Diana. My name is Diana."

"Diana of the Crossways," he said, mangling her name slightly. But he knew it. He knew *her*.

She pulled him against her gently, wishing for a future but willing herself to live in the moment, not to think of what lay beyond it. "It will work. You'll see. It has to."

Chapter 15

Christchurch Gaol, September 1647

Christchurch Gaol had been a castle once and retained both its battlements and the Murderer's Walk where archers had once been posted to shoot down unwary besiegers. He stood leaning out over the wall, bathing in the cold wind that came before the dawn.

The memory of that indefinite time of imprisonment and terror in the stifling dark was too fresh for him to bear to return to the tiny kennel they had made within these walls for Upright-Before-The-Lord. To be within walls at all was nearly more than he could stand, though he would bear it for *her* sake, to be with her until she died.

He had tried every way that he knew out of the prison, prowling barefoot and silent through the darkness that was not dark to him. He could go over the roofs; there was a place where he could climb down the outside wall, if he were willing to hazard a twenty-foot drop at the bottom.

But once outside, he could not return. And he could not take her with him by that route. She was weak; he had seen as much tonight. She would not be able to follow him over the roofs, and he could not carry her. All the ways by which he could bring her out were locked. All were guarded. Even if he could somehow steal proper women's dress so she might pass unnoticed through one of those gates, he would be with her; and all knew *him* and knew that Matthew had given orders that he was to be kept close.

He could not save her. He would not leave her. She had refused the only escape he had for her and pinned all her hope of life on his ability—*his!*—to spin a tale for mortal men's dazzling.

Denounce Matthew, she had said, as if it were a simple thing. Matthew had been denounced before. The Reverend John Gaule had published a pamphlet just last year that had made many people skeptical of Matthew's powers and authority. Despite the pamphlet Matthew had written to answer Gaule's accusations, requests for the Witchfinder-General's services had decreased to the point that Matthew's band had been forced to travel as far afield as Hampshire to find their evil employment.

So if one of his own spoke out against Matthew here . . .

He did not know if it would work. He did not think it would. But if *di'anu* were brought before the court to plead, she would be outside the prison's walls. There would be a chance then for them to run, but that precious chance was two days away. He must find a way to keep Sterne away from her until that moment. Tell them she had spoken of the book. That she would take them to where it was hidden.

Make her tell. Make her tell. Damned . . . tainted . . . The hellfire awaits. . . . soulless . . . UNCLEAN . . .

The gibbering Upright-self that he had hidden within for so long clamored for release, but he would not let it be free. It had saved him in those long years when rebellion was death, but now he courted death, the lover he would take if his *righmalkin* were stolen from him. To avert that happening he must craft a final lie for Matthew, a shining net of story that would let the two of them escape. He turned the story over in his mind as he waited for the dawn on the castle walls, and it was here that John Sterne found him.

"Master Makepeace."

There was a fatal moment of incomprehension before he answered to the name of his slavery. He turned and saw himself through Sterne's eyes—the recognition of what he was—and knew the depth of his failure.

"So the devil returns for his own at last," Sterne rumbled with slow satisfaction.

The man on the battlements stared at Sterne, wild defiance in his eyes. He could no longer bend his neck in the subservience the children of Men required, and there was nowhere at all left for him to run.

They'd huddled together in the Long Gallery for a time that seemed too short. There'd been no words, until finally Upright had told Diana that she had to go back to her cell.

"Wait for me. Wait for me there, and I will come."

She hadn't wanted to go, to surrender even this illusion of freedom, but she'd trusted him. She had to. And so she'd gone. The tension between them—of danger, of discovery—had been so great that it hadn't even permitted a kiss. He'd left the lantern behind, and its flame spread a fan of bright yellow light upon the walls, casting the irregularities in the plaster into flickering, shadowy relief until the wall looked like the cratered surface of the moon.

Diana had stared intently into the lantern's flame as the iron clashing of the lock sealed her in, willing herself not to beg Upright to take her with him, willing herself not to weep or to howl her despair as she heard his footsteps retreat along the corridor.

And then Diana was alone. But not truly alone—never again, as long as Upright-Before-The-Lord still lived.

The irrational certainty of the bond between them was nearly as frightening as her imprisonment. Love was a word her own time used without understanding it very well, a transitory thing that could be true in the moment and nothing but ash in a year's time. But a forever love, an eternal love, a passion as undying as the bones of the earth? If Diana didn't know what it was supposed to feel like, how could she be sure when she'd found it?

"Lady, by yonder blessed moon I swear.... Do not swear at all;/ Or, if thou wilt, swear by thy gracious self,/ Which is the god of my idolatry." Scraps of borrowed poetry tumbled through her mind. *"It is too rash, too unadvis'd, too sudden;/ Too like the lightning, which doth cease to be/ Ere one can say it lightens...."* The rhymes of Shakespeare's doomed lovers swirled around her, filling her cell with hungry ghosts, and finally Diana slept, still waiting.

She woke in the cold indigo light of earliest morning to a wolf-howl that had lanced through her darkest dreams to rouse her.

Upright had not come back.

Disbelieving, Diana got to her feet. She pulled one of the blankets around her shoulders like a cloak and walked around the limits of her prison as if he could possibly be hiding somewhere here. Last of all she went to the door and looked out into the dim corridor beyond.

He had not come back for her.

It was a defeat too great to be understood all at once. She had trusted him so completely that it was impossible for her to believe he hadn't returned as he'd promised. Her trust and his absence clashed uneasily in her mind, leaving her baffled and mentally off balance.

He wasn't here. He hadn't come back.

Where was he?

She didn't know. She had no way *to* know. All she could do was wait.

The sound of the key in the lock was like a reprieve, ending the hours of fearful waiting. Diana was on her feet, turning toward the door, words of welcome on her lips before she saw who it was.

John Sterne entered the room.

His sheer size made the chamber seem small and threatening. He smiled, and the hope Diana had not even known she cherished died at last.

"Waiting on that hell-babe thy lover," Sterne said with grim satisfaction. "He'll not be joining thee, Mistress, this side of Judgment Day."

Sterne stood blocking the doorway, holding a short leather-covered baton in his hands and regarding her with calm pleasure.

"What have you done with him?"

She could not keep from asking, even though she knew that the question only gave Sterne further ammunition to use against her.

"Thou would do better to consider the state of thy own soul," Sterne said. "Tomorrow day thou shalt go before the judges to purge thy soul in confession as thy body shall be purified in death."

Diana stared at him, only now realizing her own danger. With Upright gone—she would not believe he was dead; she would *not*—nothing stood between her and John Sterne's sadism. Nauseated denial made her senses waver so that she nearly missed his next words.

"I have here thy confession," Sterne said, pulling a roll of paper out of his coat. "Thou wilt sign it, Mistress Malignant; and when it is read out in thy name tomorrow, thou shall not recant it. An' thee do, I shall see thee burnt alive before the sun sets; I swear on God's holy Name."

Sterne held the paper out to her and let it drop to the floor, where it curled against the cold stone like an autumn leaf. Her confession.

He can't burn me. He can't. Witches are hanged here, not burned. He can't . . . Diana thought in terror. Her thoughts were a frantic whirl, tangled between the uncertain conviction that she'd made no such confession and the hysterical relief that this meant—surely it must mean—that he was not going to do anything to her.

"But what about the Book?" *Oh, Bright Lady!* Diana moaned inwardly. She had to be mad to tease Sterne with a question like that—no wolf he, but a rabid dog, slavering at the end of a very fragile chain.

"Ah, the precious book." Sterne slapped the end of the truncheon into his free hand, and Diana could almost feel its weight. Sterne looked at her, the slow weight of intention coalescing in his muddy eyes. "It is Matthew who seeks the Great Book of the Malignants, to his soul's peril. He thinks that with the King in Cromwell's hands, he must find high patronage or die, and studies that the Devil's own grammarie will gain it for him—but such mastery is the path to damnation."

And you're jealous of him, and you don't want him to have it because if he gets his hands on something like the Great Book, what will he need with you? Diana thought. She did not dare to raise her eyes, lest Sterne see that knowledge in them. She stared instead at the curled parchment on the floor. The document glowed yellow with August sunlight. No, September . . . It was September now, if the quarterly Assize Court was meeting tomorrow. And the parchment contained her confession.

"Which wilt thou choose, Mistress Anne? Thy mark upon the paper or to roast alive in the foretaste of hellfire?" With a careless motion of his boot, Sterne kicked the rolled parchment toward her.

Her fingers trembling with tension, Diana picked it up. It was handwritten in that ornate, print-clear secretary hand that Diana had seen on the papers on Matthew Hopkins's desk a seeming lifetime ago. She scanned the writing quickly:

I, Mistress Anne Mallow, late of the parish of Talitho, formerly of London, have entered the Devil's service these fifteen years since, making my vow to Satan in the person of his agent Adrammelech, Grand Chancellor of Hell, who has given to me for my use and comfort certain imps or familiar spirits to the number of five, their names being . . .

Her eyes flickered over the rest of it. There was nothing here but a pack of witch-hunter's lies straight out of the *Malleus Maleficarum*.

"Don't jape that thou canst read," Sterne said, yanking the document from her hands as she flinched back. He stepped past her to spread it out upon the table, using the empty lantern and the sinister weight of the truncheon to hold it uncurled.

"Aye," he said as he lifted the lantern to set it in place. "I know that Devil's mannikin was here with thee last night, filling thy body with his unnatural seed. He must burn—Matthew will see that now. His kind must be swept away so that the Kingdom of God can be made manifest in this world. Now wilt make thy mark or shall I use thee until thou begs to burn beside him?"

He was still alive. The force of that relief was enough to make Diana draw a ragged breath. Not dead, but they were going to kill him. Burn him alive. Witches were not burned in England—that penalty was only exacted by the courts for treason and heresy—but Diana had no doubt that Sterne would make good on his vow. He would not wait for a court's approval to murder her lover. Almost against her will, Diana took a step toward the table.

"I'll sign." Her voice was a hoarse crow caw.

Sterne thrust a ragged stub of charcoal at her, and Diana's fingers curled around it reflexively. She stared at the parchment. She'd sign this piece of nonsense gladly to keep Sterne from getting his hands on her. It was only a death sentence. No one who was not already in danger would be accused by her signing of it—not Mistress Fortune, not any of her fellow prisoners. The paper was nearly meaningless in any way that counted; but if she signed it, she had confessed to witchcraft—and would hang for it. Despite her avowals, her hands shook as she drew the shaky "X" that Sterne seemed to expect at the bottom of the rough vellum sheet. Mistress Anne Mallow, her mark.

The sound of satisfaction from Sterne once her mark was on the paper convinced Diana that she had made a dreadful mistake, that there was some other course of action she could have taken, if only she could think what it was. But the paper was gone, pulled from beneath her seeking hand, and Sterne was turning away to go.

Wait! Tell me where Upright is! What have you done to him? Grimly Diana bit her lips shut over that hopeless cry. Useless to think that John Sterne would tell her anything. All she could know was that Upright-Before-The-Lord was alive *now*— because John Sterne was going to burn him alive tomorrow.

Diana stood stubbornly mute as Sterne walked out, tucking her false confession into his coat. She stood until she was surrounded by silence once again; and then on stiff unfeeling legs, she walked to the bed and lay down and pulled the blanket around her to muffle her weeping. When she crossed from waking into sleeping, the howls of a trapped wolf haunted her slumbers.

She had to speak out. The conviction stayed with Diana awake and asleep, obsessing her until she had blinded herself to the consequences that would inevitably follow. Sterne held her false confession; she would be present when it was read out, and in that moment she must make her voice heard. Denounce Hopkins, as she had begged Upright to do.

It would not be as telling as an accusation by one of Hopkins own assistants would have been, but it might have some effect. But even if it did not, even if it was a futile and meaningless gesture, it was still a duty Diana owed to the Bright Lady and to the man who had risked so much for her sake. *Never again,* Diana reminded herself grimly. *Never again . . .*

Intent upon that one last duty, Diana was docile when her gaolers came for her in the morning. The day had dawned foggy and cold, as if Nature herself wept for her imprisoned children. Clutching her blanket around her, Diana stepped out of her cell to join the dejected coffle of those prisoners who would be tried and sentenced this day.

So few!

Not one of them was whole. The bruises and blisters, the burns and open sores told their own bitter story. If these were the people who had said she had the Great Book, Diana forgave them instantly. They had suffered beyond imagination, and now would die for Matthew Hopkins's greed.

Diana scanned the faces of the group, searching anxiously for familiar faces. She did not see Lettice Forster or her daughter Sarah or Pastor Conyngham or Mistress Fortune, but those remaining were familiar enough, even changed as they were by the weeks of brutal captivity.

She wanted to think that the missing ones were free, but it was so much more likely that they were dead.

The prisoners were brought into the courtyard. It was filled with bodies: a troop of mounted militiamen in half-armor, another group on foot, and others—men and women both— who just seemed to be here to watch.

In the chaos it seemed almost possible to slip away, but the wooden gates that secured the yard were closed and in her gray smock and blanket Diana would be recognized as one of the prisoners before she had taken ten steps. And if she ran, she would lose her chance to speak out before the court.

Diana and the others were herded forward and made to mount into the cart that would take them to the courthouse. The loading was a laborious process made more awkward by the nervousness of the troop of militia set to guard them and the injuries of the prisoners. As soon as she could, Diana gave her blanket to one of the others, a vacant-eyed mumbling woman who wore only the ragged remains of her smock. Diana did what she could to help the others climb up, her mind circling between fear and fury as she tried to find the words to pray. If only her accusation worked!

The sharp sound of horse's hooves ringing on stone made her stop and look up. John Sterne had come up beside the cart. He sat at his ease, mounted on a splendid horse, looking down on the prisoners for trial. In one hand he held the horse's reins and in the other, a dog-whip. When his gaze met Diana's, he raised two fingers to his hat brim in scornful salute.

Frightened and furious, Diana looked away. At that moment an animal howling broke out at the other side of the yard, accompanied by shouts and outcries. Diana hung back, wanting to see the cause, and a moment later the source of the disturbance came into view.

Upright.

He was being carried by three men, and still he fought like a maddened panther. His wrists were bound, and blood from his struggles to free them flecked his arms and chest. He was naked except for the ragged remains of his breeches, and as he twisted in his captors' arms Diana saw the fresh marks of a heavy beating crossing his back and thighs.

She looked back at Sterne. He was watching Upright with an expression on his face almost like lust. Diana could not bear to see it, but neither could she bear to look away from what might be her last sight of her lover.

One of the guards prodded Diana with his truncheon, and she obediently stepped up into the cart with the others. On the ground, a fourth man had joined the other three and was fastening a rope noose around Upright's neck. Sterne laughed and said something as the free end of the rope was handed to him, but Diana couldn't hear the words over the clatter of the gates being opened.

She knew what must come next; but before she could even cry out, Sterne swung his whip hand down over his horse's flank and the startled animal lunged from a standstill into a run. The men holding Upright released him; he fell to his knees for an instant before he was jerked to his feet by the rope and began to run.

The pure brilliant flame of hate that kindled in Diana's heart at that moment washed away all fear and weakness. In that shining instant she did not care what happened to her, as long as Sterne could be made to pay. She barely noticed when the cart lurched forward and began to move in the direction of the courthouse.

The courthouse was a large, square, new-looking building built of yellow brick, with a great crowd of people—some on horseback—gathered outside. From the moment the cart came in sight of the building, Diana could hear the cries of vendors and the roar of the multitude and realized that, to the citizens of Christchurch, this trial was the most momentous event that many of them might ever see and they intended to make the most of it.

"*'Butcher'd to make a Roman holiday,'*" Diana thought acidly. It was her last coherent thought before the crowd saw the wagon and turned upon the accused witches with a roar like the storming ocean.

If the bailiffs and the militia had not both been there, there might have been no need for a trial—although it was equally possible that the frenzied attempts to reach the prisoners and drag them from the wagon had been attempts to aid in their escape.

But the militia pushed the crowd back with pikes before it could overturn the cart and Captain Shackleton's shouted commands kept a bare semblance of order that allowed the prisoners to be passed out of the cart along a human chain that ended at the back passage into the courthouse. The defendants were pushed and prodded along the way they were intended to go, most of them happy to escape the violence of a potential mob.

The courtroom was a large, spacious chamber like a secular church. In fact, Talitho's small church and much of the church-yard would have fit neatly inside its towering, white-washed space. Diana had expected to see something like the judge's bench in a courtroom of her own time, but all there was at the front of the room was a long table with three large chairs behind it and another smaller table facing it. There was no barrier to separate the participants from the spectators, and the benches were jammed with those who had come to watch the notorious Matthew Hopkins put on a show.

Even from the back of the courtroom Diana could still hear the groaning and muttering of the crowd outside. When they were herded into a corner and allowed to stop, she looked around.

She and the others were crowded into a corner behind the crossed pikes of still more militiamen. She craned around them, trying to see. The people who crowded the benches were massed and waiting as if for the start of a play.

Because that was what it would be, Diana told herself. A play, a show, a performance—and no more truth and substance to it than prime-time television.

Diana saw Squire Alcock and the Reverend Simon Grimsby—the architects of Hopkins's campaign of terror in Talitho—in seats near to the front, obviously savoring the moment and their own importance. She saw Mary Phillips, Hopkins's handmaid, standing near the back in a cluster of admirers, tipping a flat brown bottle to her lips.

But no matter how she searched, Diana could not find Upright or John Sterne anywhere in the crowd. A bolt of pure miserable terror cut through every other emotion. Was Sterne carrying out his promise of Upright's execution even now?

At the front of the room, men were walking back and forth now, placing documents on the long tables. A richly dressed gentleman leaning on a tall walking stick came and seated himself at the long table. Diana heard him greeted as Judge Burr before he began leafing through the papers before him as if he were alone in the room.

The babble from the spectators grew louder, and Diana could make out occasional words and phrases. There would be three judges to hear the charges today, but no jury. The sentence would be rendered as part of the judgment and carried out later.

Where was Upright?

Just as Diana thought she could bear the suspense no longer, Sterne entered, striding largely, with the end of the rope wrapped around his fist. Behind him staggered Upright-Before-The-Lord, crouching, mud-and-blood spattered, clinging to the rope with hands that had been burned raw by it.

But alive.

The ringing, white-hot fury that had taken possession of

Diana's very soul rose up again as she looked at him. Stumbling after Sterne, he turned toward her as if she had spoken; and once again she had that dizzying swooping sense of being drawn from her place, of staring up at her own face over the crossed pikes of the guardsmen.

The moment shattered as Sterne gave a vicious tug to the rope and sent Upright sprawling forward across the floor in the direction of the smaller table. With quick economical motions Sterne tied the rope close about one of the table's legs, tethering Upright as if he were a dog.

Diana glanced from Upright to Sterne, and whatever he saw in her eyes erased the satisfaction from his face, resetting it into grim lines. She looked back to Upright, to where he crouched, head down and sides heaving visibly as he fought for breath. She kept her eyes on him, willing him her strength, not caring now that anyone might see.

The second judge—Massey—came and was seated. Sterne opened the document case he carried and began laying out a few books and several sheets of ivory vellum covered with dense black script. Confessions, probably, and Diana's among them.

There was a roar from the crowd outside—impossible to tell whether it was approval or rage—and Matthew Hopkins entered, sweeping up the center aisle like a visiting movie star.

Obviously he had expected to be last; he stopped in the act of sweeping off his hat when he saw the empty judge's chair. The graceful, studied movement was completed half a beat late. He turned to Sterne.

"Where is that puling lackey Falwell?" he snarled in a voice that carried clearly to Diana's ears.

"Sir Wilmot says Judge Falwell does not come today," Sterne answered in his slow, careful way. "He falls ill and will send his deputy in his place."

"Why was I not told?" Hopkins snapped. He cast a reproachful, suspicious glance at Upright, but it was obvious that even Hopkins could not hold his disgraced hound responsible for this. "How long must we wait?"

Sterne had no answer to either of these questions. Hopkins flung his hat and gloves down upon the table and approached the judges.

For all the notice any of them—judges and accusers—took of the reason for this trial, the prisoners huddled behind the pikesmen might have been inanimate objects. From that position, it was easy to overhear the conversation between Hopkins and the judges; and from her scanty knowledge of Hopkins's career, Diana filled in the gaps.

Hopkins wanted to start without Judge Falwell's alternate. He'd been counting on Falwell, a believer in demonic witchcraft and a man sympathetic to Hopkins's position, to sway Massey and Burr, who were known to hold no strong views in either direction. If a true bill of indictment could not be brought in at this session, the prisoners could be bound over for another quarter for further inquiry; but it was much more likely that the charges would simply be dropped—and the accused freed, confessions or no.

Finally, at Hopkins's urging, Judges Burr and Massey agreed to start the proceedings without the third judge present, though with the understanding that the evidence would have to be presented again if Falwell's alternate so desired it. Hopkins was counting on there being no such demand. After a brief flurry of ritual, the court was called to order and the first prisoner called.

"Bring forth Mistress Anne Mallow of London, late of the parish of Talitho," the Clerk of the Court cried.

Hopkins turned toward her, his hand outstretched in a practiced, courtly gesture. The pikesmen swung their weapons up, opening a path for Diana to walk between them.

Now that the moment was here, Diana felt her anger and her courage falter. She found them both again in Hopkins's gloating certainty. What had Sterne told him—that she'd say her part?

Diana brushed past Hopkins as if he weren't there and stood, defiantly facing the judges.

"My lords—" Hopkins voice came from behind her, with

just the right touch of obsequiousness. "—I present to you Mistress Anne Mallow, who is a witch and a Malignant and who has conspired to aid the man Charles Stuart, formerly King Charles of England, to regain his throne and defile the good people of England through the sin of witchcraft."

The spectators broke into a clamor at this unexpected development; and Diana realized that by adding treason to the list of accusations, Hopkins had made it possible for every convicted prisoner of this court to be burned alive for treason.

"No—" she began, and was drowned out by the judge's voice.

"Who accuses this woman?" Judge Burr was unimpressed by the uproar, cleaving strictly to the letter of the law.

"This man—or creature, I should call it," Hopkins said. He pointed, with an orator's polished flourish, at Upright-Before-The-Lord.

"Why is the accuser tied to a table?" Burr asked in his arid voice.

"Because I have only lately discovered that he is himself an agent of the Devil."

"That isn't *true!* Hopkins is a *fraud!*" Diana's voice was shrill and cracked, soaring over the other sounds like a raven's harsh call to judgment. "He holds no warrant from Parliament! He makes up his confessions and tells you they're the truth. You pay him to do *that,* not to find what's really true! If anyone's in league with the Devil here, it's *Matthew Hopkins!*"

The room exploded into a babble of competing voices as people jumped to their feet, arguing and pointing. The roar of the crowd outside swelled as Diana's words were relayed to them.

Sterne moved forward to stop her, murder in his eyes. Upright lunged after him, pulling futilely against the rope, but it was one of the pikesmen who barred Sterne from reaching her.

"If he had the list of witches he claims to, what would he need with his network of paid informers?" Diana shouted through the din.

Burr was hammering on the table with his gavel while Massey, driven beyond that, stood on his chair and roared out his bull-throated demands for silence.

Unable to be heard for the pandemonium, Diana shut up. She was jostled roughly backward by the pikesman; but for all its deceit and dishonesty, this was still an English court and she would be heard.

The crowd outside had surged into the courtroom; by the time the bailiffs got the doors shut again and barred, there was only standing room in the court and the ranks of bystanders were jammed up against the table to which Upright was bound.

His hands were free. Diana did not need the moment of anguished silent communication between them to know to turn her eyes away and draw no attention to him. Once he was free . . .

Diana glanced toward the bench. Burr continued hammering at the table as if that sound alone could clear the courtroom and Massey, seated now, was nearly purple with fury. It took several moments for the truncheon-wielding bailiffs to batter the spectators into some semblance of silent cooperation. The courtroom, uneasily quiet now, was like a tinderbox, and one spark would ignite a riot.

When an uneasy semblance of order had been restored, Massey spoke, though he still had to shout over the gabble of the spectators.

"Am I to understand that you—an accused Malignant— charge Master Matthew Hopkins with witchcraft?"

Diana opened her mouth to answer.

"She might as well," a new voice called out.

It came from behind her. The speaker was a young man; his brown hair hung in Cavalier curls though his dress was Puritan sober. He had entered through the side door under cover of the commotion, his easy access to the court explained by the roll of official-looking parchment affixed with dangling seals that he held. And behind him—Diana's eyes widened and she swayed with the shock—behind him, stood Pastor Edmund Conyngham of Talitho, his hand on his sword and his face a grim mask of purpose.

"Who the devil are you, sir?" Burr growled.

"My name is Daniel Merriam," the stranger said. "I am Judge Falwell's deputy to this court; but more, I have a warrant here from Parliament for Master Hopkins's arrest. He is charged with fraudulently—"

It was too much for the mob. Its members surged forward with a bestial howl, and the room exploded into violence.

When he had last been taken and chained, he had been a child. Now he was grown to manhood and possessed of all the powers of his kind—and was unafraid, at last, to use them. The mob rose up, a furious, many-throated animal, but he freed himself and passed among them unseen, moving through them as if they were no more than trees in the forest. He reached *di'anu* as she cowered back in the corner; and without effort, he cast his spell over her as well, tangling her in a dream so that she moved with him, blind and enchanted. In another moment, they were free.

The day had darkened, and he called the coming storm to cloak their passing, chanting storm-sky and sea-mist to cover their track. Dragging her with him, he flung their bodies into the maelstrom of the swarming rabble, winding through the mob to a place they could run freely. There was only one thought in his mind now. The woods. The woods, and safety.

Home.

Chapter 16

The New Forest,
September 1647

It seemed she had been running forever. The last thing she remembered was someone saying Daniel Merriam was to be arrested . . . No, it was *Hopkins* who was to be arrested and Merriam who had brought the warrant. Beyond that, everything faded into a dreamlike journey as the countryside floated past their horse's drumming hooves.

Diana blinked, staring down at her own running, mud-spattered feet. There were no horses. She was on foot, and it was raining. She looked up and saw unfamiliar fields and hedges, fences, and—in the distance—a house.

She must have slowed; there was an impatient tug on her hand. Her foot caught on a root and she fell to her knees.

When she looked up, she saw Upright staring down at her, still gripping her hand with his own bleeding one. His wild black hair was plastered to his face and neck with the wet, and his only garment was the pair of ragged breeches that rain had molded into a glistening veneer that displayed his every muscle. The marks of the whip and the rope were livid against his pale skin; he spoke one urgent sentence in a language that Diana could not understand, and then she felt the blinding, dazzling pressure begin again behind her eyes, urging her into a dream of horses.

"No," she said, pulling her hand free and waving him off. The pressure ceased at once. Diana got to her feet and looked back.

The village of Christchurch was made small by distance, though she did not know how far they had come or how long they'd been running. Both the time and the distance were obscured by the fog and the shifting veils of rain. It seemed that a veil of smoke hung over the town, though she could not be sure. Burning . . . Sterne and Hopkins had meant to burn them both.

She turned back to the man beside her, who was watching her with anxious eyes. She took a step toward him, wanting to hold him close and take what comfort she could from that, knowing there was not time. Her body trembled with exhaustion.

"Upright?" Diana asked. He shook his head, a brief sideways motion, and Diana felt the echo of that negation inside her own mind. But if he weren't Upright-Before-The-Lord, who was he?

"Di'anu, we must run now," he said in English as halting as if he translated it from another language. He took her hand again and pulled her after him, heading inland as if he had a fixed destination in mind.

In this time the woodland called New Forest was still the vast wilderness that William Rufus had claimed for his hunting preserve five centuries before. The coven had met at its edge; and in it, a man might still hide from all pursuit.

But the preserve's edge was miles away and Diana's strength, broken by weeks of ill-treatment, was not equal to the brutal pace that Upright set. By the end of another hour, her pace had slowed to a stumbling shamble; and Upright finally gave up all attempts to urge her on, simply standing beside her as she knelt, gasping for air in the dubious shelter of a hedgerow.

"I can't," Diana said. It was bitter to admit it, but she lacked even the strength to get to her feet now. "Go on. I'll follow you."

"Nay, I'll not leave thee." He crouched down in front of her, smoothing the sodden hair back from her face. "Did thou not swear thou wert mine own?"

Diana made one convulsive attempt to stand, but her legs gave way under her and she only succeeded in falling forward into his arms. "You have to go," she whimpered, closing her eyes and leaning against him, letting herself sink into the warmth where their bodies met. She was cold; she was tired; she wanted. . . .

She was jerked back to full consciousness by a drizzle of cold water down her back. As she'd lain against him in a daze, he'd scooped a small hole in the earth and let it fill with a thin soup of rainwater and mud. Now he was pouring the result over her.

The thin mud had been for her hair; he made a thicker paste and began ladling it over her skin, ignoring her feeble protests.

"What are you doing?" Diana demanded groggily.

"I must leave thee here for a time—only for a time," he said, holding up his hand against the protests she hadn't made. "Thou wilt sleep and I will come for thee and thou shalt wear this robe of earth lest others come for thee instead."

He was going to leave her. He was going to be safe. If she had to cover herself with mud to make him go, Diana thought fuzzily, so be it. She helped him rub mud into her skin and smock and hair; then he scooped a shallow trench beneath the deepest part of the hedge and coaxed her into it, arranging her body until she lay beneath the hedge with her cheek pressed against the earth and he'd covered her with another layer of mud, old leaves, and sticks.

"Wait for me," he said again, backing out of the hedge.

Forever, Diana thought dazedly; and despite her determination to stay alert and leave when it was safe, she was unconscious almost before he was gone.

* * *

She was jarred awake minutes or hours later by the jumbled sound of hoofbeats—many horses tromping down the narrow track between the hedgerow and the field. Though Diana lay within plain sight inches from where the riders passed—close enough to be splashed by their horse's hooves—they did not see her, and Diana suddenly saw the reason for Upright's careful camouflage.

The riders called back and forth in loud voices, and she thought she recognized Reverend Conyngham's voice among them. Cramped, exhausted muscles complained and rebelled when she tried to shift, and eventually Diana gave up and lay still, cold and aching. If it were Conyngham—the Magister of the Talitho coven—he would surely help her.

But would he extend his charity to Matthew Hopkins's renegade hellhound? She didn't know, and it seemed like too much effort to find out. Diana kept her silence as the sounds faded into the distance.

Would Upright come back?

Her mind kept circling back to the sore spot of that uncertainty—not that he would desert her, because she knew he wouldn't, but that something would keep him from coming back. To distract herself, she tried to decide how long she'd slept—and how soon she could expect him. It was irritatingly difficult.

The trial had begun in the morning and the two of them had been on the run for several hours, but she did not know what time it was now. Late afternoon or early evening—the days were getting shorter as the fall equinox approached. She had almost made up her mind to go looking for him when she heard hoofbeats once more.

This time it was the slow trudging cadence of a plow-horse moving deliberately over the muddy ground. The sounds came level with her hiding place and stopped.

"Come out," Upright said. No, not Upright, although it was the man she had known as Upright-Before-The-Lord. But when she named him that in her thoughts now, she felt that strange aversion, as if it were not *his* name at all.

Abandoning the fruitless puzzle, Diana squirmed stiffly out from under the hedge. He pulled her to her feet, ignoring her yelps and whimpers of pain, and led her proudly toward his prize. After the first shock, it felt good to move, even though every muscle protested.

"Where did you get that?" she demanded in awe.

That was an enormous beige horse with a flax-colored mane and tail and huge shaggy feet, and he'd led it here with no more tether than his hand upon its mane.

"I borrowed it," he said with a flash of dark amusement in his voice. "Now, mount thee, for we have miles and miles to go."

Diana stared at the animal, unable to imagine herself on its back, and then she took a good look at Upright.

From somewhere he'd acquired a leather jacket that hung on him like a tent and a tattered straw hat that was drooping and melancholy in the wet. He looked like a scarecrow somehow come to life.

"What are *you* got up as?" she asked.

"Mount," he said again.

With his help, Diana scrambled inelegantly onto the horse's back, barely managing to pull the muddy smock down far enough for decency and comfort. The grit covered her everywhere—her hair, her skin—she could even taste it, and her ineffectual attempts to tidy herself only smeared her more evenly. The rain was an irritating persistent drizzle—not heavy enough to wash the mud from her hair, not light enough to allow her body heat to dry the wool garment she wore.

Diana scraped a handful of mud from her leg and shook it to the ground, then wiped her muddy hand on the horse's shoulder, clutching at its mane for support.

Upright passed her the other thing he'd brought, a large flour sack half-full with plunder. Before she could look inside, he made a chirping sound to the horse and started off. It followed docilely along behind him like an enormous dog, moving at a brisk walk that accelerated to a bone-jarring trot. Diana clutched the shaggy mane with both hands and held on for dear life.

It was all Diana could do to keep from sliding off the wet— now wet-and-muddy—horse, and its bouncing gait jarred every one of her bruises; but the heat of its immense body was a warm comfort, easing the cold that seemed to have soaked into her very bones as she lay beneath the hedge. As she clung to the horse's mane, Diana felt the dark softness of exhaustion waiting to drag her down into it. The brief rest had only revived her enough to realize how tired she was; she had to stare at her interlocked fingers to make sure they retained their grip.

But she shared Upright's urgency that they flee Christchurch as fast and as far as they could. Their escape had been halfway between luck and a miracle, and Diana was no more willing than he was to bet both their lives on the chance that no one hunted them now—or that they could get free a second time.

After not too long a time, the horse slowed to a walk again and she could take one hand from the animal's mane to investigate the sack she held clutched against her stomach.

The first item she saw was a gray shawl. She teased it carefully free of the bag with cold-numbed fingers and shook it out.

"You stole this stuff," Diana said, though it was hard to be indignant about it, all things considered.

"Put it on."

I'll get it all muddy, she wailed mentally, but didn't bother to even say the words aloud. Working one-handed, she wrapped the shawl around her head and shoulders. Because it was wool, it began to warm her almost immediately, even while the soaking rain beaded its fuzzy surface with tiny crystal drops.

Upright slapped the horse upon the shoulder and it began to trot again. Diana gritted her teeth and held on.

They were crossing the rolling Downs of the southwest, moving through farmland and sheep pasture. Though their destination was called "forest," it was a forest only in the oldest sense of the word—wilderness—and would be much the same: stands of trees, but rolling open spaces as well. This was September—harvest time—and the weather was reasonably warm; but rain and shock and weeks of privation made Diana's teeth chatter as much with cold as with the plow-horse's bone-jarring trot. The horizon was obscured by veils of rain mist, but from her elevated perch, Diana could still see houses in the distance; and any one of those houses' inhabitants might see them and raise the hue and cry.

Diana looked ahead, in the direction they were travelling, and from her imagination and knowledge painted the vista that should be there: the slow rise of land; the darker green of standing wood lots dotting the middle ground; and in the distance, a dark wall of trees. But that refuge was still miles away.

Once more, the horse dropped back to a walk. Diana took advantage of the respite to shift her position and further investigate the contents of the sack.

It was the random thievery of a gypsy—a tinderbox, two candle ends, a knife, a stoppered green glass bottle. There was a wheel of cheese, half a loaf of wheat bread, a honeycomb wrapped stickily in a napkin, half-a-dozen fresh apples.

Hunger made her insides clench. "There's food," she called down to him, just as if he didn't know. "Can we stop to eat?"

He shook his head, not speaking. Diana tore a chunk from the loaf and tried to hand it to him. "Eat," she said, but he waved it away.

"Thou," he commanded.

She was too hungry to argue. He waited until she had finished the piece of bread in her hand before slapping the horse into a shambling trot once more.

It was dusk, and they were within sight of their goal. Upright had long since given up urging the horse to trot; now, it walked and he walked beside it, head bowed.

The rain had stopped a few hours ago, but now a thick mist had gathered in the air and in the hollows of the ground, making sight uncertain and the footing treacherous. There was forest ahead—not the deep forest where Royalty might hunt, but the woodlot on its outskirts where local villagers might turn out their pigs to forage and cull the fellwood for their fires. In the dusk, the leaves that would be gold and red and green in sunlight were reduced to a ghostly dun-gray pattern against the mist.

Wrapped warmly in the stolen wool shawl, fed enough to take the edge off her hunger, and able to leave the journey's effort to the horse's muscles, Diana had dozed and not seen how weary Upright had become.

For the third time in as many minutes he fell against the horse's shoulder, and this time threw an arm over its neck to hold himself from falling to the ground. He had refused to ride with her; the horse would not carry double, he'd said, and someone must lead it. Now the animal lifted a foot and put it down again, stopping.

"Upright?" Diana questioned. She felt the faint psychic flinching away, but she had no other name to call him by. *Hob, Robin, Oberon* . . . He made no other move, even when she leaned precariously forward to place a hand on his arm. Her muscles trembled as she did it; she was tired beyond exhaustion—and if that was so, how much more drained must he be, first beaten and dragged behind Sterne's horse and then walking all day?

"Stupid, stupid, stupid . . ." Diana muttered savagely at herself. She'd been so caught up in her own misery she hadn't even thought about him. Somehow she'd begun to feel he was some eldritch force of Nature come to her aid, instead of a very mortal man who had been pushed to the limit of his endurance.

As he lay against its shoulder, the horse began to show signs of restlessness. It raised its head, pulling its neck out of Upright's grasp.

He fell to the ground with a limp bonelessness that made Diana cry out in frightened protest. As if it had caught her mood, the plow-horse began to first back away from the fallen man and then turn back the way they had come. The flour sack slid to the ground with a faint clank as Diana dragged at the horse's mane with both hands and kicked her heels at its sides;

but no matter what she tried, she could do nothing to stop the animal.

Swearing helplessly, Diana took its mane in a death grip with both hands and tried to swing her leg over its back to dismount.

Stiff, cramped muscles refused to obey her; she floundered spastically on its broad back, spooking the horse further. When she was almost lying facedown—the only way she could get her leg across its back—the horse shied violently to one side. Diana slid off. She dangled for a moment from its mane before she remembered to let go and fell free, landing on her backside with a painful thump.

The horse cantered off across the field, a looming spectral shape in the mist, but Diana paid no further attention to it. She groped through the mist until she had collected their pitiful sack of provisions and made her way back to Upright.

He had rolled half onto his side and lain, eyes closed, as still and pale as a waxworks doll. Automatically Diana sought for a pulse, but could not be sure whether she felt one or not through her cold numb fingers.

"Don't die," she heard herself saying. "Please, don't die."

She should have made him ride; she should have made him rest. . . . Frantically, Diana searched through the sack, looking for something that would help. She wrenched the wax-covered stopper from the green bottle and sniffed at it. Brandy. She lifted his head into her lap and tried to pour some into his mouth.

His response was more violent than she'd expected. He jerked away, spraying the liquid from his mouth and coughing.

"N'haé. No ve je hela mé!" he cried, scrabbling away.

He glared at her without recognition, and his eyes flashed green in the dusk, like a wolf's.

But human eyes don't do that. . . . Diana hugged herself with tardy dread against the falling sense of shock as he dragged himself to hands and knees. Only animal's eyes glowed in that way, mirroring the available light in red or green or silver.

"Who are you?" Diana whispered to herself. "What are you?"

He heard her. He raised his head and gazed at her, wiping his mouth with the back of his hand. He shook himself, pushing his hair out of his eyes with a muddy hand before he spoke.

"Hwyfar."

Was that an answer? "Upright?" Diana asked uncertainly. She looked back the way they had come. The horse had stopped a few yards away and was grazing, head down and unconcerned, but she did not think she could catch it again. The easy tears of exhaustion gathered in her eyes. They were so close....

"No." Weariness had drawn the lines of his face into a stark mask, but the voice was again the one she knew, quiet and sane. "Do not call me by Matthew's gift-name. I renounce him and all his works. Call me in the name my mother's brother gave to me. *Hwyfar.* Shadow."

A brief cascade of shared memory: the silver valley in the hollow hills, capture, chains, a madhouse, and a smiling man— *Hopkins,* dressed in black....

"Shadow," Diana repeated, giddy with lack of rest.

The name fit him as a key fit a lock; there was no dissonance now between the mental image of him and the name. Despite this latest shock she felt strangely uninvolved, as if she'd been insulated from all the customary forms of cause and effect, as though what happened here occurred in a place outside of Time. Not Upright-Before-The-Lord Makepeace. *Shadow.*

Whose eyes glowed like a wolf's. Who could steal her senses with a look and control a plow-horse with a touch ...

"Shadow," Diana said again. She didn't care that this made no sense, that it all seemed to involve some mad logic that lay just beyond the reach of her conscious mind. She knew him. She had always known him, known him since before Time began.

"We must go," he said, but it was hopeless. He knew it as well as she did; instead of trying to stand, he simply crawled back to her and leaned against her, resting his head on her shoulder and closing his eyes.

His stolen hat had vanished sometime during the afternoon, and the rainwater from his hair made a slow, cold trickle between her breasts. Diana leaned her cheek against his hair and let her eyes drift shut, content in holding him, though she knew she shouldn't be. If they didn't move soon, they'd be dead. Exhaustion, exposure, shock . . . any one of those could finish them. Diana knew these things as well as she knew her own name, but knowing didn't seem to help. She felt as if she were floating upon a silver sea of peace, leaving the pain and exhaustion of the body behind.

Was this all it was for? a fleeting part of her wondered mournfully, until she left that, too, behind.

The electric sensation of *power* roused her. It was a half-painful tingle over her skin and senses, dragging her back from that deadly dreamless swoon. Shadow felt it as she did; he stirred where he lay against her chest, his breath a faint whimper of protest. With an effort that seemed a superhuman exertion, Diana opened her eyes.

For one dazzled befuddled moment she thought it was the moon she saw, a piercing silvery illumination that turned the mist around it to milky veils of sapphire. Then she blinked and focussed and saw it was a deer—no, a stag, a *white* stag, with branching antlers that glinted gold in the haze as it stood at the edge of the forest and held them both in its calm regard.

"*Grall'hoch*," Shadow said, raising his head to stare at the apparition. It glowed as brightly as if there were a moon that shone on it alone, its white coat shining with a light that had no earthly source. Diana felt the quiver of unease he couldn't suppress, then Shadow had pushed himself away from her, trying to stand.

She helped him as much as she could, though the sodden wool garments she wore felt as if they must weigh a thousand pounds. When he was on his feet, she stood as well, still clutching the shawl and the sack, grimly determined not to lose them.

The stag was still watching them. Diana stared at it, uncertain whether this were a vision, a hallucination, or a true sending from the Bright Lady. It was easy to believe that the creature was enchanted, but following it was beyond her strength. "Help us," Diana whispered. "Help us, please."

"Follow it," Shadow said hoarsely. " 'Tis *seely.*" He took her hand and led her forward, placing one foot in front of the other with unyielding tenacity.

The stag stood watching them until they had nearly reached it, then bounded away, stopping a few yards off and watching them with fathomless liquid eyes.

A swarm of conflicting impressions slid disorientingly through Diana's mind as she stared at it: a creature of flesh-and-blood; a fairy beast that smelled of magic and moonlight; no stag at all, but a cold-eyed woman with lips as red as the rowanberry and eyes as blue as Death. She closed her eyes, refusing to choose among them. Only the hand that gripped her own was real.

Shadow pulled at her. Diana opened her eyes and stumbled after the stag, certain that each step was the last effort she could make.

Diana was never certain afterward how long that dreamlike journey took. The wood they travelled through now was not dark, though surely the sun had set long ago, but lit with a sourceless silvery light that shone from the pale flowers that carpeted the ground between the great trees. She heard no sound but a faint sea roaring, as if a wind Diana could not feel agitated the leaves, and the path was soft beneath her feet.

The stag lingered just beyond their reach, waiting each time until they'd nearly reached it before springing away again. Shadow seemed to draw strength from the forest that surrounded them, urging her onward any time she faltered; and Diana, too, drew sustenance from some mystic wellspring. The pains of her body were a dim, distant thing; she was neither tired, nor hungry, nor thirsty. All she knew was that they must follow,

follow, follow through the endless twilight that had neither dusk nor dawn.

At last she and Shadow reached a clearing where the light was blue and chill. Different.

It's morning, Diana thought, shaking herself as though she were rousing from a dream. For a moment she could not remember how she'd gotten here, or what had gone before.

The stag! She turned and looked behind her, barely in time to catch a last glimpse of white as the stag bounded off, deeper into the wood. Where had he—? . . . The memory twisted in her grasp and slipped away.

Beside her, Shadow was moving forward. He dropped to his knees, parting the undergrowth to reveal a darkness beyond.

"What?" Diana asked. Speech was an effort, as if she had been silent a very long time.

"Come," Shadow said, crawling forward.

Within the thicket was a miracle, indeed—a warm dry den floored with the soft leaves of last year's autumn, a refuge made of a deadfall tree that had toppled against a stone, and the webwork of vines that overgrew it. The den's roof was not high enough for either of them to stand, but the enclosed space was large enough to lie comfortably in.

Here . . . safe . . . here . . . His thoughts twined around her own, striking echoes from them until Diana was not sure which of them thought.

Shadow had already spread his stolen coat over the leaves to make a bed and was in the process of pulling off his breeches to add to the pile as well. When he saw her watching him he stopped and plucked at her shawl.

"Take them . . . off."

Diana dragged the shawl from her shoulders and handed it to him. It had dried, since . . . Her thoughts slid away from the memory. Diana shuddered as the damp wool beneath turned clammy in the morning chill. Awkwardly, she dragged the smock off over her head. He was probably right that she'd be more comfortable without the smock; and whether he was or not, she couldn't bear to wear the scratchy, filthy, too-tight garment a moment longer.

The mud Shadow had poured over her had seeped through it in runnels and spots, adding a gritty dappling to her skin. She wadded the cloth up and scrubbed at herself, trying to rub away not only the mud but the memory of endless days of captivity and humiliation.

Shadow pulled the smock out of her hands, holding her gaze as he shook his head.

No. Not that way.

He shook it gently, smoothing it out and brushing dried mud from it, and then spread the smock over the leaves as well.

His movement turned his shoulder and back toward her, and she saw the livid pattern of oozing weals and black bruises against the pale ivory of his back.

"You're . . . hurt," Diana said, inadequately. She'd known he'd been beaten; but in the chaos of their flight, she'd forgotten.

Never again . . . never again . . .

He turned back to her, smiling faintly and holding out his hand. His tangled, wild joy spilled into her mind, catching her up in it until she laughed and wept and clung to him with the sheer release of freedom.

"Come and lie with me," he said, holding up the shawl. Obediently Diana lay down in the nest he'd made of their clothes. He settled beside her, pulling the thick shawl over them both.

His body was cold at first when he pressed it against her, but the contact warmed it almost at once. He put an arm across her, pulling himself to her and clasping her leg between his thighs, claiming her with his touch. The intimate embrace pressed him into the hollow of her hip; he shifted against her, seeking a more comfortable position, and she felt the soft, heated pressure of his body as it hardened against hers, its blind, seeking insistence; but he seemed content just to hold her and nothing more.

The aftermath of that last emotional spasm had left her completely exhausted. Diana clung to him as trustingly and thought-lessly as a child. *Warm and safe . . . warm and safe . . .* The litany circled again and again through her mind, leaving no room for anything beyond it. His breath was warm against her neck, and slowly their body heat trapped beneath the shawl began to warm them.

Diana lingered on the edge of sleep, feeling a faint sense of something left undone. The man lying half across her was a blessed living weight. She wanted to press him close, to hold him forever so that nothing could ever hurt him again, but she was afraid to put her arms around him lest she hurt him herself. At last she compromised, placing her hand on what she remembered from the evidence of her own eyes to be unblemished skin.

The weight of her hand on his thigh rocked him against her, and she heard his breathing change. His leg pressed harder against the tickling ache that had begun between her thighs, and she felt the heat that was trapped against her hip increase.

Her hand slid up the back of his leg to cup him against her, an action as unwilled and automatic as her heartbeat. He rocked against her again, this time with conscious intention in the movement; and with dreamlike slowness they shifted, their bodies sliding over each other until she had taken his weight upon the cradle of her hips. He pushed slowly into her, groaning softly with the pleasure of it. The sound was as erotic as a touch; she opened to take him as deeply as she could, feeling the liquid warmth of his presence as he eased inside her, a heat that grew with each beat of her heart.

This was what she wanted, this intimate absolute print of his body upon hers. Diana smoothed her hands over his unmarked flesh as if she would learn every contour of him past all forgetting. He cradled her in his arms, holding nearly still, his face pressed against her neck as the radiance kindled by their joining grew into a blaze as steady and inexorable as the burning of the sun, until its incandescent tide swept though them like a thing not of their making, binding them irrevocably together even as it released them into sleep.

Chapter 17
The New Forest, October 1647

Diana crouched over the small fire, feeding it from her hoarded store of twigs and keeping a watchful eye on the brace of rabbits roasting over the flames. Her hair—freshly washed and braided with stalks of autumn goldenrod to reduce its betraying shine—was tied back with a black strip of cloth that had come from Shadow's breeches. More strips of black cloth, braided into a cord, held the wool skirt that had been made from her smock in place around her waist. Over the skirt she wore an apron of rabbit skins for added warmth, and the wool shawl was wrapped across her breasts and cross-tied behind her back. If unconventional, the costume was warm, even in the chill of early autumn.

She added another stick to the fire, wondering when Shadow would return from his foraging. He meant to move their camp again soon. They moved constantly so that they would leave no lingering scars of habitation on the forest, and they'd been here three days. Perhaps tomorrow.

He said they needed a place to winter, something more weather-fast than their temporary camps, where they slept in a blanket-lined hollow beneath a turf-covered windbreak of woven branches that could be jerked down to conceal them in an instant. She did not question the need for such exacting caution; all Diana wanted was to blot out the memory of the nightmare that had begun with the arrival of Matthew Hopkins in Talitho.

Diana poked hopefully at one of the rabbits with a peeled and whittled wooden stick. Savory juices rushed out, and she carefully sprinkled the meat with a bit of their precious store of hoarded salt. Putting the salt box away, she added another twig to the tiny fire and resisted the temptation to check the rabbits for doneness again. They would be done when they were thoroughly brown; she'd learned that much by now. Shadow had taught her.

He'd taught her everything that had let her survive in the forest from how to locate edible roots, berries, and grasses to the trapping of the rabbits, squirrels, and birds that made up their diet. He'd made the skirt and apron that she wore as well as the travois that transported their growing store of possessions, its bearing surface salvaged from the remains of the leather jacket he'd stolen. They slept through the light of day, when it was warmest and they were most vulnerable to discovery, and rose at dusk to hunt and forage and build their small, carefully concealed fires.

It was an existence as bizarre as it was idyllic, so divorced from what had come before it that Diana had trouble believing in any world beyond the greenwood. The night, as Shadow had prophesied so long ago, had come, and everything was utterly changed. The sane orderly course of her existence had been wrenched out of true too many times, last of all with the revelation of Shadow's true nature.

She heard the snap of a twig and rose to her feet, smiling. He was back; she knew it as much from the touch of his mind upon hers as from the deliberate sounds he made to warn her. Each time he returned she felt a rush of sheer, joyful thanksgiving—that he was back, that he was alive. In another moment, he appeared at the edge of the clearing, as suddenly and completely as if he had materialized out of nowhere.

He was nearly naked, his only concession to modesty the scant leather loincloth that was the other relict of the sacrificed leather jacket. His skin was colored green with a mixture of plant juices, berries, soot, and animal fat; and against that verdant background, a careful pattern of lines and circles and dots was drawn in charcoal and ash—a camouflage that made him able to vanish at will into the forest.

Braided strips of rabbit fur made the belt from which a stolen knife in its leather scabbard hung. His hair was braided back, studded with the long, gray wing-feathers of an unwary gull in a pattern like branching antlers. He looked like something out of a fable—or a myth.

"Shadow," Diana said aloud, though there was no need. She had already learned that he could sense her feelings as well as he could project his own. She held her hands out to him, her whole being carried on a wave of gratitude for his simple presence.

It was ridiculous to feel these things so strongly, she told herself. It was maudlin sentimentality brought on by shock, and surely it would pass.

Only it had already been more than a month—the moon had waxed and waned and would soon be full again—and she still craved his presence the way her body craved breath.

Shadow came and knelt at her feet, smiling up at her, drawing forth his scavenged treasures one by one from the sack knotted at his waist to present them to her.

A comb—Diana snatched it up with a cry of delight—a proper comb to replace the unsatisfactory wooden one he'd so painstakingly whittled.

"You shouldn't go near people!" she scolded unconvincingly.

"I don't," he said.

Diana frowned at him doubtfully, not sure whether to believe him or not. He would not lie to her, but his definition of the truth was maddeningly exact. If she took him up on this, she knew from experience that she could spend a fruitless hour arguing over the precise definition of "near."

"What else?" she questioned, giving up.

A pot of honey, a flitch of bacon, a tin spoon, a small pouch of tobacco, a handful of unfamiliar silver coins, five eggs still warm from the hen—all wrapped for safe carrying in a linen shirt that would have to be dyed somehow before either of them could wear it; the snowy linen would show up too well against the green of the forest. Except for the eggs, he must have gone inside a house to get these things; they weren't the sort of items a homeowner would leave lying out.

Though neither of them had seen any sign of a search party in their weeks of hiding, Diana knew that Shadow was desperately careful to avoid discovery—keeping them to the deep forest, avoiding people even when he went to raid for the supplies he could not make: blankets, salt, bread.

And combs and honey.

"You promised!" Diana said in despair.

"To stay away from people. Yes. There was no one there. And these were left," he said, pointing at the coins.

"Left?" Diana said.

"By the stones."

She knew the place. It was as close to civilization as he would let her go, and all their camps had been within a mile of it: three stones arranged in a rough triangle about nine feet apart. The tallest of them came no higher than Diana's shoulder, and they would have been easy to overlook as a natural formation, save for the fact that this part of England was not particularly rocky and their composition bore no resemblance to that of the local stones.

But who could be leaving silver coins there?

"That isn't the point," Diana said, knowing she'd lost the argument.

He laughed—a short fox-bark—and rose up to kiss her.

She held him against her, sealing his open mouth with her own and reaching greedily for his tongue. His skin was warm and smooth beneath her palms, and he made sounds of pleasure low in his throat as she stroked his back. The marks of his beating had healed quickly; all that was left now were swiftly fading scars.

Another time, their kiss would have escalated quickly into the loveplay that occupied much of their nights-turned-day, but he'd been gone since dusk and, at the moment, the spitted rabbits demanded the attention of an appetite of another sort. With a growl of genuine reluctance he released her and squatted by the fire to take the rabbits from the spit.

Diana had been starved so long in her captivity that food was always now of interest, even though Shadow's skills ensured that they always ate well. With deft motions of a whittled fire-spoon, she buried the stolen eggs to cook slowly in the embers and then crouched, watching him, as he wrapped one rabbit for later eating and disjointed the other into equal portions upon two curling trenchers of bark.

Diana touched her lips with her fingers. He was like a drug. His mouth on hers could make her forget anything, delay anything, abandon any plan. When he held her, when they made love, Diana lived entirely in the moment, without worries or fears or plans for the future. She suspected that Shadow lived in the moment always.

Who was he?

Or should the question really be, *what* was he? He did not belong anywhere in the textbook history of seventeenth-century England; the tale of Cavaliers and Roundheads and the English Civil War. Not this wild child, her forest lord.

He passed her one of the portions and then waited, with odd courtesy, to see that she ate. Grudging the moments it took the sizzling flesh to cool, Diana devoured it greedily. Shadow joined her, and soon there was nothing left of the carcass but picked bones. She sucked rabbit grease from her fingers and looked up to find him watching her with grave interest.

The question of what he was intruded again, and this time it wouldn't go away. Diana wiped her hands clean upon the grass. *Ask him,* she told herself. He would never hurt her; that much she knew, and trusted in it absolutely. In fact, he attended upon her with a single-minded devotion that bordered on worship. It made Diana faintly guilty when she thought about it. She had done nothing to deserve such love.

If that was what it was. If she knew the meaning of the word. She didn't even know if she loved him. All she knew was that every moment he was away from her ate at her heart with a fear like grief.

"So," Diana said. "I've been meaning to ask. Where are you from?" It wasn't the first time she'd asked these questions, but she'd never gotten answers, only kisses.

The determined brightness of her tone wavered toward shyness, falling awkwardly flat somewhere between. She looked away. The light was growing stronger. Soon it would be time to bury the fire and go to ground, hiding the day away.

He stared at her unreadably. *Why did she ask when she knew?* his expression seemed to say.

"I mean," Diana blundered on, "I don't know very much about you."

His steady gaze mocked her clumsy words. She had slept against his heart each day for a month; he had dared torture and death for her. And though she sought for it, she did not find anywhere within herself an equal gift of fidelity to give him in return.

Shadow wiped his hands clean against his thighs and reached for the comb. "Take down your hair," he said.

He did that sometimes—ignored what she said or countered it with a demand of his own. She didn't know if it were because he didn't know the answer or simply thought that the answer was obvious. It didn't matter. Diana was suddenly ashamed of her questions and wanted nothing more than to forget them.

She untied the length of cloth, and her hair in its unsecured braids fell forward around her face. Shadow moved behind her, lifting the tousled mass of it off her neck and painstakingly unbraiding it from the stalks of wildflowers, running the strands through his fingers until it fell loose and free.

The touch of his hands on her neck kindled a spark of arousal, of a desire whose embers were never extinguished; and Diana arched her back, thinking of his hands on her body.

Carefully he began to comb her hair, the elegant silver-and-tortoiseshell comb easing the tangles that had eluded Diana's impatient fingers.

"I come from . . . a place," he said softly minutes later, when Diana was lulled into a sensual reverie by the rhythmic movement of his hands on her hair and she was certain he'd forgotten the question.

The memory of the silver forest valley bloomed behind her eyes: a valley filled with silver mist, where Time could not come.

"What happened?" Diana asked, as softly as she could.

"I don't remember." There was a confused blur of nets and shouting in Diana's mind, and a child's terror, as vivid as if he'd spoken of it aloud.

"You'd gone hunting. There was some kind of trap," she suggested. Her heart ached, thinking of the forest child who had so innocently blundered into Man's world.

"They put me in a cage." The anger at that event so far in the past was still a harsh weight beneath the softness of his voice. "They said I was *daoine sidhe*. They took me away."

" 'Danna shee'?" Diana repeated blankly, distracted for the moment from her daydreams. It was a moment before she realized what she'd said. *Daoine sidhe*—the Fair Folk.

But the Fair Folk were . . . not a myth, exactly; but it was hard for Diana to reconcile the Celidhe Court, the fearsome lords of the Wild Hunt, with the strangely primitive existence that seemed so natural to Shadow—and besides, Wiccan tradition held that the Fair Folk had left the world of Men long before, in the early days of these islands' Christian conquest. Certainly long before the seventeenth century.

But if he weren't an erlking, a fay, an elf, what was he? Or was it her preconceptions that were at fault? Mistress Fortune had mistaken Diana for one of the Fair Folk when she'd first arrived—were they still in the world? Not creatures of fantasy after all, but an ancient clan, a survival of an earlier race as unrecorded by history as the witches themselves were? History, Diana mused, was written by the winners, most of whom in this time were city-dwelling, upper-class, male Protestants. It would be easy for them to overlook what it didn't suit them to remember.

The comb moved freely now through her hair in a slow soothing stroke, lulling her with the promise of pleasure to come, urging Diana just to *be,* without thought, without regrets.

"And now I will go home," Shadow said. "It lies west of here, across the sea."

"You mean Ireland," Diana said languidly. The pictures in his memories told her that much, combined with her twentieth-century knowledge. But were Shadow's childhood memories enough for him to find his way home?

"Ireland, then. And we will go there, thou and I, and live among my people in freedom once again."

But later, after he had loved her, it was only Shadow who found unquestioning oblivion in the aftermath of pleasure, not she. Diana lay awake, listening to the calm rhythm of his breathing as he lay curled against her, a boneless sleeping-panther weight, and the questions did not go away. He spoke so matter-of-factly of taking her with him to find his home and his people again. . . .

And she didn't know if she wanted to go.

Diana stared upward as the morning sun made the interwoven boughs above her head into a canopy of stars. West, across the sea—Ireland. The journey, while long, would not be impossible. They could walk as far as the coast; Diana's knowledge of English geography was shaky, but she thought the Irish Sea wasn't very wide and they could surely hire a boat somewhere to take them across it. There were no passports for them to worry about, no ID papers they would need to produce; they could buy—or steal—horses once they got to the other side, or even walk the rest of the way.

But she didn't want to go to Ireland. Diana wanted to go home.

She tried to remember home and all the familiar things of

her life, but Salem and her bookshop and her life in the twentieth century had all taken on a frightening remoteness, as if they were incidents in a story she'd read once a long time ago, an account unreal as fiction.

No, no, no . . . She turned and burrowed into Shadow's shoulder, trying to shut out the frightening truth.

She didn't know where she belonged anymore.

Diana was awakened an hour or two before sunset by the sounds that Shadow made moving about their campsite, readying them to relocate the camp. Diana kicked aside the blankets, reaching for her shawl and sitting up.

It was chilly here under the forest canopy. In a month's time, there would be frost, and what would they do then? Tying the shawl around her, she crawled out of the nest.

Her breakfast was waiting for her: cold rabbit, roasted eggs, and a mound of watercress and wild onion Shadow must have gathered today, all laid out neatly on a curl of bark. Diana found her skirt and tied it around her hips before picking up the food. She looked around, absently peeling an egg.

The traces of their fire were gone, dug under and carefully disguised with forest litter. The fruits of their scavenging were piled carefully together for loading. Once the blankets had been rolled up and added, their sleeping place disguised and the boughs he'd used to screen and line it scattered, they could go.

"Shadow?" Diana looked around for him and did not see him, though she had heard him only moments before. Finally she located him from the sounds and saw him pulling a log of deadfall timber into the clearing.

He had not painted himself today, and the green dye was wearing away from his skin, but he still looked like what he was—a forest lord, a wild thing not meant to be seen by human eyes.

When he saw she was awake he smiled and raised a hand in greeting before returning to his task. Diana smiled in return, finishing her breakfast quickly and turning to the matter of the blankets.

There were four of them: one brown, one gray, one woven with a green stripe, and one dyed a red that had faded to pink long before Shadow had stolen it. She folded that one inside the brown one and the stripe inside the gray before rolling them into bundles that she lashed together with another piece of carefully braided cord.

The preparations to move were a familiar thing and when they moved it was never very far, but what was acceptable and even fun in the warm days of St. Martin's summer would become a grim struggle for survival once winter came.

As she worked, Shadow filled in their sleeping-pit and dragged the fallen tree to cover the spot, then pulled the travois over to Diana.

"Where to?" she asked, knowing he would have scouted the place the day before. He could see in the dark as well as any cat; it was a part of being . . . what he was.

"Not far," he promised, as he always did. "It will be safe."

It will be safe. It was an odd thing for him to say, but she understood it after they had been walking awhile and the forest thinned to allow her glimpses of bushes and the meadow beyond. The thought of venturing out of the forest into the open land filled her with a reflexive apprehension, a leftover from the terrifying days of captivity. Why were they coming so close to the edge of the forest, where anyone might see them?

She had her answer a few moments later when he dropped the poles of the travois and gestured proudly.

"A pool!" Diana ran over to it.

It was deep and perfect—a spot where the brook had, by accident or design, become broad and deep enough to swim in. It had been dammed to back it up, and the water spilled over the sticks and stones of the dam with a purling chuckle. Even at this hour, sunlight still dappled the pond's surface;

Diana glanced at the unobstructed vista of blue sky above and
dipped a cautious toe into the water. Cool, yes, but the sun had
been shining down on it all day. It would be warm enough.

"Do you like it?" Shadow asked, coming to stand beside
her.

"It's perfect," Diana said honestly.

She had been able to bathe several times in their journey
and even wash her hair. Shadow was fastidious in that regard
and bathed even when the cold would have given Diana second
thoughts, but the procedure had involved a small tin pot and
a lot of laborious standing and pouring. The streams and springs
they'd found had all been shallow, nothing she could immerse
herself in. When she thought about it, Diana could not remember
the last time she'd been able to take a real bath.

"Here is a present for thee," Shadow said, holding out his
hand.

On his palm rested a cake of soap, perfumed and white and
stamped with an elaborate monogram. He must have taken it
when he stole the comb and saved it for this moment.

Again she felt the desperate clutch of tenderness at her heart.
She took the soap from him and rose up on tiptoe to kiss his
mouth. "You can scrub my back," she offered provocatively.

He smiled and began untying the cords that held his knife
and loincloth in place.

The crisp shock of the water as she plunged into it made
Diana whoop. Just as she surfaced—the pool was five-feet
deep, if that, at its deepest part—Shadow jumped in after her,
with more enthusiasm than skill, drenching her all over again.

They sported like otters. Diana had accepted Shadow's assur-
ances of her safety with unquestioning trust and splashed noisily
through the water, scooping handfuls of it to throw at him,
squealing in feigned dismay when he dove beneath the water
to pounce upon her in mock attack.

Finally, warm and panting from her exertions, Diana waded
back to shore to retrieve the soap. The last light of day would

be gone soon, and the water was cold enough to make her not want to linger; it was time to move on, to set up their camp.

After she'd had her bath.

Diana held the soap high over her head as she walked back out to him, as though she were afraid to get it wet. Shadow dealt with that simply, tackling her and dragging her under; and when they surfaced again, it was he who held the soap.

"I will scrub your back," he said with satisfaction.

He ran the soap over her skin and rubbed the shining track it left behind until his fingers slid through the creamy lather as if it were oil, through her hair, over her shoulders, her belly, her breasts. . . .

She stood quietly, letting him caress her; but for once the inevitable response of desire that warmed her at his touch wasn't an answer, but another question: What was she going to do?

What was she going to do with *him?*

She pulled away finally, ducking quickly beneath the water to rinse herself and then rising to claim the soap from his hand. She would not think of the future now, she promised herself; but as the soap in her hand glided over his body, washing away the last of the green, leaving his skin warm and pale and clean beneath her hands, the question she had managed to avoid for so long refused to be set aside again.

What were they going to do? What was she going to do with him? It was 1647; England was about to settle into a decade or so of uneasy Commonwealth, followed by the Glorious Restoration and the reign of Charles II, and none of her sketchy knowledge of the next few years was any help at all. She and Shadow were fugitives, probably wanted by the law—and even if they weren't, where could they go? Diana could not think of a single place that would take both her and Shadow in.

And even if such a utopia existed, she didn't want to go there. She wanted to go home. Home, home, *home* . . .

She wanted to stop thinking. Diana wrapped her arms around Shadow, pressing herself against him on the excuse of soaping his back. His hands rested on her hips; he dropped his head to nuzzle at her shoulder and rubbed his jaw against it in wordless communion. She rubbed herself against him, their soapy skins sliding over each other, the frictionless touch slowly creating its own heat.

Pressed against him as she was, Diana felt the moment his muscles tensed with alarm, felt the unsettled surprise that spilled from his mind into hers. Carefully he pushed her away, sliding from her embrace and sinking down into the water. Only his head showed above the surface as he moved toward the shore, his gaze still fixed on something behind her.

Shadow's silent, deliberate advance upon whatever he'd seen behind her was the stuff of which nightmares were made, and nothing—not even Hopkins himself with a band of mounted militia and a loaded cannon—could be as frightening as her imaginings. Gulping down her fear, Diana turned, trying to make as little noise in the water as Shadow did.

She was ready to be shocked, ready to be terrified, but what she saw in the clear blue light of the October dusk was . . . nothing.

No, not quite nothing. As her eyes adjusted, she could see movement beyond the tangled screen of trees. There was something there—not a deer. Not from Shadow's response to it.

From the corner of her eye, she saw the white flicker of Shadow's body as he slunk swiftly past her on the bank. Diana saw the knife in his hand—a faint, silvery flicker—as she stared unblinkingly at the movement through the trees, the swing and flutter of the gray skirt hem.

Skirt hem . . .

A person. A woman.

Gray skirt hem, somehow familiar, dipping and bobbing through the trees . . .

"Wait!" Diana sucked air into her aching lungs for the shout even before she moved. "Wait!" she cried again, floundering forward out of the water. "No!"

She was nearly too late. By the time she broke through the trees into the clearing beyond, Shadow was already there, half-risen from his crouch before the kneeling woman, with the knife bare in his hand.

"Don't kill her!" Diana cried, grabbing his free arm to pull him back. "She's a friend!"

"A friend?" Shadow straightened and stood up, unconscious of his nakedness. His muscles were still hard with tension. He seemed willing to believe Diana but wasn't entirely certain she knew what she was talking about. "A friend to us?" he demanded of the intruder.

"The covenant stands thy friend, Shining One, as thee knows." The woman rose stiffly to her feet, brushing dirt from the skirt of her gray dress, and looked past Shadow to Diana.

"Ah, Mistress Diana. Did I not say thy own would come for thee out of the Hollow Hills?" Mistress Fortune asked.

Diana had not recognized the Talitho coven's dancing ground from the direction that they had approached it, nor had she realized until now that the pool that they had bathed in belonged to the same stream she had drunk from her first morning here. Mistress Fortune crossed the stream with them, waiting beside the pool while Diana rubbed herself quickly dry with one of the blankets and then dressed.

Diana kept darting glances at her mentor. She'd been so certain Abigail Fortune was dead, killed in the Lammas Night attack on the coven, or dead in prison thereafter, that to see her here, alive and whole, was a constant series of shocks.

"What are you doing here? What happened?" Diana asked helplessly.

"I did but come to see that all was well for the dancing—"

"No!" Diana burst out in mingled frustration and relief. "What happened to *you?* Hopkins . . . those men—"

She took a step toward Mistress Fortune. Behind her, Shadow noiselessly retreated, stopping at the edge of the trees to gather together the materials for a fire. Mistress Fortune regarded the two of them steadily—an act of bravery, since Diana knew that the older woman believed with absolute certainty that both Diana and Shadow were Fair Folk from the Hollow Hills with powers beyond mortal comprehension.

"I thought you were dead," Diana finished helplessly.

Mistress Fortune turned her head and spat. "I take more killing than the likes of Hopkins could manage. Nay, I ran, as did all of us who could, and stayed well-hidden until Master Hopkins was well away about his mischief elsewhere. And now that he is dead—"

"Dead?" Diana echoed blankly. "Matthew Hopkins is dead?"

She ought to feel something—some triumph, some vindication or relief. But all she felt was a curious blankness, as if she looked into a part of herself that ought to contain something, and didn't.

"Aye—swum as a witch at Christchurch with his own tricks and died of it before the warrant laid against him could be acted upon. T'was our own pastor, Edmund Conyngham, who was there and bears witness and saw the body laid on the dead-cart. They'll bury him at Manningtree, though whether within the churchyard or outside remains to be seen."

To be "swum as a witch," the accused was tied hand and foot and thrown into the nearest large body of water to see if he floated. Floating, supposedly, was an infallible proof that the innocent was a Witch; Diana knew that there were ways to arrange for the victim to float—or drown.

"So everything . . ." Was all right now? Was that what she meant to say, when she knew how many had died even before the day of the trial? "What about Sterne? What about the other prisoners?" Diana asked instead, trying to rally her emotions into a rational order.

"Those who were taken up are freed, their confessions set aside by the warrant that Judge Merriam did bring from London to accuse Master Hopkins." Mistress Fortune shrugged. "Pastor Conyngham did not bring news of Sterne, nor of Goody Phillips, but I think they may lie quiet and low for many a year to come, now that thou hast exposed Hopkins's villainy."

Chapter 18

The New Forest,
October 30, 1647

Mistress Fortune had stayed only a few moments longer, promising to return in the morning to bring supplies and the Magister's word on when the coven would meet. She was anxious to leave and Diana did not keep her; she already owed Abigail Fortune a debt greater than any she could ever repay.

When Mistress Fortune was gone, Diana and Shadow stared at each other across the fire. Most of their jackdaw's hoard of possessions still lay piled on the travois Shadow had built. The blanket Diana had used to dry herself was flung carelessly over the lot: a bottle, a tin pot, a spoon, some green-tanned hides, some stolen clothing. What had seemed a treasure trove only a few hours before was reduced by the meeting with Mistress Fortune to . . . junk. A pitiful collection of oddments, even by the standards of Talitho—the gleanings of a seventeenth-century bag lady.

No one could live this way. It had been stupid of them even to try.

Diana's eyes filled with tears, but this time Shadow did not move to comfort her and soothe them away, as if he already understood the depth of her betrayal.

''Don't look at me like that,'' Diana snapped. At once he dropped his eyes and turned his head away. The promptness of his compliance only fed her angry guilt. ''Stop it,'' she said. ''Don't *humor* me.''

Shadow said nothing, only rising silently to his feet and moving away. Going to get more wood for the fire, Diana supposed. She stood and stared into the flames. Her eyes ached and burned, but the tears did not come freely.

''It isn't even going to work, probably,'' she told the fire, then reversed herself almost at once. ''It's my last chance. Don't I have the right to go home?''

''Go home,'' Shadow echoed from behind her. ''To *thy* home?''

She wasn't surprised to find he'd circled around behind her. It was part of what he was—he approached nothing straight-on; everything was oblique, subjective. She turned and looked up at him. His eyes caught the firelight, glowing redly. Alien.

Every time she thought she'd accepted his difference, she found she'd only managed to forget it. Each time she was reminded of it, there was the same faint, unpleasant shock.

Home. Alone? Perhaps it was only her imagination and not his thoughts that supplied the next question.

''You could come with me,'' she offered reluctantly. ''Back to the future. If it'll work for one, it will work for two.''

But would it? Another time warp would only send her back where she belonged in the first place: Could she carry someone who'd never been there into the future just as the coven's Great Book had carried her into the past?

And if she could, how would a creature of deep woods and forests adjust to the asphalt jungle of twentieth-century Salem?

''No.'' His refusal was quietly firm. ''I will go home.''

Home. The pain and longing in that last word was enough to make responsive tears well up in Diana's eyes once more.

''Yes,'' she whispered. *Go home to your silver valley, Shadow. Be safe and happy there.*

He put his hands on her shoulders, and she leaned back against him, putting her hands up to cover his.

"And thou wilt go to *thy* home," he finished for her, his voice flat, "and not with me. But thou art mine. Thee belongs to me—thou saidst so." There was a long pause. Shadow drew his hands from beneath hers and stepped away.

"But thou didst not promise," he finished bitterly.

When Diana turned around, he was gone.

She realized the futility of running around the woods shouting for Shadow to come back almost at once. If he didn't want to be seen, he could disappear inches in front of her face and she would never find him. Diana cast about for another half an hour, telling herself she was only gathering fuel for the fire and not looking for him, but at last her arms were full and she went back to sit by the small fire. It seemed she sat for hours, wrapped in the blankets and feeding its flames automatically from the pile of sticks she had gathered.

"But thou didst not promise." The quiet finality of those words made her heart ache: sentence and judgment and acceptance of her treason all in one.

I'm sorry. Diana hung her head. Her eyes ached with unshed tears. *Sorry, sorry, sorry . . .* The words spiraled around within her head in a meaningless, lonely ache. She'd *never* told him she'd go with him to Ireland!

"Thou didst not promise."

He didn't really want her anyway, she told herself. He really just wanted to go home. Diana took a deep breath, gulping down the heartache as if it were tainted food.

How did she know if she loved him if she didn't know what love was? How would he get to Ireland and home without her help?

Diana closed her eyes and rocked back and forth in sheer misery. It was almost impossible to imagine Shadow travelling across England alone, walking into Liverpool, buying a passage to Ireland. He'd never be able to pass for a native Englishman. Even as Upright-Before-The-Lord Makepeace, he'd been . . . eccentric, and the ghost of Upright was long-exorcised from

Shadow of the Shining Ones. He could not pass for human. He could not get home without her help.

But if I don't go back to Salem tomorrow, I won't get another chance, she moaned to herself. Tomorrow was Samhain. Tomorrow the coven would raise the power to send her back where she'd come from. It would be her last and only chance.

She could get Pastor Conyngham to help Shadow find his home. The compromise was unsatisfactory even to Diana, but it was better than nothing and she could see no other way; even if the time-travel spell didn't work, she didn't think Shadow would want her back.

"Thou didst not promise. . . ."

She could explain everything, Diana thought hopefully. She could make everything all right if she could just talk to him. But she waited until all her firewood had burned and the moon was gone from the sky, and still Shadow did not come back.

Shadow prowled through the woods all night, trying to understand what she had done so casually, without a word of warning to him. These woods were familiar to him now; he knew the places for rabbits and watercress, for mushrooms and herbs, clean water and brack: a good hunting ground, a good living-place, if only it were not so near to Man's world.

And it was not home.

How could she do what she had done? He tried to understand; but when he thought about her actions, they made less sense, not more. She was his *righ-malkin;* she belonged to him, and he to her. How could she leave him? Her body and her mind both acknowledged their bond, and still she said she would go away from him, to a place he could not follow.

How could she say one thing and do another? His own folk could not lie; the act itself was an amazing thing, nearly unimaginable. In his captivity he had learned to do it, though badly, and he would gladly have forgotten how. But humans lied as easily as they breathed, changing the shape of the very world with their casual words, as if alone of all Her creation, the Bright Lady had not laid upon them the duty to see and to witness and to tell the truth.

He had believed *di'anu* when she had said she belonged to him, and now she planned to set her words aside as if they were casual things. *She was going to leave him.*

He thought of going into the village, of finding Mistress Fortune and taking from her a promise that she would not help his *righ-malkin* to leave tomorrow night. But he knew in his heart that it would do no good, even if he had faith any longer in a child of Man's ability to keep her word. It was *di'anu's* will that she leave him, not Mistress Fortune's.

Why? He had done nothing to make her cast him out. He had fed her and kept her and made a home for her; there was no other whose touch she preferred to his—yet she would leave him.

It made no sense.

He flung back his head and sang his confusion and despair to the Bright Lady in the sky. The thin, wavering cry rose into the chill October night, then faded and died, finding no echo save in the scattered barking of distant dogs. It was the autumn, the Dying Time, when his folk danced so the Dark would come to give birth to the New Year. They danced even here, these Man-children to whom his people had given the secrets and the dancing so long ago.

At home they would dance tomorrow night, dancing in the New Year, building fires upon the hills to welcome their kindred, the dead who rode the wind and brought the Dark. A longing to be home filled him—and a fear that home might be there no longer, destroyed somehow in the years he'd been away.

But in the end his thoughts always came back to *her.* Diana. *Di'anu.* She belonged to him; she was his *righ-malkin.* He had fed her; she was his—and she said she would leave him.

The moon had set when he walked soft footed into the clearing where she lay sleeping, bundled insecurely into the blankets without a proper bed to comfort her, her face drawn by unquiet dreams. His heart ached with the need to cherish her. He reached out his hand and brushed a strand of bright, tumbled hair from her forehead. She stirred, but did not wake.

He could dazzle her, lay the waking dream upon her until she moved to his will and not her own, take her away from here tonight and be miles away before the moon rose tomorrow and the Dancing Time began. It was his *right* to take her with him to his home and keep her.

He reached for her again. A touch—that would be all he would need to weave such a spell around her mind and body that would let him carry her away from here, far beyond the coven's reach. He could not hold the enchantment long, but a day would be enough. She would not go. She would be his to do with as he would.

Only a touch.

He could not do it. It was his right; it was his duty by the only law he recognized, and he could not do it. He had been a captive among strangers for too long to ever hold another being prisoner.

He drew back his hand. She was free to go where she chose.

But Shadow's heart was filled with fear that she would make the wrong choice.

There had not been a carefully constructed canopy to sleep beneath when Diana finally abandoned her vigil, and so the morning sun awoke her after only a few hours of troubled sleep.

Diana sat up, the echoes of the latest nightmare fading as she opened her eyes. She winced with the stiffness that came from a night of sleeping in her clothes on the hard ground with only a few blankets for padding and rolled stiffly over onto her stomach.

"Shadow?" Diana whispered. But there was no answer.

She sat up. The pool where they had bathed yesterday was covered with a heavy white mist. It hung above the surface of the water-like steam. The lighter ground mist had already been dispelled by the sun, but the day had not yet melted the season's heavy dew; it made the ground silvery so that footprints showed dark against it.

Diana got to her feet, clutching the blankets around her and shivering in the early-morning cold. The terrain around the pond was relatively open—in the deep forest she would have been warmer, in a sheltered nest lined in blankets with Shadow beside her to warm her. Diana looked down at the twisting line of footprints that showed plain against dew-silvered ground. The tracks crossed the stream and passed near where she had lain sleeping before turning back on themselves and wending away again.

Someone had been here.

Diana's heart pounded with the automatic panic of a wild animal. Someone had been here. Who? What did they want? Should she call out for Shadow or stay quiet? Was the intruder still here somewhere, lurking?

Suddenly Diana realized she was shaking, clutching the blanket around herself so hard her fingers hurt. Waves of reasonless irresistible terror washed through her. Someone had been here. . . . Someone had been here. . . .

Suddenly Shadow appeared through the trees, running crouched low to the ground, summoned by the terror she felt. When he saw Diana was alone he stopped, obviously puzzled to find no enemy in sight. She pointed toward the footprints on the ground, shaking too hard to speak.

He understood at once, backing up in his own tracks and circling around, vanishing again among the trees. Diana stood where she was, her heart slowly resuming its normal rhythm now that help had arrived. She swallowed hard and took a deep breath, willing herself calm. There was no danger—and if there were, Shadow would be able to handle it. She was safe.

Rationally, Diana knew that both her lingering nightmares and the panic attacks were relics of her torture and imprisonment at the hands of Matthew Hopkins. Over time these emotional seizures would fade and she would be all right. But she would never be the same woman she had been before all this had happened.

There was an ostentatious crackling of twigs as Shadow returned. He was carrying a large basket in his arms, one of the tall cylindrical sort that Diana had seen used as backpacks or saddlebags here. The basket lid flopped open untidily, evidence that he had already investigated and knew what it contained.

Shadow set it carefully at her feet, as though it were fragile, and opened the lid. Diana could tell he was amused, but could not fathom the reason for it.

Oh.

There was a loaf of rye bread studded with currants, a silver goblet, a wedge of cheese and a meat pie, a stone jug of cider. . . .

"Offerings," Shadow said, as if this were an explanation.

"Mistress Fortune!" Diana exclaimed.

"She did come and bring thee provision, as she did pledge," Shadow admitted.

Mistress Fortune had done far more than that, Diana realized as she unpacked the hamper. Beneath the food, there were clothes—a dress and underclothing for Diana, a coat and breeches for Shadow. He sneered when he saw them, a silent expression of scorn.

"Don't give me that," Diana said, holding the green wool dress up against herself to check the fit. "You'll be glad enough to have them on the way to Ireland."

The quick look of hope he darted at her was enough to destroy all her joy in the morning. He thought she'd changed her mind.

"Whoever you end up going with," Diana added quickly. "I mean, you're going to have to be able to try to pass as a—"

The look of betrayal on his face was too much for Diana to bear. She gave up the sentence and let it drop. Shadow looked away. To cover her shame, Diana turned back to the basket.

Shoes and knitted stockings. Mistress Fortune must have tithed the entire coven to gather these things together; there were far too many items—and far too rich—for them to have been all her own gift.

Shadow stood watching as she unpacked in a silence more eloquent than words. Diana's cheeks burned. She refused to look at him.

It wasn't fair that she felt so guilty. She couldn't go with him, she told herself as she dug down to the bottom layer. The last things in the basket were two leather-wrapped packets.

Concentrating fiercely on them to keep from thinking of anything else, Diana reached in and lifted them out. She could feel the shapes through the thin leather that wrapped them: a large ring, heavy for its size, and some kind of beads, oddly light. . . .

The morning light shone down on the ring as Diana shook its wrapping free. The sun's rays struck blindingly off the glistening yellow surface of a necklet of pure gold.

It was in the style the Celts called a *torc*—a hollow tubular shape of chaced and twisted gold, bent in a circle and ending in two finials of stylized dragons that snarled at each other across an inch-wide gap.

It was priceless—an antique even three-and-a-half centuries before Diana's own time.

Why had they given it to her?

Shadow lifted the torc gently from her hand and stared at it intently. With uttermost caution, already suspecting what she would find, Diana opened the second bundle. Its contents were as familiar to her as the silver pentacle she once had worn.

It was a necklace. The beads were large, round, and acorn sized, polished smooth. Half of them were as black as Shadow's hair, their surfaces showing the iridescent rainbows of oil-slicks and ravens' wings. They alternated with beads the bright straw color of crystallized sunlight.

Amber. And the black stones were jet. It was an amber-and-jet necklace, distant ancestor to the one Diana wore in her coven. But when the coven had met here, she had not seen anyone at the regular wearing such a necklace, not even the woman who had acted as the Maiden.

"Di'anu." She thought Shadow was speaking to her, but when she looked up, he was staring at the necklace in her hands. He stretched out his fingers to touch it, then picked it up.

"Di'anu," Shadow said again, sliding the beads through his fingers. The amber glowed in the sunlight, and the jet glittered darkly. *"Diw—di'anu."*

"What do you mean? Shadow? Do you know why she gave them to us?" Diana said.

From his expression, he seemed to feel that he'd already made a complete explanation. He sighed faintly at her look of puzzlement and groped for the words he needed. *"Diw,"* he said, holding up the torc. *"Di'anu."* The necklace.

"The Lord and the Lady," Diana said slowly. "But why give them to us?"

"So that they may go home again beneath the Hill," Shadow said. Ignoring Diana's automatic yelp of protest, he twisted the golden torc open and fitted it around his neck. The metal glowed against his skin like sunlight on water.

He held out his hand, and for a moment he seemed to be about to ask for the necklace as well. Diana clasped it against herself, unconsciously unwilling to relinquish such a beautiful thing. Shadow dropped his hand and turned away, walking off into the woods.

Frustration and resentment made a cold weight in Diana's chest. Why did he have to show his feelings so plainly? Why couldn't he be happy for her? She wanted to go home; was that such a crime? He wasn't being reasonable. She'd never said she'd stay with him.

"Thou didst not promise. . . ."

Diana aimed a furious kick at the empty basket. It was too lightweight to provide a satisfactory target; when her foot struck it, it simply toppled over and rolled a few feet away. Diana sat down on the blankets.

If she could be sure of getting a second chance to go home, she would be glad to escort Shadow to the ends of the earth first. *He* was homesick. Why couldn't he understand that she wanted to go home, too? It wasn't fair that she should have so little time to make a choice that was so irrevocable. It wasn't as if they could date or she could change her mind later.

I have as much of a right to go home as you do, Diana told the empty clearing, but saying so didn't leave her feeling any better. *It's tonight or nothing. Stay or go. No turning back.*

If only she could be sure that what she was doing was right.

There was no solution. She felt cross and uncomfortable with missed sleep and the feeling she'd lost her own good opinion of herself. Finally she uncorked the jug and poured the silver cup full of Mistress Fortune's cider. The drink seemed to help, making the problem less urgent even if it didn't solve anything.

A cup of cider also seemed to restore her appetite, and Diana breakfasted in solitary splendor on rye bread and mutton pie, scrupulously putting half of everything aside for Shadow, just as he would have for her. She folded up the suit of men's clothes and put it back into the basket and wrapped the necklace up in the leather and tucked it in on top. The dress and underclothes lay in a pile on the blankets. The sun was high overhead now, but there was a coolness in the air that hadn't been there a few weeks before. Winter was coming.

Diana looked at the clothes—smock and stay, bumroll and petticoats, even knitted wool stockings and stout leather shoes. And a cap of fine white linen with an embroidered whitework pattern running around the edge. Finer clothing than any she had worn here yet.

She ought to put them on. They'd be warmer than the make-shifts she was wearing—and certainly more seemly for appearing back in twentieth-century downtown Salem in.

Thinking about the timeslip made Diana remember other things that she didn't want to leave behind here. She hunted around until she found a digging stick and walked back across the stream to the dancing ground. It took her a few tries to find the spot where the turves were loose—where the fire was laid on dancing nights—but once she did, she began to dig. After a strenuous hour's work she had them—the things Mistress Fortune had buried for her when Diana had first come here.

Her clothes. Diana held up the ragged remains of the orange silk blouse and the black wool slacks. They seemed skimpier than she remembered, less well made, and were ruined past possibility of wearing them anyway. She set them aside and dug down for the rest. Wadded up in her underwear she found her watch, still running—*"Takes a licking and keeps on ticking,"* as the Timex people were so fond of saying—her gold crescent earrings, and her silver pentacle.

Diana held up the tiny circled star. So stupid that people should have to die for this. Diana unhooked the clasp with awkward fingers and hooked the pendant around her neck. But that was over now. She was going back where witch-hunters were the stuff of Saturday-night horror films, where—at least in Massachusetts—people didn't have to die because of their religion anymore.

Diana put in her earrings and buckled on her watch, telling herself that this meant her decision was made beyond regret. It was the sensible choice. It was the *only* choice. When she was finished, she bundled up the rags of her clothes and went back across the stream.

The basket, the clothes, and all of the blankets were gone; only the half-loaf of rye bread remained, buried in the leaves as if it had been kicked. She wondered what he hadn't liked about it and then gave up wondering when she saw the small spark of a fire a few yards deeper into the woods. When she reached the fire, she found Shadow squatting beside it.

The gold torc gleamed against his white, unpainted skin, and his hair was braided back and studded with feathers. His scars were only a faint uneven pattern against his back now, hard to see unless you looked for them. He was intent on his work.

There were piles of herbs lying on a cloth beside him, the fruits of his morning's gathering. The tin pot that had been the dearest prize of their scavenging expeditions was placed close to the fire, warming the liquid it held. From time to time Shadow poked at the pot's contents with a spoon. Diana recognized the recipe from the smell; he was brewing another batch of the skin-dye he used to make himself invisible in the forest.

"Fat lot of good that's going to do you with Tiffany's show-room window hanging around your neck," Diana muttered. She shook out a couple of blankets from the pile and spread them on the ground before the fire, seating herself where she could share its heat. Shadow pretended not to hear her. His artless sulking made Diana want to laugh and cry at the same time. Why couldn't he be happy for her?

Maybe someday he'd understand.

Diana watched as he blended powdered charcoal, soot caught on the inside of the tin pan, animal fat, and crushed plants into a thick viridian sludge, and slowly it came to Diana what she was actually seeing.

"Eye of newt and toe of frog, wool of bat, and tongue of dog . . ." Herbs, fat, soot . . . the recipe for the Sabbat ointment that witches used was the same as that of the salve Shadow used to vanish into the forest.

Why? What was the connection between Shadow's people and the Wicca?

It didn't matter, Diana told herself brutally. It was just another question she wasn't going to be around to ask.

Chapter 19

The New Forest, Samhain 1647

By the time the salve was cooked to Shadow's satisfaction—thirty-five minutes, Diana had a wrist watch now to time it exactly—her feelings had turned from sorrow to anger. Once again Shadow had managed to go away from her without leaving, vanishing inside himself where she could not follow. Diana missed him. She missed the easy comradeship of the previous weeks they'd spent here in the forest. She was tired of being ignored.

"I need to talk to you," Diana said when he'd set the unguent aside to cool.

Shadow glanced up at her from beneath his lashes, a sullen stubborn anger about his mouth. "Aye—wilt talk to me, and then wilt leave me," he said.

"Why won't you be reasonable? I don't have any choice!" Diana cried. It was too close to the truth to make pleasant hearing. She flung herself to her feet. "If I don't go now, there won't be another chance. I'll make sure you get home. Tonight, I'll talk to the coven, and they'll—" She hated herself for babbling on this way, as if he were a spurned lover she could buy off with favors.

"I will have no more of Man's promises. I will make my own way, with no help from such as they," Shadow said brusquely. He picked up the pan and dipped a finger into the liquid, testing its temperature. Shutting her out.

Unfairly, his withdrawal made her want to hurt him, as if something inside her selfishly demanded a devotion from him that she would not provide herself.

"You'll be caught," Diana said. "You'll never make it. They'll—"

She stopped, her imagination failing. He was an adult now, not a frightened boy. She could not imagine what the good people of England would do to Shadow if they caught him—Shadow, with his green-dyed skin and wolf-glowing eyes, wearing only a loincloth and a fortune in gold about his neck.

"You might consider looking at it from my point of view," Diana muttered rebelliously.

Shadow lifted his gaze from the pan and stared directly at her. In the morning sunlight the firelight gilded the black amber of his eyes, making them seem to burn.

"Thou dost not want me," he said simply.

"No!" Diana protested before she thought.

She was leaving; wouldn't it be better for him to think she didn't care? Kinder? *I love you,* her mind said, but she did not say the words aloud. He would not understand how she could leave him if it were true.

But love was not kind, Diana was discovering. Not kind, not easy, not gentle. Love demanded, and love hurt. And somehow she could not bear to lie to Shadow, even though the truth seemed infinitely crueller.

"That isn't true. I do . . . want you. But I want to go home, too," she said plaintively. "My whole *life* is there, and—You don't understand. How could you? But it's the future; we have cars and doctors and indoor plumbing—"

Suddenly it seemed unbearably stupid—saying she was rejecting the man who loved her, the man that she loved, for flush toilets. "This isn't my home," Diana whispered.

"The past is a foreign country; they do things differently

there.'' Diana thought of spending the rest of her life in an alien land, cut off from every safe familiar thing, and knew she wasn't strong enough to face it. She was a coward. If the time she had spent in this century had taught her anything, it had taught her that. She was afraid. *Afraid.*

''I don't belong here. I belong there,'' Diana said in a dull voice.

Shadow regarded her for a long moment over the flames. ''Thou belongs with me. It is time that thee left the home of thy childhood and fashioned a home for thyself. With me.''

Diana hung her head, unable to share his simple certainty. *I can't. I'm afraid.* ''You want me to give up everything I have to go chasing *your* dream,'' she said. ''You want me to go running off after your Hollow Hills. At least I know *my* home exists.''

She was instantly ashamed. No matter how much she hurt, it was not fair to taunt him.

''It may be that I do not find it again or that my people have all gone,'' Shadow said evenly, admitting what must be his worst fear. ''If that is so, if the Hills are empty, then I and thou will make a life together as the Lady wills. But I would take thee there, if I can. It is not right to be alone, nor would I leave thee naked to the winter's snows.''

Diana shook her head silently, brushing his words aside. He did not understand. He never would. She was afraid; she did not have the courage it took to survive in his world, and someday he would hate her for it.

That was what she could not face. If she left him now, a part of her could always believe in his love.

''Do I offer thee so little?'' Shadow rose from beside the fire and came to stand behind her. His breath was warm upon her cheek. Diana turned her face toward him, and his lips brushed hers. ''I offer thee all I am,'' he said against her mouth.

A wild desperation seized her then, a blind denial of even the possibility of the bereavement to come. This would be the last she ever had of him, one final memory to keep when he was gone. She wanted to fill her heart and her senses with him, make these hours a treasure house of memory that could last her the rest of her life. Diana turned toward him and opened her mouth against his.

He tasted of fruit and woodsmoke, of the green savor of the forest. Tears made Diana's eyes burn as she put her arms around him. She felt the warmth of smooth skin and muscle that shifted and slid beneath her hands as he breathed, the faint roughness of fading scars. She wanted the man in her arms as if he were the air that sustained her, the food that nourished her—this elvish creature of moonlight and mist, a welcome, solid, living weight in her arms. Why couldn't she tell him she would stay? She loved him. She would always love him.

But would she love him when she was irrevocably marooned in an alien culture among people who had lived and died before she'd been born? Could she keep their love alive through the grinding dailiness of being together in unimaginable circumstances, through disillusionment and misunderstandings? Could she bear the possibility that someday he might not love her, that in coming to know her she might disappoint him?

I love you, Diana thought. *I love you, but I can't face that. I'm not strong enough. I love you—but I'm afraid.*

"I would thou saw my world," Shadow said, his voice a soft whisper against her neck, "and saw what I have to give thee."

His hand slid up her body beneath the cover of the shawl, curving around her ribs to cup her breast.

Diana arched against him as his thumb circled, seeking out the sensitive flesh of the nipple and brushing across it. Her whole body tightened as a pang of pleasure flickered through her. Her breath caught, and it seemed as if there were no air in her lungs. She felt the pressure of his hand against her skin as he curled his fingers and brushed the knuckles gently back and forth against her breast, content simply to begin the slow kindling of her flesh that would end in ecstasy, to destroy the future and the past, and leave only now and forever.

He bent his neck, leaning forward to nuzzle at the softness

of her throat. "I shall show thee wonders," he whispered against her skin.

But what she expected next did not come. He released her and turned away, lowering himself to the blanket and motioning her to join him.

When she was sitting beside him, he reached for her shawl, untying it and pushing it from her shoulders. In the sheltered grove and close by the fire she was warm enough, but Diana was hungry for the heat of his body against her own, the caresses that would blot out all thought.

"Now I will show thee," Shadow said. He reached for the tin pot, dipping his fingers into the mixture it contained and reaching out toward her.

His fingers slid down over the curve of her breast, leaving a glistening green trail behind. The touch of the oil on her skin was almost frighteningly intense; and when his fingers found her nipple, the pleasure it gave her made her cry out and jerk away.

"Concerning the matter of that elixir which commonly is held to bestow and confer the grant of invisibility," Shadow said, his words echoing some unknown treatise on sorcery, "it must be understood that the operator not only rendereth his self invisible, but by his craft sojourns in realms formerly invisible, made manifest to him by this same elixir."

He would not let her escape his attentions; each time she retreated, he advanced until Diana could withdraw no farther, only watch as his oiled fingers glided over the pink, puckered tips of her breasts, slipping in circles about the sensitive flesh, rolling the aching, engorged peaks between thumb and forefinger. With each repeated passage of his fingers over her skin, the glistening trails he left darkened as if they were being overlaid layer by emerald layer with the thinnest wash of watercolor, painting her with the colors of the forest.

"And what happens then?" Diana asked breathlessly. Her flesh tingled warmly where the salve had sunk into it, seeming to burn with a separate heat. She could feel her pulse beating just beneath the skin.

"Those barriers which exist in the visible world are dissolved, and all things seen and unseen are made manifest," Shadow said.

He took her hand and dipped the fingertips into the oil and placed them against his chest. Diana slid her fingers over the hard pad of muscle, then pressed her palm hard against him. She could feel his heart beat against her hand.

I don't want to leave you. Don't let me leave you. She arched against him, wanting the reassurance of his kiss. He put his hands on her shoulders, his hands slippery with oil, gliding over her skin. His lips gently brushed her mouth.

Her breasts tingled where they brushed against his chest; they felt swollen and heavy, almost unbearably sensitive, and she was reduced to heat and ache and liquid arousal, wanting a consolation she could not give in return.

His hands moved down to her waist, loosening the ties of her skirt until it slid loosely down over her hips. He traced a line down her body from her breasts to the dimple of her navel, then raised his hand and ran his fingers over her lips.

The sharp flavor of the liquid seemed to strike through all her senses at once. It was in her nose and mouth, a green scent bright and bitter and curiously sweet, tingling along her tongue. When she opened her mouth against the taste, he touched his oiled fingers to her tongue. The ticklish contact made her recoil; he smiled to see her reaction and she smiled bashfully in return.

"Only let me show thee," he said, his body urging hers backward.

He slid slowly into her, his body bringing with it an unfamiliar sensation of oil and green heat. He was slick where she clasped him between her thighs, and his body slid over hers like a falcon skimming the winds of heaven. When he kissed her, Diana tasted the forest—sorcery and alchemy from the inward life of plants, intoxicants sinking through her skin into her blood, into her breath, making her one with the forest. The roughness of the blanket beneath her back, the fire's uneven heat, dissolved to nothingness as her consciousness expanded, making her a part of everything that lived.

Shadow touched her as if he knew this was the last time, as if he knew this one afternoon must last them both forever. The slow conflagration that grew from their coupling bore them both upward on its wildfire heat until Diana was swept high above the world on a shimmering carpet of desire and all the turning world was a child's toy she could hold within her hand. Nothing was hidden; all was distinct. There could be no secrets in this world to which Shadow had transported her.

She wanted him.

It was a hunger that was kindled rather than slaked by the slow, connected dance of their bodies. There was something more, something beyond what they had, and Diana instinctively hungered for it—for a bond, a completeness that would bind her to him, to his world and her place in it, and leave no room within it for fear, for uncertainty, for secrets.

Far beyond their tangled bodies Diana reached out for him, and he began to fill her in a way he never had before. She felt the cool shock of bathing in a summer stream, saw the midsummer stars glittering above, felt the security of sleeping in a chamber far beneath the earth, and knew, suddenly, that he was seeing into her as she did into him, that all that she had been was open to him—as if, when this blending was completed, there would not be two, but one. One soul eternal and indivisible, bound as one until the end of time.

Trapped, a small unworthy frightened part of her said.

Diana began to struggle, rejecting the communion he offered her with the swift violence of panic. With the immediacy of dream-turned-nightmare, heat became cold and desire turned to pain; no longer carried above the world, she seemed to fall for miles, twisting and turning and seeking futilely for escape.

The shock of her impact jolted Diana back to an awareness of the world as it was, to the weight of Shadow's body pressing her down, to the sound of wind through the autumnal branches and the smell of the fire. She opened her eyes and saw his face, eyes closed, still blindly seeking her in that invisible world to which he had admitted her.

"No!" Diana cried. She pounded her fist against his shoulder; and when he made no response to that, she dug her fingers into his back as hard as she could, savaging him until she thought she could feel blood beneath her nails.

He opened his eyes and looked at her, not understanding, and lowered his head to kiss her.

"Stop it," Diana said, trying to throw him off. "Let me *go!*"

Slowly, she saw him begin to realize her distress. He stilled himself against her, but she could still feel his body locked within her own, suspended in the act of love. The erotic undertow within the tides of her own flesh pulled her down, urging her back into that bliss, to sink, to drown. . . .

"I did but seek to show thee." His voice was plaintive, ragged with the need that made his body tremble against hers. In another moment she would give way to him, ignited by his desire for her into a blaze that would leave her nothing of herself.

"No!" She began to struggle, unable to explain what she wanted, what frightened her so. "Let me *go!*"

The words echoed between them, as if Diana had said something far greater and more irrevocable by that demand than she had intended. Shadow pulled away from her and got to his knees, turning away.

"I did but seek to show thee," Shadow repeated. He was breathing hard; his skin sparkled with sweat and oil.

"I . . . can't," Diana said.

Her cheeks burned hotly, and she could not bear to look at him any longer. She drew her knees up beneath her chin and hugged herself tightly, unable to understand how everything could have gone so wrong. Until Mistress Fortune had come back they'd been happy. There had been no choices to be made. And now when Diana had to choose, every choice she made seemed wrong.

"I can't be what you want."

"Thou dost not know," Shadow said painfully, "what I want of thee."

I know enough, Diana answered silently. But for the first time she wondered if it were true.

Shadow rose slowly to his feet, his back to her.

"Don't go," Diana said before she could stop herself. But there was so little time left; and when these brief hours were gone, her time with him would be gone forever.

Shadow stopped in the act of tying his loincloth around his waist, the line of his back an elegant rebuke.

"I know it isn't fair," Diana said miserably. "I've never been fair to you. All I've ever done is make trouble for you. But . . . please stay." *I can't bear it if you go.*

Shadow turned back and knelt beside her again, hiding his face against her neck.

"Ah, fair," Shadow said against her ear, his voice trembling between laughter and despair. "What in my life have I ever known of fair?"

It was possible that she simply did not understand, he told himself. He had been so long away from his home—when he was taken by Man, his time to choose a bride had lain years in the future, and his uncle had not yet seen fit to tell him all that lay in the way of it. And so he had done all he knew how to do to wed his *righ-malkin,* and still she said no and yes and no again, spinning like a lodestone on a string and rushing toward ultimate disaster.

He had tried to show her the world as he saw it, and even that had failed. All that had been left to him was to serve her in the only way she would permit, granting her the oblivion she sought. The labor of their bodies was no true communion, though it brought him a small temporary ease, and afterward he awoke, to watch over her where she lay sleeping, painting himself as he waited to pass unnoticed through the forest.

He would make his preparations to go on alone, because he must, but he still hoped. There was still time for her to choose.

He would wait for her until all hope was gone, until the sun rose in a world that no longer held her presence.

And then he would go on alone.

It was the cold that awoke Diana at last. The sun had set, and all light seemed to be gone from the world. Even the fire was reduced to a puddle of dark red embers and white ash. It seemed as though the whole planet had been forsaken as she slept, as if Winter had come and she had awakened into a world of barren frost. She groped for Shadow's body beside her.

He was not there.

Diana sat up, still groggy with the soundness of her sleep. She clutched the blanket around her, feeling feverish and light-headed, as if some part of her mind were still asleep and spilling its dreams into her waking mind. Habit alone made her search around herself for twigs and bark chips as she shivered in the chill night air.

There were enough dry sticks within reach for Diana to be able to rekindle the fire and make it shed enough light for her to find larger pieces of wood. Soon she had it burning brightly once more, radiating its globe of protective warmth.

Shadow was nowhere in sight. Diana looked around and did not see any of their small store of possessions. Even the basket Mistress Fortune had left was gone. All that remained by the fireside were the blankets Diana was wrapped in and a pile of cloth laid on the bare ground.

She could see the white gleam of a linen smock and automatically reached for it. All the clothes that Mistress Fortune had sent were in that pile, and Diana put them on with the habit of long practice: canvas stays and bumroll, woolen winter petti-coats and dress. It didn't matter where Shadow had gone; she must not look for him. He had gone, and this was how the rest of her life would be, day after endless day of all the years she had left to her. Alone. Without him. Diana steeled herself to accept that.

The world seemed to expand and contract, carrying her attention from a fierce concentration on the tiny action of lacing her stay one moment to an unfocussed meditation that left her staring off into space in the next, the task of the moment forgotten. It took Diana a long time to dress, but at last she was done. The hem of her green wool skirt brushed against her ankles with tickling unfamiliarity.

In all those bulky layers of clothing Diana felt as though she were some sort of fragile object swaddled in layers of padding, insulated from the world and all that was in it; but once she was dressed, the acuteness of the autumnal chill receded and some of her disorientation seemed to pass. Diana stooped to pick up her shawl and fling it about her shoulders; and once that was done, she felt almost too warm, feverish and restless.

She picked up her discarded skirt, the one that had been made from her prison smock, bundling it in her arms and looking around, her mind sliding off in that random half-distracted fashion again. *I must be coming down with something,* she thought to herself.

That was when she saw him.

His skin was painted a dark dappled green, and the feathers in his hair made spiky branch-shapes that blended him with the body of the forest. Against his skin, the gold torc gleamed like captive moonlight.

This place was too near the witches' dancing ground; he had been moving the camp farther away, so that it would not be discovered. Shadow watched her with a level, unsmiling gaze— remote, unapproachable, wary, and alien.

But never to her.

Diana hugged herself close. It was as if that afternoon's last frantic denial had exhausted a blind obstinate resistance. Something in her that had been closed before was open now— as if he had taught her a road that, if she had not yet followed it, she was certainly capable of following. Diana felt a power, a connectedness, a certainty that she could never remember having felt before. All he asked was her trust.

She reached for him.

There was a sound behind her, and Shadow vanished in a flicker of the light.

"Mistress Anne, it is time," Abigail Fortune said.

Diana blinked, unable to remember what she'd been thinking the moment before. She felt feverish, dizzy.

"Come, Goodniece," Mistress Fortune said again. She plucked at Diana's sleeve, and Diana followed her out of the clearing.

The coven was already gathering when Diana stepped unsteadily out onto the dancing ground. Fewer were gathered here tonight than had been gathered for the last meeting Diana had attended, and there was a tense air of calm expectancy among all those assembled. Their faces and voices seemed to waver in and out of her sight, like visions seen through candle flame or mist, until Diana began to worry that they would all dissolve at any moment and leave her . . . where?

None of them would meet Diana's eyes, though all of them wished to touch her—her dress, her hair—as if Diana were some talisman of unimaginable power, a changeling from the Hollow Hills in truth. She looked around for Mistress Fortune and didn't see her; but surely the older woman had been right beside Diana a moment ago?

Diana felt flushed and feverish, certain now that some combination of food poisoning and allergy was making her feel so strange. Breakfast seemed an eternity ago, but the rye loaf she'd eaten then seemed to sit in her stomach like a vengeful, indigestible lump. And as for that unguent Shadow had rubbed into her skin—well, maybe it really was flying ointment, though he'd never seemed to show any effect from it.

Thinking of Shadow made Diana feel she'd left something undone. Where was he? She tried to remember if she'd seen him tonight, only to be distracted by the carved-turnip lanterns that were hung in the trees around the circle, casting their faint firefly-light. The flickering hurt her eyes. She looked away and saw that the flames of the bonfire were elusively blue with salt and sulphur, making the world before Diana somehow less than real.

Concentrate, Diana told herself fiercely. She had a sense that time was slipping through her fingers, that there was something forgotten, but what it was, she could not remember. She looked around at the members of the Talitho coven who had gathered here to dance this Samhain night. *The gate between the worlds is open,* Diana thought fuzzily, *and the dead ride.* It seemed as if it would take no Wiccan magic to cut her loose from this time and place and send her spinning through a tunnel of time, but there was something she had to finish first.

Diana sought out Mistress Fortune, finding her on the far side of the clearing. Mistress Fortune, at least, was solid and real and met Diana's eyes unflinchingly. Diana stepped up to the older woman and hugged her hard.

"I can't thank you enough for all you've done for me," Diana said, and knew that no matter how trite the words sounded, they were the simple truth.

"Remember us to the Hill and to thy Queen, when thou hast returned there," Mistress Fortune said gruffly. The older woman hesitated for a moment, then said shyly, "Of thy kindness, Mistress, before thou art gone, do thy arts lend thee word of the King?"

"The King?" For a moment Diana did not know who Mistress Fortune was talking about, then comprehension came. King Charles I, the king who was now in Cromwell's keeping, the king for whom the witches of England had fought.

There was no reason not to tell Mistress Fortune what little Diana knew of the near future. It was small enough payment for all that Mistress Fortune and the coven had done for her.

"King Charles will be beheaded, and Cromwell will become Lord Protector. When he dies, his son succeeds him, but only for a year or two. Charles' son will come back from France to be King, and England will never have a Commonwealth again."

It was not much, but Mistress Fortune's face glowed with joy.

''The boy is safe then? Lady praise him, that he will be our bonny king.''

What else Mistress Fortune might have said was cut short by the rattle of the drums, and the coven turned as the masked Forest Lord stepped out through the trees.

''This night we meet together to perform a great working,'' the Magister began. Try as she might, Diana found herself unable to concentrate upon his words. They seemed to dissolve into a high, sweet ringing just as the fire turned from a ruddy gold with salt blue lights to a strange, deep indigo that rippled and billowed like cold silk.

The drum began to strike and the coven to circle about her, but Diana stood as if she had been turned to stone. In the figures of the dance it was not the villagers of Talitho who frolicked about her, but weirdling creatures of the wood and forest, shining and animal-headed, horned and crowned and wrought of fire and shadow. The power they raised was a tangible weight upon her skin to do with as she chose; Diana was a part of it in a way that she had never been before, the source and the consummation of its force.

The dancers danced, and the veil between the worlds thinned, and all times and all places became one. Diana's doubts were gone as if they had never existed. She had only to step from the circle and she would be home.

But twentieth-century Massachusetts was home to Diana Crossways no longer. She had been obsessed with returning to her own time for so long that it had become a habit, a certainty she hadn't questioned, but she finally realized that she could not take up her previous life again. She'd just assumed she still wanted to go back to her own time because she had wanted to in the beginning, but that life was not something she wanted any longer. Shadow had been right. It was over.

Her mind cleared at last, and she remembered seeing Shadow just before Mistress Fortune had come for her. She'd made her decision. Everything was so simple, suddenly so clear. She'd wanted guarantees, but there weren't any in life. Though Diana was afraid of the unknown world that lay ahead, it was where her only chance for happiness lay. Going back to Salem had been a dream, an ideal; but now she was awake at last and she would not sacrifice a living breathing man to an ideal. Home was where he was.

But even as she realized that, Diana felt the undertow of enchantment pulling her deeper into the dance. Once she succumbed to it, she would be lost, driven away from this time and place against her will and separated from Shadow forever. She had to leave. Now. Leave the circle before the spell was complete or be lost forever. It was almost too late.

Diana opened her eyes wide, though the light seemed intolerably bright. The dancing figures were a blur, faceless and bodiless, and the edges of the clearing seemed to waver and retreat. The branches of the trees were now winter stark, now summer lush, spring flowers and autumn leaves following one after the other in an insane succession.

Move! Diana told herself desperately.

The ground seemed to have turned to quicksand beneath her feet. It was an enormous effort even to lift one foot from the ground, and with that simple effort her body was wet with sweat, burning even as Diana was racked with chill. As if she were poisoned.

The bread. Shadow wouldn't eat it. It was the bread. . . .

Churning nausea rose up in her throat. All she wanted was to lie down in her tracks, to let the sickness have its way with her.

But she could not. There was no time.

It might already be too late. The ground lurched beneath her feet like the deck of a storm-tossed vessel; and no matter how hard Diana tried, the edge of the trees never seemed any closer. She was trapped beyond her power to free herself—but if she could not get free of the coven's enchantment, Shadow would never know that she had chosen to stay with him. He would think until the end of his days that she had left him willingly.

The anguish of that thought was like ice water on Diana's skin, and for a moment the picture before her became distinct, the unearthly dancers only the Talitho villagers, no spirits here but what the Magister and his acolytes impersonated.

There would be no second chance. Diana flung herself forward against the wall of bodies with all her strength.

Through a river of blood, through a wall of fire, through a hedge of thorns ... The shock of the unreal impact stole the air from her lungs. Diana ran blind. She had no idea how or where or what surface lay beneath her running feet. She ran through the night, her path laid out by the track of the moon.

After a little while she could see again—trees and hedges and shocks of grain that stayed as they were and did not flow and shift to become something else. The full moon hung overhead, a frost-halo about it, and the midnight air was cold upon her skin. Diana found she was running through the meadow beyond the forest, her heavy skirts clutched up in both hands.

She slowed to a stop, inhaling deeply. The chill of the open air was an arctic shock to her lungs, restoring reason and self-control and banishing the nausea that she had felt in the circle. She turned around slowly, looking for something that would tell her where she was. The only light was that of the moon. Diana saw no sign anywhere of a fire, though a blaze as big as the one that burned in the midst of the dancing ground should be visible a long way off.

Only then did Diana really realize what she'd done.

She'd given Shadow no reason to believe beforehand that she would make this choice. Even if he had waited where she'd left him, he would have been too far away to see her leave the circle. All he would know now was that she was not there—not that she'd run to join him. If she did not find him—and soon—what could he do but give up and move on, and then he would be lost to her in truth. She might search for years and never find him again.

No! Diana refused to give in to that easy despair. She loved Shadow with a love stronger than fear or enchantment. Though she had rejected so casually everything he'd tried to give her, there must be *some* vestige of that link between them that would serve her now.

Slowly Diana turned in a circle again, seeking some hint, some intuition, of the direction she should go. For a long breathless moment she sought, then Diana lifted her skirts and began to run again—toward the standing stones.

The three stone guardians at the edge of the New Forest had always been the lodestone of their wanderings, as if they had held some special meaning for him—and now Shadow had taken refuge in a place that he was certain no human would approach on this goblin-haunted night. Hope and intuition melded together; Diana sensed his presence there, a lifeline calling her to him.

Soon the stones were visible, ghostly white shapes in the distance. She could see their shapes rising up from the field, glowing frostily in the moonlight like the bones of the moon, and knew with an unquestioning and passionate faith that he was waiting for her there. She felt for his mind, called to it, cried her message to it silently as she ran.

He stepped out from behind the nearest stone, the dark lines and dapples on his skin making him weirdly insubstantial, a creature of moonlight. In her mind she felt him as recognition turned to relief and then to joy, the sorrow and bewilderment of the last few days healed in an instant by the reality of her presence—and her promise. Diana threw herself into his arms.

The hard solid impact of flesh against flesh, the sinewy clasp of his arms, all served to assure her senses that he was real, that he was here, that she was . . .

"Home," Diana said breathlessly, holding him so tightly she could not take a breath herself. "Shadow, take me home."

AUTHOR'S NOTE

Matthew Hopkins, John Sterne, and Mary Phillips were all real people who were in fact known in their lifetimes as the Three Unspotted Lambs of the Lord. Little is really known for sure about Hopkins, though he and his associates certainly behaved very much in the manner I have portrayed them, even if for my purposes I've set this last campaign of Hopkins's a few counties to the west of his usual Essex and Cambridgeshire stamping grounds.

During his brief yet bloody career, Hopkins produced the seventeenth-century equivalent of a media circus. Almost solely through his own efforts, he created widespread hysteria over the dangers of witchcraft (something that had not particularly bothered most of England prior to Hopkins's clever publicity campaign).

Panic-stricken towns begged for Hopkins's services—and paid highly for them. Hopkins was paid to come and investigate, paid for all his expenses, and paid for each witch found and proved guilty. Estimates of his total income vary, but it is clear that during the three years in which Hopkins operated, he became the seventeenth-century equivalent of a modern millionaire. Some reports place his earnings as high as 20,000 pounds sterling, a staggering fortune for the time.

Matthew Hopkins claimed to be a lawyer; he claimed to have in his possession the "Devil's Book" containing a list of all witches in England; he claimed to hold a commission from Parliament creating him "Witchfinder-General."

There is no proof that Hopkins ever studied law, and the book and his commission existed only in Hopkins's inventive imagination. What *is* known is that during the years 1645–1647, Hopkins carried out a wildly successful campaign against

"Malignants." By the time the hysteria died down and the witch-hunts were over, several hundred people, mostly women, had been tortured, drowned, and hanged.

And Hopkins had become very, very rich.

Not everyone supported Hopkins's self-serving campaign. The Reverend John Gaule, who had himself written against witchcraft, found Matthew Hopkins and his cruel crusade even more objectionable than witches. In June 1646, Gaule published a pamphlet, *Select Cases of Conscience Touching Witches & Witchcraft*, which was a direct attack upon Hopkins and his methods. Gaule also preached and wrote against Hopkins, and other indictments of Hopkins and his methods soon followed.

This was the beginning of the end for Hopkins and his career. In May 1647, Hopkins published *The Discoverie of Witches in Answer to Severall Queries, Lately Delivered to the Judges of Assize for the County of Norfolk,* a rebuttal of Gaule's pamphlet containing more unverifiable information about Hopkins's early career. According to Hopkins, the Devil fondly addresses his alleged worshippers as "my delicate firebrand darlings." This may reveal more about Hopkins than it does about either the Devil or witches.

And after the summer of 1647, Hopkins disappears from history completely.

What really happened to Matthew Hopkins? My warrant for his arrest is fictional; in fact, no one really knows. There's a popular folk tradition that holds that Matthew Hopkins was eventually accused of witchcraft himself and questioned by the same fraudulent methods he had used to gain his convictions, dying as a result of having been "swum" as a Witch. Another theory that has been advanced is that Hopkins fled to America, there to inspire the Salem witch trials some forty years later.

And John Sterne? In a 1648 pamphlet, he claimed that Hopkins had died peacefully after a long illness. Sterne retired from the witch-hunt business that same year to live in Hopkins's home town of Manningtree, Essex, as the new owner of the Thorn Inn (you can still see it in Manningtree today) that Hopkins had bought with the proceeds of his witch-finding campaign.

And by all accounts, John Sterne ended his days a very wealthy man. . . .

Although he is such a famous—or notorious—historical character, Hopkins is amazingly difficult to research. However, for those readers interested in knowing more about Matthew Hopkins, I suggest the following:

Matthew Hopkins: Witch Finder General by Richard Deacon—the classic biography on the subject.

The Discovery of a Witch Finder by Catherine Jane Hertzig. An excellent overview of witchcraft in England and Hopkins's notorious witch-hunt. (A 1994 thesis; tell your interlibrary loan librarian it's listed on OCLC.)

Poisons of the Past by Mary Kilbourne Matossian. A sobering examination of the correlation between weather, crops, and witches. It is no coincidence that the rye-growing areas of southeastern England were also the location of Matthew Hopkins's most lucrative witch-hunts: Spoiled rye contains *ergot,* an hallucinogenic poison that also causes spontaneous abortion.

Hopkins in fiction:

The Devil on the Road by Robert Westall. Fantasy novel. Hopkins and his team supply major background to strong but poignant time-travel romance.

The Conqueror Worm. Lurid and only semi-accurate horror movie starring Vincent Price as Matthew Hopkins and Ian Ogilvy as the romantic Roundhead hero. Warning: graphic portrayal of Hopkins's and Sterne's violence against women. (Available on video; aka *Edgar Allan Poe's Conqueror Worm* and *Witchfinder General.)*

I enjoy hearing from my readers. *You* are why I write, and your feedback is important to me. My address is:

Rosemary Elizabeth Edghill
P.O. Box 364
Lagrangeville NY 12540-0364

Please enclose an SASE is you'd like a reply—and please be patient! Like most writers, I mean well but I'm always playing catchup with my correspondence.

Or you can check out my Webpage on the Internet:
HTTP://WWW.SFF.NET/PEOPLE/ELUKI

With warmest good wishes,
Rosemary Edghill
Spring, 1996

ROMANCE FROM JANELLE TAYLOR

ROMANCE FROM FERN MICHAELS

DEAR EMILY   (0-8217-4952-8, $5.99)

WISH LIST   (0-8217-5228-6, $6.99)

AND IN HARDCOVER:

VEGAS RICH   (1-57566-057-1, $25.00)